The Sachem Tales

INITIATION DREAM

Marc S. Hughes

BookLocker

Trenton, Georgia

Print ISBN: 978-1-64719-962-3
Ebook ISBN: 978-1-64719-963-0

Published by BookLocker.com, Inc., Trenton, Georgia.

Printed on acid-free paper.

If you give any type of medical, legal or professional advice, you must also include a disclaimer. You can find examples of these online using your favorite search engine.

BookLocker.com, Inc.
2022

First Edition

Library of Congress Cataloguing in Publication Data
Hughes, Marc S.
The Sachem Tales: Initiation Dream by Marc S. Hughes
Library of Congress Control Number: 2021924578

For Jasmine & Skye

And for the support of Stephanie Douglas

Prologue

Colin licked the excess blood from around his mouth, sliding the remains of his dinner to the side. He dropped his legs over to the rock ledge that faced the little town he called home and sat there enjoying the calm of the evening.

It was still fascinating Colin on how well he could distinguish particular smells around him; mushrooms under decaying leaves, the fresh, mountain water from the stream to his right, wild apples just below the ridge and, of course, the two hungry coyotes behind him in the brush.

It was the perfect night to be out, unusually cool and crisp with a full corn moon rising above the distant mountaintops. Colin breathed in deeply knowing full well he deserved such peace, especially after such a crazy week. His mom was fine with this impromptu excursion, even though it was a school night.

"Is your homework done?" she had asked.

"Yes."

"Well, all right then," Colin's mom finally said and then winked, "Maybe bring something home for me?"

"Ha, you bet."

She squeezed his arm and smiled, "Go enjoy."

Yes...enjoy. He thought as he sat there. *I have enjoyed, and besides, it had been a long time since he had hunted for fresh meat.* In fact, he hadn't had a kill since Great Grandmother Carrier's wolf lessons.

One of the coyotes applied its weight onto a stick, snapping it.

"Yes, yes, I hear you," Colin whispered. "A simple *please* would do."

Colin turned towards the two canines and they quickly lowered their ears and tails in sync. Colin smiled at their respect. He again thanked the old doe for its nourishment, tore off a section of thigh and

5

leg for his mother and then tossed the rest of the deer carcass into the brush for the coyotes to finish. He could tell from their scent that they hadn't eaten for a while, it made him happy to be sharing her with these two grateful scavengers.

Colin returned his attention towards town. Between the growls and gnashing of hungry teeth behind him, Colin was able to hear someone's television far below. It was announcing enthusiastically, "*American Transformations*- The reality show about totally wild events that have changed people's lives! Tonight, we have..."

Colin grinned as he heard this, reflecting on his past, "You have no idea what 'totally wild events' look like."

Chapter 1:
The Misrepresentation of Wolves

Remembering his childhood, Colin was only four when his mother would read specific children's books to him and his younger sister, April. They always contained similar themes, though Colin had never noticed. Looking back now, however, he understood why his mom told those stories and how he, to the delight of his mother, consistently sided with the tale's common villain.

Anne Trask had other children's books, but she repeatedly read *Little Red Riding Hood*, or *The Three Little Pigs*, or *Clever Polly and the Stupid Wolf*. The stories bothered Colin more than April in usually the same way. Colin simply felt that the mean and ugly *big, bad wolf*, who frightened the animals and children, had been grossly misrepresented. Though Colin was never conscious of it at the time, his mother seemed very pleased by his opinion.

Then at the age of seven his mother pushed the idea of him watching the horror film, *An American Werewolf in London*.

"*Werewolves?* That sounds really scary," he had reasoned.

"Oh, it'll be alright if you and I watch it together," Anne responded.

"You and I?" Colin asked curiously. "How come you're not asking April? She's only a year younger than me and watches everything I watch."

"No...no, I guess you're right. Maybe you are too young to watch it," Colin's mother had mysteriously replied. "I just thought you'd be interested, being a boy, *especially* with the special effects and make-up that they do." She paused. "I also thought you might be a bit curious at how *these* types of wolves are depicted in movies." Then she said the one thing that changed Colin's mind, "Besides, April already saw it."

Colin would find out later that this was a lie, but, of course, he *had* to watch the movie. Colin snuggled close to his mother and courageously observed every bit of the film to the end. When the credits rolled, Colin sat there confused. *Why would a perfectly nice guy, who becomes part-wolf, turn mean and ugly and terrorize all of those people?*

"It *just* seems stupid," Colin eventually said. "Maybe if this guy, David, was actually a big, mean jerk. Now that would make it believable."

Colin never did question the big smirk on his mother's face.

Anne's smiles, however, slowly disappeared as the years passed. In fact, if Colin had ever taken the time to notice, he might have seen her wince, scowl, or just plain shake her head. At the age of twelve Colin had turned his adamant opinions about misrepresented wolves into the misrepresentation of all creatures, large and small. It began with simple requests for money to help the "Save the Moose" campaign or the makeshift street signs Colin had made to caution drivers about crossing cats and squirrels. What ended any secret expectations his mother had for Colin happened on his thirteenth birthday, the day he announced he'd become a vegetarian.

As the years went by, vegetarian/activist Colin had gained more and more confidence with every new encounter he faced. This would be important since his next big challenge wasn't about creatures, it was about him becoming a high school freshman. Colin knew he needed this extra self-assurance having made his fellow classmates wonder about his pro-animal views; and now, thanks to an abrupt growth spurt, he would be facing them as a gangly *six-foot-one* animal hugger.

I'll use my height to be seen, and heard, and be awesome. Colin had thought, staring in the morning mirror and clenching his jaw in determination. It was at that point Colin decided, with confidence surging, that freshman year would *not suck*. It would be the year *he* stood out. In fact, it would be the year that *he* would become part of "the popular crowd."

Colin had his hummus and lettuce sandwich up to his mouth, but instead of biting down he had clenched his jaws and narrowed his eyes in a stone gaze ahead. His chest shot out.

Across the cafeteria table an audible "*Uh!* Not again," could be heard. "Seriously, Colin? You're thinking about *that* again?" Jasmine questioned for the umpteenth time; eyes rolled. "Why do you care so much about being part of that group?"

This was Jasmine Rainville, one of the only other vegetarians that Colin knew. She was a West Coast spitfire, the size of a sixth grader, who Colin had known since she moved to their small town of Cochran, Vermont two years ago. The two of them became instant buddies after Jasmine defused a fight between Colin and Colin's biggest nemesis, Quentin O'Reilly (*She had literally kissed the bullying O'Reilly on the lips, after which he walked away in total shock*).

Jasmine Rainville was part Hawaiian and part white, but she liked to tell people she was *hapa* (with no further explanation). Her father was a professor in Sociology and her mother was an Oncologist. The family transplanted itself from California to Cochran after her dad took a teaching job at a local university. Jasmine's mother found work at a cancer clinic not too far out of town. In California Jasmine had been homeschooled since kindergarten, but she had insisted on experiencing public education once they made the big move to Vermont. "I would like to further my understanding of the human race in a traditional environment," she had said to her parents. "Besides, I read that Vermont is quite progressive, down-to-earth and unpretentious. I'm sure I'll fit right in."

What Jasmine quickly learned was that her *unpretentious* classmates found her far too alternative and never made much of an effort to become friends. Luckily a gangly animal-hugger, and his loyal sidekick, had come along to offer some hope for the human race.

"I just want to finally fit in," Colin had answered Jasmine. "Just like you see in any high school movie."

"*What a cliche*! You know damn well that the geeks and the anti-heroes end up always the cool ones," said *the loyal sidekick*. "So, why would you give a crap about the 'in-crowd'? They're *normal* types. You're *not* normal."

The sidekick was Skyler Dillon, who, like Colin, had lived in Cochran all his life. Skyler's parents ran a small farm that raised grass-fed cattle for beef and sold their meat and vegetables at various farmer markets around the area. Colin had known Skyler and his parents since pre-school with many hard-working sleepovers where Colin had to join in helping with the farm chores. Colin, being a devoted friend, didn't stop helping on the farm, even after becoming vegetarian. Even Jasmine accepted Skyler's parents and their livelihood once she met the family and discovered their adamant humane treatment of the animals they raised.

Skyler, nevertheless, was hardly a farmer. While his older sibling's main focus was to help around the farm, Skyler concentrated on *screens*; cinema-screens, the television screen, his computer screen and, of course, his cell phone. In fact, Colin couldn't remember a time where Hollywood wasn't somehow a part of the games he and Skyler played as kids or the conversations they had.

On this particular day, however, Skyler had focused on his other past time that he reserved only for his bestest-besties: *administering brutal honesty*. "Colin, again, you *really* aren't normal. I mean, look at that nose, and those cheekbones, and your giraffe-like frame. Your version of the popular crowd would most likely be with the aliens from *Avatar*."

Colin punched his thick, freckled arm.

"Listen," Jasmine uttered to Colin, her eyes rolling again, "What *Mr. brash-mouth* is trying to say is that you're *unique*. A person like you doesn't need *that* crowd."

"I *just* want to fit in, okay?" Colin had stated again. "I want us *all* to fit in."

"What if *we* don't want to fit in? Are we terrible people because of it?"

"Like, dudes, be serious here. *I* pretty much fit in already," Skyler insisted. "Just recently I got a high-five from Jake Sullivan. Huh? Huh?"

"Yeah, and later I pulled off the "Kiss my Fat Ass" poster, stuck on your back," Jasmine said.

"Oh, right," Skyler responded, pondering the moment. "*Bastards.*"

"Come on, Jazz," Colin reacted, ignoring Skyler. "*Why* can't I want this?"

"*Because* you're a guy who looks at life differently," Jasmine explained. "You like to play sports, but you appreciate sunsets. You watch blood and guts action films..."

"Yeeeah-baby!" Skyler interjected.

"...yet," Jasmine continued with a grin, "you also enjoy an occasional rom-com."

"*What?*" Skyler blurted, glaring at Colin.

Colin gave a flushed smile.

"*And,* on top of it all, you care about things like internet petitioning for the protection of the Boisduval's Blue Butterfly in Oregon or the Plymouth Red-bellied Turtle in Massachusetts."

"Wait, how did you..." Colin mumbled.

"See?" Jasmine finished, waving a hand across the whole of the cafeteria. "You're not some *teen-clone* in the latest fashion, regurgitating sports-talk, living life through Instagram or TikTok every half-a-second. You're someone who cares. In other words, *you're not normal*."

"Yes, which was what *Mr. Brash-mouth*, here, was trying to say," Skyler added. "Besides, you're just too shy anyway. You should really become an actor. Do you know that sixty-seven per cent of actors and actresses are wicked shy?"

Colin remembered smiling at his two friends (despite the interrogations). He liked how Jasmine was such a keen observer while Skyler...well, Skyler was Skyler. On that particular day in late September, Colin had decided he would hold off questioning his high school status. It was these two misfits who were just the crowd he needed to be part of for now.

Chapter 2:
Impressing Julia

Colin had found himself concentrating on his status in school only two months later. This occurred after he miraculously made the Cochran High School basketball team.

"Yeah-Yeah, you're welcome," Coach Rushlim had said while Colin enthusiastically shook his hand. "Just to let you know, it was only because we caught Sagbush drinking at a party this past weekend. So, understand this, Trask, *all* I want from you is to stand there and look all tall and threatening..." The coach looked at Colin's skinny frame. "Well, *look* tall."

After spending the fall sitting on the bench for most of the soccer season, Colin had believed that this would be his chance at popularity.

The first few weeks of his basketball career had gone just fine while doing his best to look *tall*, and his reputation did improve with every win the team attained. Having enjoyed the constant fist-bumps and female attention, Colin understood that all he had to do was to stay focused. If the team won, he would win. *Popular Crowd,* he happily imagined. *Here I come!*

"*Hi*, Colin," Julia had said one day in art class. "I saw you play last night."

Colin slowly looked up from his pen and ink drawing, blinking hard to see if he was dreaming. He had known, without looking, who was attached to that voice long before Julia Baker finished the *h* in "hi". In fact, without acknowledging it, he had smelled her sweet scent first. He just was dumbfounded that the "hi" was directed at him.

Colin had fantasized about many crushes before, but Julia Baker was one of his top ten. She was a visual masterpiece. Her delicate peach skin, her flowing chestnut hair, hazel, magical eyes and those lips; more than once that combination left Colin in frozen wonderment.

That wonderment, however, had been from a distance. On this particular day she was *actually* talking to him.

"Colin?" she repeated.

"Yeah, uh-hi, *Julia*," he stammered.

"You did a good job last night, you know, in the game," she smiled.

He coughed to regain focus. "Game, yeah, well...I kinda just stand there, don't I."

"You do your job well," she cleverly added, putting her hand on his shoulder. Colin remembered feeling his face flush with fire.

"What are you working on?" she asked, tilting the illustration towards her and leaning close to his face.

"Oh, um, I'm just copying a style of drawing from this fourteenth century artist, named Durer," Colin said, fumbling with a large book containing artwork. He showed her the delicate etchings.

"Wow, your pencil strokes are sweet," she praised. "So, you're using a fourteenth century style to draw the Three Little Pigs story? Where's the big, bad wolf?"

"Well, you see, ah, in place of the wolf I'll be depicting *man* as the true wolf in how he treats animals and nature."

"Oh, yeah...the vegetarian activism thing," Julia said softly. "You know, I'm pretty much a vegetarian, too...*mostly* fish."

She then gently placed her hand back on his shoulder, said how much she liked the drawing and went back to her friends.

Colin sat dazed from the whole experience. *Wow, she's almost a vegetarian.* He thought.

***

As a result of that encounter, *dazed wonderment* did not end, or more specific, did not end well.

"The score's too close, Trask," the coach had said, readying Colin to get onto the court, "so keep those arms moving right over their heads. If we win this, we'll make it to the championship...Now *go!*"

The Friday night game moved along at a normal pace with a missed shot by the visitors, a basket by Cochran, one in for their team, one for Colin's team. Back-and-forth it went until the final countdown.

"You're doing great, Colin!" The voice had floated from the stands, that distinct voice belonging to only one person.

The visiting team was up by one point and they had the ball. Colin was on defense. The ball was passed to his right so he took that chance to glance into the bleachers. He saw Julia waving and cheering him on.

Suddenly, like lightening, the ball was deflected by a teammate and fell into Colin's hands. Knowing all too well that he was supposed to pass it off, the flicker of grandeur simply fogged his decision. He leaned forward dropping the ball to the floor towards the opposite end of the court. Coach Rushlim went into hysterics, yelling at him to pass the ball.

As time slowed down, Colin's brain decided to sprint ahead of itself imaging excellent dribbling skills, the leap towards the hoop, making the basket with the crowds screaming their cheers of excitement, *and then*, the running into his arms as Julia Baker gives him a congratulatory hug and kiss. The brain, however, was rudely awakened by the sudden reality of fumbling feet. The left decided it wanted to go on the other side of the right. Colin took to the air as the ball spitefully tumbled out of his hands. He landed hard on the wooden floor scraping both elbows and knees. The ball bounced off the far wall as the final buzzer blared.

The other team's bench and fans burst into cheers as the Cochran section stayed silent. Coach Rushlim glared with rage, as the rest of the team shook their heads. Only Quentin O'Reilly had something to say. He stepped over to pick up the ball, "*Fucking idiot.*"

Colin remembered clearly how he refused to look into the stands to see Julia's disappointed face. He had, instead, gone straight home without showering.

***

Mr. Richard LeClaire was the owner of the LeClaire Hardware Store in Cochran where Colin worked three to four times a week. Mr. LeClaire was a burly seventy-year-old who had the energy of an adolescent on coffee and the strength of a forklift. In fact, Colin had caught him several times lifting wood or bags of cement that would have sent the youngest and strongest employee to the chiropractors.

Richard had been a friend of the Trask family for as long as Colin could remember. He had become Colin's adopted grandfather since both sets of grandparents had died early in his life. The title of both employer and step-grandfather gave Mr. LeClaire the right, and responsibility, to teach his weekly-life-lessons. They were conveniently wrapped in stories about Richard's own personal past.

"It was the autumn of 1957 when I was playing varsity football for my high school in Colebrook, New Hampshire," he began, pulling over the plastic, waffled milk crate he always used to tell his stories. "I was only fifteen. Not as tall as yourself, but much thicker and heavier."

Knowing full well that this had something to do with his basketball mishap, Colin slowly put down the small boxes of nails he was stacking and turned towards the older man.

"Football?" Colin remarked, to indicate he was ready to listen.

"It was the Twin State Championship game and I was one of the defensive tackles," he continued. "So, there we were going into the last minutes of the game, all tied-up, with the other team in possession of

16

the ball. There was only enough time for one more play. The center snapped it to the quarterback who stepped backwards to pass. Myself and the other tackles smashed into their blockers, but I was the one who broke free. Had a perfect beeline to the quarterback who had his eye on one of his own. *Wham!* I steamrolled-him to the ground, popped the ball right out of his hands and into my own. I peeled myself up off the ground, tucked the ball in, and got my legs pumping towards our end zone. No one was there to stop me. That's when it happened...My right leg decided it didn't like what my left leg was doing. I tripped and fell. And worst of all, I fumbled that pigskin! The other team scooped it up and ran the whole length of the field, winning the game."

"And you stood up to see disappointment all around you," added Colin. "Feeling the size of a black fly."

"It could have happened that way, but instead I became quite the hero in Colebrook."

"Hero?" Colin questioned, sitting up straight. "How could you become a hero after messing up a championship touchdown?"

"Well, then, my boy, I'll tell you," Mr. LeClaire continued, a twinkle in his eye. "It so happened that the high school football field was built near an old smuggling route from the mountains to the rail road tracks. During prohibition in the early '20s men used to sneak loads of contraband, like liquor and cigarettes, back and forth from Canada for lots of money. There was a well-known raid on one of those caravans one evening. Two of the smugglers had dashed off, one carrying a sizable metal box of their bountiful earnings. After they got caught a rumor transpired that they had buried that box between the railroad tracks near the school to just beyond what was now the football field. 'Course the whole area was dug-up for years, way before even the school was built. The money was never found until...until my so-called, *messed-up attempt at a championship touchdown.*"

"You found that money...right then...after falling?" Colin queried.

"Literally right under my nose," Mr. LeClaire smiled. "While the other team's fans were cheering and yelling, I realized that my dirt-covered helmet had unearthed the top of that metal box. About thirty thousand dollars in coins and bills was found that day. Being on town property at the time, the money went to the school district allowing them to make several building renovations, plus buy text books and even team uniforms."

Colin remained silent for a little while, just looking for the slightest flicker of half-truths appearing in Mr. LeClaire's expression, but there were none.

"So... Mr. LeClaire," Colin finally responded, carefully considering what may have been the words of wisdom. "So, what you're saying is that something *good* can come out of something so messed up?"

"Indeed."

"Okay. Then what good could have come from *my* mess-up? Should I have torn up the floor boards where I fell on the court to see if there was treasure underneath?"

"*Ha!* Well, my boy, probably not," he had said, pushing the old crate back into its corner and standing. "No, but...something good coming out of what seems to be bad, now that, my friend, is always possible. It's the age-old saying, *things happen for a reason.* Why you tumbled and fumbled...well, there might be something there you just can't foresee, like humility, maybe, or the admiration for the skills of others. Or, *even,* that at some point *you* will greatly improve, shocking yourself, and others. Who knows?"

"Thanks, Mr. LeClaire," Colin said, standing up with slumped shoulders, "but what I'd like to improve is being rid of all the hate-mail I'm getting on my phone."

Chapter 3:
Victor's Revenge

At thirteen Victor Dawes had been lucky enough to have the Initiation Dream that was once a common event for the youth of his native tribe. But unlike other born Wolf Shifters, his particular dream conveyed the news that he would be different from the others. Victor learned that he had been given a unique gift that had not been seen for decades, and when it took less than a year for him to become comfortable with his new self, it was only reasonable that this powerful fourteen-year-old would use the gift to avenge his mother's unnecessary death.

Just over a year ago Raven Dawes was to have an operation for enlarged kidney stones that, according to what was told to Victor, was a simple procedure. But the doctor, a Dr. Fylus, had somehow caused an unnecessary infection during the surgery, a mistake that cost the life of Victor's mother; the mother who did her best to protect him from his father's incessant rampages. Then, suddenly, she was gone and all Victor understood was that the judge excused the doctor of any criminal wrongdoing. Victor's father screamed and cried that it was because the man was white and the judge was white *and* the jury was white that the doctor was never charged. Victor quickly learned that *abuse* did not only come from his father's attacks.

So, twelve months later, on a stormy August night, Victor bounded into the nearby forest. There, along a narrow, paved driveway, winding towards an exquisite six-bedroom Colonial, Dr. Fylus was suddenly apprehended, indicted, proven guilty and executed inside his black BMW Gran Coupe. The authorities never found the person, *or animal*, that had done the killing.

***

The first of May had Colin very glad that his freshmen year was coming to an end. He had joined the baseball team hoping for a sports reprieve from his basketball follies, however, it ended quickly when Colin broke his right wrist tripping over second base during the first game of the season. Colin decided at that point it was time to stop entertaining his callous fans with incessant clumsiness and avoided all high school events from then on. He avoided Julia as well; believing a goofball like him could never have such a beauty. Instead, he would finish his spring semester focusing on his grades and his two, *true* friends.

"Have you started this paper yet?" Skyler asked Colin as they reached the library.

"Ah, no, I haven't," he answered as Jasmine took a seat at a table, opening up her laptop.

"And you're just starting, too, I'm guessing," Skyler directed to Jasmine. "What's *your* theme?"

"Witch Hunts," she answered.

They were referring to a final project in social studies that involved the writing of a fictitious story using historical events. It was the only class all three of them had together.

"I've decided to write about a young, bright woman living in sixteenth century England," Jasmine continued, "so I need to find information from around that time period."

Colin looked over her shoulder as she Googled *witch hunts*.

Skyler, as quick as lightning on his cell phone, pointed to the Google searches he just looked up. "Write, *Inquisition time in Europe* along with *witch hunt*."

"And you know this why?" Jasmine asked as she pulled up the website's page.

"Saw it in a movie," answered Skyler. "The Inquisitions and witch hunts went pretty much hand-in-hand. Try that one, *Heretics of the Inquisition.*"

Jasmine pulled up a page filled with a variety of choices such as nature worship, Wicca, herbalism, Satanism, religion and heretic punishments. "Yeah, this should work," Jasmine said, following her finger down the screen. "*Witch burnings*, witch burnings-here...Now, get this, I had read a little on this earlier. These, so-called, *witches* were typical women who knew how to heal people or who dared to speak their mind...Right here- *'between 1400 to 1792 about fifty million women were burned at the stake for being labeled a witch'.* Isn't that sick?"

Unfortunately, right then, Quentin O'Reilly picked up the last few words.

"*Huh-what?*" Quentin said aloud, "Who's been labeled a witch? Could it be you, Princess Tofu? ...Or is it our favorite Chubby-bear?" excessively displaying Skyler to his entourage of compliant apes, "The *Hog* of Hogswarts?"

Colin stood silent, not wanting to face the equally tall freshman who had had a ceaseless vendetta out for him since the fateful basketball game.

"Oh, then we must be talking about this *witch*. Or is this just a broomstick standing here?" Quentin announced, causing his buddies to guffaw to the point of tears. "Oops, can't be. If he *were* a true witch, he'd surely trip over his own feet, turn himself into a chicken and then poor Chicken-Colin would be devoured by all of us vicious *meat-eaters*!"

Quentin nudged Colin just enough to send him sprawling to the floor. Colin was luckily able to avoid falling onto his hurt wrist. Quentin's followers continued to cackle as Jasmine sprang up and hissed, "Get the hell *out* of here you little piece of *fecal* matter!"

"Mr. O'Reilly? If you would please," the librarian, Mrs. YuLong, finally intervened. She pointed to the door and the troupe pranced out of the room. Quentin gave a smooching gesture to Jasmine and then a defiant smile to Mrs. YuLong on the way out.

"You alright?" Jasmine asked while Skyler pulled Colin up.

"Yeah," Colin barely answered, blushing through his walnut skin.

"Oh, man, Jazz, I liked the way you said, *fecal matter*," Skyler applauded. "*That* was brilliant."

"I should have punched him," she growled.

"Or kissed him...again," joked Skyler.

Jasmine gave him a look.

"Let's just get out of here," Colin insisted, noticing others in the library were still looking at him. "Besides, I better get going with digging up information for *my* paper, especially since I'll be typing with one hand."

"What did you finally decide for yours?"

"I'm considering writing a story based on the Native Americans of our area," Colin answered.

"I didn't know you were interested in that," Jasmine replied.

"I'm not, but I know Mr. Benson is."

Jasmine scowled, "You're sucking-up to the teacher?"

"Hey, it's his hobby," Colin argued. "He collects different artifacts and researches tribal lineage. *And* with that theme, along with some cool drawings, I just might get myself a decent grade for a change." He guiltily smiled towards Jasmine, and then quickly turned to Skyler, "So, how 'bout you, big guy? What did you decide on?"

"Like, *dog*, get this," he began with enthusiasm, flipping through his phone to get the Internet page he wanted. "I'm doing a major, twisted historical-fiction that takes the early nineteen-hundred eugenic laws and has them enforced in modern times."

"What's eugenics?" Colin asked.

"Simply put...It's the science of hereditary *improvement* of humans by controlling breeding, like, having babies, dude."

"I know what breeding is...*dude*."

"This *so-called* improvement," Skyler continued, "is all done in a way that selects who and *who can't* have kids, so society will birth and raise *better* humans...Something like that."

"Really?" Jasmine reacted, staring at his phone. "Tell me this isn't real history."

"Afraid so. The main idea of eugenics was to stop mental and health defects from continuing to occur in a family's bloodline by sterilizing the people that they called 'degenerates, feeble-minded or defective'."

"So, these were all *sick* people they did this to?" asked Jasmine.

"Well, no. That's the creepy part," Skyler continued. "They also ended up including regular people onto their list of *degenerates*, like blacks, Italians, local Indians, even *French Canadians*..." Skyler looked at Colin. "But, *hey*, this severe level of sterilizing got really unpopular quickly, so laws totally changed. So, in reality it's just fricken crazy shit."

"Horrible," Jasmine reacted.

"With that said, what, possibly, is *your* story going to be about?" Colin asked.

"Like, you see, this elite group of people, maybe white-supremacy-types, start up their own eugenics thing, without anyone knowing, for the sole purpose of getting rid of certain groups of people, and they literally make whole cultures disappear."

"And *whom*, may I ask, will be your *certain groups of people*?" Jasmine dared to ask.

"Haven't got that far, yet," Skyler bashfully smiled. "But these elite dudes are bad, so any other people; maybe hippy-types or democrats or-or...*free-thinking vegetarians*."

Colin punched him in the arm.

***

Colin had just entered the living room as Colin's father was reaching for the newspaper on a far tabletop with his *Accordion-Grabbing Tool*. It was cleverly assembled out of odds and ends he found at the dump one day. "Hey, slugger. How's the wrist?" he asked as the grabbing tool's spring-loaded clampers dropped the paper onto his lap.

Dr. Philip Trask was the sole dentist in the small town of Cochran, but he also had a passion for inventing unique gadgets made out of useable and unusable junk.

"It's fine," Colin answered. "Seems to be healing pretty fast."

"Ah, to be young again."

Colin's thirteen-year-old sister, April, bounded into the room with her long, dark brown hair swimming across her face. She came to an abrupt stop in front of her dad. "Look, Daddy, I got a *ninety-five* on my Nigeria project," she cheered, flashing several sheets of paper, creatively bound, in front of him.

April always loved announcing her school accomplishments, especially when she wanted something, but mostly to spite Colin. "Yeah, and my *full* presentation is going to be the main exhibit inside our lobby's display case at school."

"That's wonderful, dear," her dad smiled, giving her a high-five.

She turned and presented Colin with an exaggerated smirk then quickly asked her dad, "So, can I *finally* get a cell phone?"

"No," her mother simply said as she entered from the kitchen holding a cutting board full of cut garlic. She had been putting the final touches to two spaghetti sauces simmering on the stove (a spicy garlic sauce for Colin and one total meat sauce for everyone else). "You're still too young." Colin's mother said, then turned to him, "I saw you were focused on one of your anti-meat protest drawings. Don't you have a big research paper you're supposed to be working on?"

Anne Trask was the quintessential stay-at-home mom who (besides being extremely aware of all school work needing to get done) had the energy of ten stay-at-home moms. She was always helping with school events, fundraisers, several charities and full-time volunteering at the Cochran Retirement Home. In fact, she had been labeled *Supermom* long before the newspapers documented it as evident fact.

As local reporter, Jeannine Granda, put it:

Mrs. Anne Trask is widely known around town for carrying the load between running a family and helping the community. Today, however, she had gone far and beyond her daily contributions. The thirty-nine-year-old homemaker had come upon a group of elderly men and women from the Cochran Retirement Home, trapped in their excursion van. Trask had been on her way to volunteer at the facility when she found the van turned on its side slowly sinking into the Texas Hill swamp. The driver was completely unconscious. In what seemed to be the well-known phenomenon of "sudden strength", Mrs. Trask was able to slightly lift and drag the van to dryer ground, allowing access to the petrified senior citizens inside. When police and fire crews showed up minutes later, Trask had already escorted the seven members out of the van to safety, as well as the unconscious driver. Mrs. Anne Trask simply said, when interviewed, "Our Senior friends, here, sure love to exaggerate", but she was very glad to have been there to help.

"Oh, for goodness sake," Colin's mom would say (anytime the subject came up). "I *believe* Ms. Granda also stretched the truth a little. Don't you? A kid could have slid that old van out of there in all that greasy mud with proper leverage."

No one, of course, ever asked what the "proper leverage" was *or* tested that theory.

"A research paper?" Colin responded to her question. "Like, no, it's really just a writing project," he explained.

"A writing project that will be graded, right?" Anne continued to press as she headed back into the kitchen.

"Um, yes...I'm going to write about local Indians. You know, maybe the Abenakis or something."

Suddenly Anne had stopped dead in her tracks, spilling garlic across the floor. When she realized how reactive she was she swiftly produced a big smile, saying, "Um, huh, *Indians*? What gave you that idea?"

Colin got up to help her as he admitted, "Actually...it's Mr. Benson's, um, hobby. He's insane about anything to do with native cultures. He supposedly has books, maps, pottery, even a hatchet and an old army rifle that was given to a Mohican chief in exchange for..."

"An antique rifle?" Colin's dad interrupted. "Harvey Benson has an old rifle like that? *Well*, I'll just have to ask him about this gun of his."

Needless to say, Colin's dad liked junk that could shoot and go bang, too.

"So," Anne continued to inquire, "you're picking that subject because of Mr. Benson's interest in it?"

"Ah, yeah," answered Colin, realizing this decision to tell the truth wasn't going to earn him any claps on the back. He read his mother's look of disappointment as being due to his quest for an easy grade. He had been wrong.

Anne instead produced her famously fake smile again and said softly, "Well, just don't start it late this time and get yourself in trouble."

"*Geezum crow*, speaking of trouble," Philip exclaimed, looking into his newspaper. "There's been another mass murder down in southern Vermont. That's got to be the third or fourth one in that area within months."

"Put that negative newspaper away," Anne exclaimed. "It's time for dinner and to focus on something positive, like giving thanks to what nature has kindly given to us."

"Gladly," Colin's father responded, throwing the paper to the side.

Chapter 4:
In Search of the Family Secret

Since that vengeful act against Dr. Fylus, Victor Dawes had developed a liking for being judge and executioner of the area's more pathetic *Europeans* (a term Victor's father always used for white people). The particular Europeans that Victor, and his small pack of Shifters, had chosen to focus on almost always had an exaggerated belief that they were superior than others. Victor would find this blatant arrogance very amusing every time they were in the middle of a kill, especially watching some grown men cry like baby boys. What he didn't find amusing was how his fellow pack-mates could actually see these humans as food. He, himself, could barely stand the smell and taste of their liquor or chemical infested bodies as he ripped them apart.

On this particular evening, Victor and his five subdominants had just shifted back to their human forms by the edge of the Connecticut River where they had stored their clothes. They squatted by the shore wiping off the blood and sweat, and then quietly put their clothes back on. One of the Shifters cleared away any evidence of paw and foot prints as the rest of them climbed into Victor's Jeep Cherokee (completely acquired using money from the dead and a forged driver's license). The group silently left the grassy parking space and got back onto the main road.

Maul was the first to cheer from the back seat, "*Shit*, man, that was great!"

"They didn't even have time to mutter a sound," Talon added, his arm around his girlfriend, Fang.

"It was fucking hardly fair," said Beta. "We could have taken those bitches in human form."

"Fuck, no!" shouted Trapper, squatting in the far back. "The fun is always in the newspaper descriptions the next day about how *'they found animal fur in the fists of the mangled dead'*. They think somebody is killing these people with *dogs*! I fucking love it!"

"*Shut the fuck up*, you idiots!" growled Victor, as he tried to focus on his driving. "You need to remember the purpose of these kills. Our century old revenge is not just some fucking game. *Tonight,* was a good night! There are ten less European bastards living on *our* land!"

"Bye-bye, whiteys!" added Fang.

"*AAAOOOooooo!*" the group howled as they made their way back home.

Victor drove on, quietly recalling how he had reached this pinnacle of authority. Looking back, he could say that his pursuit for justice had been violently molded by a struggling blue-collar father with strong ties to his American Indian background. This native background was the excuse used by Victor's dad, Baird, to amplify the resentment for anyone better than him (which he mostly saw as the *Europeans*). An otherwise tall man, with the cavernous lines of strong opinion etched in his face, Baird Dawes would passionately explain to his son, or anyone else willing to listen, that his anger was *"towards the governmental mistreatment of all Native Tribes throughout the U.S. They took our land, they took our spirit, and suppressed our native ways."* Which was, he always added between shots of whiskey, what has kept him and his family so poor.

When Baird's wife died at the hands of an *incompetent European doctor* his rage tripled. He numbed his feelings with even more drinking, releasing a daily barrage of fury on the closest things he could get his hands on, his only son. The abuse was daily, that is, until Victor turned thirteen.

One drunken evening in October Baird had become suddenly sober after he found himself sprawled out and bleeding on his front lawn. He stared back towards the house with blurred vision at the creature in the shattered sill, having been thrown out of the living room window.

Victor had accidentally shifted in rage when his father was pelting him with slaps and kicks. He had simply grabbed his father's collar and tossed him like a stuffed garbage bag.

The humbling of this angry man was swift and he was immediately reverent of his eldest son from then on.

Victor recalled these pleasant household changes as he drove his green SUV down the dark, country road. His father had kept his word to stay sober and had become very energetic in working towards a healthier quest that Victor would soon learn about.

Victor dropped off his energized and satisfied pack, and then calmly drove his vehicle back to the family farm. Driving down South Main Street in Eureka, at the respectable hour of 9:30pm, Victor jokingly thought, *With still enough time for homework...Ha! Right.*

***

Dr. Philip Trask had been sipping his coffee when he opened the morning newspaper that following day. The front page bore the horrific news about more murders in southern Vermont. He threw that segment to the floor and opened to the comic section instead.

***

Colin, Jasmine and Skyler took advantage of a warm spring Saturday to hike up to Lookout Rock.

"Like- *hello*? I'm way back here, dudes! Th-thanks for including me in this little jaunt!" Skyler uttered between breathes. "*Text* me when you're there to see if I'm still alive, okay?"

"Do you hear something?" Colin chuckled.

"I heard that...V-very funny!"

Skyler had crested the next hill when he saw the other two settling in at the top. When he finally reached them, he sat heavily down on a felled log and began to rummage through his pack for his water.

Jasmine was on her cell phone with her dad while Colin sat relaxing on the scenic ledge.

Finally relaxing himself, Skyler eventually said to Colin, "So, dude, are you putting in a lot of hours at the hardware store this summer or are you going to chill?"

"Lots of hours. I'm trying to save some money for a mountain bike that fits my size frame," he said, slowly pulling out a sandwich made of cheese and Tofurkey slices.

"*I'm* going somewhere this summer," said Jasmine proudly. "I'm spending two weeks in Arcadia, California with my grandmother. She's the local town witch there, you know, a midwife and herbalist. She was my inspiration for my social studies paper."

"Nice," Colin said.

"Yeah," Skyler nodded. "*California*...cool. Maybe you'll bump into some movie stars."

"I'll keep an eye out," she replied.

They sat breathing in the fresh warmth, kicking the dirt off their shoes to the wild apple trees below. Skyler pulled out a big bag of trail mix and gingerly took two handfuls then passed it on.

"I'm staying local, myself, so you don't have to worry, home-boy," Skyler had said to Colin. "I'll be working at an *actual* coffeehouse-slash-video store that is just opening in town."

"A video store?" questioned Jasmine. "Why?"

"They're the hard-to-find movies. DVDs not streaming on your TV, filed into a massive shelf-load of genres; indie films and international films, you know. The owner even rents the DVD players...brilliant."

"But, guys, you can't be working all summer," Jasmine argued. "Come on, go somewhere. Somewhere different than *here*."

"Hmm, you're right. Like, maybe we could get over to that swimming hole up in the Northeast Kingdom. With the awesome cliffs, deep pools...what's it called again?"

"Perkinsville Falls," Colin answered.

"Perkinsv- *Ug!* That's just an hour away," said Jasmine, shaking her head.

"Okay," Colin replied, not wanting to sound too small-town-trapped. "*We*, my family and I, are going to a *somewhere*. It's no big deal, though. Early August we're all heading out to a family reunion in the White Mountains."

"New Hampshire sounds a whole lot better than *just* Cochran," Jasmine said, mussing-up Skyler's hair. "You'll be seeing different relatives. That'd be cool. Whose side of the family is it?"

"My Mom's side. I've probably only met a quarter of them. My mom's dad came from a family of thirteen kids. So, I imagine they all had kids. I'll be seeing cousins and second cousins I never even knew existed. A lot of them from Canada."

"Canada? Do they speak French?" Jasmine asked.

"Yeah, some, I guess," he answered. "Mom said they pretty much speak English. But I remember being very young and listening to great aunts and uncles talking to each other in a language that sure wasn't English, and I don't think French. Some of them had quite a unique look about them, too."

"Like what?" asked Skyler.

"Different," Colin said, standing up slowly to stretch his legs. "Some were just big, well, tall like me, but Eskimo-like. Tall, but round."

"Ha-like me," Skyler chuckled.

"Except without so many freckles," Colin smiled, giving Skyler a friendly tap on the head. "No, *Native-American*-like...*Hey*, I never thought about it before! Do you think we could have Indian blood in our family?"

"Well, since you're bringing it up," Jasmine began, "I've always thought you and your mom had a unique look, not as much April. I mean, back in California I did a homeschool project on the Cheyenne and Crow Indians of the northern plains. I drew some of them and, you know...you do, kind of, have certain features that could be American Indian."

"Seriously? You're just admitting this to me now?" Colin questioned.

Knowing Colin might see this as a self-image-issue to dwell on, Jasmine responded with, "*No*, you're right. Your features aren't at all like my drawings. Seriously, *forget anything I said*. Besides, we're basically *all* mixed raced, right? Look at me, Asian-like features with olive skin, dark auburn hair and greenish eyes. What am I?"

"An alien from Uranus?" Skyler answered.

She rapidly punched Skyler in the shoulders.

"Damn, woman!"

"*My* mother..." Colin began, but stopped.

"What about her?" Jasmine asked.

"*Okay*, so back a few months ago she acted funny when I first told her I was writing my social studies paper on Indians, you know? *So*, how about *this* as a theory...*what if* we have a family secret that she never wanted to tell me and April? What if she *acted funny* because she didn't want *me* to uncover anything about local tribes...*because* her side of the family has some type of connection to them?"

"Like, dude, *did* you uncover anything like that?" asked Skyler.

"No."

"You probably found most of your information in only a few books, right?" Jasmine questioned. "And one Wikipedia search?"

Embarrassed, Colin said, "Ah, yeah."

"Seriously?" Jasmine reacted. "I bet Mr. Benson has a lot more materials you could have borrowed."

Skyler decided to interject. "This *really* is interesting, though. What you're suggesting, Colin, is that maybe great-great Grandfather Trask..."

"No, my mother's maiden name was Sachem," Colin corrected.

"*Which* she never mentions," Jasmine added.

"I know, right?" Colin responded. "That's weird, too."

"Anyway..." Skyler continued, "here's my theory: great-great Grandfather *Sachem* had a fling with one of the local natives making *you* all a bunch of half-breeds that your mom's family doesn't talk about."

"Wow, if you look at it that way," Colin said, "maybe that's why my mother would want to keep it a secret."

"So, why don't you ask her?" Jasmine suggested.

"I don't know. Her reaction to that Indian paper had been a bit harsh. Of course, she seemed relieved when it was done, but didn't seem to care that I got an *A*."

"You got an *A* on something and she didn't ask any questions?" Jasmine said.

"I get *A's* sometimes, and, no, she barely even read it," Colin said. "She did say something odd, though, after glancing at it. She had casually whispered the names of the tribes I wrote about, 'Abenaki, Penobscot, Narragansett and Iroquois.' Then went, *'hmmm.'* And that was it. She just put my paper down and went back to some sewing."

"That is a bit strange," responded Jasmine. "I wonder why she only focused on the names and not what you wrote." She paused at the thought and then suddenly jumped to her feet with a determined look on her face. "Okay, I'm officially curious. I say we have some fun looking into this. It'll be like a mystery. You in, Sky?"

"Sure. I like mysteries."

"*I know*, we'll both help you dig up some answers this summer," Jasmine gleamed. "It'll be our birthday gift to you."

"That's right. That's coming up, dude," said Skyler, getting to his feet, too. "Fifteen! 'Bout time. Jasmine and I have been enjoying fifteen for several months now."

"Did you know that many cultures see the teen years as a turning point into adulthood," Jasmine smartly said. "They all have different rituals to celebrate the big changes. Maybe if we uncover a "native" background of yours (if you truly have one) there might be some type of traditional coming-of-age ritual we could do for your birthday."

"Yeah, something like in this old Richard Harris movie...you know, Richard Harris, *Dumbledore*, Harry Potter one and two? Well, in *A Man Called Horse*," Skyler resumed with enthusiasm. "Harris, playing an English aristocrat, gets captured by a western Indian tribe. He eventually gains their respect to the extent where *he* is to be *initiated* into the tribe as a warrior. Now to do this he has to get wooden pegs shoved into bloody slits just above his nipples."

"Gross," exclaimed Jasmine.

Skyler pinches skin just above his chest and continues, "From there the pegs are tied to ropes and the ropes are pulled toward the ceiling of some ceremonial building that they're in, right? So, John Morgan, *Harris,* is then lifted up off the ground where he has to hang for hours. If he can survive, he proves to the tribe that he is truly one of them. Now wouldn't that be a neat ritual!"

This time, Colin and Jasmine smacked Skyler across the head.

***

Later that day, at 1111 Bridge Street in Cochran, a curious threesome asked Anne Trask their burning question about the Sachem families' possible past.

"Well, that is some question..." she responded in a slow, monotone voice. "But, no...no, I don't think so," Then, with a sudden look, she had turned to Colin and said, "Has this anything to do with that paper you did for Mr. Benson?"

"No. Not at all," Colin answered, having wanted to question the evident intensity of her response. "We were just curious. Something we saw on a show- no big deal. In fact, we were going to now ask Skyler's mom if he's got Viking blood in *his* family."

They left the house without another word and walked towards town.

"*That* was weird," Jasmine finally said.

"Yeah...like, *Viking-blood*...my family?" Skyler responded. "Really?"

"I kind of panicked," Colin admitted.

"There *were* certainly major vibes there," offered Jasmine. "What do you think it was all about?"

"Don't know," Colin said, looking down at the ground. He stopped and turned towards the others. "Did you see her pupils suddenly shrink? She seems to do that when...I don't know, when emotional?"

"Eyes do that, don't they?" Skyler offered. "Well, they do in the movies."

"It *really* feels like *she's* hiding something," Colin blurted, looking frustrated.

"Let's think about it. What could be so bad about being part Indian that your mom would almost flip-out over you finding out about it?" Jasmine asked.

"Okay, *I've* got this one," Skyler began with animated flare. "White settlers of the area looked at the natives as below-human...*savages*. One day the Indian's raid their small village. Some women are kidnapped, you see, maybe one or two from the Sachem family. And they're forced to be wife-slaves, and-and they have children, because of it, but eventually they all get rescued, but by who? Soldiers? Local militia, maybe? And when they're brought back to their village, the families are embarrassed by these tainted members, and their offspring. So, they all make a vow to never talk about it again...Hey, this is good."

"Great. Look who's already positioning himself for the movie rights," Colin replied. But, still, as they continued to walk to town, Colin had already decided to devote himself to an all-out search for the truth, with or without the approval of his mother.

Chapter 5:
Murdering Canines

After Colin and his friends had left, Anne Trask immediately called Richard at the Hardware store on the house's landline.

"Okay, talk about a weird day," Anne began. "First, Colin shows up with his friends asking if we had any Indian blood in our family."

"Did it come from that paper he'd done?" Richard asked.

"I'm not sure," she responded. "That paper was mostly about known tribes, not ours. Do you think an innate curiosity could simply surface, even without the gift?" she asked.

"I suppose," Richard pondered. "What did you end up telling him?"

"I said, no, of course."

"You know, Anne, he still has a chance to receive our talents. He'll be only turning fifteen soon."

"Oh, I suppose, but if he *doesn't* have the gift, I don't need a Waabishki'inini son of mine accidentally finding out about *our* special talents."

"No harm done," Richard said. "He'd have probably stopped right there and have just found it pretty neat to be of native blood. What else was weird?"

"Well, get this, no sooner do the three of them leave do I get a phone call from a Baird Dawes," Anne continued. "He claims to know I'm of native heritage and had found some type of document that could really, how did he put it? *'Boil a person's Skiri blood'*. Now how could he have known I was of that clan? Did he call you?"

"No, no, he didn't. *Dawes*, huh? I think I know the name," Richard considered. "I'll have to look it up, but I believe their line are descendants of the radical rebel group that left the Sachem tribe centuries ago. Had you ever heard of this? Their leader was the

Superior named Makade'ma'ingan. This particular band of Indians had been the murderous branch of our Skiri Tribe. Always attacking settlers.

"Now your Grandmother Carrier is one of our best record keepers. She might know about this Dawes fellow."

"So, what do you think this document is that he's all upset about?" Anne questioned.

"Can't figure," Richard answered. "What did he tell you?"

"Sorry, I didn't wait to find out. I refused to listen to him anymore after he said; *'You'll be hating those arrogant white folks once you've heard what they've done to us!'* I probably should have indulged him, huh?"

"If you didn't agree with him, how did he respond?"

"Something about *'your loss, but you'll come around soon enough.'*"

"Well, let's keep our ears open for any more activity," Richard said. "I'll get the word out to our circle and any other small packs around. Maybe you could call your grandmother about that name."

"I will," said Anne, "Do you think something's up?"

"Never can tell," answered Richard. "I don't believe any of the Makade'ma'ingan descendants have rebelled in years."

"Until now."

"Let's hope not."

"Then you must sense something wrong about those murders in southern Vermont."

Richard didn't speak at first, but eventually said, "I was going to tell you this sooner or later, but here it is: I sent Johnny down there to take a look. He's our spy right now. For our sake, I truly hope it's a bunch of trained dogs doing the killings like the papers say."

***

Police Chief Mitch Porter had become fully involved with the recent murders in the area after his half-brother was mauled. Several newspapers had dubbed these attacks *The Pack Dog Murders*; Mitch saw them as messy mass killings. Even with the State Police now part of the investigation, and that he, himself, had not been very close to this low-life brother of his, Mitch felt obliged to help his mother uncover the truth.

Mitch Porter had grown up in the small town of Ascutney, Vermont, but advanced to Police Chief in the larger town of Eureka that sat just south of it. As rugged now as he had been in high school, the slowly balding officer still earned respect from the out-of-hand locals or visiting tourists. The offenses Mitch usually dealt with were common year after year, domestic disputes, drunkenness, bar fights, vandalism, wife, child and animal abuse, and a once in a while, murder-suicide by a disgruntled husband or lover. That had all recently changed. The cases coming in now were *groups* of people being murdered in and around his jurisdiction.

Sergeant Stephanie Harrison, the BCI Detective for the State Police Department, was the individual assigned to look for the smallest pieces of evidence concerning the case.

"Hello again, Police Chief Porter," she said when she joined him and the other officers at the scene of the crime.

"Please, call me Mitch," he replied.

"Mitch, fine, so what do you know so far? Is it similar to the others?" asked the sergeant.

"Yeah," Mitch responded, having handed her his notes outside of the pale-yellow raised ranch. "The victims were between the ages of nineteen and twenty-eight. They were found here in a basement gym that was used for their power lifting workouts and, ah...white supremacy meetings."

"Muscle bound skin-heads. Interesting," Stephanie remarked.

Mitch looked over at her and smiled.

Stephanie Harrison had come to Vermont after being in Boston for five years. This Bureau of Criminal Investigations job was to be a vacation compared to dealing with urban violence. Now she was dealing with bizarre, bloody murders that surpassed anything she had seen in the city.

Stephanie had gone on to higher education wanting to stay true to her love of animals, especially dogs. With exceptional grades she pursued the profession of veterinarian. However, her keen observation of an animal's condition and a knack for pursuing small details drove an admiring professor to suggest a new direction for her to take, Forensic Sciences. Skeptical at first, Stephanie found the area to be very fascinating and stayed with it, leaving her veterinarian dreams behind. Now, looking back, she chuckled at the thought of this past dream. Here she was ironically part of a crime scene *possibly* involving dogs.

"What's fascinating about this murder," Mitch continued, "is that there were ten of them weighing a *muscular* two-hundred and ninety to three hundred and sixty pounds each. Not a trace of canine blood around, but fur and paw prints were everywhere. You know, even a bunch of trained, killer dogs would've had trouble taking these guys down."

"Maybe it was the element of surprise, a whole pack of dogs at once," offered Stephanie. "The fur was examined, right?"

"Yes, husky or malamute," answered Mitch, "but the lab will probably push the wolf-mix idea again."

"Maybe real wolves...trained to kill people," Stephanie said. "Is Jack, from Fish and Game, involved yet?"

"Yeah. They're looking into anybody who may be raising or breeding large canines."

"There's got to be a *somebody* involved," Stephanie said, as she ducked under the tape. "I'll go see what I can find."

"Good luck," Mitch responded. "It's really ugly."

Chapter 6:
Mr. Benson's Basement

The first weeks of summer were either spent working their jobs, swimming or frequenting the small library in town. Colin was enjoying diving into this family mystery, looking for that one clue that could *crack the case*. Jasmine had enjoyed the whole mystery, too, taking the job of historical sleuth very seriously. As for Skyler, he just wanted to finish uncovering Colin's family secrets so he could start digging up some dirt about his own.

Within the town library Jasmine had been looking through a thick book concerning New England folklore as the other two searched library shelves and the Internet. She asked earlier if Colin had ever found anything interesting in his own house. His findings uncovered some French-Canadian cookbooks, hiking guides and maps, ugly clothing from the eighties, some unsuccessful inventions and the usual saved volumes of National Geographic.

"The National Geographic had book marks in chapters on Indian cultures, but they were also tabbed in sections about things like Colorado, wolves and even different breakthroughs in science."

"Hey, wait...Check this out," Jasmine suddenly said, lifting the hard-cover tome and carrying it over to the boys, "It says here in Fascinating Vermont History: *'Early autumn of 1864, after serving in the Union Army during the pinnacle part of the Civil War, Conway Sachem returned to his home in Newport, Vermont with an Honorable Discharge.'* It says here that *'a variety of town reports documented several complaints about Mr. Sachem suggesting that Conway's personality had drastically changed. With bouts of anger and incessant 'growling' noises, local doctor, Theodore Martin, attributed the symptoms to the inevitable horrors of war. The violent behavior, however, got Private Sachem shot and killed after he went on a bloody rampage one night attacking several men within McDougal's Pub on Elm Street.'*

"Phew! Are you related, Colin?" Skyler asked.

"Darned if I know. Never heard of a Conway Sachem," Colin said. "You don't think that's the big family secret, do you? A family member going berserk?"

"It was family history over a hundred years ago," Jasmine replied. "Any family could have had one raving lunatic from their past, and made sure they'd forgotten about it."

"So, in other words, along with Colin here, the Sachem family has had approximately *two* lunatics," Skyler sniggered.

Colin whacked his arm.

"Wow...check this out," Jasmine butt in. "It also says that it took the sheriff and other officers several rounds of ammunition to bring the raging man down."

"But it all doesn't help us with our mystery," Colin said. "We still haven't found much Native American stuff."

"Besides, dude, you said your grandfather was of a family of thirteen," Skyler said. "How many were girls?"

"Gee, like eleven," answered Colin who suddenly caught on to what Skyler was saying.

"Like, duh. The Sachem name would have changed throughout history, of course."

"Uh, like to *Trask*," followed Jasmine, feeling stupid.

"Yeah, so, what we need is your lineage," Skyler pointed out.

Colin and Jasmine had looked at each other and both said simultaneously, "*Tribal lineage*. Mr. Benson!"

***

Jasmine, Skyler and Colin walked up the slate pathway to their teacher's radiant pink ranch home. When Mr. Benson answered the door, Colin asked if he could research some more stories concerning the tribes he wrote about in his paper.

"Geezum-moses, Mr. Trask. You have doubly shocked me this year," Mr. Benson said with a broad smile.

The three of them had not been used to seeing Mr. Benson in casual clothes, especially since he wore a suit and bow tie to school every day. Today he greeted them in jeans and a plaid shirt with a massive belt buckle displaying a jumping deer. "And to think you're all doing this during your summer break, too," he beamed. "Well, come in, come in, you guys," Mr. Benson gestured. "Did y'all watch the parade yesterday? Whadya think? Pretty simple, huh?"

"I always like it," Skyler commented. "I mean, it's the parade, then the food and then music in the park, *and*, of course, the fireworks. The fourth is always awesome here."

"So, summer Indian research, huh?" Mr. Benson smiled. "All three of ya caught the *bug*, didn't you? I believe I was almost your age when I became fascinated by the native cultures of the Americas."

The low, deep barking of two obviously large dogs erupted from the kitchen, accompanied by a voice. "Who is it, dear?"

"Some of my students, Honey," said Mr. Benson. "They wanted to explore my collection downstairs." He had quickly turned to the threesome and reassured them that the dogs were harmless.

A middle-aged woman strolled into the entry hall wearing a light pink Red Sox baseball cap, bell bottomed jeans and a t-shirt that read: *Coed Naked Bocce*. She gripped two giant, black and white spotted Great Danes by their thick collars. They both *did not* give off a look of "harmlessness".

"Would you folks like a beer and some chips?" Mrs. Benson asked, over the barking.

"Sweetie, they're underage. Maybe some sodas, Hun," Mr. Benson suggested, ushering them towards the stairs. "My wife's used to dogs, not teenagers," he smiled.

In the basement they found themselves in a semi-organized mini-museum. An American Indian museum with head dresses, shields, deerskin pants, hatchets, knives, photographs, framed documents, jewelry, and animal skins everywhere. Artifacts were on the floors, on the ceiling and scattered among tables and bookshelves.

"Just remember to put everything back where you found it," he proudly said. "And tribal lineage is in this filing cabinet. Enjoy. I'll see about those sodas."

"Thanks, Mr. Benson," they all chorused.

The three had first just stood there admiring this incredible find, and snapping a few pictures with their phones, but once the sodas and chips arrived, they dove head-on into their research.

"Dude," Skyler said from the filing cabinet. "He's got Indian information on tribes I've never heard of. Kickapoo... Nipissing... Chickasaw."

"Any family names?" Jasmine asked, having flipped through eleven files already.

"Ah, no... nothing," Skyler said. "You know, I bet the stuff here *can't even* be looked up online."

"I'm glad. We wouldn't be in this neat room," Colin replied. "I mean, *amazing* room."

Hours went by long after the sodas were drunk. The three grew tired of the intense focusing.

"I'm getting the feeling our theory is wrong," Colin said, sounding disappointed, but suddenly stood, pointing to a thinly bound manuscript, "Oh-my-g-...Mi'kmaq, Membertou, and, *here...Sachem!* Right here on the cover."

The other two gathered over Colin's shoulder after he sat back down.

"This has to do with a Mi'kmaq chief, a Chief Henri Membertou," Colin read excitedly. "Mi'kmaq? That's definitely Indian, isn't it?"

"Totally," Jasmine said.

"But, *Henri?*" questioned Skyler.

"Keep reading," Jasmine pressed.

"'*In 1610,*'" Colin read aloud, "*Chief Membertou, his extensive family, and tribe had all converted to Catholicism thanks to the French occupying the Mi'kmaq territory. This was the area in and around today's Nova Scotia.*'"

"Wow, that far north?" Skyler commented.

"Anything about the Sachem name?" asked Jasmine running her fingers across the page. "Anything about later history or migrating west to this area, closer to Vermont?"

"Maybe. Check this out," Colin read on. "'*The eldest son of Chief Henri protested the decision to follow the ways of the French Catholics even though his father...*'"

"But why Henri?" interrupted Skyler again. "Why not Flying Osprey, or Crouching Badger?"

"It says here that Henri became the Chief's baptismal name, given to him by the French," Colin said and then continued. "'*...the eldest son*, his name was Sa...'se'-wa'sit...Well, *he protested following the French even though his father was simply seeking to make peace with the outsiders so to have access to the French trade. The son was angry with his father for giving up the Indian ways. By following the French and their religion Chief Membertou had to renounce his position as Shaman and any of the magical rituals and practices that were associated with that position.*'"

"So, what did that do to the family and tribe, I wonder?" Jasmine asked.

"Right here: '*Along with the rejection of the French and their beliefs* Sa'se'wa'sit *appointed himself the new Mi'kmaq chief for any tribesmen and women who chose to follow his decision to separate from the others. Though Chief Henri refused to challenge his son's choice, he insisted that he and his followers move off to another territory.*

"'*By spring, the eldest son, with almost half his family and tribe members, moved their community southwest into the region between what is now known as Quebec, Canada and Vermont. It was here that he changed his last name to...*finally, here, Sachem...*and they would be known as the Sachem Tribe.* Wow, so there it is!"

"Their name, your mom's name, oh, my," Jasmine cheered, jumping up and going back to the filing cabinet. "We've got to find this Vermont area Mi'kmaq tribe!"

"Hey, guys?" It was Mr. Benson from the stairs. "You'll have to excuse me and my wife, but we've got Square Dancing lessons at five, and it's just now 4:30. Did you find some fun things? I've got a lot, don't I?"

They all said yes, shuffling the documents and pages back into their folders.

Jasmine quickly said, "But we do need some more time on one area we found."

"Maybe I can help," he offered, coming into the room.

The three looked at each other, but Colin decided he'd take a chance and ask. "We were curious about a Mi'kmaq tribe that settled northeast of here."

"Mi'kmaq, huh?" pondered Mr. Benson. "Why, yes-yes. That's the small group who had separated from the Nova Scotia area, if I remember. I don't have much about them...Mysterious tribe according to some stories."

"In what way?" Colin asked.

"Oh, you know, Indian folklore...A hodgepodge of little stories here and there, if you want to believe them," Mr. Benson said, pacing. "I only have one piece of documentation of them up at the school. It's in an old notebook. I could try and find that. Yes, Mi'kmaq, though they did go by a different name."

"*Sachem*," Skyler responded.

"Right, Sachem, and that folklore stuff had something to do with shaman practices." He turned to them and said, "Is *native magic* what's got your curiosity? I have some great stories of Ute and Hopi and some other small tribes near Alaska...but, hey, got to go. And about that document...My wife and I are taking a trip to Arizona and Nevada for three weeks. We're leaving Friday. Mixed vacation, you know. I'm checking out some Navajo reservations and sights and my wife is heading to Las Vegas. In other words, I'll get back to you guys about that notebook, okay?"

The three of them put back their files, scooped up their notes, soda cans and the bag of chips and headed for the door.

As they walked down the street Skyler went wide-eyed and said, "*Dude*, this tribe may be into *native magic*. So cool."

"We're after Colin's family background, Sky. Remember?" Jasmine insisted.

"Which might include magic, get it?" Skyler responded.

"What it totally suggests is that our theory about my Native connection is really true," said Colin excitedly. "But it's looking like my Indian background might have nothing to do with raids and kidnappings...I'm actually from an honest-to-goodness tribe."

"Well, not just *plain* Indian. It is clear that some tribe members mixed with other people, you know, like your mom and dad," said Jasmine, then she turned to Skyler. "Sorry, that destroys your little complex movie idea, doesn't it?"

"My *foot* was in the door. *Goodbye*, Hollywood," Skyler said, theatrically throwing up his arms.

"But why the big secret?" Colin questioned. "Could having a native background really be so bad as to keep it a secret from me and April. There's gotta be something else."

"Well, there's no knowing without that actual notebook Mr. Benson has," Jasmine said, "*and* we won't see that until he gets back- *Oh, shit*."

"What?" they both said as they turned to see what Jasmine was looking at.

"*Damn*- O'Reilly," Colin said.

Quentin and his gang had just left LeClaire's Hardware Store and were walking across the parking lot towards Colin and the others. Several girls were in the group, and to Colin's surprise, one of them was Julia.

As the entourage got closer, Quentin was about to blurt out his usual corrosive words when suddenly Julia waved a big, "Hey, Colin!"

Quentin's face turned an incredibly reddish purple, which gave Colin only a moments pleasure. Quentin gave Julia a deplorable look and then directed his attention to his henchmen. He pointed to Colin and simply said, *"Boys!"*

Instantly the O'Reilly Gang was wrapped around the three. Tony Sagbush and Spencer Whimer pulled Skyler and Jasmine out of the circle to make the attack *O'Reilly-style*, a fair five against one.

"Why don't you *Neanderthals* crawl back into the cave you came from?" Jasmine fervently hissed, not having realized the extra *punch* she just gave the situation.

Colin got a sudden glimpse of Julia about to protest when a quick hand from one of the other girls fell over her mouth to quiet her. Quentin, however, witnessed Julia's concerned face. He turned back to Colin, squinted his eyes into angry slits and then pounced, crashing his fist into Colin's cheek and nose. Colin was too busy feeling the effects of the blow to have noticed he had tumbled into the other gang members who added their own punches. They muscled Colin back into the arena, dropping him onto his hands and knees in front of their leader.

Quentin sniggered as he threw back his right leg for a damaging kick to the ribs.

It never happened.

Instead, an unexpected force parted the bullies like a sudden tornado. With precise positioning, this mysterious savior intercepted the flying foot of Quentin's, flipping it over his head with his body following behind. Quentin landed hard on his back and shoulders, hitting the hot, dirt parking lot.

Through the one eye that hadn't already swelled, Colin could see the shape of a rounded, older man. When the man turned to face the other troublemakers (who had already fled the scene), Colin realized it was Mr. LeClaire.

Quentin slowly peeled himself up off the parking lot. He swore through his teeth about how much trouble his parents were going to give Mr. LeClaire, and then he, too, ran off to join his cronies.

Mr. LeClaire said nothing as he strolled over to Colin, giving him a handkerchief to wipe his bloody face. Jasmine and Skyler came over to lend a hand, too. The group of girls still stood to the side in shock.

"You guys may want to pick who you hang out with a little better," Jasmine suggested.

"Shut-up, *granola*-bitch!" chimed one of O'Reilly's worshipers.

Colin caught Julia's eyes. She looked away shamefully and split from the others towards town.

He turned to Mr. LeClaire and said with awe, "How did you do...?"

"What? That? *Old* karate," Mr. LeClaire chuckled. "Just some army training, that's all. Ha! And I've still got it, don't I?"

Chapter 7:
The Dream

It had been the night before Colin's birthday and he had reluctantly offered to help his father with one of his new inventions. He knew he wouldn't be much help since he was still healing from the O'Reilly confrontation.

Sure enough, by eleven, Colin was aching and exhausted, having rebuilt the third mock attic space to test his dad's converted muzzleloader. He called it *The Foam Insulation Shooter*. The shotgun was designed to shoot out an encased liquid tube of highly expandable insulation in and around an attic where it would fill in those hard-to-reach areas. This would help the homeowners from having to climb deep inside their dusty attics to get the job done.

Again, Colin's dad reweighed the gunpowder amount so as not to blast another hole into the pretend structure he was *trying* to improve. When the shot still sent the foam blasting through the plywood wall, Philip admitted he had had enough for the evening.

Colin's bed was a welcoming sight and he dropped to sleep immediately. With a hard rain pounding the roof above, Colin slept peacefully and heavily. It wasn't until the early morning hours that the dream had begun.

Colin found himself walking through a neighborhood of closely stacked homes, all having small driveways and yards. He made the choice to squeeze down a thin stairway between two of the houses to reach the backyards of the neighborhood dwellings. As he descended the stairs, he noticed a squirrel walking along the top of a stone partition above him (this was not at all important to what he would remember later, however these minor events were so vivid it was as if he had truly experienced them).

When he reached the opposite side, past the small back yards, he came across a dirt road that ran parallel to the row of homes. The road moved along the remnants of what seemed to be old, abandoned factory buildings. Colin focused on his dusty bare feet walking on the gravel, but quickly looked up when he felt he was being watched. He turned towards the far end of the street and saw a man standing about one hundred yards away looking at him, smiling. Colin could see that the man was dressed in American Indian clothing of buckskin and fur. The man stood tall and lean, being partially draped by a pale-yellow pelt, his long black hair blowing in the breeze. But as quickly as he focused on this figure being a man, the form converted into an incredibly large brown and white timber wolf, articles of clothing dropped to the side.

The wolf sat there staring at him for a few seconds before it abruptly sprung to its feet going into a run directly aimed at where Colin stood. Colin felt no fear, but still dug in his heels. Galloping now, the wolf's paws pounded the dusty roadway as it came closer and closer. Then, within seven feet of Colin, the canine took to the air heading right towards Colin's chest. He braced himself for the impact, staring into the wolf's amazingly light green eyes that bore into his own. But there wasn't any impact; instead, the wolf was absorbed into Colin as if swallowed by the chest itself with only a vague jolt to his body.

Dazed and amazed at what had just happened, Colin felt his whole body go stiff; every muscle, from his ear lobes to the bottoms of his feet, seemed to tighten and expand. After that he shook with a cold-less tremble, electricity pulsating throughout his body. He bent his knees and felt long toenails dig deep into the dirt road. Then, with amazing force, he sprung high into the air, higher and stronger than the wolf he just absorbed. Higher than...

Out of the bed Colin had flown, still half in his dream, with sheets sprawling. He dropped quickly to the floor, but caught himself on his fingertips just before his face would hit. Breathing heavily from the excitement, Colin merely whispered, "Oh, man- *that* was sick!"

***

Colin had returned to sleep only to awaken an hour later refreshed and extremely energized. When he went to brush his teeth, he realized his left eye and nose were no longer bruised and his body's black and blues were barely visible. He casually brushed it off as being due to his healthy, vegetarian lifestyle and headed downstairs.

"Happy Birthday!" a choir from his mom and dad rang out.

"Happy Biiirthdaaay," April barely breathed, rolling her eyes.

Colin ignored her.

"Wow, do I feel great," he proudly announced. "All that heavy plywood work last night must have been good for me, Dad. And I've gotta tell you..." Colin suddenly cut himself short, rethinking whether he should mention his dream to his mother. He suddenly considered how she might connect it with his curiosity about family history and didn't need the intense inquiry this time.

"Tell us what?" his mother asked.

"That-that I think my *fifteenth* year is going to be a great one for me," he said instead.

His mother gave Colin an odd glance, but went on to say, "Well, I hope so. Anyway, I've got some birthday French toast ready for you, if you're hungry."

"I'm famished," he said, sitting down near his dad's plate of eggs and bacon. Suddenly Colin had an incredible urge to ask for some bacon, but bit his lip. He concentrated instead on his French toast.

"I promised Mr. LeClaire I'd help him change some fluorescent lights that were out around the store," Colin said, after he finished his breakfast. "Then he's giving me the rest of the day off. Jasmine, Skyler and I were thinking about going swimming down at the river."

"Just be back here by six tonight," his mother suggested. "I'm planning your favorite veggie Lo Mein dish."

"LooooMeein! Gag, Moooom-" April protested.

"Oh, April, stop the whining and talk it out," Anne said.

"Okay, well, *I know* it's Colin's *birthday*, but *why* can't you also make..."

Colin left the house while April continued with her far-too-common grievances.

At the hardware store, Colin found the owner already up on a ladder juggling three of the long, white fluorescent bulbs.

"Happy Birthday, Colin," Mr. LeClaire called down to him.

"I did promise to help you with those today," Colin said.

"Oh, these few lights here were really bugging me," he replied, trying to line up one of the tubes into place as the ladder shook slightly. Suddenly one of the long bulbs under his arm slipped out and had begun to fall to the floor on the opposite side of the ladder. With flawless grace Colin whipped around the ladder and caught the bulb centimeters before it hit.

Colin stood there in amazement at how well he had maneuvered. He looked up to see if Mr. LeClaire had seen what had happened. At first the older man simply stared down at Colin. His expressionless face took Colin by surprise, especially since he had just made the *snag*-of-a-lifetime. But just as quickly, Mr. LeClaire went into a broad grin, waddled down the ladder and smacked Colin on the shoulders. "Great catch! That woulda shattered all over the floor, what a mess *that* would have been. So, I want you to appreciate what just happened."

"Well, sure," Colin said, but then he was not sure, "Um, like, appreciate how *cool* that was?"

"The feeling of success, my boy! The fact that your feet, just now, didn't mess up. You may have tumbled in that-there basketball game last winter, but this might be a sign that things have, let's say, *shifted.*"

"The *improved* me? I don't think it works that way, Mr. LeClaire," said Colin.

"You might be surprised how things happen...over-night," he grinned. "Now, let's take care of these other dead bulbs."

As he helped with the rest of the lights, Colin had a funny feeling Mr. LeClaire kept a watchful eye on his every move, but he completely forgot about it once his friends came to get him for their afternoon outing.

"Did you get my text, dude? Like we're heading to Perkinsville Falls instead," Skyler exclaimed to Colin. "Jasmine's dad offered to drive."

"Sorry, I forgot my phone, but that sounds great," Colin said, grabbing his things. "I'm heading out, Mr. LeClaire."

"Hey, thanks for the help this morning," he returned, "And enjoy this special day! I'll see you at your home tonight."

They were off in Mr. Rainville's old Volkswagen bus, which sported two big magenta daisies on both sides. Jasmine quickly noticed the lack of bruises on Colin's face, but Colin flippantly bragged about being a fast healer. Instead, he wanted to mention his dream.

"I hafta tell you about something else...It's kinda about our research."

"What are you folks researching?" asked Jasmine's dad.

"Oh, just some things we're looking into about...the Inquisition time period in Europe. You know, the stuff I wrote about in my paper. The witchy things," Jasmine quickly lied.

"Cool, your Grandma Rainville would be proud," her father remarked. "Did Jasmine tell you guys that her grandmother is a practicing Wiccan?"

"I did, Dad, thanks," she replied, then whispered softer to Colin, "Tell us later."

Once out of the van and heading to the swimming hole the group waved goodbye to Jasmine's dad and followed the trail down to the river. Colin had asked if Jasmine's father wanted to join them, but she said he was happy exploring the local bookstore and sipping on a latte instead.

When they got to the water's edge, they noticed they were not alone. There were three other groups of people dispersed along the rocky edge. Four teenage boys were hanging out above the falls, a young couple with a black lab had blankets along a side ledge, and one lone college-age guy with a tall bag of corn chips and a six-pack of beer had parked himself against the edge of one of the larger pools.

Perkinsville Falls was actually three swimming holes in one. Rushing waters that had slowly eaten away long stretches of rock and earth formed the top two holes. One was large and round that was great for jumping and diving, while the smaller, deeper pool sat just above it. The smaller pool, eight feet wide in diameter, was where the falls tumbled in the hardest. Most anyone knew to leave this upper pool alone after heavy rains, and last night's rains had caused quite a deluge. So Jasmine, Skyler and Colin were perfectly content to be wading in the chest-deep pool just below the rest of the bathers.

Having suits already under their clothes, they laid out their blankets on a flat, sandy section along the riverbanks and took off their extra layers.

"*Whoa*, dude! Have you been lifting extra lumber at the store?" questioned Skyler once Colin's shirt was off.

"What?" Colin answered, looking down to a more solid, ripped set of abs. He flexed his arms showing well-defined biceps and stood there in amazement. Colin had never been heavy so the closest to looking truly fit was little versions of all the important muscle groups attached to a tall, lean frame. That day, though, he looked a whole inch thicker.

"Cool," he said, bending into the traditional muscle-man flex.

"Yeah, right. Like you didn't know, Mr. *Popular-Crowd-Pursuer*," Jasmine responded. "Now stop with the showing off and tell us what you were going to say about our research."

"Well, it's not really about the research, but it's kind of related," Colin began, still staring at his arms. "Have you ever heard about vision quest dreams?"

"Maybe," Skyler answered. "There was this movie abo..."

"Yes, I have," Jasmine interrupted.

"I remember reading about how young American Indians would go out into the wilderness for days without food or shelter waiting for some sign, usually in a dream, to tell them the direction they should follow in their adult lives."

"And..." prodded Jasmine.

"And usually, they had some type of animal visit them physically or within their dream, and that would be their animal guide."

"And..."

"And I think I had one. I mean it was *so* vivid," Colin explained, then continued to describe every detail of the dream he had the night before.

"You said you could feel the wolf sink into you?" Skyler eventually asked. "Like, *that* is so sweet."

"Did you recognize the Indian character?" Jasmine asked.

"No, he was too far away," said Colin. "But he was *totally* Indian."

"I wonder what your dream meant?" Jasmine pondered.

"I know my *mom* would love to analyze it," Colin had said. "She used to always ask me about my dreams. But...this time she'd probably suggest it was all about us asking family heritage questions, then wonder what we've been up to."

"I wouldn't tell her, Colin," Jasmine replied. "Besides, the dream probably is just about all our research."

"Yeah, you're probably right," Colin answered as he dipped his whole body into the water.

"It's still an awesome dream," Skyler said jumping out of the water and looking above him. "*This* area is boring. Let's head up to the diving hole and see who can make the biggest splash."

Suddenly loud shouting started to come from the teenagers high at the top of the falls. They were all pointing down to the upper pot hole. Colin noticed quickly that every group was accounted for except for the beer drinking college guy. They pushed out of the water and up onto the climbing rocks to reach the upper section. The young couple with the dog had already climbed up to the side of the dangerous pool.

"He just jumped in and hasn't come back up!" one of the boys yelled over the thunderous sounds of tumbling water. "He's probably being pressed against the side walls and can't get out."

The man with the dog paced along the circumference for a better look, but couldn't see the swimmer.

"It's all that water pressure, bro!" yelled another teen above.

Colin and the others had almost reached the hole from the lower pool when they heard one of the boys yell out, "*Yo, dude! No way-don't...!*"

Colin looked up just in time to see the young man jump into the bubbling pool. When he, too, didn't resurface his girlfriend began to scream.

The three had reached the pool and peered in. No sign of any movement could be seen through the bubbles and foam from the falls. Suddenly, an arm shot up, but disappeared just as fast.

"*Oh, my god! He's going to drown!*" the woman cried out as her dog frantically barked at her side.

Colin's first thought had been to find a long stick to shove into the churning water for the two men to grab. He just knew he didn't want to risk his own life with such evident signs of danger. But then the feeling of danger was gone, replaced with an absolute confidence in himself.

Colin glanced to the ledges on the other side where the trees hung over the river's carved cliffs. He jumped across the pool and scurried up the rock face to grab the tallest, thickest sapling he could find. Colin jumped back down to the pool's rim, stripped the sapling of its branches and dropped the tree across the smooth stone sides like a bridge. He sat himself in the middle of the tree's trunk facing away from the falls, which splashed loudly against his back. With the movement of a gymnast, he plunged himself forward into the bubbling waters hooking the back of his legs around the tree's perimeter as he went upside down. With his sense of touch on overload Colin swiftly shot his hands to the area behind him, rapidly feeling around for skin. He followed along what he knew was the two swimmer's chests and grabbed for their outside arms. He used every muscle in his body to slide the victims from the rocky wall and away from the water's determined, pressing power. In seconds he had both men up to the surface with the boyfriend coughing and sputtering, while the college student floated unconscious.

Jasmine quickly ran to her bag to get her cell phone. She hopped back up the rocks typing in 911, getting a dispatcher once she was standing near the pool again.

Skyler had just pulled the student onto the rocky edge; lying his head to the side. Being very glad to have had several years of Boy Scout training, Skyler tilted the insentient swimmer's head back, pinched his nose and administered mouth-to-mouth. Four puffs of air later the college student coughed up water and stale beer.

Colin helped the other man out of the water. He assisted him over to a warm, smooth rock to sit. Jasmine walked over to where Colin and the man were, still on the phone and giving directions to their location. She noticed Colin made a funny face as he rolled a finger around in his ear. Jasmine got off the phone and was about to say, "Are you okay?" but was quickly interrupted. Colin had suddenly found himself in an emotional hug from the young man's girlfriend.

"*Oh-my-god-thank you!* Thank you *so* much!" she gushed through streaming tears. She let go of Colin and knelt down to do the same to her boyfriend, telling him how stupid he was.

"I'm fine," Colin finally said to Jasmine. "Heard some weird buzzing sound, that's all."

"Shake your head," she said, pointing to Colin's ears. "You probably have water in them."

Colin shook for a second and then turned back to the man, "How are you feeling?"

"Good," he muttered, still coughing. "Fucked-up move...trying to be a hero. I owe you my life, man."

"No, hey, that was totally brave of you," Colin said, only to be inundated again by admiring fans.

"*Like, DUDE! You-were-awesome!*" the group of fellow teens chimed after they traversed down from the top. They patted Colin on the back rehashing the whole event.

"Yeah, like, *we* all so messed up leaving our phones on our towels!" admitted one of the guys. "Shoulda taped that whole shit, big time!"

"*Woulda* totally gone *so* viral, dude!"

Within minutes an ambulance and two police officers had arrived. The officers questioned Colin and the others about the incident, congratulated him, and then assisted the ambulance crew. A very grateful college student waved goodbye from his gurney as he was carried to the parked vehicles above.

Eventually Colin looked at his friends and shyly smiled, "Um- enough fun for one day?"

"Yeah," they both agreed.

As they went to get their clothes, Jasmine had the strangest feeling she saw the couple's black lab bow low as they passed. It was easily forgotten once they were on their way home.

"You really did that, Colin?" Jasmine's dad inquired as they finally left Perkinsville Falls.

"It was like, so amazing," Skyler had said again, recollecting the whole scene. "You just tore that tree out of the ground as if it were a daisy."

"It wasn't *that* big of a tree," Colin tried to argue, even though he knew the truth. Colin had brushed the tree incident off as probably being the same unexpected strength that his mother had when she saved the senior citizens in the swamp. So, just like her, he wanted to downplay it. "Besides, the tree was half dead...*ish*."

"Right, all dried and brittle, huh?" Skyler added.

"You took a big chance back there, Colin," Jasmine eventually said. "It, well, it wasn't like you."

Colin couldn't think of an argument for this because he knew she was right. "Yeah, I know. Kinda weird. Maybe it'll be my fifteen minutes of fame. Ha, a fifteen-year-old's fifteen minutes of fame."

"Hey, that's funny, Colin," Mr. Rainville said. "Did you know that phrase was coined by Andy Warhol?"

"One of Dad's hippy-*ish* celebrities from the past," Jasmine whispered.

***

Once home Colin had decided to be cautious. He simplified the facts of the day to his mother who was happily putting together his birthday dinner. He mentioned the drowning scenario, but left out certain details of the rescue.

"That must have been scary to witness," she reacted. "Are the two men okay?"

"Yeah, I think. The college student went to the hospital, but he seemed alright," Colin said, then decided to add, "*And* you *should* have seen Skyler. He pulled that guy out, did mouth-to-mouth and totally revived him in seconds. Just to let you know, he'll probably play down his heroics tonight."

Jasmine had come to the party nicely dressed in a dark maroon skirt and a white peasant-shirt. Skyler, on the other hand, showed up in a pair of red and yellow plaid shorts and a t-shirt promoting the local video store. Mr. LeClaire followed right behind along with Colin's dad carrying balloons.

"Never too old for balloons, are you, Champ?" he happily announced.

Colin had given him a thumbs-up at the same time lifting his eyebrows to his friends. When he knew he had them alone he whispered, "Let's not get too detailed about the day, okay?"

"Why not?" Skyler asked.

"I don't know, just don't want it to be the focus," Colin answered.

"Colin, phone call for you," his mother said from the kitchen. "Some woman from the Burlington Times. Probably wants to know about the incident. Hi, you two, dinner's almost ready."

"So, you already told your mom?" Jasmine said when his mother went back into the kitchen.

"Well, yeah, a little. I mean, a short version of the story."

Colin's mother popped her head into the foyer again and said, "Great job, Skyler. I heard about you resuscitating that college student. Maybe you should talk to the reporter, too."

"Yeah, I should," Skyler smiled oddly and then whispered to Colin, "*What* did you tell her?"

"Gotta get the phone," Colin said, quickly walking away.

When he had come back, everyone was seated for dinner. He took his place next to Jasmine and Mr. LeClaire as his mother and father passed out plates of Lo Mein and spiced tofu.

"Colin, *what* an incredible experience! Your Mom just told me," Colin's dad blurted.

"What- what happened?" April quickly asked, sensing the situation may require her to compete with her brother again.

This time Skyler interrupted Colin before he could speak, "*It* was unbelievable! We reached the pool these two dudes were drowning in and Colin, like, *snapped* into action."

Skyler proceeded to describe the whole scenario including leaps and climbs and tearing out trees. He finished with, "He *grabbed* the two swimmers like they were wooden puppets."

"Hey-yeah, but, Skyler, here, pulled the unconscious one from the water," Colin jumped in, attempting to match Skyler's enthusiasm, "and he totally *saved* the college dude's life. M*outh-to-mouth resuscitation*. Incredible."

"Is this true? You did all this, Colin?" his dad asked, ignoring the whole Skyler part and sporting a big, proud smile. As his father was saying this, Colin had watched his mother give a sudden wide-eyed look to Mr. LeClaire. Mr. LeClaire didn't take notice, but instead turned to Colin with a curious glimmer in his eyes.

"*What* a story, you guys," he slowly said, scratching his chin. "Those heavy rains from last night must have easily filled the rivers and streams. Ain't no surprise that a person could get caught in one of those pot holes."

"Totally," Skyler agreed. "The water was streaming down hard."

"I'd been to Perkinsville Falls once or twice," Richard continued. "They were pulling out the body of a far less fortunate person that day. Some big construction worker was stuck up against that pool wall for hours."

"Ah, Richard...? April, you know," Colin's dad said.

"Oh, it's all right, Daddy," she smiled. "I've heard worst."

Colin, however, thought it funny that his mother hadn't said a word. She just stared at him and at Mr. LeClaire, who had quickly thrown her a glance that was like a *wink-less* wink. Colin sensed something odd between them. This all happened so fast that the others had missed it entirely.

She eventually did speak, as she slowly served herself some salad, "I am so impressed by what you did, Colin. And *you,* alone, pulled out these two swimmers?"

"Ah, no, like I said, Jazz and Sky hel-..." Colin tried to say.

"Yes, Mrs. Trask, Colin pulled them to the surface, we just helped afterwards," Jasmine intervened.

"*Why* didn't you tell me this seemingly important fact earlier?" his mother said, still expressionless.

"Right! I mean...it's so awesomely-great," his father added.

"I- ah, well, I didn't want it to be a big deal," Colin confessed, giving his friends the evil eye.

"I think it's fabulous and that *all of you* are alright," his mother quickly said, with an odd relief in her voice *and* a cheerful twinkle in her eyes that Colin hadn't seen in a while. "We can talk more about this later, but the food's getting cold. Now let's say thanks to the good earth for its gifts and nourishment, and be thankful that no one was truly hurt today."

Chapter 8:
The Documents

On the same evening as Colin's birthday celebration, one hundred and eight miles south of Cochran, a gathering of twenty people had taken place in Baird Dawes' old barn. They had all been sought out and recruited by Baird to fulfill what he felt was *destiny*. A destiny, he believed, was connected to the fact that his son's gift was no accident.

According to tribal history the emergence of a Chief Born usually occurred for a reason, a *warring* reason. Young Victor, *this once skinny, hopeless brat*, suddenly had the special component of their tribal bloodline that created the next leader. It was this very bloodline that had once evolved to perfection only to become muddled by the interbreeding of other tribes and white settlers. Baird had, for a long time, figured that *this* was why there were fewer and fewer Shifters left in the area. Now with Victor's special gift unveiled, the promise of a new era for the tribe had evidently been born.

Baird had been determined to help by finding former tribe members who actually had the ability to shift, and were hungry to make use of it. Of course, Baird's other intention was to find a strong pack for Victor to lead. It was what a Chief Born was *born* to do, and this graying, reformed Indian was going to see that the positive omen of an actual living *Superior*, existing today, became total justification to go to war with the *Europeans* again. But before this fateful meeting of like-minded warriors was to take place, Baird had accidently come upon even more evidence to go to war.

In the late winter months, after Victor physically announced his big changes, Baird had remembered that a high school buddy of his was a custodian in the University of Vermont's library. He had called to ask him if there were possibly any listings of Indian families in the area that he could get the records of. Francis Galton had called him back to apologize saying he'd only located an old book of addresses from the basement archives that may or may not be of help. Besides the addresses, the book did contain the person or family's name *and* race.

Baird had agreed to come up and look at it anyway. What he found was a scatter of information that *did* contain the names of American Indian families throughout Vermont, but they were only recorded from around the early half of the 1900s. Baird decided that it was at least a start, even if the information could have changed since then. By mulling over the large, leather-bound tome, he discovered that its contents were comprised of more than just addresses. It was also filled with several loose sheets of field notes, detailed studies, multi-paged letters, and small folders of 4x6 cards labeled "pedigree charts". Baird had begun to realize that this book had been purposely placed in the basement for a reason. Through some more thorough research Baird eventually understood that what he had was undisclosed files of the State's Eugenics Program from the 1920s and '30s. It was an accumulation of data compiled by the late Henry F. Perkins and his team of researchers.

The data outlined how Mr. Perkins had begun to collect family's specific bloodlines throughout Vermont to form records of the *social* "inadequates" and their "defective germ-blood". His quest was for "human betterment through selective breeding" and became determined to enact a sterilization law to stop, what he and his people believed was, "the polluting of the blood of the pure and civilized", also known as "the well born".

Also known as the Europeans! Baird had thought.

Perkins' findings, though focused mostly on the poor, produced a variety of racial categories he also labeled as the "feeble-minded" of the state. These included the French-Canadian, the Polish, Italians, the "Negroes", as well as several families under the label, "of Indian descent". Each category specified the area and address on which these families had settled in and around Vermont. Why this particular book was out of view of the public, Baird surmised, was that it included extensive letters of racial bias by prominent philanthropists, politicians and public policy makers of the time, as well as the recipe for an unauthorized sterilization formula that was given to patients in a local mental hospital.

All this information would have been enough to keep Baird's poor opinion of *Europeans* consistent, however, he was soon to realize that there was much more. Though the last written eugenics report was recorded in the early forties, Baird stumbled across a hidden sleeve tucked inside the back cover of the book. Inside he found a firmly wrapped manila folder containing far more modern documents.

What Baird had learned was that the original "Eugenics Sterilization Plan" had been pushed along through legislation in 1926. The eugenics supporters had the inflated belief that people would just volunteer to be part of the program, but the plan had totally failed. After several attempts to test the unauthorized formula on mental patients, resulting in several deaths, the eugenics program was temporarily stalled, then discontinued completely. Discontinued, that is, until the early 70s. It was then that a newly formed group emerged and secretly revised, improved and implemented another eugenics sterilization plan without the knowledge of the public or its recipients.

With eyes blazing and temples throbbing Baird thoroughly read through every page containing minute details of how they accomplished their goal. There were names of the people they sterilized, the very formula that worked after six tries, *plus* a fancy parchment that displayed the names and signatures of prominent doctors, lawyers, politicians, and other families of wealth who must have been proudly part of the whole scheme.

When Baird was done reading the "of Indian descent" list and found his family's name, as well as his wife's parent's name, he sat there in silent rage. Regaining his composure Baird grabbed all the documents and quickly drove home to begin building his plan for tribal vengeance.

***

Back in Cochran, on the same night Baird had gathered Victor's pack of supporters, Anne Trask was finding herself in an extra good mood. She had pushed everyone into the living room to open presents so she could pretend to be cleaning dishes. The thrill of gifts distracted Colin enough to miss Richard slipping into the kitchen unnoticed.

As soon as he passed the threshold, Anne grabbed him with excited force.

"*Richard?*" Anne whispered with wide eyes. "Do you think *he's* got it?"

"It sure seems it," Richard smiled wide. "This morning, when he came to help me, he caught a falling florescent bulb I dropped as if he'd performed ballet all his life. Along with their description about saving those men from drowning, I'd say your son might just be joining us after all."

Anne paused, walking over to the dirty plates to load in the dishwasher. Her arms were full when she suddenly turned to her old friend and said, "*Let's* call the relatives. I want to perform the old coming-of-age test at this year's reunion."

"The *famous* Sachem Obstacle Course?"

"Yes, to see just how many new Shifters we have in the family. I'd love you to come."

"Well, now," Richard considered, helping with the dishes, too. "I haven't seen something like that in years. You bet I'll make it. It will thoroughly help Colin adjust to his new self."

***

Before Baird gathered the recruits for the *Victor-Army*, he had recorded the Indian family names, addresses and information from the found documents and had begun contacting each family or individual of native background. By asking just the right questions, he was able to find people from his own tribe. Once he had found fellow descendants and fellow Shifters, he quickly spread his information (and anger) to any of them willing to listen.

"Oh, yes, believe it. It was called, 'Operation Eugenics'," Baird would say to the tribesmen or women over the phone, "Rich, white people, here in Vermont, put it together. I can send you an email on it, or mail it to you. You won't *believe* what you'll read, it could boil a person's Skiri blood, I tell you! And *your* parents were on the list, Carl. Oh, yes. Alice and Harold, right? You were the only child? Well, your mom and dad were vaccinated with the formula in '72, and so were you after that. It was *mixed* in with the polio vaccine. Can you believe it? ...Kids? Yeah? Only one? We did, too, but I've talked to several couples who couldn't conceive at all. Guess we were lucky to have one kid. Complications? Yeah, same with my wife. Is she all right now? Good. Must have been a glitch in their sterilization drug. Otherwise, we wouldn't have had any, either. *So*, did your kid become a Shifter? No? Just you? Well, I've heard that from many families, too. Messed with our blood, *our genetics*, I bet. Makes sense why there's far and few of us now, huh? Piss you off, right? Me, too! Oh, yes, I've heard all about those murders. You think it's a few of our own? Wouldn't be surprised...No, the killings don't upset me one bit either. Tell you what, Carl, we're going to gather a handful of us, who still have the skill, right here at my barn in Eureka. Sure. We can vent some of this anger. You interested? July seventh at eight pm. No, no, let's not do anything that harsh, maybe not yet, but we can talk a bit more about those murders. *Great*, see you then."

So, on that particular July night, a purposeful Baird Dawes stood tall in front of one of the largest gatherings of the Skiri Clan he had seen in many years. To his left a young, confident Victor Dawes stood even taller.

The Chief Born's obedient subdominants sat among the group of twenty in the far back. Talon, Fang, Trapper, Beta and Maul were all lounging with their feet up on chairs, quite relaxed and feeling entitled. They were the only teens there, dressed mostly in ripped jeans, black t-shirts and baggy hoodies. Victor, on the other hand, had his hair neatly pulled into a ponytail and was sporting two dangling feather earrings. He dressed far more formally, accentuating his strong physique with a black muscle shirt.

The others who had gathered were between the ages of twenty-five and fifty-five. Six women were present (including Beta and Fang), the rest were men. These men were all tall and strong, bearded or just scruffy, showing battle scars of some sort on their faces and arms. Now together, as a group, the men and women felt bonded by their native background and increased anger at the information Baird had told them. Together as a group they felt like a solid pack. Everyone, that is, except one brawny, fifty-four-year-old man with a long, thinning ponytail.

Johnny Dumont, the informant that Richard LeClaire had sent to investigate Southern Vermont, had stumbled upon the meeting only by chance. After purposely joking about the local murders to a fellow tribesman over a beer, he was told of the gathering to be held and that it would unite them all again. He, however, had not received Baird's initial phone message about the documents or the passionate call to battle, so Johnny was there at the meeting to prove his loyalty, and to learn more.

"Welcome my brothers and sisters of the Clan," Baird had begun while he paced back and forth in front of the seated party. "As I had mentioned over the phone, I believe our time has come to finally assemble ourselves into one powerful, organized body. What we have learned of these Europeans...*is a fucking damn good reason to teach them and their descendants a lesson.*"

The group cheered Baird's words. Johnny joined in, too, looking like he understood, but racking his brain for any recollection of recent *white-man* transgressions that would have been bad enough to upset everyone here.

"With these names of doctors, lawyers, state representatives and other Europeans of distinction, we can finally use our buried skills as Shape Shifters to wreak fear and vengeance onto those who had *attempted to destroy our tribe!*"

The group once again hooted and hollered at his proclamation. Even though Johnny was still completely in the dark, he suddenly noticed a tall, thick man off to his side not standing or cheering at all.

Once the others were quiet the tall man eventually stood and questioned Baird's words, "And *what* good will that do, Mr. Dawes?"

Johnny suddenly realized who it was. It was Richard's LeClaire's son, Bobby. He was the owner of a successful lumber company up in the Northeast section of Maine. Besides Baird, he was one of the oldest at this meeting, and, as Johnny assumed, was one of the only ones who harbored the bloodline's highest status.

Bobby LeClaire was a long-forgotten Chief Born, or, in the tribe's language, he was a *Ma'iingan inini*. Bobby's father, however, had tried to suppress his son's special gift for the sole purpose of keeping their peaceful lifestyle in the small town they had lived. After the night Bobby decided to use his gift to scare some older classmates who had bullied him throughout most of his earlier school years (the four boys received only cuts and scratches, but were thoroughly traumatized for life) it was enough for Richard to demand no further shifting around their town. Because of this the strong-willed boy decided his gift was far more important than his family, so, at the age of sixteen he decided to leave home.

He traveled to the forests and mountains of Northern Maine, found two young subdominants to form a small pack and lived in the wild. Their animal skills helped them survive in the backcountry for several years.

After some time, however, Bobby began longing for human needs. These types of needs required the making of money and making money required him to live among the humans. So, he made the decision to leave the wilderness, repress his own shifting skills and work towards monetary freedom. He used his "gift" to muscle his way into a large lumber business in Maine which he eventually owned and operated right after several freak accidents killed the original owners. This allowed him a lavish home, expensive vehicles and an impressive trophy wife. He was very content with his non-shifting life until he happened upon a fellow tribesman having had received Baird's phone call. Bobby, however, knew nothing about Victor.

An interest in witnessing what would come about at a meeting of fellow Shifters brought Bobby to Eureka, especially after hearing about Baird's sterilization story. Though he had his luxurious life, Bobby and his wife were never able to have children. With this news that their reproductive capabilities may have been tampered with made Bobby angry enough to come out of hiding. His plan, now, was to try and understand his tribesmen's passion to rebel so *he* could lead them into battle; a kind of battle that he would personally shape and form.

Bobby now had everyone's attention, "I'm curious *why* we are to terrorize these people when it all happened so long ago?"

"Because it has affected all of us here in this room tonight, *Mr. LeClaire*," Baird said while he stood his ground as the organizer. Out of proper respect, though, he bowed. "*And* many of these people are still living. I've researched this list thoroughly. These arrogant families still run the state's legislation and county politics. They are in the positions to make their lives and their children's lives easy as they continue to make *ours* more difficult. The fact that they successfully went through with this plot to stop us is grounds for a war. Who knows what other secret programs they're planning?"

"So, the plan is to attack these families and their offspring," Bobby continued, in a calm voice, "Do you think they, the authorities, will accept that? You'll eventually be discovered and be hunted down by them *and* their government. Our kind will be *exposed*. What would be the purpose then?"

"To see the fuckers *suffer!*" Maul yelled out.

Bobby LeClaire spun on his heals to face Maul. His pupils shrunk to pinpoints with nostrils flaring. "Know your place, *sub!* You are not in the position to speak!" Bobby growled.

Victor had made a move towards the taller man, but Baird held his arm out to stop him. Victor complied.

Bobby turned toward the front again. "*I* am not against retaliation. If this secret experiment on our people is true, there is reason to fight back." He looked at those around him. "*However*, what I am against is the *blatant* recklessness of it all. Senseless killings *without* a future."

"And *what* do you suggest, Mr. Leclaire?" Baird asked.

"Precision planning," Bobby explained, believing his born position as leader had now placed him in full control. "We will develop an underground organization that uses its mental and physical strengths to slowly take over specific, indispensable businesses, like construction, trucking and trash removal. Money could be the power we need to mess with our oppressors and become strong again by cleverly gaining a position of hierarchy. We could, as a tribe, become similar to the Mafia, the *Skiri Mafia!*"

"And *whom*, may I ask, would be the *Godfather* of this Mafia, Mr. LeClaire?" Baird asked.

At first Bobby was shocked by such an impertinent question, then said, "You dare question my position of authority, Baird Dawes?"

Victor finally stepped forward and boldly said, "No, *I* dare question your position."

Bobby, at first, stood silent, breathing slowly to control his anger. "I assume that all present here tonight remember and understand our old tribal traditions," Bobby LeClaire said, directing his words to Baird and the other adults, completely ignoring Victor. "So, Baird, as the oldest and the father of this...*pup*, I believe *you* should have better taught your son the ways of respect for his *Superior!*"

"Speaking of old tribal traditions that you, yourself, must know," Victor said, holding his ground, "certain unique circumstances can place an individual in a position to challenge a Chief Born."

"*Unique circumstances?*" Bobby repeated, incredulous.

Victor stepped away from the taller man, at the same time peeling off his shirt. "You do know of the ritual battle which was how the *old ones* determined who would be their next leader *if* there was ever to be two Superiors, Mr. LeClaire?" he hissed through sharpening teeth, compressing pupils and lengthening arms and legs.

"*Wha*-it can't be!" said Bobby as he stepped back for the inevitable fight.

Chapter 9:
Three Dead Soldiers

Jasmine was out in California and Skyler was working a full day, so Colin had to take it on himself to go back to Mr. Benson's house and collect more information about the Sachem tribe.

Having just come home from his trip out west, Mr. Benson had kept his promise of finding the old booklet in his classroom and letting Colin know. He greeted Colin at the front door of his house wearing a black cowboy hat and a thick leather belt with a new, shiny buckle proudly displaying the word *Navaho*.

"Got it just outside a reservation in Arizona. Pretty spiffy, huh?" he said as he invited Colin inside.

The low, powerful barks of the two Great Danes were suddenly heard from the kitchen, this time unattended by Mr. Benson's wife. They barreled towards the front door ready to take on whoever dared enter their domain. Colin braced himself for the attack after seeing the apparent shock on Mr. Benson's face. But as soon as they were in view the huge canines came to an abrupt stop, sending the oval rug underneath them sliding down the hallway with the two dogs on top. With frightened eyes, both Great Danes gave a quiet whimper and cowered away slowly; their heads down. They never ran off completely, but laid low to the floor, eyes looking straight at Colin.

"Well, *I'll be*," Mr. Benson had finally said, his hands on his hips. "Honey, where are you? Ya gotta get in here and see what Tweety and Bam Bam are doing! It's the darnedest thing."

Tweety and Bam Bam? Colin thought.

Mr. Benson's wife came into the hallway looking like she expected some trouble. She was dressed in hot pink denim shorts and a black t-shirt displaying an airbrushed Elvis on the front.

"*What* did you do to them?" she asked her husband, though she seemed to have directed it more towards Colin.

"They just stopped dead in their tracks," Mr. Benson said, hands still on his hips. He turned to Colin and said, "Are you wearing some strange cologne?"

"No, sir," Colin answered.

"Well, whatever it is, they seem strangely respectful of you," said Honey Benson, curiously smiling now. "You must be emitting some powerful aura that they're picking up. These dogs are psychic that way, you know."

"Hmm, yeah, that's probably it, dear," Mr. Benson said, seeing that the conversation was about to get weird. "Well, we've got a bit of work in the basement, Honey. Could you see if there's any sodas in the fridge?"

Colin let go of the strange dog incident as soon as he was back in the Benson Indian Museum. There he found the center table devoted to a small, battered, leather notebook.

"Here's what you're looking for, I think," Mr. Benson smiled. "I know it was over a whole century after leaving Nova Scotia, but this is the only documentation about that half of the Mi'kmaqs who had split, *and* where they had migrated. It suggests this Skiri Clan settled around the area somewhere northeast of Seymour Lake. Well, there's a crude lake drawing...looks most like Seymour."

"I know they switched their name to Sachem, but what's this Skiri Clan name?" Colin asked. "I mean, you'd think they'd stick with calling themselves Mi'kmaq."

"Very good question, my man," Mr. Benson said scratching his head. "'Skiri', or 'Skidi' was the name of a Pawnee *group* from Nebraska. Maybe this Chief Sachem heard of the Pawnee word, Skiri, and felt a connection to its meaning of wolf. Wolves in Vermont have not been around since the late 1800s, *and* within this little notebook, discovered in the late 1700s by a group of trappers, there's references to wolves in it, so maybe there is some connection to the Sachem people."

"But if the Pawnee were out in Nebraska area, how did this Chief Sachem hear the word?" Colin questioned. "On the television one night?"

"*Ha, jocular*...well, there were scouts within the tribes...*maybe* some traveled far...Maybe stories from the west traveled east."

Mr. Benson continued as he opened the pages gently. "Okay, so these trappers found the notebook tucked inside the boot of one of three dead soldiers. According to some research I did, the soldiers were probably part of a small governmentally funded census group sent out into that territory. These census people were to document the land, the settlers and any indigenous peoples still in the area. This booklet was dated, 1779, but wasn't discovered until 1782."

"It sounds like they never accomplished their job," Colin commented.

"True," Mr. Benson said. "According to the trapper's, the cause of death must have been coyotes, or wolves; traces of fur were everywhere. Anyhow, this one educated soldier had watched the tribe from a distance and wrote down anything he observed. Maybe he was trying to determine who they were before they tried to make contact. He was killed before he could approach the tribe and meet the chief. From the extra information I read in his notes, I would say that the guy was a bit of a drinker, too."

"But how did anyone know it was the Sachem's Mi'kmaqs? I mean, the *Skiri* Clan?" Colin questioned.

"See these quick sketches by the soldier?" said Mr. Benson, pointing to rough circles and symbols, "They were the same glyphs found in Nova Scotia used by Membertou and the Mi'kmaqs there. Now this new symbol, however, never matched, but was seen much later in Abenaki stories and writings. It's been suggested that this new Skiri Clan had changed their symbol along with their name, and the *Wolf Clan* stories also suggest having wolves as *pets*. So, it is ironic that these soldiers may have been killed by wolves."

"How come there wasn't any more documentation on this tribe?"

"No one's quite sure," Mr. Benson said as he rubbed his chin. "Speculators believed that they had died out or were killed off. Others thought they just began to mingle among the other tribes and settlers. All I know is, I'd have wanted to learn more about that shaman-magic stuff I had mentioned to the three of you earlier. It would seem that even though the father, Chief Henri, renounced his shamanic ways for the sake of French Catholicism, his eldest son made sure he continued to practice it. It sounds like he may have taught others of the mystical ways, too, if I read the words correctly. Taught practices or not, the documenting soldier, according to what he *claimed* to have seen, really insinuates *magic*. OR my drunk verdict. But, *hey,* I'll let you take a look yourself, and jot down anything you find that may quench your native thirst."

"Thanks, Mr. Benson," Colin said.

He settled into a chair as he focused on the script. He realized he first had to learn how to decipher the rough scrawl, though it was in English. Once he learned the chopped-up pattern of words the soldier was inscribing, Colin was able to gather what the man was writing about so long ago.

He began to read the soldier's passages:

First entry for indigenous peoples of New York's most northeastern territory.

Day one.

Classification: Tribe six

The fourteenth day of August 1779

I sit in a low cluster of pines overlooking the small aboriginal village. I busied the hours with observation and notes and am now ready to register my findings. I will henceforth compare Tribe six to those previously documented by my fellow soldiers and myself. The following is thus noted:

-Elm-bark longhouses scattered around the small village, similar to that of the Abenaki tribe...Tribe four.

-Hair, mostly long and tailed with colors of blacks and dark browns. Thick brows are more prevalent than any I have witnessed from the other tribes.

-Strong family ties, children seem respected, much loyalty. Elders and sick all cared for. The whole of the tribe seems to be helping in the raising of the children.

-Meals include a bit of foraging for berries and roots, but mostly meat hunting as their main food source.

-Somewhat similar traditional dances of ceremony and gratitude. Hooting and growls seem unique to this village.

Day two entry for Tribe six

The fifteenth day of August 1779

Have observed the Chief and other higher ranked males and females doing 'still-sitting' for hours. Might be a form of dream-visions I have read in my studies. Also, what I can only surmise as a ritual drink, was given to three boys and two girls. It made the individuals wild and uninhibited. The Chief steadied their behavior with authoritative focus.

At the twilight hour the same adolescent children danced for the tribe wearing wolf skins. The adults chanted outside their circle with smiles and praises.

Day three entry for Tribe six

The sixteenth day of August 1779

Today I was the closest I've ever been to the encampment. My curiosity had got the better of me with the incredible sighting of five young wolves entering and leaving this village as if domesticated dogs. I hadn't noticed them before. Hours later I see the return of several hunters with some of the young who were just initiated. I hastened to notice that four of the older hunters easily dragged the day's kill of two heavy bucks and one Bull Moose on traditional travois as if they were dragging goose-feathered pillows. And this, too: not one of them carried weapons of any sort. No bows or arrows, knives or spears. They somehow, from what I could see from the animal's wounds, took down these creatures by using grappling hooks, and then some other sharp object to cut their throats. They could easily have weapon storage outside of the village, or could they have trained the wolves that I've seen do their killing? Curious. I will try to further investigate, but it still indicates a unique display of indigenous hunting thus far.

Day four entry
The seventeenth day
I believe myself to have been seen, though not one tribe member has acknowledged such or has called me out. I just sense they're moving more carefully now. They are much more cautious. Yet, today a smallish Indian girl turned in step and immediately gazed in my direction, her mother corrected her focus with fear on her face. I will keep my distance for now, until I can safely make contact.

Day six entry
The nineteenth day of August 1779
I have hidden in a new location; am writing while observing a loud argument between two of the tallest tribesmen and the Chief. I have determined that one is the father and the other, his eldest son, maybe. The Chief, however, seems very surprised by their bold, verbal outcry, though I understand not a word that they speak. Many villagers stare from their huts with opened mouths. This must be a rare display of defi—   I am not sure what I see! A trick of the sunlight, perhaps?! The two aggressors, the two in front of the Chief they changed

They are getting hairier   muscles
        they're shrinking to all fours and
Their mouths -TEETH. The teeth- they have, shaped
sharpened!
Witchcraft! ??? It's got to be.
Even the Chief steps away, yet unafraid.
He glances MY way- Why? A warning?
He knows I'm here. They know
I must go.

Day seven entry
The twentieth day of August 1779
I am determined to make contact today. I shall bring along
Privates Samuels and McIntosh to meet with the Chief. I did
not tell the Privates of the strangeness I saw. But what I have
witnessed of the elder Chief, his signs of integrity and altruism
makes me believe we will be welcomed.

I await the exit of the two aggressors as a precaution hoping
that the two are preparing a band to go for another hunt.

Yes. I was correct. And a similar group as before, the
father/son are among the band. So relieved.

For peace offerings we have little, yet are prepared with two
Boston-made knives, a metal shovel and a strong pick-ax. I
pray our gifts to the Chief and his people will gain us trust.
Perhaps then may we explore the witchcraft I have witnessed.
A moment longer we shall wait.

I will breathe with ease knowing tha

The writing ended. Colin could not see the slightest indentation of the next stroke. Something had happened quickly, but not quick enough to stop the soldier from slipping the booklet into his boot. It seemed to Colin that the notebook's contents would hint to the fact that the *aggressors*, the angry tribesmen, had attacked the soldiers. But then Colin remembered that Mr. Benson had said there was fur all over the place.

What about the mention of witchcraft and how it made the aggressors hairier? Colin thought. *So, it could have been the aggressor's hair!* He emitted a laugh and considered the fact that what he saw was probably due to the soldier drinking, as Mr. Benson had suggested. Of course, there was still the possibility that the tribe had domesticated and trained those wolf dogs to do the hunting *and killing* for them.

Wasn't there a story about this in southern Vermont? Colin suddenly thought.

Colin suddenly noticed the time and quickly jotted all the main information down, forgetting the Southern Vermont connection. He had also written a reminder note to himself to *Google* shaman magic for the fun of it. Skyler would at least get a kick out of that.

He hopped up the stairs and said goodbye to Mr. and Mrs. Benson, who were still talking about the strange reactions of Tweety and Bam Bam. As Colin walked out the door, he played with the idea of how the Sachem Tribe might have trained these two Great Danes to kill. The thought had seemed quite creepy.

Chapter 10:
The Body of Bobby LeClaire

Police Chief Porter and Sergeant Harrison passed under the strip of police tape to yet another murder scene within the past month, except this time it was only one person.

"Found him by the river this morning, Chief. Well, what was left of him. Pulled the body out half an hour ago," Officer York said, as Mitch and Stephanie maneuvered through the tall grass and rocks.

"But it wasn't a drowning?" Mitch questioned again, though he had hoped it was.

"Nope. Got the same markings as the rest...but this one's a *bit* different," Officer York replied as he pulled back the sheet. "Besides the fact that he was found buck-naked, this big fellow seemed to have put up a fight."

"How do you know?" Stephanie asked, kneeling beside the bloated body.

"I'll tell ya, Sergeant," the officer continued. "This time we found fur under the fingernails and, get this...*In* the mouth."

"*Mouth?*" Stephanie repeated as she slowly separated the dead man's lips with her rubber-gloved fingers. Sure enough, small tuffs of fur sat between the front teeth. Then she found tiny fragments of flesh, fur and blood crammed inside the man's long fingernails. Stephanie glanced at the multiple claw marks on the body and could tell that he had been part of the fight. The wounds were mostly from the chest up; the other murders had been clawed and bitten all over their bodies. However, death for this burly man had occurred from a massive wound to the stomach. In fact, the whole stomach was ripped out of the body.

Not knowing why, Stephanie had knelt down to lift up the eyelids.

"Hmmm," she responded.

"What?" Mitch asked.

"Well, you know, a person's pupils, when dead, are almost always dilated," Stephanie said, reaching again for the lids. "His are just tiny pin-pricks."

"Could be drugs," Officer York suggested.

"That could be checked in the lab, but it doesn't get us any closer to who is doing this," the police chief remarked. He pointed to officers Grunwald and Henderson. "Go up river and look for the location of a possible struggle. Officer York, get back to the station and check missing persons. Let's find out *who* this guy is. If this murder is different from the others, maybe the clues will be different."

"Wait. What's that?" Stephanie reacted as Officer York was sliding the sheet back over the body.

"What's what?" he asked.

"Look, a small tattoo on the back of his forearm," the sergeant said. She pulled out her pad and quickly sketched the unique symbol onto the paper.

"It sure isn't one of those Irish-Celtic tattoos," observed Mitch as he looked over her shoulder. "It looks American Indian."

***

At the hardware store Mr. LeClaire had begun to demand tougher jobs for Colin to tackle. To Colin's surprise, he enjoyed the heavier, challenging work and was excited that his *Mountain Bike* goal was almost in reach.

He walked home on that warm August evening and continued to the back of the house to see what his father was up to.

"Hey, Col," his dad smiled with his shotgun invention in his hand. "Your mom is in quite the happy mood. She's been packing all morning."

He lifted the gun and blasted a glob of his specially mixed sealant that was incased in a plastic cylinder. It broke open on impact spilling the sealant into the cracks of their chimney. This was his *next* big idea.

"Well, I may just have something here, by golly," he proudly said. "How was work?"

"Great," replied Colin. "I'm finally lifting more lumber stacks than Mr. LeClaire. He got some sort of bad news, though. Gotta let Mom know."

Colin jumped onto the porch and through the door in time to see his giddy mother (while holding beach towels, sunscreen and their landline phone) suddenly drop her smile.

"Are they *sure* it was him?" she said trying to maneuver away from Colin. "But he was a..." She looked at Colin. "Really? The stomach? Hmm-yes, okay, try for Monday. We can wait. We'll talk then."

She got off the phone and looked up at Colin.

"It was Mr. LeClaire, wasn't it?" Colin asked. "I saw how upset he was earlier. Someone died?"

Colin's mother didn't answer right away, but eventually said, "Yes, his son, Bobby."

"I never knew he had a son," Colin said.

"Yeah, that's one story he doesn't mention freely. They had a falling out many years ago."

"Did you know him?"

"Oh, yeah. Big, tough Bobby LeClaire. He owned a lumber yard in northern Maine," Anne explained.

"How did he die? You mentioned the stomach."

"Ah, *shot*...it sounds like."

Colin was about to ask what had happened between this mysterious son and Mr. LeClaire when his mom said, "Richard had always preferred peaceful solutions to events; Bobby, on the other hand, did not."

"Was he involved in the Mob, or something, and got himself killed?"

"No, um...maybe," Anne sputtered. "Change of subject, okay? How 'bout you go get your bags packed. And remember, lots of old clothes."

"Ah, why?" Colin asked as he moved towards the stairway.

"We Sachems like to get dirty," she announced, actually giddy again.

***

Stephanie Harrison had been off in the lab studying the fleshy fragments found under the latest victim's fingernails with Fish and Game Warden, Jack Richmond. Police Chief Porter made himself busy at the station, playing detective.

Mitch opened up the folder embarrassingly labeled, *The Pack Dog Murders* and spread the files over his desk. He had understood that the murders were all connected, that *maybe* dogs were involved, and that, for some reason, the victims were mostly white males. But now, with the news of the latest murder, Mitch had a new twist to the mystery. They discovered that the latest victim was Bobby LeClaire, that he was a high-powered businessman and, according to his wife, had an American Indian background. The two young officers Mitch had sent to look for clues had discovered the car in a small open field on the New Hampshire side; it was two miles up the river and had been set on fire.

LeClaire's body was identified due to the keen eyes of Officer Grunwald. She had caught sight of two small pieces of a *LeClaire Lumber Company* business card that had fallen from the vehicle before it was set on fire. The young officer also found the evidence showing that Bobby LeClaire must have died from his wounds earlier, was driven to the river in his car, then dumped into the water. What was difficult to comprehend, Mitch realized, was the fact that the tracks from his car showed signs of only one person leaving. The prints sunk deep into the soil as if the offender was carrying a heavy load, but Mitch just couldn't believe a single person could have supported the weight of such a husky man all the way to the river.

He turned the partially damaged business card over in his hand and noticed pieces of an address on its backside.

"*Bair-* and *-6 Edge-*. Damn," Mitch said to himself as the phone rang. "Yes?"

"Sir, it's Officer York. Nothing much else about this LeClaire-guy 'cept I did a Google search for that possible Indian tattoo of his and found an expert who could probably help."

"Great. Email me the name and number, I'll call him later," the police chief said.

"Well, Chief, this guy is *right* here in Vermont. A Mr. Harvey Benson, up in Cochran."

***

Johnny Dumont sat across from Richard LeClaire in the hardware store office. Johnny was a tough looking individual, but on this particular day he looked exceptionally drained and haggard.

Richard had sat there quietly after hearing the news, digesting what he had just heard. Finally, he responded, "It explains how Bobby could have been so easily killed."

"He had fought admirably," Johnny tried to reassure.

"But got scared enough to change back to human," Richard replied.

"He thought his money could get him out of the ritual battle," Johnny offered.

"Hmmm, yes," Richard said, a sad smile on his face. "Bobby fought so hard as a teen to not be human, only to die because he became *too* human. Okay, then...it seems we now have a strong and angry Superior among us. That's as shocking as Bobby's death."

"My mouth dropped at the sight of the boy transforming," admitted Johnny.

"The son of Baird Dawes, huh? Lizzy Carrier told me what little she knew about the father," Richard said as he stood and looked out his window. "She explained him as a self-deprecating martyr for the mistreatment of Indians. He obviously sees the arrival of a Superior as a sign to fight back. *And*, as we all have speculated, he and his son are obviously involved with the murders in the south. The battle has already begun."

"Yeah," agreed Johnny.

"It makes sense why this *Victor* would be so vicious having grown up under Baird's hatred," Richard continued. "But how are they convincing others to be just as angry and to fight along with the two of them?"

"Documents," Johnny said, recalling Baird's words. "Something about documents. I would have mentioned it earlier 'cept I had to tell you about Bobby first. Dawes has information concerning some troubling events that were carried out by wealthy, Vermont people...decades ago. So, whatever is contained in those papers is the main reason for the group's rage."

"You couldn't ask about it?" Richard inquired.

"No, this was somehow explained to the others from Baird's initial phone call. Since I wasn't personally invited, I haven't been told shit. Been spending my time playing tough and mean to prove myself."

"Are they planning to find and go after these people?"

"I think so," said Johnny as he rubbed his temples over-and-over. "I do know one thing about the documents, there are names on them identifying the people who had been involved with whatever they're angry about."

"So, whatever they've discovered is bad enough to form an army of Shifters and risk exposure of our kind," Richard said irritably. He stopped and breathed a sigh. "And an angry army like that, led by a young Superior, is going to be hard to stop, even by some of our strongest tribesmen and women."

Staring seriously at his friend, Richard eventually said, "We need you back down there to find out their next move."

"Yeah, I thought as much," Johnny replied. "I'll do my best."

Richard smiled sadly. "Be careful."

Chapter 11:
The Sachem Family Reunion

The trip to Flying Pheasant Campground, just east of Lancaster, New Hampshire, took a mere two and a half hours. To Colin it seemed much longer.

"Again, *why* are we doing this?" asked April for the umpteenth time.

Colin rolled his eyes at her for the *umpteenth* time.

"To see some of my relatives who I haven't seen since your father and I got married," Colin's mother repeated. "Come on, April. It'll be fun. There'll be kids of all ages there."

"Yeah, any cute boys?" April asked, her arms tightly crossed.

"Well, probably-but..." Anne began.

"Probably-but *related to you*," Colin finished. "Just quit the damn complaining!"

"Colin," his mother said, "Mind your words."

"Her whiney screeches are hurting my ears," Colin responded.

"*Nnneeeaaah!*" April shrilled.

"April, *stop*! If you two have a problem, talk-it-out."

This had always been his mom's solution, Colin knew, but it never really worked.

"*Hmmph*," April remarked as she grabbed one of her teen magazines, but not before sticking her tongue out at Colin.

Anne eventually turned to him and asked if his ears had been sensitive lately.

"Yeah," Colin answered, thinking about how he could now hear everything so crystal clear. "I can hear the weirdest sounds. Even my cell phone makes a noise I can't stand. I don't even want to use it anymore."

"I'll take it!" April volunteered.

"I didn't bring it," Colin admitted and continued. "I'm thinking my ears are clearer from having less allergies this summer. My nose sure is clearer."

"That's right, you used to sneeze up a storm this time of year," his father replied.

"Well, let me know if it gets too much," his mother said with a mysterious smile. "And, April, like I said, this reunion is going to be fun and interesting."

"Yeah, right," she mumbled.

"Why *interesting*?" Colin asked curiously.

She turned back to him and smiled, "My family has a long line of wildness in us."

Colin smiled and nodded, but didn't make a comment. He considered the use of the word "wildness" and wondered if these seldom seen relatives of his still followed their traditional *native ways*. Colin had begun to get excited about this whole reunion thing.

***

The tanned, but weathered face of Connie Smith stared over at her hung-over husband, Irwin, as they drove onto the road to the Flying Pheasant Campground. She slowed to a crawl to examine the visual layout of the place they'd be staying. Connie smiled at the vast potential of its grounds. This particular camping area bordered protected National Forest that allowed a huge span of uninhabited terrain for the wildest of her family to roam. Then she frowned at what she knew as *the family*. Blood relatives, sure, but very repressed for a bunch of Shifters.

However, she thought to herself, *that's not the reason I've come to this ridiculous thing.* "Wake up, Irwin!" her raspy voice bellowed. "We're here."

"Wha-Huh?" he sputtered, shimmying upright to peer out the windows. "Think their serving dinner yet?"

"It's three in the afternoon, you idiot," Connie barked, "and we're camping, remember?"

"Gee, Hun, do you really want to connect with these relatives of yours?" Irwin asked. "All you've done is complain about them since I've known you. Whadya call them? *'Damn European Domestics'.* Whatever the hell that means."

"Close the trap and go ask the manager where 51N is," she ordered.

"If you ask me, you've been pretty damn vicious ever since your trip to Eureka, *geezum-moses*," Irwin mumbled as he waddled towards the campground office.

***

Colin's father drove slowly down the rows of trees and campers in search for their site. April was especially anxious to get out of the car.

"Here it is," exclaimed Colin. "I'll get out and direct you."

'What are you trying to get, *brownie points*?" April sneered. "Or are you really excited to be here?"

Colin didn't answer as he hopped onto the pinecone laden gravel road. While he helped his father back their pop-up camper into place, he began to realize how excited he was to be out in this natural setting. His mother had always had them go on camping trips since he first remembered. She seemed to be at the peak of excitement any time they got near a wilderness location, whether it was to stay overnight, hike for a few hours or simply stop and stare out from a roadside overlook. Eventually, when Colin was old enough to complain, (like April), he insisted on the luxury of hotels and motels with in-ground pools and dinners out. But on this day, with the smell of fresh cedar in the air and the scent of Flying Pheasant Lake just down the hill, Colin had got plain fired-up about being there.

Colin's mom had been dropped off at the main office to sign them in. She had come back up the dirt road skipping like a schoolgirl. "I just saw Aunt Trisha and Uncle Bill. *What* a cute couple," she smiled happily. "You two go off and explore. I'll help your dad prepare the camper and all. Some families have signs up, so go introduce yourselves if you see any."

"*Oh*, joy!" announced April. "We're supposed to walk up to total strangers."

"*Not* strangers, April," her mother corrected. "Maybe you can find a distant cousin to connect with."

"*Can't wait*," April remarked, but started down the road.

"Hey, I'll join you," Colin said, having wanted a reason to see the sights.

"Why? So you can fend off any attacks from distant cousins?" she smirked.

"No, so I can protect you from this wild, scary wilderness," Colin said, baring his teeth and raising his arms like some tall, *thin* bear. "I've heard the mice and squirrels are ferocious around here."

"You're *such* a twit," April responded. "Seriously, why are you following me?"

"I'm not following you, *Willis*," Colin said, insulted. "Besides we're in a new area with relatives we hardly know."

"*And?*"

Colin had struggled wanting to tell April anything about his summer extracurricular activities. He thought he should wait until he got more information by seeing if these relatives would prove his Indian research correct. He decided to at least tweak her curiosity a little.

"Well," Colin smirked, bending forward and raising his eyebrows, "who knows...there just might be more to Mom's ancestry then meets the eye."

"*Oooo,* family secrets?" April exaggerated, waving her arms.

"Yeah, well, maybe we'll find out Mom's not *just* French Canadian," Colin dared to say.

"Like, maybe she was raised by elves, but was later adopted into the Sachem family," she jokingly deliberated. "And *she* only ate Lucky Charms cereal and drew rainbows as a child."

"And grew up to only date boys who wore green," Colin joined in.

He accepted the fact that April was not ready for his theory.

"*Oh, my god-* that's right," she replied. "Remember that old picture of Mom and Dad in college going on one of their first dates? Dad *was* wearing that atrocious, green polyester suit!"

"Ha, yeah, I do."

"Dad wore green a lot," giggled April. "She must have influenced him."

It was good to see April finally coming out of her stubborn shell, Colin realized, she could actually be fun when she wasn't focused on complaining or attacking him.

They had eventually reached the lake and began to encircle it towards the wooded shores to its right. Even as he and April continued to talk about fantastical possibilities of their mother's background, Colin couldn't help but be aware of the minute events going on around him. The frog that had just caught a fly by the marshy section of the lake, the ants pulling a large wasp into their tiny hole, the mother skunk with three babies keeping perfectly still as the two intruders walked past her den. Suddenly, reacting to no sound, but sensing something, Colin looked at a shadowy clearing in the woods ahead. He grabbed April and quickly hushed her silent, making her kneel to the ground. He pointed to the clearing. April followed his finger, and then gave a little gasp. In front of them, at about one hundred and ten yards, were two wolves. Both had been staring at them with their white and gray fur waving in the wind.

The two large canines peered for one last second, then bounded towards the deep forest, playfully nipping at each other's hindquarters.

Colin and his sister watched the empty clearing for a little longer.

"*Whoa!*" April finally said. "*That* was awesome. I didn't know there were wolves in this area."

"I thought I had heard about some groups wanting to reintroduce them back into the wild here," Colin said. "It must have happened."

"Where's your phone?" April suddenly said. "I want to text a friend about this."

"Remember? I didn't bring it."

"*Really?* Who doesn't carry their phone? When I get mine..." she began and then trailed off. "I'll tell her later. *Still,* that was pretty cool."

"Remember what Mom said once, 'Seeing certain animals were good omens, especially wolves and eagles.' I guess we just got a good omen about this weekend."

"*Right*," April said as she looked back up towards the campsites. "Well, I just *hope* Mom starts cooking soon. I'm as *hungry* as a wolf."

***

Colin and April had found themselves meeting many cousins and second cousins as well as aunts and uncles they never knew existed. Some were very round and stout; some were tall and lean like Colin, while others were rather short. Colin's mother had explained that the short ones were of their French-Canadian side, and then realized she had put her foot in her mouth. "I mean, the *French* side that is traditionally shorter than our English-speaking-Canadian-side."

Colin let this go without questioning it, smirking at the fact that their American Indian background was bound to slip out this weekend at some point.

To Colin's dismay, though, the weekend meandered by without a hint of any native heritage implied. April had found two other gloating teen cousins to complain with (unaware she was actually enjoying herself), while Colin mingled among as many relatives as he could.

His search for the truth began with the jolly, beer-drinking uncles.

"So, your Annie's boy? Ya look like your great cousin Clarence. Had logs from a truck fall on him back in '62."

"Tall for your age. Play basketball?"

"Ya play hockey, I hope. Not that sissy basketball!"

"Let me see those muscles, you hamburger."

Every comment or question was followed by slaps on his back. Colin endured the slaps as well as the lengthy talks about United States versus Canadian sports.

From there he moved on to some of the grandfathers, and even great grandfathers, who told embellished stories of bygone days. Colin tuned in to any terms that might talk of rituals, dreams or even hunting experiences. He instead heard about how the milk was delivered by horse and buggy, about building and maintaining a town square skating rink, how they used to sled down Casey Hill and across Elm Street until Chester Owen got hit by Mr. Byron's Model T and broke both his legs. Plus, there were the many stories told by Dr. Sachem (*Dr. Grandpa*, to everyone) who used to get paid with live chickens and ears of corn for his optometry and ENT work. The eighty-four-year-old spoke of how he even had to turn down a 550-pound sow once.

All this mingling didn't accomplish much until Colin introduced himself to Great Grandmother Carrier.

It had been early afternoon that Sunday as a group of relatives, including his mother, had just left the campground's assembly hall building. Colin slipped in through a side door, having escaped yet another game of horseshoes with three highly competitive cousins. He had noticed the gathering of elders entering the building earlier because of an argument by one of the aunts near the playground. She had been asked, Colin overheard, to help keep the teens busy on the beach while the *Games* committee prepared for some special family race they were planning. This particular aunt (one who Colin had not met personally) was extremely upset at the fact that she was not part of the committee. She hissed some words that Colin couldn't decipher and stormed off. Instead of eavesdropping on the meeting, Colin busied himself until he found the opportunity to visit with the oldest member of the Sachem family.

Having recently heard so much about Great Grandmother Carrier, Colin had questioned himself as to why he hadn't gone to her in the first place. He didn't remember her when he was younger, but was told by his mother that they had met years ago when he was about two. Since then, she had kept to her dairy farm in the northeast tip of New Hampshire, which she ran by herself, since the death of her husband. "Sadly, we never found the time to all get up there to visit her," his mother had said just before the reunion.

According to his mother's stories Lizzy Carrier neither resembled, nor acted, her age. Anne Trask's favorite way of describing her was that she probably still got carded in grocery stores for trying to buy beer. She was ninety-two. In these few days of the reunion Colin understood what his mother was saying having observed this older woman moving about with ease. Though she used a cane, Colin was convinced it was merely a prop.

He entered the assembly hall and saw her cane leaning against a soft leather chair in front of the fireplace. Colin took notice to the cane's exquisitely polished surface, exhibiting a well-crafted wolf head at its crown. He approached Great Grandmother Carrier from behind ready to seat himself on the couch beside her. He admired, as he got closer, her sweet flowery scent; unlike the smell of the elderly people, he had met, at his mother's work. In fact, he remembered this very scent as being an incense fragrance that his mother would use in their home a lot.

"Annie Trask's boy. Colin, is it?" she spoke without turning to see.

"Yes, but how..." Colin began as he slid himself onto the couch.

"I still have powerful ears, and it's the way you walk on the wood floor, dearie. You're very sure and strong, yet still very youthful. I've been watching you, as well as your other cousins," she said with a smile, displaying, as Colin also recognized and admired, her own teeth. "It's what I do at my age. I sit and watch, listening and getting to know the next generation of our family. It is so good to finally meet you."

"Yes, me, too, Mrs... Grandm-," Colin stammered as he shook her weathered yet firm, gripping hand.

"Oh, just call me Lizzy..." but then she paused. With a twinkle in her eye she said, "Or, perhaps, *you* would like to call me by my birth name, *Nashoba*."

"*Nashoba?*" Colin repeated, perking-up in his chair. "That sure sounds like..."

"Indian...maybe? *Yes*, it means *wolf* in Chickasaw. My mother enjoyed learning the different native languages," Lizzy said. "I sense there's a touch of curiosity on the subject for you?"

"Oh, *yes*, I've been...investigating *our* link...as a family, to natives, like, in this region. But nobody has said anything all weekend," Colin had confessed, feeling excited about finally getting answers to this mystery. "I *know* about the secret," he then whispered. "I just wanted to know if what I've researched was true."

"About what, my dear?" she pried as she questioned the depth of his knowledge.

"About our ancestry, about an Indian connection from our past. I want to know if we're a bit more than just Canadians and why we keep it such a secret."

"*A bit more?*" she responded with a wide grin. "Oh, yes. The Sachem bloodline is indeed a *bit* more. *But* let's not fill your head with too much information today, dear boy. Very soon you'll know far more. Yes, indeed, you will."

Chapter 12:
Listening, Smelling and Touching

Monday would be their last day at the campground with a late afternoon checkout time. This allowed most of the day for the big event the family members called *The Sachem Challenge* (complete with t-shirts and, for the winner, one wood-carved trophy displaying a bare foot). It was to be held from noon to three, followed by a quick awards ceremony, and the traditional feast of roast pig. The news of the pig made Colin's mouth water.

They were told that the race was only for the young relatives between thirteen and sixteen and was traditionally quite difficult and possibly dangerous. Colin thought this was a ploy to get any teenager to want to attempt it. What he couldn't figure out was why the adults developed this whole event *only* around the teens.

"Excited, Colin?" his dad asked as he entered the camper in his fishing vest and waist-high boots. He had just returned from the lake with a self-made rod that, according to Colin's dad, could send out sound vibrations of a wiggling worm, instead of using a worm. He caught nothing.

"Excited? Yeah, kind of," Colin mumbled with a cream cheesed bagel in his mouth.

"It's supposed to stay in the seventies today so it won't be a scorcher," his dad announced, always up on the weather. "Partly overcast, but fairly breezy. *That'll* keep the bugs away, 'cept for in the woods."

Colin looked at him for a moment then said, "Are you practicing to be a meteorologist, Dad, or are you nervous about something?"

"Nope-nope...just want you and April to have fun...with this race."

"Do you know something about *this* race?"

"Ah, well, a little...I got to see it once at the one other reunion I went to," his dad said between the tugs of his waders. "I remember the kids doing lots of running and jumping over stuff. *And* there was this boy...he almost, kinda slipped off the swinging rope into the river. Your Great Uncle Bill caught him. Huh, *that* was fascinating."

"*Fascinating?*"

"Yeah, I kinda got to see it. Wasn't supposed to, I found out later, but *they*, your mom's family, kinda all seemed upset that I saw it."

"Upset? Because you saw swinging ropes and rescuing uncles?" Colin questioned.

"Well, to put it simply, Uncle Bill...*kinda* just came out of nowhere and grabbed the boy before he fell. Rather miraculous...really. He obviously was agile for his age...for even back then. I'd have probably thrown my back out."

"So, that's it? You weren't supposed to see that?" Colin wondered. "Maybe this particular kid wasn't a good swimmer, plus Uncle Bill was, say, an ex-football player or something?"

"Actually, he *did* say he played football," his father said. "As for your mother, she insisted that every part of the course had been completely thought-out and safe. So, she asked me just to forget about it. And, I did...until now."

"But what did you see that you thought wasn't safe?" Colin pursued.

"Um, well, as a racer, in *that* race, you were to swing across the section of the river that sat over a... well, a hundred-foot drop. But-*hey*, don't you worry, big guy. You're Mom has more than promised me that there wouldn't be steep gorges over rivers in *this* race."

Colin stared at his dad again, then returned to his bagel. "*Great,*" was all he said.

***

April paced back and forth near the horseshoe pits, hands on her hips and red in the face. "*Mom,* I *don't* want to do this," she kept saying. It was just minutes before the starting time and she refused to put on her sneakers. "*I* don't race...*I* shop!"

"Sachem rules, dear," her mom calmly said. "You're thirteen, everyone else is doing it and it's gonna be fun. You might even surprise yourself."

"What? Find out *I'm* just as much a klutz as Colin is?"

"I promise it won't be embarrassing," her mother assured. "And anytime you want to stop, you can let me know."

"I know, how 'bout *now*," she responded.

"Tell you what, I'll give you a hundred-dollar gift certificate to your favorite clothing store when we get home, as long as you do at least the first three sections of the course."

"Seriously? A gift card, like from Bella Boutique?"

"Yes."

"And a cell phone."

"April," Anne protested and then considered it. *If all goes well, here, Colin won't want his phone. If all goes really well, April won't want the phone either!* "Fine." She finally said.

"*Really*-Wow! Alright, then, I'll do it," April exclaimed as she finally sat to put her sneakers on. "So, like, what will Colin get?"

Anne glanced over to her son who was tightening up his shoes near the starting line. In his shorts and the Sachem racing shirt, she could see the muscular changes that had taken place after his birthday. She would soon be seeing how his gift would affect his performance. As for April, she didn't think her daughter had received the family gift yet, but she had learned from past reunions that this simple physical test could sometimes bring out unexpected skills from the least likely candidates.

"I'll ask him later," Anne eventually said. "Besides, he *wanted* to do this. And, who knows, he might reward himself by winning the whole race."

"Ha! -*Right!*" April responded instantly, then saw her mother's expression and said, "Well, yeah, that *would* be special. Wouldn't it?"

The race official was Aunt Trisha who had her *Race Official* t-shirt on and a starting pistol. She had just announced to all participants to line up. The thirteen-year-olds were placed in the front of the line, so Colin was almost to the back. There were only two sixteen-year-olds behind him. Colin had recognized the two as the Carrier twins, Benjamin Junior and Benson. They had been the buzz-cut cousins who were so competitive the day before at horseshoes. Of course, within this family of competitors was the third and youngest brother, Benny, who was lined up with the fourteen-year-old group. Benny was the only one of the three whose hair was longer than a hundredth of an inch; his thick, dark eyebrows gave him a devious look he made use of throughout the game. During the horseshoe matches, Benny would perform an obnoxious dance every time he got a ringer against Colin. He actually howled when he threw the horseshoe so hard that it bent the post. Colin brushed the incident off as a lucky shot and cheap equipment.

The overall tally of racers had been eleven. They were lined up between two long ropes that opened at the far end leading them down to the lake.

April gave a nervous look over her shoulders to Colin, who smiled back with two thumbs up. When he looked beyond where April was standing, he caught the eyes of Great Grandmother Carrier sitting in a rocking chair on the grass. She smiled back raising her old, wrinkly thumbs up to him. Colin then bent forward having expected the gun to be raised right away, but instead saw his mother and several other women come around with blue bandanas in their hands.

"*Mom*?" April blurted, "What the heck. You're blindfolding us?"

"It's an important part of the first three sections," one of the other aunts announced. "To test your senses."

"*Senses*?" Benny joined in, "I thought the course would be running and jumping and stuff! I want a race that calls for speed!"

"The Race is more than just running and jumping," came a familiar voice.

Colin turned to see Mr. LeClaire, who was also sporting an official t-shirt, walking towards the racers. Colin's mother gave him a welcoming grin.

Mr. LeClaire smiled back at her as Colin heard him quietly say, "We *need* to talk."

He returned his attention to the contestants again and said, "The course for this race will contain many levels that will test areas of yourself you never knew existed."

"*Like,* who are you?" Benny boldly asked only to falter with his defiant stance when Mr. LeClaire approached him.

"I am a long-time friend of the family," he smiled, but gave off an air of status all the racers could feel. "*And* I just happen to be the non-biased outsider who will judge and record the results. Mr. Carrier, is it?"

Benny lowered his shoulders and stepped back in line.

"Now listen carefully," Mr. LeClaire said to the others again as blindfolds were tied tight. "You will first be tested with your listening, smelling and touching skills. These three skills will lead you to section four where your blindfolds will come off. From there the skills needed will be more about *speed* and agility."

Colin gave a brief shiver at the word agility, but had quickly reminded himself that *that* was the old Colin.

"Your parents and relatives will be stationed around most of the course," Mr. LeClaire continued, "to help those who might not be able to go on or who may find themselves in precarious positions" (Colin quickly thought of the boy about to fall one hundred feet into a river). "However, for those," he turned in the direction of Benny, "who feel so competitive as to make risky, unconscious decisions along the way, be advised that such hasty actions may possibly place you, and other racers, in unnecessary danger."

Colin could imagine Benny rolling his eyes under his bandana. Having worked with Mr. LeClaire for so long, Colin was going to believe everything he was saying.

"*Let the race begin,*" Mr. LeClaire announced.

The gun went off and Colin grabbed the rope beside him carefully maneuvering himself out into the field. But before he could reach the opening the Carrier twins trampled by him making him fall hard to his knees. Colin cussed angrily to himself, but then stopped. He suddenly remembered Mr. LeClaire's instructions. *Listening* had been the first thing he mentioned. So instead of peeling himself off the ground, he sat with his ears alert.

All he heard at first were his cousins screaming, tripping and breathing heavily, moving away in a downward direction. Then he perked-up his ears beyond their sounds and heard a woman's repetitive words, *"Colin, Jasmine, Colin, Jasmine, Colin, Jasmine..."*

Colin couldn't understand why his friend's name was being repeated along with his own. Then it occurred to him, *smell* was the second section of the race.

Colin went into a protected strut down the grassy embankment concentrating on the teens around him as well as the whispering woman. He suddenly tripped on a large stone and cursed under his breath again as he fell.

He was about to get back up when he thought. *I'm wearing sneakers, the trophy showed a bare-foot.* What if that was it? His bare feet would feel the ground underneath him far better.

Colin tore off his shoes and found he could now go into a smooth, conservative run. He was better able to anticipate the rocks, bushes and trees under foot by sensing change in the terrain. He followed the repeating name of *jasmine* and then figured that it was the specific scent he was to smell to reach the subsequent sections ahead.

The ground had felt moist from the obvious closeness to the lake so Colin followed its edge to the whispering woman who was now quite close to him. He could also hear the bustling of fellow racers all around him fumbling or splashing along the water. He bumped into someone unexpectedly and realized by the smell that it was April.

"Oops, sorry," she politely said.

"Hey, it's me. How're you doing?"

"Good, I guess. It's hard, but exciting," she exclaimed between breaths. "You hear it, right? That's where I'm going."

"Yes, follow *'jasmine'*," Colin answered, hoping he wasn't being too helpful.

"Jasmine? You mean *'rose'*."

Colin was about to protest, but April had already moved off to his right. He, in turn, continued towards the faint sound of what must be *his* particular flower. Within seconds, though, he had to stop, having found himself surrounded by hundreds of flowery fragrances. The incredible variety of sweetness floated all around him as he just turned in place confused by the attack. He realized that he hadn't considered the actual smell of the jasmine flower until that moment.

What was it? He thought. Where had he connected the word jasmine to the smell he had experienced from his past?

Colin had felt like he stood there for hours, confused and probably blowing the whole race. He thought of how he was going to disappoint his mother who he had overheard at the start telling April about his possibility of winning. In the middle of the thought about his mother one individual fragrance stood out among the others. By focusing on it alone, he connected the smell to his own home of oils and incense that his mother usually used; it was the smells of roses *and* jasmine.

Then he remembered. *Jasmine was the same smell that I smelled on Great Grandmother Carrier just yesterday!*

Colin was off again, using the accuracy of his bare feet to proceed. He went into a jog towards, what he remembered from his walk with April, was the direction of the deep woods. The terrain was now laden with sticks, pine needles and pinecones, but his feet were somehow perfectly callused, as if he were barefoot all his life. Colin was too busy to wonder why.

The jasmine smell grew stronger as he wove through brush and forest. He now had mastered how to focus on the scent, though the smell of pine pitch, trampled gravel and even April's rose fragrance was still all around him. He kept his feet low to the ground to anticipate any changes, but got careless when the fragrance seemed just above him. Colin leapt over a low section of ferns only to smash his body into a tree. He dug fingernails into the furrowed bark, as he held strong to its cylindrical sides. Pausing only for a second, he shook his head to gain clarity as to how the heck he was gripping this tree with nails.

The whole race, and how he had adapted to its obstacles, was beginning to make little sense to him.

Ahead of Colin he heard the recognizable voice of Benny cheering the loss of his blindfold. "See you later, *losers*!"

At any other time, Colin wouldn't have cared about the challenge, but a powerful urge to beat this cocky cousin had pushed him to move harder. He was about to drop back down to the ground when he realized the jasmine smell was truly right above him. Slowly he extracted his effectively sharp nails from the bark and began to climb. He climbed with swaying arms, checking for branches above him. When his hand brushed against an unnatural form, he traced around it to understand the shape.

Ah, the next sense is touch. He thought.

The shape was a freshly cut wooden arrow, pointing up.

Colin sprung up the tree, brushing his hands in various directions to see if the arrows continued and to grab the next branch, or knot. He felt a vague angle change for each arrow, as if it wanted him to encircle the tree. At one point one of the arrows had directed him to the right. Colin reached out to touch a thick branch. He tried to crawl on its top, and then decided instead to shimmy along it, hand-over-hand. He couldn't comprehend where this was taking him and he had to be at least several feet above the ground, but the scent he had been following was now extremely prominent. When his hand hit cut wood again, he realized that it pointed down.

"*Down?*" Colin questioned aloud.

That was when he sensed that another person was nearby. Actually, he could *smell* this person. It was Dr. Grandpa. He remembered his scent from the day before.

"Um, hi? Dr. Grandpa? Do I, like, just drop?" Colin asked this indiscernible presence.

"Yes, Colin," came his voice. "Very good job. Now you can take this off."

When Dr. Grandpa pulled off the blindfold Colin found himself on a well-made platform cleverly braced to the side of the tree. Peering over the edge he could see the ground far below. He was about to ask how this eighty-four-year-old man had climbed the tree, but was interrupted with the next instructions.

"Listen carefully, young man," Dr. Grandpa began as he raised his finger towards a distant location. "Your destination is the top of that mountain there, Mount Madison." He pointed to the first of several peaks that outlined the horizon. Though the closest of all the peaks, Colin's mouth had dropped at the amount of territory he was now supposed to cover.

It's got to be at least three or four miles! Colin thought.

"Speed and agility are what you'll be needing to finish," the older man said.

Mostly to himself Colin said, "Yeah, right. If I don't drop dead from exhaustion."

"Mr. Trask, I am not at liberty to encourage or dissuade you, however, I must remind you of where you are and how you got here. Think about what you have already done and find it in you to know that you will do more. There are only five others who have made it this far, so go. Oh, and your color is green."

"What's the color for?" Colin asked quickly.

"It'll be your path to and up the mountain. You must leave a check on each colored marker with the provided pens. The others have different colors. Your first marker is there. Now go!"

Colin didn't stop to contemplate the advice, but sprung from the platform back onto the tree and quickly maneuvered to the ground. He found the green marker, checked it, then saw the second fifty feet away on a small sapling ahead. He sprinted in that direction.

Chapter 13:
Incredible Feats

Ahead on a cliff overhang, two miles beyond the first section of the race, Connie Smith watched and listened to the proceedings below her. She was just as curious as the others to see who of the young hopefuls would have *the gift*. Her intentions, however, were strictly for recruitment. To do this she tried her best to act interested in everything about the reunion and get involved. However, the insinuation that the others still did not trust her was evident.

She couldn't blame them, really. She *had* been an unruly teen, especially compared to her younger sister. Both parents had been Shifters from various descendants of the original tribe, but *she* was the sibling that received the gift. Her father had encouraged her animal side. He had always told Connie that her mother had become frail and weak from denouncing her true self as a Shifter. "She *chose* to mingle peacefully with the simple humans, along with your sister, rather than honor her tribal *wildness*," he had said. In the end her mother had *"selfishly given in"* (in her father's words) to wounds from a fall down the basement stairs. "It *never* would have happened if the bitch had *remembered* to shift!" he complained to a younger Connie only minutes after the fall. So, Connie learned to appreciate her talents and abused them like any teenager would, like killing farmer's livestock, leading domestic dogs out of town or just scaring the local boys.

The grudge, this weekend, by her mother's relatives, had to do with her involvement in this very similar race years ago near Mount Washington. *She* had won it, as simple as that. Why they all refused her the glory, she couldn't understand. Connie had performed the race like all the others, except she had already known that she was a Shifter and knew how to use it to her benefit. So along with the speed needed, jumping challenges and agility, she added a bit of her own personality by using *cunning* as a tool. *What was the big deal?* She thought. *A trap here, a sabotage there.* Connie had assumed that the use of *clever cunning* was an honorable trait of the wolf. *But-no! The Elders did not.* Well, she had to admit, the judges did have reason to be somewhat perturbed by the possible disaster she had helped make happen. I guess she did chew *too much* fiber off that rope swing that was to carry her cousin across the river gorge.

But, hey, she thought, a smirk covering her lips, *I knew that cousin was a Shifter too, and he would have been fine with the fall...I think.* Besides, he *was* catching up to her far too quickly, so she *had* to do something. In the end, after Uncle William prevented his fall, this cousin continued on to get second place, but was later awarded the first-place trophy instead of her.

"Ah, who gives a shit?" Connie hissed.

She had understood her place in this unique, but passive group. These people did nothing with their gifted bloodline. They were weak. They were domesticated. Her true place was with the bloodline that took action in the past and is finally taking action again. *Why? Because that group of Wolf Shifters was no longer going to take it anymore!* It had never wanted to accept the European ways in the first place. This branch of the Skiri Clan honored their gift by using its strengths, magic and cunning to terrorize the Europeans who had stolen their land. Connie knew where she belonged. Not with the *Sachem* descendants, but with the descendants of the true leader from their past, Chief *Makade'ma'ingan.* Her place was with the ever-growing pack of *Victor Dawes.*

***

Back at the beginning of the race, Richard LeClaire had found Anne in a secluded area near the lake. She had been whispering the word *rose* for her daughter to follow.

"What is it, Richard?" she said, in a barely audible voice, especially in this crowd.

"I saw Johnny on Saturday," Richard said, his tone sullen. "He told me a little about what was going on with the man who had called you a month ago, Baird Dawes, as well as explaining Bobby's death."

"Oh my god, are the two related?" Anne responded.

"They are, and because of it, we have a serious problem that needs to be reported to some of your relatives as soon as the race ends."

"Does it involve Johnny? Is he all right?" she questioned.

"He's all right, but he's going to need our help," he explained. "Mention it to your Uncle Bill, he'll know who to gather."

"How did Bobby die?"

"Baird's son is a Superior."

"But Bobby is... Two in one place," Anne paused. "A Ritual Battle."

"Yes," Richard answered. "The Dawes boy is sixteen."

"To have beaten Bobby he would have to have been..."

"*Very* strong. Yes," Richard said.

***

Running along the forest ground as if it were plush carpet, Colin had taken the time to glance at his fingernails. They were definitely longer, but what struck Colin was how thick and strong they were. He'd barely had the time to wonder about the changes he'd been seeing in himself. Were these maturing qualities one received once fifteen or had his organic and vegetarian diet proved highly beneficial to his young body? All he knew was that Dr. Grandpa was right, he *had* done some amazing things so far that his friends and classmates would have been totally amazed at. What would Quentin and the others say about him now?

A branch suddenly skimmed his ear.

Stay alert! Colin thought as he went into a faster sprint towards another green marker. He checked it off and then quickly scanned the horizon for the next. When he spotted one, painted on a pine about a hundred and twenty yards up a slight hill, he made a dash in that direction.

Set in the rhythm of his pace Colin's mind had begun to wander. This time he thought about Julia. *If she could see me now!* Colin smiled. *Sprinting barefoot! My awesome agility-Damn, she would totally...*

Colin had smoothly cleared a row of thick underbrush, but immediately found the ground disappear underneath him. The drop was fifty feet into a gouged-out ravine with felled trees dispersed along its bottom. Colin could see no rope or hanging branch to grab as he plummeted towards what he thought was his end. Wanting to accept fear as the emotion-of-choice, Colin instead, found himself concentrating on the fall and the impending collision with tree trunks. He prepared himself for a three-point landing, focusing on one horizontal trunk. His body tingled. *Oddly,* he just knew he'd be all right.

Colin relaxed certain muscles while tightening others as he made contact with the leveled trunk. His legs were spread shoulder width apart as he quickly dropped a knee and a hand for balance. The other hand wrapped around a side branch with grappling fingernails.

He landed hard, but safely.

Once secure Colin stood upright. He returned his attention to the marker location above him and shook his head. He was now close to the bottom of this steep ravine that could have been avoided if he hadn't had his mind on Julia. This was obviously what Mr. LeClaire meant by *precarious positions.*

Colin looked down at his prominent fingernails, then up to one tree clinging half way up the side of the ledge by stubborn roots. He guessed it was about twenty feet above him. Near the top he saw a protruding rock, and just above that was the east side of the ravine's top ledge. If he could just reach those two areas he'd be out of this deep gully in no time.

Bending low, Colin prepared to put all his energy into a standing jump to reach the side of the clinging tree. He pressed hard off the trunk with such force that instead of reaching the dangling tree he bypassed it completely and settled onto the extended rock. Having hopped easily to the top ledge Colin stared back down the ravine in shock at how he just got out. He checked the marker, and then began to run to the next green symbol.

***

Benny Carrier was totally in the lead and he knew it. What had helped this lead was that he already knew about his native past *and* the gift. His father had told Benny and his brothers, years ago, of their possible special inheritance, but it was only Benny who had the Initiation Dream and the physical powers that came with it. Though he had learned of his new talents at the age of thirteen, Benny *had yet* to be able to actually shift. He had mastered the strength, hearing and sight, and the incredible agility of the wolf, but could not change into a wolf.

Benny smoothly traversed the mountain slope where he was able to see several markers, this enabled him ample time to know his next direction. It also enabled him to listen for any other racers, in case they were getting *too* close. Minutes earlier he had heard the scream of his second cousin, Mark, a thirteen-year-old who had cleverly flown through the senses-part of the race, but must have messed up on that horribly loose rope bridge. Benny smiled picking at the fibers still caught in his teeth. He had also heard Colin and another at one point, but lost the sounds of their pounding strides. He figured they must have made their own mistakes and were both out of the race.

The only other worry he had was Sasha, the fourteen-year-old girl who was bounding up the slope to his right. Having pin-pointed the distance of her crushing branches and turning stones, Benny knew that he had time to have a bit more fun with this last opponent. He scanned the terrain ahead for the next obstacle Sasha would have to face. The various rope swings, bridges and jumps were all to gauge the animal-like abilities of the newly gifted young. Benny's father had already told him of the hurdles they were to face making it easier for him to know what to look for.

Benny surveyed the rocky, thinly treed horizon from his vantage point and spotted a red marker, Sasha's color. He sprinted to that location and looked beyond. Sure enough, Sasha's next task was to climb a jagged rock face, grab the aptly supplied rope, then vault sideways around an overhanging precipice to a safe ledge on its other side.

Benny looked and listened for any relatives who could be observing, then bounded up the cliff's edge. He considered chewing on more rope, but instead devised another antagonistic scheme. Having noticed that you couldn't see the ledge to swing out onto until you did so, Benny realized how he could set his next trap.

"Let's call it a *delay*," he told himself.

He straddled the rock ledge, consisting of one big slab, gripped its sides and shook it barely loose from the cliff's stubborn grasp. The slab was left to teeter on the uneven surface, ready to tumble. Benny smiled at his scheme and then jumped to the sloping ground below.

It's a thirty-five-foot drop. Benny thought. *Any fellow Shifter could handle that without getting hurt.*

***

Connie had left her vantage point, and her clothes, behind to gain a new view from up on Mount Madison. As a wolf, though much older now, she could cover a lot more ground.

She had just observed the rope-bridge shenanigans of her little nephew, Benny, and was much impressed by his trouble-making ways. *He could be a perfect candidate.* She thought as she climbed higher.

Having silently settled under the low boughs of junipers, Connie witnessed how her cunning relative was to commit yet another ill deed. She had to stay and see if his fiendish scheme would work.

***

Colin had regained a lot of lost time after the ravine debacle. He had come upon several other obstacles and now understood that these markers were placed in specific spots on purpose for the runners to make mistakes. These mistakes, which he had avoided since the ravine, could have easily resulted in serious injury.

Now why would my relatives set up such dangers? Colin thought, while still highly focused on his stride. *Unless they knew we'd have the abilities to avoid them. But Mom promised Dad there wouldn't be...Oh-wait. She promised there'd be no "steep gorges into rivers"...How sly!*

Colin came to a sloping field of tall boulders and scattered spruce weaving haphazardly up the mountain. They each stood about ten to fifteen feet apart. He had noticed that the markers were intermittent among the large rocks and trees, indicating that hopping from boulder to boulder would be the fastest way up. But on observing the actual path he saw that the spruce trees were blocking the way. *So, besides believing we would not hurt ourselves the relatives must somehow know we can perform incredible jumping feats, too!* Colin curiously considered.

He stopped his pondering and began to spring from boulder to boulder, hurdling any interfering spruce and pines along the way.

"I've got *a lot* of questions for Mom when this is finished," he whispered to himself.

When he catapulted over the last tree and landed, he quickly heard the running footsteps of another racer. With an opponent nearby and another green tree tag ahead, Colin propelled himself in that same direction.

The various trees, smaller juniper and red cedar, indicated that the summit was getting closer. The terrain had become rockier with far more steep ledges and uneven ground. Colin saw that his direction was to go up the middle of a crack in the side of a cliff.

To his right he saw a girl running, someone he had met very briefly before the race. *Sasha, I think her name is.* He watched her smoothly hopping along a jagged rock face. She was fast.

Colin dashed to his next task, but not before seeing Sasha effortlessly swing out and around a large hanging slab on a thick rope, and then she was out of sight.

Colin had just been ready to climb the severed ledge when he heard the scream.

The rumbling and crashing of falling rocks came from the direction of where Sasha had just been. Colin flew out of the cliff's impression and ran towards the location he had last seen her in. He stumbled around the cliff wall, just below what used to be a jutting precipice, and came upon a frightening sight. Ahead of him sat a boulder the shape of a long, but thick, rectangular tabletop, heavy dust floated all around it. On the backside he could see one flailing hand digging and hitting the large stone.

Colin leapt over to the stones' far side and found Sasha wiggling and growling furiously, trying to free her crushed left leg. She angrily whipped her head towards Colin.

The pupils! Just like my mother's eyes when she's angry. Colin thought.

Sasha quickly calmed down, and then said with a struggling voice, "It just collapsed. I landed at my marker and the platform just pulled away from the cliff...the wall just...Hurts *really* bad."

"Okay-okay," Colin said, quickly surveying the scene. "I'm going to do my best. Others should be here soon."

He grabbed the rounded front of the rock and attempted to lift. The battered slope underneath his feet was uneven with broken stone, so his feet couldn't find secure ground. At that point a massive boulder careened down just missing Colin's head. He looked up to where the slab had broken away from the cliff and saw that it was unstable, ready to avalanche at any time.

He straddled the boulder placing his feet firmly on two balanced rocks. Though he had been stable, his struggle to lift the stone was still feeble. When another boulder bounced by, just missing Sasha, he quickly found the courage to try again and dug his fingernails into the hard surface. His muscles tensed so tightly he could feel them ripple and move, his t-shirt tearing from the strain. Every bit of his skin prickled with the intensity of his purpose. He pressed his eyes shut to focus, feeling movement in the large stone. The rock had been so heavy that Colin thought his fingers were elongating from his efforts.

Then he heard Sasha make a screeching sound and quickly assumed that he had just rotated the boulder onto her leg more. This infuriated Colin so much that he tightened every aspect of his body, put his fingernails deeper into the stone and lifted with fierce determination. The boulder effortlessly took to the air, as if made of paper mache, rolling several times away and down the slope until it settled to a stop.

Unfazed, Colin jumped out of his straddled position to examine the leg. When he turned to her, she looked traumatized.

"Dammit! I hurt you, didn't I?" Colin said angrily, his voice hoarse and rough.

Sasha looked like she was trying to move away from him, digging in her hands, but going nowhere. Feeling that he must have caused more damage he turned towards the injury to see how bad it was. When he reached for the bleeding appendage, he saw what had been scaring her. His fingers and arms *had* gotten longer, larger. The heavy rock hadn't seemed like it was stretching his arms, his arms and fingers *had* grown to a different length. As he watched they slowly retracted to their former size.

Colin stared back at Sasha. "*What* did you see?" he asked cautiously, still a little hoarse.

"Nothing...nothing now," she stammered. "You just...AUGH! *Lookout!*"

Another boulder crashed towards the two racers, but Colin arched his body over Sasha and the jagged stone bounced off, lacerating his exposed back. He fell to the side, surprised more than hurt. He quickly jumped back up and said, "We've got to get you out of here."

He leapt towards a small group of trees and (recalling his rescue at the swimming hole) effortlessly tore a sapling from the ground. He peeled off the branches and ran back to Sasha. Colin then ripped his already shredded t-shirt off and gently raised her injured leg into what would become a supporting splint. After some squeals and grimaces Sasha was lifted and carried away from the hazardous spot and transported to safer ground.

As Colin lowered Sasha onto a small patch of moss the cliff wall gave way to a mass of boulders, gravel and dust. They stared in awe at the ripped and damaged slope they had just been on.

After the rumbling calmed Colin turned to Sasha and asked if she was all right. Then, eventually, questioned her again, "Really. What did you see?"

Two men suddenly leapt into their clearing with concern on their faces. One of them, Colin understood, was Sasha's dad, Desmond Sachem.

"*Are you all right, Sash?*" he fervently asked.

She looked up at him with a nervous smile, "I think it's pretty bad...but the pain seems less. Colin *saved* me."

Sasha's dad looked at Colin then looked at her leg. He gave a partially concerned expression to the other man, and then calmly said to Sasha, "You're going to be all right, my girl. Thanks to who you are."

Colin moved closer to the other man, a younger uncle of his, and whispered, "What does he mean? That leg is a total mess."

The man looked at him respectfully. "We came off of the summit just as you had flipped the rock off of her. You must know *now* how incredible your gift is."

"I'm not talking about *me*," Colin said. "*Sasha* has a *crushed* leg. Why does he tell her she'll be okay? To protect her?"

Then the younger man did an odd thing. He stepped back, did some strange bow by placing his fingers to his forehead, and simply asked, "How's your back?"

Confused again by the change of subject, Colin was about to reply harshly, then stopped. He arched his back and pressed a hand behind himself to feel around. *Nothing.* No cut, no pain.

"I *don't* understand," blurted Colin, "*any* of this...*this* whole race. What *I*, and probably the others, have been able to do. What the *hell* is going on and what do you mean *'Thanks to who we are?'*"

Colin swore the man had bowed again, but all he said was, "Be patient, Colin. You'll find out soon enough."

Sasha's father gave him a similar gesture, and simply said, "Thank you."

***

The awards ceremony had taken place a half hour after all racers (intact or injured) had returned from the course. Benny, Colin and Sasha sat at the winner's table along with Uncle Bill, Sasha's father, and Great Grandmother Carrier.

There had been an argument by some of the relatives about why some obstacles had been faulty and why no one had been watching the cliff section of the race. It had resulted in the worst injury they've ever had to date; the elders had noted. They asked any non-participating relatives if they had witnessed any problems, but all of them shook their heads. Lizzy Carrier was not convinced. She looked for signs in the eyes of her young, great grandson and that shifty granddaughter of hers, Connie. Neither flinched.

The ceremony had continued with Benny winning the official *Sachem Challenge* trophy to the sound of clapping while Colin and Sasha received second and third places. Sasha had begun to argue the fact that Colin might have won if he hadn't helped her, but Great Grandmother Carrier hushed her concerns. From under the table the older woman produced a new, smaller trophy, carved also in wood, and held it up for all to see.

She proudly said to the others, "Colin Trask, son of Anne and Philip Trask, dropped all chances of winning this race to help a fallen participant. His concerns for Sasha's safety and keen ability to save her from further injury, requires a new award for our long-celebrated tradition here."

She stepped towards Colin and gestured him to stand, handing him a carving of a howling wolf. At the base it read, *Superior contestant.* She reached for his hand in a handshake, but instead leaned over and kissed it. Embarrassed, but flattered, Colin couldn't help but notice that wood chips were caught between her long fingernails, and the smell of freshly cut wood came from the trophy.

The group of relatives burst into loud clapping and cheering, far louder than that of Benny's first place win. Colin had felt bad for his cousin so he made a look of confusion towards Benny to ease the circumstance. Benny only scowled back. Colin shrugged it off and returned to his seat. He wanted to see how Sasha's leg was doing, but the clapping continued, now followed by some low murmurs and surprised stares. He got a glimpse of his excited mother saying something to Mr. LeClaire as he bobbed his head in acknowledgment.

Colin gave a simple nod to everyone and raised the trophy. He sat back down.

While the group still made gestures of added attention in his direction, Colin leaned over to Sasha and asked about the leg. It was still in the splint with extra tied shirts and towels around it. Why her father didn't just send her to the hospital, he couldn't understand.

"It's feeling so much better," she smiled. "Before it was totally throbbing with pain. Now it just feels stiff and tight."

"Here, let me peek, since I put it on," Colin said as he reached for the t-shirts. He had just untied the ripped fabric when Sasha's dad suddenly appeared beside them saying, "Hey, wait, you might not want..."

But it was too late. Colin unwrapped the bandages.

"It's *almost*...healed," he said, completely dumbfounded.

"Ah, yes, well," stammered Desmond.

"Dad? *How* can I...?" Sasha began.

"You've *got* to be kidding, right?" Benny interrupted. "Of course, *you* can heal."

"Why?" Colin quickly asked as he noticed Sasha's dad try to intervene.

"You're *Shifters*," Benny blurted. "Come on!"

"Benny, ah..." Desmond attempted to interrupt.

"Your *abilities*, shit-heads? Isn't it obvious? You two can change into *wolves*."

Chapter 14:
Wanting Explanations

Connie Smith and her husband had quietly, and quickly, left the campground with not one farewell.

"Why so soon, my love," Irwin asked. "I was just 'bout to play horseshoes with your nephews Bill Jr. and Benson. Probably coulda won this time, since they're both hurt from the race."

"Just *shut up*," Connie responded even though she bristled with thrilling news. "I just needed to get the fuck away from that domestic hoard. Anyway, I found what I came for. *Ha!* And then some."

***

The family ride back to Cochran had only two excited people in the car, April and her dad. They had spent the last half hour speaking with exaggerated enthusiasm about the race.

"It was, like, I could *really* tell where to go," April said for the third time. "I mean, *me*-blindfolded."

"You did very well, dear," her mother quietly said.

"*I* moved through a forest with *just* my nose and ears!"

"Did *well*?" their dad joined in. "*I'd* say, Sweety. *Geezum-crow*, the both of you did great...sorry about the bad tumble into the brook, April. How's the head?"

"Seems better. The bleeding stopped," she answered.

"And, *you*, Colin...Wow," Philip continued. "*What* you did for that cousin of yours was beyond admirable. I never did hear how you got that rock off her leg."

"What? *Mom* didn't fill you in," Colin said.

She shot him a nervous look then softened her face with a begging expression, *"Don't say anything."*

"Honey, what do you know about it?" Philip pressed.

"Oh, Desmond just told me that our clever son, here, made a lever out of thick branches, rocks and logs."

"*Ha!* An inventor, just like his dad," Philip responded and then he looked over his shoulder. "So why the long face then, sport?" But he didn't wait for an answer, "You *really* wanted that win, didn't you? Ever since that basketball game, I bet. I don't blame you."

"Yeah, damn...*wanted* to win," said Colin, as he burned an angry stare into the back of his mother's head.

April saw his intense expression, but read it all her own way, "Colin, you didn't find out about my shopping deal, did you? I mean, *yeah*, I enjoyed the race once it was all happening and everything, but Mom really had to bribe me to run, you know, and you, well, you ju..."

"April," Colin said, producing a smile, "it's okay. Mom and I just need to talk about... what she expects of me, now that I can run through forests barefoot and blind."

"*You* ran barefoot?" April responded. "And you didn't get hurt?"

***

Once they were home and unpacked Colin and his mother stepped out into the backyard where they could talk in private. Colin did so with raised shoulders and crossed arms.

"*What?* What more would you like to *shock* me with?" Colin said.

It wasn't until Colin's father and sister had gone up to their bedrooms did Anne take him by the arm to explain *most* of what was going on.

Colin was tired after the crazy day, but couldn't wait to hear what his mom had to say.

"Please sit," Anne said as she pointed to the picnic table.

"I don't want..." Colin protested.

"*Sit,*" she demanded.

"Is that an order?" he daringly asked.

Colin's mom paused. She looked down and smiled. Without looking up at him she said, "If I were not your mother, no, I wouldn't have ordered you."

"*What? More* mysteries about this Sachem family?" Colin expressed in breathy hisses, his pupils slightly shrinking as he sat himself down.

His mother saw Colin's eyes and once again couldn't help but smile. Anne Trask had wanted to have a Shifter in the family from the start, and had been so disappointed by the lack of visible signs, from both Colin and April, that she had accepted the fact it would never happen. But now, now there was proof, even with April showing evident skills. And then there was Colin, who, without a doubt, had become *so much more*!

"What?" Colin asked again, annoyed by her untimely smiles. "*What* is so amusing about my...or is it *our* situation?"

"Yes, 'ours', Colin," his mother said calmly. "Myself, some of the relatives you met this weekend and, *you*. We all have this gift. Maybe even April."

"Gift?" Colin said, standing again. "It's an oddity, Mom! I was an oddity before this, now I'm a *freak*. A freak who can become...what? *A wolf?* That ought to go over well in school."

"Please keep your voice down, Colin. As for your classmates, they don't need to know, *ever*. We have hidden our shifting skills for ages."

"Hidden it? *Come on!* We're supposed to hide this great *gift* after you and your relatives so kindly tested us all to find the truth?" said Colin. "Wow."

He had fallen back into his chair, exhausted from the day, exhausted from the overload.

Eventually he said with his fingers to his temples, "*Yes,* we have to hide it. That makes a load of sense. *But* I still don't get it. All I wanted to do was solve this mysterious Sachem secret of the family being...*right*...American Indian. I obviously missed some key details."

"We descend from the Skiri Clan, *skiri* meaning wolf," his mother explained.

"Oh...right," Colin responded shaking his head.

Colin's mom stood up and put her hand on his sagging shoulders. "It's going to be all right," she quietly said, then sat down next to him. "You had the dream the night of your birthday. I'm curious what you saw?"

"The *dream*?" Colin considered. He had completely forgot the obvious correlation. "*That's* part of it, isn't it? You always asked about my dreams. You were waiting, weren't you? *You* knew."

"Actually, I didn't know," she responded. "In the last few decades, none of us in the clan ever knew if our special bloodline would continue into the next generation, especially...to *your* degree. We only..."

"And this? What is this *other* thing?" Colin stood, getting exasperated again. "*'...to your degree'.* What is different about me?"

"You have, let's just say, a rare, but special part of the gift. It's an honorable and fascinating part. But not something I can talk about without the help of some elders."

"Elders? What *elders* are going to tell me more?"

"Who would you like?" Anne suddenly asked.

Colin paused to consider this then easily said, "Great Grandmother Carrier."

"A wise choice," she responded. "And maybe Richard LeClaire. He's a great teacher and a great trainer."

"He's one...one of us, too?"

"He is. He's been a friend and part of our pack-of-four for many years."

"Four? Who are the other two?"

"Johnny Dumont and Carolyn Royal."

"Oh, that wilderness outing group of yours? So, all those getaways were the times you guys...changed?"

"Yes, those 'getaways' were our *wolf-time*. We always had lots of fun. But, hey, it's late and there's still so much more to explain," Colin's mother said, getting up out of her chair.

"One thing," Colin began. "Sasha told me I began to change, I mean *shift,* when I needed to lift the rock off of her leg. Does that mean *I* can shift...any time?"

"Yes, but it will take practice to control it, especially around strong emotions."

"Can you show me how *you* do it?"

She gave him a concerned look. *Showing him might be a bit too much for one day.* She thought. *But he's a Superior. He can handle it.*

Anne first looked up to the bedroom windows to see if there were any curious eyes watching and then spread her arms out as if to offer a hug. As Colin watched in amazement his mother's pupils almost disappeared completely with her nose and mouth slowly altering. They expanded forward with her human teeth becoming longer and sharper. What was previously bare skin now filled in with multiple sprouts of hair; *fur?* Her arms began to shrink as she faltered slightly on shortening legs. She dropped on all fours, her clothes loosening and draping haphazardly around her. Then she reverted slowly back to herself as Colin stared at her dog-like paws changing back into human hands.

Colin had been sitting there slack jawed the whole time until he said, "Like...*damn.*"

"I made it quick. I'd otherwise have to put my clothes to the side for a full shift," she explained. "They get entangled and uncomfortable."

"I guess they would," Colin responded. "So, the wolves April and I saw near the lake, three days ago...They were relatives of ours?"

"Yes, probably Aunt Trisha and Uncle Bill. They love to run off and frolic in the woods as soon as they can."

"Ha, yeah, *frolic*...This is gonna take some getting used to." Colin responded, moving towards the house.

His mother put her arms across his back and asked again, "So, what did you see in your dream?"

"You mean, besides the wolf jumping into my body?"

"Yes, we all get to experience that."

"Well, the wolf was a man first."

"Really? What did he look like?"

"An *Indian*-looking man, with only slightly tanned skin. He was tall, lean and strong, with long black hair," Colin recalled. "And a friendly smile."

"Wow," Colin's mother responded. "That must have been Chief Sachem, himself."

Chapter 15:
Different Eating Habits

At the Pleasant Street Grill Colin had met up with Skyler and Jasmine for the first time since visiting Mr. Benson's basement and the weekend reunion. He found it difficult to face his friends and not be able to tell them anything about what had happened to him.

"Dude, like, how are you?" Skyler exclaimed as he put Colin into one of his massive bear hugs. "Seems like it's been years."

"Haven't forgotten that hug, though. *Whew,*" said Colin. He turned to Jasmine and said, "Hey."

"*Hey*-back," she smiled, giving him a hug, too. "Was the reunion so boring that you couldn't text us?"

"Sorry, bad, or no reception. But forget that," Colin quickly said. "I want to hear about California."

"Yeah, any earthquakes?" added Skyler as they sat around a table.

Jasmine gave Skyler an exaggerated grin then turned to Colin. "It was great. My Grandmother's *so* cool. We walked the warm beaches, picked herbs along cliff-covered hillsides, ate great vegetarian dishes and met all these cool, progressive people who think so radically. It's *so* alternative there, that it makes Vermont seem fifty years behind the times."

"Actually, in most movies Vermont is depicted as..." Skyler began.

"*So*, Movie-Man, what've you been up to?" Colin interrupted.

"Not much without my *team,* dude. Just working. But, hey, like, I've seen some great films."

"Shocking," Jasmine muttered.

"Yeah, well, this one, it was so chill," Skyler continued. "It was about this league of vampires at war with a growing population of werewolves, you see, and this one vampire girl was..."

"You guys ready to order?" interrupted the waitress.

"Hi, Christine," Skyler answered. "For me- three slices of pepperoni pizza, please,"

"Why not get the *whole* pie, Skyler?" the waitress asked as she rolled her eyes.

"What a great idea. *You* convinced me again, Christine, and with fries."

Christine didn't bother to write it down.

"I'll have the grilled cheese and a small salad," said Jasmine.

"And you, Trask?" the waitress spoke in a monotone voice. "Let me guess, *veggie burger*."

"Um," Colin said with a blush, pausing. He looked nervously at his friends and then said without hesitation, "The double cheese burger and, ah, some chicken wings...*please*."

Jasmine produced a barely audible, "*What?*" while Skyler dropped the two chair legs back on the floor and announced, "*Whoa-dude.* Did *you* just say what I think you said?"

Even Christine stood there believing it was a joke.

"Seriously, yes, it's what I want," Colin answered the staring faces. "Hey, people change."

The waitress walked off as confused as the others while Jasmine prepared her artillery of questions. "And *what* about all those poor cows, calves and pigs in the factory farms being abused and slaughtered?"

"I know, I know," Colin answered. "I am still upset with those factory farms. It's just something I need in my diet now, that's all."

"'*Just something I need*', he says...*what the frick,*" Jasmine huffed as she stared in disbelief.

The stares continued once the food arrived as Colin used all his strength not to gobble every bit of meat in one bite.

Skyler decided, however, that his friend had finally got some eating sense and proceeded to talk about the werewolf and vampire movie again. It had lasted only a few minutes until Jasmine interrupted. "*So*, did these big changes occur before or after your family reunion?"

Colin accidentally bit into the whole chicken wing, bone and all...and swallowed. After two coughs he eventually mumbled, "Well, I..."

"Hey, like, I get what happened, dude," Skyler chimed. "It was the *Indian* thing. You found out the truth about your heritage and, *boom*, you decided to do as the natives do, right?" He then said (in a terribly cliché-Indian accent), "Big hunter mean big meat eater means big changes for this *Many-Moons-Vegetarian*."

"Ha, like, truly, that's what happened," Colin replied as he tried to look honest.

Forgetting for now about the meat, Jasmine recalled their whole *mystery-quest*. "Then it's true? Did you find out you're truly Indian?"

Colin smiled and realized that this would nicely end all focus on the subject, "Yeah, I really am."

"Was it at the reunion or from the documents at Mr. Benson's house?"

The notebook! Colin suddenly remembered. *It mentioned the wolves. The wolves the soldier saw, they were the tribe members! That means the aggressive ones must have murdered the soldiers as wolves!*

"Colin? *Colin?*" Jasmine repeated.

"Wha-what?" he said snapping out of his daze.

"Like, hello? Jazz was asking what had happened," Skyler added.

"Oh, sorry...I learned it from both," Colin answered. "Wait till you see these papers of Mr. Benson's. *Interesting* stuff. It seems I'm from a *typical* tribe from up north here in Vermont. Dancing, hunting, rituals, you know, plus the shaman/magic thing had to do with acting like animals to, like, to feel their energy and stuff."

"That it?" Skyler responded. "No cool hocus-pocus kinda things?"

"Naw, not really...Oh, and the reunion," Colin continued quickly, "well, there was Great Grandmother Carrier, *she* was the one who finally told me the truth."

"So, was it the Mi'kmaq tribe we read about?" Jasmine asked.

"Oh, yeah. But they called... themselves the Skiri Clan."

"'Called'?" Jasmine repeated.

"Well, they eventually mixed with settlers and other tribes," Colin explained. "French Canadians, Abenakis and such. That's why they, we, aren't, like, an organized tribe...anymore."

Colin struggled hard not to say more, eating meat had been shocking enough for these two.

"And members of your family needed to keep *that* a secret?" Jasmine added, playing with her salad. "Sad."

"Hey, I bet it has to do with that push to keep the *white-man's* blood pure," said Skyler. "So, when that mixing of the races took place, they probably all decided to lie about their own Indian background."

"Yeah, and you know this because of what?" Jasmine questioned.

"Well, besides that eugenics stuff and pure-blood stuff that I wrote in my paper...I also saw something like it in a western. You see the people of the town discriminated against anyone who was different than they were, especially if you were a mixed family. *And* especially if you had mixed with them-there *savages,*" Skyler exaggerated as he eyed Colin with silly intenseness, then leaned back in his chair. "Not saying that *you're* a savage, of course, *dude!*"

Colin had given him an extended stare, and then returned to the luscious taste of chicken flesh. Eventually he smirked and said, "*You'd be surprised.*"

Chapter 16:
The Education of Benny and Colin

Connie Smith dropped her husband off at Lebanon's Mega-Burger Palace where he was manager, drove quickly home, and then called-in sick to her cashier job at the Kwick & E-Z Mart. She grabbed a cold piece of bacon and a glazed donut and then hopped back into her car. She got on the highway and headed off to meet with her young nephew, Benny.

Thanks to Connie, today would be Benny's first, true lesson in the art of changing into a wolf. Connie knew just what it would take to push Benny towards success. She was banking on the smoothness of the shifting lesson, the boy's inevitable gratitude, and, of course, the easy persuasion to join Victor's pack. She could tell by his personality, and his performance in the Sachem race, that he would be a perfect candidate.

As she pulled into the gas station where they were to meet Connie considered the *other* candidate and *his* personality. *Colin Trask.* Anne's son, however, unfortunately showed traits that would make him harder to convince.

Of course, there's the other issue of adding Colin to the pack. Connie thought. *Victor, a Superior himself, would have to be convinced about a nontraditional, unique opportunity. Could this young Chief Born disregard the Ritual Battle to gain a fellow warrior for the cause? Or would he kill him like Bobby LeClaire?*

Nevertheless, Connie knew that the power, strength and combined intelligence of two Superiors would be incredible and she was going to suggest the idea fully. Two Chief Borns guiding their subdominant soldiers into battle would mean an easy victory. Though this would have to be delicately proposed. Deep down Connie knew she had a good idea, and she finally deserved high recognition for her efforts.

In any case, counsel with Victor about Colin Trask would have to wait for now. Today was to be Benny's day.

***

Great Grandmother Carrier turned onto the Trask dirt driveway early Saturday morning. She parked her purple Volkswagen Beetle next to their ramshackle garage that showed many a scar from failed experiments. Lizzy Carrier was probably one of the oldest drivers to hold a New Hampshire license, and would jokingly explain how she planned to give it up at ninety-nine so as not to attract any more attention.

She felt honored this day to have the position of educator and counselor for their first known Superior since Richard LeClaire's son (not including, of course, the one Richard had heard about from southern Vermont. *Because* of this alleged Chief Born, Richard felt it pertinent that they teach and train Colin as quickly as possible).

The whole Trask family, and Richard, were there to greet Lizzy as she slid out of her car. After the hugs and small talk Colin's dad excused himself and April. The two of them were having a day trip to nearby Burlington for shopping. Anne's excuse for Lizzy's visit, and their outing, was to improve Colin's skills that he learned he had from the Sachem race, and Richard was going to coach him with his own personal athletic wisdom.

"We believe he can improve his agility and confidence for any sports this coming school year," she cleverly had lied. Philip, of course, was too excited by this idea to question any it. Besides, April saw this as an opportunity to make use of her $100 gift certificate and look into a new cell phone. Dr. Trask saw it as important father/daughter time.

After April and her dad had finally left, the older woman turned to the others and said, "Okay, for the days ahead, I'd like all of you to be calling me by my birth name, *Nashoba*." Then, turning to Colin, she dropped her head and placed her wrinkled fingers to her forehead (it was the same bow the older men had given him on Mount Madison, Colin recalled). "And, dear, Colin, I am *very* honored to be here for you."

"I'm glad to see you again, Grandmother Ca-..." Colin began.

"Nashoba," she corrected.

"*And,*" Mr. LeClaire exclaimed, "I'd like you, Colin, to officially call me Richard." Richard gave a slight bow, too.

"And I'd like you all to get inside," announced Anne. "The bacon, sausage and eggs are getting cold."

As they shuffled into the house, Colin admitted, "All this, ah, hierarchy stuff is a little weird for me. How am I so different from the rest of you?"

"You will see by the day's end," Nashoba answered.

"It's going to be a lot to get used to," his mother said.

"*Especially* the dogs," Richard added.

"The dogs?" Colin questioned.

"Haven't you noticed the behavior of dogs around you, Colin?" Nashoba asked as she sat herself at the table.

"*The Great Danes,*" Colin blurted.

"Great Danes?" his mother responded.

"Yeah, Mr. Benson's Great Danes, Tweety and Bam Bam. They stopped dead in their tracks when they saw me the other day, just whimpering and staring."

"What were you doing at Mr. Bensons?" Colin's mom questioned.

"That just might be where he discovered his roots, I'd gather," Richard smiled.

"Um, yeah," Colin returned, slightly blushing. "Jasmine, Skyler and I did some snooping."

"*Those two* don't know, do they?" Anne seriously asked.

"No-no, only the Native American connection," Colin explained.
"We like to use American Indian," Richard corrected.

"Right-American Indian. But honestly, it is hard to keep my obvious changes from them," he continued. He then pointed to the bacon and sausage on his plate.

"You must keep the *obvious* secret from them, as you know," Nashoba replied. "We have come this far without being discovered. Only exaggerated stories and fables hint of our existence through the ages. So, remember, with cleverness and control we must hide this special talent inherent in us, yet still use its magic when we can. And we, as your teachers, are here to guide you."

***

Connie parked her car at the Lake Morey Inn. The older women and teenager walked along the grassy shore of the lake and then proceeded to climb a mile or more up the hillside beyond the lake's western edge. Connie's plan was to demonstrate her ability to shift once they reached a choice location.

"Just one thing," she said as she came to a stop. "Take this address and don't let anybody see it. This is the group, or *gang,* if you prefer, of like-minded Shifters. I think you'll like their company and they might be able to use your youth and cunning ways."

She handed him the paper, which he put into his pocket, and then took a step back.

Connie held out her arms and transformed down into a wolf of dark tan, white and grayish fur, within a matter of seconds. Benny watched, with childish excitement, itching to try it himself.

Slowly she switched back to a human and eventually said, "I can change form in five seconds, if need be. It's just harder to control the clothes from falling off and putting back on...and you don't need to see an old fart like me without clothes."

"Yeah, okay, now *me*," Benny said, getting impatient. "What's the trick, anyhow?"

"First lesson- *I* am your *Elder*," Connie quickly snapped. "In *this* particular pack, that I've invited you to join, *you* had best learn your place. It could save your life. *Do you understand?*"

"Yes," Benny said as he dropped his head.

"Okay then. The most important thing to know is that *strong* emotions can set off the change. Everything from anger, hate, jealousy, fear, even love can start your shifting. It's urgent that you learn to control these emotions so you don't shift in the middle of your school's playground or something."

"I'm fourteen, *bitch*! I don't *play* on playgrounds," Benny reacted.

Connie whipped her ring fingered hand across the side of Benny's head.

"*Jesus Christ! Fuckin'- Ouch!*"

"It'll be *a lot* harder next time if you don't learn how to *watch your god-damn-mouth*!" she warned.

Benny made a sulking face, but agreed.

"*Again*, the control of emotions is *very* important," continued Connie. "Once you master control, changing into a wolf will be as easy as spitting. But being your first time, *I'm* going to have to get you to feel some *big-time* feelings. This'll be the only way for you to finally experience a real shift."

"Ah...wait...is it okay to speak?" Benny cautiously said.

"Yeah," Connie answered.

"Like, *how* are you gonna do this?"

"By you trusting me," his aunt said as she pushed him against a birch tree and pulled out a long piece of chain from the canvas bag she had brought. Benny had wondered what the jingling sound was. He now wished he didn't know. As his aunt began to wrap the chain around him and the tree, he felt more and more uncertain about this *day of lessons*. When she was done Connie attached a lock to its end.

Benny felt evident slack in the chains so he bravely said, "They're pretty loose. If you were going to scare me into a shift, don't you think you'd have to tighten the chains so I don't just wiggle out?"

His aunt gave him a devilish grin, reached into her bag again and pulled out a pair of handcuffs.

Benny gave an audible squeal as Connie roughly pulled his arms around the back of the tree and locked them together with the cuffs. He was beginning to get scared at the thought that his crazy aunt had tricked him into some sadistic circumstance. *This* made him mad; the fact that *he* was so scared.

I'm a goddamn Shifter, dammit! He thought. *Wolves don't get scared.*

Benny closed his eyes tight and attempted to focus on emotions and shifting. He breathed heavily and clenched his teeth, squeezing with all his might against the metal chains. Nothing happened.

Benny reopened his eyes to find himself completely alone. His aunt was nowhere to be found as he began to notice the thick, deep forest suddenly closing in on him.

"Is this fucking *it?*" Benny yelled, fighting back the fear again. "*This* is your *fucking* lesson; *scare* the nephew?"

There was still no sound of movement, except the constant caws of overhead crows. He used his exceptional hearing to listen for the slightest footsteps or even quiet breathing. There was nothing. He yanked more at his shackles, rested, yanked again, then stood and listened.

"*No fucking way!*" Benny shouted as he tightened his muscles while yanking yet again. He pulled at his locked wrists, wiggling his whole body in frustration. "No goddamn fucking way I'm going to be left out here!"

Once again Benny stiffened his body with much more force, biting down hard. This time, however, the teeth had bitten into his lower lip with unusual sharpness. This made him notice that the handcuffs had loosened considerably. He could now feel muscles and bone shrinking and transforming as the definite sound of bodily changes could be heard from within. Even the growing of fur made a noise.

In no time at all the chains *and* the cuffs had fallen to the ground around him. He fell away from the tree and dropped to all fours. Benny wiggled himself out of his clothes and looked, as best he could, at his new self.

In that same moment, Connie stepped out from behind a large elm, wearing a satisfied smile. "Took you long enough," she smirked, bending low to be at his level. She stared into his bluish-green eyes and said, "I'll join you so we can *now* continue our lessons."

She quickly shifted, kicked her clothes next to her canvas bag and gestured to Benny to follow her deeper into the forest.

Benny bounced, leaped and danced around like a happy, rambunctious pup until his aunt nipped at his ankles to stop.

***

Colin and his mother sat in the extended cab of Richard's Nissan truck. Nashoba sat up in front enjoying the four-wheel-drive power as it pressed up the rough dirt road.

"We're hiking Mount Mansfield?" Colin asked.

"Yes. On the southwest side, off the Nebraska Notch Trail," answered Richard as he followed the old road to the trailhead parking. "We'll split from the trail two miles up. There's an out-of-the-way clearing about one and a half miles into the forest that will be great for our classroom."

"Your wife, Sally, loved to run in this area, didn't she?" Anne said to Richard.

"She sure did. She loved the autumn time the best. Sunny, cool days, with all those bright colors on the leaves."

"She was a Shifter, too?" Colin asked.

"Oh, yeah," Richard smiled. "Weren't too many of us who married fellow Shifters. It sure made it a lot more fun running through the forest together as wolves."

"Hang on," Colin suddenly considered. "You mentioned autumn colors. If you were shifted...I thought dogs, canines, only saw in *black and white*. Wouldn't that include wolves?"

"Well, *I* can see colors as a wolf," said Richard. "How about you, Nashoba?"

"Sure can."

"Me, too," exclaimed Anne.

"Well, that's cool," said Colin as they pulled into the parking area. "It would be too much like watching something on one of those old televisions I heard about that *you guys* grew up with."

"Don't knock our past," Richard commented with a smile. "Besides, we didn't know any better. It was just the way it was."

As they piled out of the truck Nashoba smoothly maneuvered across the lot onto the rocky trail with her trusty wolf-head cane (which Colin now, of course, understood its meaning). Anne grabbed the one backpack from the truck's bed.

"Did you pack some food?" Colin asked her.

"No food. We will find something to eat as wolves."

"Then what's in the backpack?" he questioned, noticing how full it was.

"Never you mind," she smirked, displaying a wide smile as she scanned the surroundings.

Colin remembered that smile. It was the giddy side that would always come out when she was in natural settings. *Makes sense!* Colin thought.

The group merrily hiked along the path as the adults told funny stories about wolf experiences they had in their past. Richard eventually suggested that they pick up their pace by going barefoot. They could hide their shoes in the brush somewhere safe.

Colin was amazed at how well Nashoba was doing. She said that being barefoot felt more *wolf* to her.

Richard pointed into the deep forest when they reached a curve in the trail. "This way," he said.

They moved briskly around boulders, trees and an occasional flowing stream. Colin realized how he was totally pumped to be out in nature again...barefoot. He also took in the smells that further increased the thrill of this educational adventure.

In no time they reached an open clearing where Richard stopped the troupe. Colin's mom immediately shifted, galloping and hopping all over the grassy field.

"She's got to be the fastest shifting *Shifter* I've ever met," Richard said as he shook his head at her silliness. "Your mom told me she had you watch a transformation already."

"Yeah," Colin answered, as he watched his gallivanting mother and finding it still a bit weird.

"Any questions concerning this little phenomenon?" Nashoba asked.

"Well, sure," Colin responded. "Lots. Like, *why* change into wolves, why not other animals? Plus, how can a physical body shrink and change into something totally different? Why hasn't anybody seen any of you through the centuries, besides that soldier I read about at the *Benson* Museum, who happened to be *killed*, by the way! *Oh...* or is that how it works? Do the *mortals* (is that what you call *regular people?*), do they get *killed* if they've seen too much?"

"Killed? *Oh, my!* Slow down, my boy," Richard laughed slapping him on his back. Nashoba gave him a look of shock.

"Oops, sorry," Richard quickly said, giving the fingers-to-the-forehead bow.

"Hey, and can you *please* stop with all this-this superiority stuff?" Colin said, embarrassed.

"Our word for you *is* actually *Superior*," Richard explained.

"'*Superior*'...that was carved on my trophy."

"Yes, it was," Nashoba winked.

"I don't necessarily feel superior," Colin considered. "I'd prefer that you all treat me the same, like an equal."

Richard looked at Nashoba, as Colin's mother joined in as a wolf. "Well, *that* sounded like an order, didn't it?" Richard smiled.

"Yes, it did," Nashoba responded, as Anne shook her wolfish head up and down and dashed off again. "So be it. We'll treat you like an equal. Great. Then have a seat. We've got questions to answer."

They all got comfortable while Anne dashed off again into the woods.

"First let's talk about how and why it all happened," Nashoba began. "As you might have learned from your brief studies about our tribe, our people split long ago from the *Membertou* family because of French influence. When the original Mi'kmaq chieftain, Henri, discontinued his shamanic practices his youngest son, Sa'se'wa'sit (he had refused a baptismal name) broke from the group, bringing along with him several men, women and children, and traveled to the area north of us. This is where Sa'se'wa'sit became the new chief. *This* is the person you saw in your dream.

"Once they had settled, this passionate and kind leader took his knowledge of Shamanism, that he had learned from his father, and taught the whole tribe the mystical ways. This included meditation, herbal healing, the reading of dreams and, of course, animal shifting.

"You had also asked, '*why change into wolves*'...Our tribe and its leader had studied the ways of the wolf ever since their days in the land now known as Nova Scotia. Their respect for this creature stemmed from the fact that they were so much like humans. Wolves are highly social, they live in packs almost like a village, they follow rules within that pack so the common good of the pack will be upheld, they have strong family ties, they respect the territories of other packs and, curiously enough, they like to play. The wolf, therefore, was the animal Chief Sachem and the others most revered, so in a unanimous decision the tribe members chose to become this animal. Hours and hours our people practiced and meditated, visualizing how to make the change happen smoothly. Daily they concentrated on *wolf energy*. They killed the old or weak of nearby packs and wore their skins as if it were their own, imitating the wolf's behaviors in dance. Eventually the ability to shift slowly took effect. Somehow the mental imaging, along with the tribe's ancient knowledge of shaman magic, allowed them to finally transform. Within time every member had become an expert at shifting.

"They began to call themselves the Skiri Clan and they taught each generation, that followed, how to shift. *Now* they were a tribe of both human and wolf, having the combined attributes of both. This mixture doubled our senses and strengths. We even received the ability, as you learned from Sasha's hurt leg, to heal quickly and easily. This is why we call it a *gift*.

"Generation after generation became better at being both species from the ritual exercises taught to them until one day, they began to notice that the ability had begun to come naturally. At the age of thirteen, the time period an adolescent was consider an adult, the innate ability to shift was beginning to show."

"Thirteen?" Colin reacted. "So, I was late."

Colin's mom had shifted back to human and was dressed when she overheard Colin. She responded with, "So now you can understand my years of frustration that you hadn't received the gift. *Especially* when you decided to become a *vegetarian.*"

"Sorry," Colin smirked. "Rebellious teen?"

"Of course, these natural abilities to change *is* now more common for ages fifteen and older; ever since the 1960s or so," Nashoba explained. "In fact, a lot of families since then...too many families, really, have raised only *non-shifters.*"

"I've attributed the lack of *shifter* tribe members to *so much* mixing of cultures," Richard commented.

"We truly don't know the reason," Nashoba said, leaning on her cane. "However, let us continue... *So,* in the beginning of natural change, these young men and women were describing dreams about wolves coming to them and the next morning they *had the gift,* without the usual training. They could shift into wolves after simple concentration or great feelings of emotions. They mastered the change in no time."

"*Then,* another interesting change happened," Richard joined in. "Around the same time that the exceptionally old Chief Sachem had died and the tribe was warring with one of the Iroquois tribes...the Mohawks, I believe, *another* phenomenon took place. An adolescent boy had had his Initiation Dream that announced his position as the next chieftain. It became known because he had the ability to convert into a *man-wolf.* It was said that several girls, too, had become Chieftain born..."

"Wait. Back up," Colin interrupted. "What do you mean by *a combination of man and wolf?*"

"Or *woman* and wolf," Richard corrected.

"No-*seriously,*" Colin pressed. "Do you mean, like...a *werewolf?*"

"Well, *yes.* Our term for this is *'Ma'iingan inini',*" Nashoba said, and quickly continued. "The imperative need to find another leader had somehow incorporated into the tribe's ability to shift. What was created was the birth of a unique individual within that generation who found out that he or she was a Ma'iingan inini, and, inevitably, the next leader, the tribe's *Superior*."

Finally absorbing the actual words of what was just said, Colin gasped. "Wait! *Superior? Leader? Me?... I'm a werewolf?*"

Chapter 17:
The Ma'iingan inini

Hyman and Darryl LaPierre knew they weren't supposed to be out with their rifles, but the last few days of cooler August weather had got them excited about the upcoming hunting season. They had loaded their packs with five bags of potato chips, a box of beef jerky, six Twinkies, ammunition and fifteen cans of beer. So, they were ready for a successful day.

From their parent's home the two men traversed along the northern ridge of the rolling hillside. They knew that if they hiked about six miles north into the forest, their gunshots, if any, would not be heard. They knew this to be true because Darryl had sent Hyman out about every few miles starting at 3 miles, in that same direction, then stood there and listened for any gunfire that Hyman purposely shot off at each mile. When Darryl couldn't hear any more blasts the two mapped out a trail, brought out a bunch of wood and tools and built a comfortable blind. They eventually supplied the space with two folding lawn chairs, a small table and one centerfold from a girlie magazine to pin to the tree, laminated, of course.

"Ya know, Darryl, *I'm* feeling pretty lucky today," Hyman remarked as they made their way through a thin patch of maples.

"Why's that?" asked Darryl.

"'Cause last night I had a dream about three naked women sitting on a tall, brown and white horse," Hyman said.

"And *that* means you're gonna be lucky today?" replied Darryl.

"Sure," said Hyman, "horses are supposed to be lucky."

***

Great Grandmother Carrier and the others had been standing around accomplishing nothing while Colin paced up and down the field.

"Colin, please understand. It's not what you think," his mother said, trying to calm him. "Remember how you hated the children's cartoons and books depicting wolves when you were younger?"

"I remember," he said, wide-eyed as he looked around, trying to find a way to escape.

"Then remember, *deep down,* in your gut, how you knew that the explanation of *'the big, bad wolf'* was wrong," she responded. "*Now* remember how disgusted you felt when you saw the *werewolf* movie"

Colin stopped his frantic pacing and focused on his mother. "*That's right. You* had me watch that movie, like, when I was *just* seven. About the shocked and scared man who was bitten by a wolf and became *'cursed'*...He mutated into this-this *hideous, deformed creature* and went *crazy,* out-of-control. It attacked everything and everyone, tearing them apart and eating them! *Do I lose control? Do I eat people?*"

Colin's pupils had begun to shrink while arms and legs slowly lengthened. But they quickly stopped.

At this point Nashoba stepped in front of him and grabbed both shoulders hard. "Look at me, Colin. Look at Richard. *Look* at your mother. Do *we* seem like the types who would *lose* control? Do you think *we* would use our gift for *murdering* and *killing* people?"

Colin stood still, staring straight ahead. He eventually lowered his shoulders and said, "No..." But raised them again explaining how none of *them* were this *Ma'iingan inini*-thing!

"*We* call *you* our Superior," Nashoba said, throwing her chest out with pride. "*I*, personally, would not call an out-of-control killer *my* leader."

Colin stared at Nashoba, absorbing what she had said. She gave him the slightest grin. He lowered his shoulders again and looked over at Richard and his mother and laughed, "*Ha*. I guess you wouldn't call me *leader*, would you?"

"Okay, then," Richard exclaimed as he clapped his hands together. "I say we get back to your lessons."

"So, seriously, I won't lose control?" Colin quietly asked again.

"No," Richard smiled, continuing on, "If we haven't already indicated, Colin, the ability to change into a Ma'iingan inini is very unique, but, just like us, it's a coordinated change. That is, once you *control* your emotions. Those intense emotions you felt when you and Sasha were threatened by the falling rocks were what made you begin to shift in front of her."

"Like I almost did just now," Colin said. "But when fully changed, will it be into a hideously disfigured, wolf-like monster?"

"Hardly," Richard corrected. "My son was a very handsome man-wolf...Pain in my butt, but...handsome."

"Your son was a Superior?" Colin replied. "Do you mean the one who just died?"

"Yes."

"So... though we can heal well, we still can die easily," Colin said.

"Not easily. We have miraculous bodies. You especially," Richard explained. "And, as you've probably learned, we have incredible senses, too, to help extend our lives, especially our ears."

"Even though our hearing helps in keeping us alive," Anne joined in with a chuckle, "it isn't always good in today's society." She then explained how most machinery, electronics; even radios and televisions, had extra noise they all had to put up with. "And the *cell phones, whew*, do *they* make quite the buzzing noise. We just choose to not have them."

"Buzzing?" Colin repeated. "Like a screeching humming sound."

"Yes. They emit a high frequency, especially close to the ear," Richard said. "The sound is like a thousand bumble bees."

"We can use them," Nashoba added, "but they are loud and annoying."

"I thought my phone was broken," Colin commented and then turned to his mom. "What about Dad's phone for his work, or April's soon-to-be phone? They'll be all around us."

"I've done my best to have less phones in our house," Anne replied. "I even convinced your dad that I hear horrible sounds from it due to an eardrum accident I had as a child. He uses our landline at home and his cell outside or at his office. We'll have to come up with a new lie for April."

"And speaking of the *inevitable*, let's talk more about dying," Richard interjected. "Aging is still a factor, but, for those *other times*...

"You see, Colin," Nashoba continued, "we are protected by muscles, agility and heightened senses, but we can still be killed by injuring two specific areas: the head and stomach."

"Okay, I can see losing your head a bad thing," Colin surmised, "but the stomach?"

"Think about it," Richard said. "What would be a wolf, or dog's, most important organ?"

"Ha. You're right, the stomach," Colin answered.

***

Up in the mountainous surroundings of Lake Morey, Connie had been allowing Benny time to enjoy his new wolf self. They spent several hours just dashing around the rocks and forest, while Connie kept an eye out for food. She knew the lesson of killing would be just as important as any other, besides getting to have the luscious taste of forest-flesh.

It sure beats night-after-night of Mega-Burgers! She thought.

Finally, in the middle of demonstrating the skill of long, powerful leaps, she caught sight of a doe in a clearing. Connie quietly barked to Benny, "If you can remember the skills you've used today, we *could* have meat very soon."

Benny's mouth watered at the sound of this. When he finally tried to speak, he said, "Where?" though all he heard was a slight whimper from his snout.

"Just a few feet away," Connie yapped. "Stay quiet. We'll approach at separate sides"

Benny had then moved to where she said the doe would be, excited by the idea of killing something. He lowered to his haunches as he spied the doe grazing on a small patch of grass and clover. Benny waited for his aunt to get into position, but became impatient. He instead moved slowly towards the unsuspecting prey, deciding to use the *powerful leap* to catch the deer off guard.

***

"Speaking of stomachs," Colin eventually admitted, "I'm hungry."

"No- not yet," Nashoba intervened. "Superior or not, you do not eat until you have successfully shifted. Then and only then will we track down any food."

"Track-down? Like little forest animals?" Colin replied.

"We could," Nashoba giggled, "but I'd prefer something bigger."

"Big forest animals...right. Okay then, let's do this," Colin finally said, and then paused, "Ah, will it hurt?"

"It actually tickles," his mother answered as she moved to the side to transform.

Richard joined her as they both raised their arms and shifted on the spot, changing immediately into their four-legged counterparts. His mother, Colin noted, had feminine-like qualities exhibiting light features of white, off-white and tannish fur. Richard, on the other hand, had areas of dark brown fur, sporting a gray-white mask that framed his face and snout, sliding back under his belly. To Colin's surprise, their eyes had kept their own personal colors of blue and green.

The two stood there on all fours looking at him with anticipation. Colin gave a little laugh and bent over to scratch the tops of their heads. He couldn't help himself.

"Are we ready, my dear boy?" Nashoba announced beside him.

"Yeah."

"The technique we will try today is an old one I had learned from *my* grandfather," Nashoba said, as she stepped away from Colin and slowly raised her arms. "Be ready to laugh."

Great Grandmother Carrier immediately shifted, flicked off her clothes and leapt, with ease, towards the others. From an old woman to wolf, she had taken on qualities slightly different than his mother and Richard. Nashoba was much more plump and stockier, with the whites and grays around her face and body more prominent. Colin could easily see that her ability to move as a wolf was not at all hampered by her human age.

As he watched the threesome *frolic* around the grassy field Colin casually thought. *This totally is a fascinating scene, but what is there to laugh at?*

In that moment the three began to run around Colin like a bunch of happy puppies. Believing that communication with the others was over, Colin crossed his arms to wait for what was next. Suddenly Nashoba butted her head onto the back of his knees, making them buckle as his mother pounced towards his left arm, gently grabbing it with her mouth and pulling it back. Down he went, going into a roll so as not to fall on anybody. From there they all jumped on top of him, gently biting, pulling at his t-shirt and pants, then licking his face when he wasn't looking. Colin got into the act and began to perform headlocks around their necks, or low swings with his arms to knock their legs off balance. He rolled, and then pounced at them, laughing every time someone got in a full-face lick.

Being so focused on this canine wrestling, Colin never noticed that something had been slowly happening to him. He had begun to grip the ground and change directions quicker using longer fingernails and toenails. His dodges and wiggles advanced in their intensity as arms and legs lengthened and transformed. Colin stopped his playing when his clothes began to rip and tear from his expanding muscles. He began to focus instead on his lengthening nose and mouth, plus the evident feeling of growing fur all over his body.

Colin jumped to his feet with excitement and shock, fragments of clothes falling to his side. What he first had noticed about himself was that the sensation of his growing and shifting body was so subtle. The tugs and pulls of physical lengthening had *indeed* tickled him.

In no time the transformation had stopped.

Breathing heavily, he looked at the three staring wolves and then down at himself. Over his evident snout he could see that his arms were still somewhat human though longer, muscular and furry. His legs, however, had changed considerably. The dense muscles of his hips and thighs were human, but his knees reversed in direction into canine hock joints. His fur was a slight dark brown and black, turning mostly white near his feet. *And his feet*, they were only half the length of their original selves, with rounded toes sprouting sharp, black nails. The black pads of his feet were heavily callused and dog-like, but he still had his human heel. This allowed him to stand upright.

Colin then reached up to touch his face. His new nose and mouth were not the full length of a wolf, but he understood that the look must still be very canine with his pronounced muzzle. He slid his fingers along his sharp teeth, pinched his wet, black nose, and then reached up to bristly, pointy ears. The ears did not point straight up, but tilted and pointed backwards at a slight diagonal direction.

Finally, Colin wanted to check two other areas. Sensing the continuous stares of the watching wolves, he slowly turned his back on them to peak down. He sighed with relief when he saw a thicker patch of fur filling in his, otherwise, exposed maleness. Then, for kicks, he reached behind his back to see if he had a tail. *Huh, nothing.* He thought. *Just a fur-covered butt.*

"That must look cute," Colin said aloud, scaring himself when he heard his coarse and husky voice. "*I* can speak?"

"Of course," Richard yapped.

"Wait, I understand you!"

"Ha, welcome to the pack, Colin," Nashoba barked. "You are *truly* a Ma'iingan inini...Ready to eat?"

***

Benny sprung into the air with full force to kill the grazing doe, but not before snapping a twig on his takeoff. The doe quickly looked up and skirted to her left to escape. She would have succeeded if not for Connie positioning herself precisely in its path. The wolf engulfed the struggling doe's neck into her jaws, bit down hard and shook her head until she heard a snap. The doe crumpled to the ground.

Benny trotted over, gleefully excited to finally eat, and barked, "Hey, we make a great team."

Connie whipped her head around, flashing bared teeth. "*You idiot!*" she growled, "*We* wouldn't even have *food* if it weren't for *me*. Snapping a twig. Come on!* I have a mind to..."

The blast from the gun had come so suddenly that Connie was left staring in shock. Benny looked up in time to see a hunter aiming at him. He swiftly sprinted to his right with full force, dashing into the forest and out of range.

Connie attempted to call out to him but could barely bark. Her legs collapsed under her and she fell dead to the ground.

"Holy McMoses, Darryl, it really *is* a wolf!" Hyman shouted, running out from behind their blind. "I didn't know we had wolves in Vermont."

"Well, guess they reenlisted them 'cause it's *definitely* a wolf, ain't no *Ki-yote*" remarked Darryl as he cautiously looked around with his gun in case the other came back. "Died awful quick. I only shot it through the belly."

"Oh, I can't wait to tell Daddy," Hyman said only to be hit on the side of the head by Darryl's barrel.

"No way, dumb-scull!" he said, grabbing Hyman's shirt. "We *ain't* supposed to be hunt'n, *remember*. Just imagine us getting caught with a deer *and* a wolf. Jeezum-crimany!"

"Whadawe gonna do then?" Hyman asked, rubbing his head.

"Let's cut-up the deer meat here," Darryl advised, "put it in our packs, then maybe with the wolf we'll just keep ourselves some souvenirs, like a foot and the tail. We'll bury the rest."

"Good thinking," Hyman responded.

* * *

Three large wolves sat around the felled deer savoring every bit of it. Beside them, still awkward by his size and boney-clawed fingers, was Colin.

"See," Richard had barked to Colin, "You heard and saw this old buck long before any of us did."

"Yeah, but you brought him down," Colin said in his rough voice. "With help from mom, of course."

"Glad you noticed," she replied. "You just need some practice in getting used to your Ma'iingan inini self."

Colin had a hard time getting used to ripping off deer parts and eating them. Staring at the bloody leg in his hand he recalled the rest of the family at Thanksgiving dinner eating turkey legs as he ate his tofu dish.

Big changes! He thought.

Colin had smiled at the Thanksgiving memory, beginning to realize how much he was enjoying himself in this bizarre situation. He chuckled again at imagining the traditional school essay question of, *"What I did on my summer vacation"*.

"Well, I've had enough," announced Nashoba. "This buck had a good life. I could tell by his taste. It's truly respectable in this day and age for a buck to have lived this long."

"Now we'll have his spirit in all of us," Richard responded.

Colin quickly ate around the rest of his leg and put down the bone. He gave a thumbs-up to indicate he was done, too. This had to look funny coming from a werewolfish-being.

"We already thanked this creature for its nourishment," Nashoba said to Colin, "so it is important to offer the remains for the Elders above, as well as to the scavengers around us. Our Elders have watched over our kind for many generations. It is *they* we give thanks to for our many gifts. We honor ourselves when we honor them."

The four bowed their heads to the last of the kill, and then Nashoba began to walk back to the clearing where their clothes had been left. As she did so she simply turned to say, *"That,* dear, Colin, would be one of the most important lessons of the day: giving thanks for what you received. But let's head back home, the sun has moved across the sky far enough."

"Um, what will *I* wear?" Colin asked remembering his torn clothes.

His mother appeared to his side and replied, "Another good lesson to learn for yourself, once you can control your own shifting. *Take* your clothes off first."

"Fine, but what about now?"

"It was *clothes* that I had in the backpack," barked Colin's mom.

Chapter 18:
Pinket Worthington

Stephanie had pressed what looked like a new doorbell that, instead of ringing, sang the first stanza of *"Hound Dog"* by Elvis Presley. A chorus of two large dogs immediately followed the doorbell's song. They heard a woman wrestling with the dogs on the other side of the door, and then were finally greeted by Honey Benson.

"Hello, ma'am. I'm Police Chief Porter of Eureka," he said, showing his badge. "And this is Sergeant Harrison. We'd like..."

"*Oh, damn,*" Honey suddenly blurted. "Vinny's Vintage Vinyl is lying, Officers. I did not steal that *'Guns and Roses'* record."

"Um, Ma'am-Ma'am, it's okay...Right now we just want to talk to your husband," Stephanie reassured her, "about Native American information."

"Oh, ha! Well, then please come in," Honey said as she blushed through her makeup. She moved away from the entrance while holding back the dog's collars. "Dear, you've got visitors!"

Both Stephanie and Mitch slid along the farthest side of the entrance as the Great Danes tugged and growled. Stephanie couldn't help but think how several of *these* types of dogs, if trained, could do a bit of damage to a group of unsuspecting people.

"Hello, hello. How can I help you?" said Harvey Benson, entering the hallway.

"We're from..." Mitch began.

"Oh, I heard," said Harvey. "Over the barking, of course. *Eureka, Vermont*. Nice little town."

"We'd been told you were a collector of Native American artifacts and a part-time expert on the subject," Mitch replied.

"I am, indeed. It is a big hobby of mine, besides teaching," Harvey said, gesturing to his basement. "My museum, if you will, is down here."

"We have had some incidents in our area," Mitch began as they stepped down the stairs.

"You must mean the dog attack stories I've read about, right?" Harvey responded.

"Yes," Mitch said as he stood there in awe of the vast Indian display scattered throughout. He continued, "It has to do with one of the victims. He had a specific tattoo on his arm. Identifying it could help with our investigation."

"We believe it to be a native symbol of some sort, Mr. Benson," Stephanie explained while eyeing a leather dress.

"Please, call me Harvey, and that was a Penobscot woman's buck skin dress. Very fashionable at the time," Harvey smiled. "So, ah, do you have the tattoo symbol?"

Mitch handed him the folded paper that had the sergeant's sketch on it.

Harvey gave it a look, said a long, "Hmmm," and then moved off to a filing cabinet. He pulled out two books and some folders and rummaged through them.

"Sorry about this old-fashion searching," Harvey said as he scanned the many pages and notes, "I suppose if I were twenty years younger, I'd have put all of this on my computer *and* a web site."

Mitch and Stephanie laughed.

"Oh-wait...yes. Right here, or close to it," Harvey announced as he displayed his findings. "It almost looks like this Iroquois symbol here, but I'd say it's closer to this northern Abenaki clan."

Mitch took a look, followed the design's curves then realized they didn't truly match, but were indeed close.

"Not quit the same, is it," he said.

"It's pretty close, especially considering how each tribe likes to uniquely represent themselves," Harvey suggested. "Or, simply, it was a special design based on one of these original symbols that this person created himself."

"How about this?" Mitch said, "Is there any documentation of where, say, today's Abenaki or Iroquois families might be living in the area?"

"Abenaki, yes. Iroquois, less likely," Harvey said, thinking out loud, but then he quickly turned and said, "Wait, I was told once that there was a documented, state-wide program that contained the names and addresses of a variety of races in the state from, um, oh-right, *now* I remember, from some *eugenics project*."

"Do you mean that experiment from the early nineteen-hundreds where they tried to sterilize certain people?" Stephanie questioned, having read about it once in the newspaper.

"But wouldn't that information be from the early nineteen-hundreds?" Mitch pointed out. "We'd need more up-to-date addresses."

"Yes, I know-I know," Harvey responded, with his hands behind his back. Then he looked at them sideways. "But there may be another piece to this puzzle...I never did go see if it were true, but I remember it being said. It was a Dr. Carol Baker who had hinted of it.

"Okay, bear with me. It happened at a ceremony for the high school honoring the newly refurbished library that the husband, Dr. Kenneth Baker, helped fund. At the Holiday Inn Conference Center, where the ceremony was held, Ms. Baker came over to me to talk...*obviously* not *too long* after visiting the cash bar. She must have been drinking a wee bit because she was giddy and *very* talkative. She had somehow heard I was into Indians and had asked me if I knew of any living around here today, then immediately began to giggle, saying, 'bet you don't know any, do you?'

"So, she *proceeded* to whisper that she had a way to find some if I were terribly interested. She claims to have known about some stashed away papers containing fairly recent addresses of *'those types of people'* living in Vermont. She then suggested that I *go look them up soon...before there weren't any of those types around anymore.* Very cryptic, huh?"

"Did she say this was connected to the old eugenics program?" Stephanie asked.

"No," Harvey said. "Just that it was possible addresses to local Indian families."

"But she *did* say where these papers were?" Mitch questioned.

"Yes. The UVM library."

"Who should we talk to about these rumored documents?" asked Mitch.

"A Mrs. Pinket Worthington is in charge over there. I had gotten permission to see several old books in the archives section once, and she was the one who escorted me. She seemed quite particular on who got to enter that part of the library. But, hey, all you'll have to do is flash your badges and say 'police business', I bet."

"Yeah, something like that," Mitch said with a grin.

"Thanks for your help, Mr. Benson," Stephanie smiled.

"Harvey...Glad to be of service."

"Thanks-Harvey."

***

It had been 4pm in the afternoon by the time Mitch and Stephanie found the University of Vermont's library to search for the specific papers Harvey had suggested. Mitch called ahead to the campus security for directions and special parking privileges. When they got there, they were escorted to the location and to the appropriate librarian.

Mrs. Pinket Worthington had been head-librarian for the university for forty-nine years. She wore her gray hair in a gripping bun and stood a mere five-foot even. But as small as she was, Mrs. Worthington had the look of someone who was to be seriously heard and obeyed. When the officers asked about material containing addresses for multi-racial families (after they, of course, showed their badges and said *police business*) Pinket asked, "Do you mean the Henry Perkin's program from the twenties?"

"The eugenics program," Stephanie began, "Yes, but..."

"We *do* have papers from that particular project," Mrs. Worthington exclaimed. "Just downstairs."

"You see, we heard that the library might have more recent addresses," Stephanie added. "We're looking for people of Indian origin."

Mrs. Worthington pursed her thin lips, then, just as fast, produced a big smile. She instantly looked like an all-knowing grade school teacher when she said, "Oh, my, *no*. I've *never* heard of any such thing. But, come now, dearies, follow me. I can show you what I do have and I believe it'll include just the addresses you need."

They accompanied her through locked doors to the basement below. As they descended the marble stairs, she said, "That was an interesting piece of history, wasn't it, those eugenics experiments? The idea that people could create their own special paradise."

"Paradise?" Stephanie questioned.

"Oh, sure," Mrs. Worthington said. "It was the aristocrats of Vermont, and other states, who wanted to make their inhabitants healthier and smarter by purifying their bloodlines."

"*Yes*, by getting rid of those *they* felt were too unfit to be in their *hierarchal* presence," Stephanie responded, and then apologized. "Sorry. I haven't eaten much today."

"That's all right, dear," Pinket smiled, opening a second door leading to stacks and rows of endless shelving. "Now, let's see," she pondered looking at the isles. "We had just moved things around recently. The files used to be over there." She pointed and then hesitated. "But they could have been moved to two other places. If you two officers could try the dates section over to your right, I'll look in the paper file area in the back here."

Stephanie and Mitch went to their area and began to scan shelf after shelf. When they finally found a section of books, folders and plastic wrapped newspapers, concerning that particular time period, they worked at opposite ends pulling single groups out and skimming the labels.

Across the room and to the back, Pinket kept glancing over her shoulder to see if the officers were going to come back her way for more questions. She could hear the sound of a broom to the floor and had realized Francis, the custodian, was slowly passing by. As soon as he was out of ear-shot she quickly went to the tucked away filing cabinet. She had purposely left it dusty and messy so as not to attract any attention to it. This was because Mrs. Worthington had known *exactly* what the officers were looking for.

And such documents were not going to be seen by them...or anyone else...unworthy! She thought smugly.

Pinket had been guarding the special files from the beginning of their existence. Its folder of delicate information could never go public or the truth could hurt the reputation of important families involved. Of course, it would also hurt her little paycheck she received monthly for her troubles. Not that she needed compensation for keeping the secret of such a worthwhile project.

A program that literally prevented the breeding of social inadequates! Very worthwhile, indeed. Pinket passionately thought. *The fewer of them the better.*

She listened one more time for any footsteps before she pulled open the latched drawer. That was when her jaw dropped in utter shock. Her gasp could be heard from across the room.

"Anything wrong, Mrs. Worthington?" Stephanie asked.

"No-no. Nothing that concerns our search," Pinket explained with a controlled tone. In truth her heart was racing, completely understanding the horrible situation she was now faced with.

Francis Galton (peering through the thin slits of folders on the bookshelves) had known exactly what Mrs. Worthington was looking for and what was missing. He knew that he had better get himself, and his broom, quietly out of there, to let Baird Dawes know she had discovered the loss.

Pinket, in the mean-time, continued to shuffle frantically through the other files and folders to see if she had misplaced the documents for some reason. In doing so she came across trivial Eugenics papers that could get the police officers off her back. She looked over its content and found that the papers did indeed have addresses. Though the census study was taken between 1923-1929, she would simply say it was the most recent information she had on file.

"I believe this is all we have here that, I hope, will help you both," Pinket said aloud. She quickly arranged the folder and papers away from the dusty filing cabinet that she would later have to pull apart to keep up her much-needed search.

Mitch and Stephanie came around the corner anxious to see the information that could help their case.

"I can have my assistant upstairs make copies for you to take. However, I have a 5pm meeting to attend to so let us move along and get you two back to your police business."

The three of them ascended the stairs to the main lobby of the library and found the assistant. Once copies were in their hands the two went on their way.

Pinket, on the other hand, had hurried back to her office until closing. She was to have a long night in the archives.

Chapter 19:
Benny Meets Victor

A group of twenty-one Shifters had gathered again within Baird's barn. It was almost the same group that had met weeks before minus one of the women. Connie Smith did not return. She had not been seen for several days according to her worried husband, however, the newcomer, Benny Carrier (who stole his mother's money for a cab ride there) had told the group of Connie's unfortunate death. It wasn't a sympathetic crowd.

"She was teaching you how to shift for the first time?" Victor Dawes said as he repeated Benny's story. "Then got shot...*in the stomach*...Pretty bad shot for hunting standards, I believe. But, let's get back to something. Somehow she trusted you to come and be part of us...Why?"

"Because, *sir*, you were a-a gang of fellow Shifters that she thought I should connect with," Benny cautiously said having remembered the painful advice about respect.

"A '*gang*', she said," announced Victor, as the group laughed. "So then, pup, why do *you* think she wanted you in *our*, so-called, gang?"

"Well, like," stammered Benny, "it's because I won a race at our reunion. The Sachem Challenge. I used some fricken clever..."

"Did you say *Sachem*?" Baird interrupted, having been seated off to the side.

"Yes, it was a family reunion in..." Benny tried to explain again.

"What's your last name again?" Baird had continued to inquire.

"Carrier... sir."

"A relative to Lizzy Carrier?"

"She's my great grandmother," Benny answered, "but I..."

Never letting Benny finish his sentence Baird stood and addressed the group, "For those of you who aren't up on your native history, this part of the Sachem Tribe's descendants of Chief Sa'se'wa'sit, himself, who we can honestly thank for our gift. However, for those who do not know, it would be our next-in-line, Chief Makade'ma'ingan, who would first make the battle cry that *we,* ourselves, plan to continue! The Sachem descendants, for *centuries,* have remained ridiculously obedient to our European adversaries. But *not* today...Let us welcome our newest, and I hope, trustworthy addition to our... *'gang',* Mr. Benny Carrier. An obvious traitor to his own *descendants.*"

Johnny Dumont moved uncomfortably in his seat from this unfortunate turn of events. He had heard from Richard about the reunion and the results of this race. Johnny had also heard about Colin and that he was their best hope in stopping this madness in front of him. The problem, now, was that the Carrier boy knew all about Colin. Johnny had to somehow prevent the mentioning of Colin and how he, *like Victor*, was also a Ma'iingan inini.

"But could *they,* these Sachem Shifters, give us any trouble?" asked a burly man in the back. Baird stepped towards the man, smiling.

"Carl, is it?"

"Yeah."

"*'Could they give us trouble?'* Hmmm, trouble from the Sachem clan?" Baird responded, looking pensive. He turned to face the others, "Did any of you ever hear the story about Bobby LeClaire and two of his subdominants spending time in Alaska? He had wanted the experience of being a Superior in the vast wilderness there. One day, as the story goes, they were suddenly charged by two full-grown grizzly bears. One of the subs was badly hurt, while the other whimpered by his Superior's side. Bobby, alone, took on those massive bears, killing them both in a matter of seven minutes."

Baird stood there to allow the Alaskan tale to sink in.

Benny, however, suddenly stood up, recalling the rumors told to him after the reunion. "Shit! Like, wait! Th-..."

"*Yo!*" Victor growled putting up his hand. "There's a story being told! Didn't Ms. Smith teach you manners? *Sit!*"

Victor calmed himself down and then turned back towards his father, "*You* were saying...Dad?"

Baird paused, glaring at Benny. He then raised his arm towards his son. "Bobby LeClaire took on those bears, killing them in *seven minutes.* Victor, on the other hand, took Bobby down in *three!* No one, especially fellow Shifters, are going to give us any..."

"*But- there is a-...*" Benny attempted again.

Benny gasped as he was swiftly lifted into the air by Talon.

Victor hissed as he walked over and held Benny's face between his long fingernails. "*Little annoyance,* you're not a very good listener, are you?"

"Yes, I mean, *no,* but..."

"*Shush!*" Victor demanded as he put a sharp nail to Benny's lower lip, making it bleed. "I'm beginning to *lose* my patience with you."

"*But...!*" Benny began to yell, feeling certain the knowledge of Colin was probably going to be the most important information of the night.

Talon put his hand over his mouth.

"Drive this *uneducated parasite* back to his home until he can learn to *shut up!*" Victor said.

"Hey, like, I haven't got my driver's license yet," Talon answered.

"Then *take* your girlfriend along to help you!" Victor threw him the keys to his Cherokee. "And, pup, we *don't* want to *hear* from you until you hear from us, *get it!*"

Talon and Fang carried Benny out of the barn.

"Okay, no more interruptions," Victor continued, brushing his hands together. "About my worthy adversary, LeClaire...he made an important point before he died. *How* do we wreak our vengeance on those who had tried so hard to be rid of us? You, there, what's your name again?"

"Vincent Sinclair," Johnny Dumont said as he bowed with his fingers to his forehead.

"Carl introduced you to us, didn't he?" Victor asked. He walked towards him as if he were much older than Johnny. "So, Vincent, what do *you* think is the answer?"

"Maybe we should do the same thing you and your friends have been doing," Johnny said as he tried hard not to exude a bit of fear since Victor would have easily smelled it. "Quick attacks on small groups."

Victor had stared hard at Johnny, but then returned his gaze to the group. "Yes, it does seem to have worked. The police departments haven't moved beyond their killer-dog theory, and thanks to the help of our friend, Officer Henderson, here, we at least have some ears on the inside allowing us to know their next move." He pointed to a young man who sat in the back of the barn wearing regular street clothes. The officer tried not to show it but he was feeling very uncomfortable with this group he sat among. "*However,*" Victor continued, "they now have some paper fragments of what could be our address, here at the farm, that they matched to an old county homestead listing. Because of this we need to form a different plan. My dad will explain."

When Baird stood up, he gripped a set of papers in his hands as if he were holding solid gold. "My friend at UVM has recently informed me that *our* Police Chief Porter has been snooping around the library archives in Burlington, the very library where my informant found *these* documents. Now Officer Henderson has confirmed that this is true, but without these *more* recent race-specific addresses," Baird held up the papers, "the police have very little to work from. Because of this, though, we must do our best to stay far from their radar."

"I know that some of you," Victor continued, "have been *salivating* at the possibility of making use of your carnivorous skills, *but* we have decided to lay low for a few weeks. So, no communication for that time period."

There was a sudden bustling of angry disappointment. Victor enjoyed their enthusiasm.

"We wait for only a few weeks...because we have a plan," Victor smiled, though his eyes resonated a touch of menace that made Johnny shiver. "There will be more to say later, but I'll give you this, as Mr. Sinclair suggested with the '*quick attacks*' idea, *we* plan to execute such an attack on a handful of Europeans. *And*, get this- it will be some of the *actual* Europeans listed within these very documents."

Chapter 20:
Shifting Mantras

"Where's April been?" asked Colin. They had begun day three of *"Werewolf School"* (as Colin had been calling it).

"She'll be staying with her friend, Paige, for the next two nights," his mother said as she prepared a big breakfast of steak and eggs. "Your dad's been busy with work. Good morning, Lizzy."

"Good morning to both of you," she said in an excited voice. "Today, dear Colin, *you* get to learn to change at will."

"Without the playful attacks?" Colin replied. "Or the forced anger?"

Yesterday's lesson had been held right there in the Trask house using the emotion of *anger* to make a successful shift. This time Colin had stood around in his dad's baggy sweat pants and top so as not to rip through his perfectly good clothes. The sweat pants and top never survived.

In the anger-lesson his teachers wanted Colin to recall something fairly recent that had made him mad. Colin immediately thought of the day Quentin and his gang attacked him near the hardware store. Richard congratulated him on his choice and then proceeded to play the part of Quentin. He stood close to Colin's face saying certain put-down words and nudging him hard against his shoulders.

After this scenario had gone on for several minutes Colin eventually accepted the fact that he didn't get angry easily when someone was bothering *him*. It was how poorly others were being treated that got him mad. The way Quentin had treated Julia that day was what truly pushed his buttons.

"The mind triggers all shifting," Nashoba eventually said. "So, see what upsets you in your mind and focus on it."

With that Colin concentrated on Quentin yelling at Julia and pushing her around instead of himself. With every image of the bully's scowling expression, along with Julia's helpless and scared face, Colin slowly stretched and transformed.

Once shifted the teachers had him do useful skills around the house to get comfortable in his new body. Things such as changing light bulbs without breaking them, doing dishes, carrying laundry down to the basement, clearing cobwebs off the ceiling and lifting the washer and dryer so his mom could clean underneath them. Colin *knew* he was really just being asked to do work he would have otherwise complained about.

"Today we'll be heading up to Lookout Rock once Richard arrives," Anne said.

"I like it up there," Colin replied with his mouth full.

"The ability to shift when we choose comes in very handy, Colin," Nashoba said. "Especially when you don't want to scare the locals or *you* want to return home in the clothes you first wore."

"Trivial setback," Richard added as he stepped through the door. "I remember shifting back to human buck-naked just as a bunch of women were..."

"Richard..." Anne interrupted. "We haven't the time."

"That's right. We've got to get started," Nashoba said.

"Do I get breakfast?"

"Take the steak with you, Richard."

In no time the group had gotten themselves up to Lookout Rock, with two picnic baskets in hand (killing their food would not be part of the lesson that day).

The first exercise was about quieting oneself. Simple meditation.

The four of them sat still on the ledge, their eyes closed and breathing normal, but steady. Colin was to try not to think, but listen only to his breathing. He realized he wasn't very good at this, being distracted by the simplest flutter of butterflies nearby.

Eventually Nashoba whispered softly about how this meditation was a large part of their ancestor's everyday rituals. It was to calm the body, mind and soul before the day's big decisions were to be made. She had also said that it was a good way to stop and relax after a hard event in one's life, since such an event could set off an unnecessary transformation.

"So, now, while in this calm state," Nashoba continued, "I would like you, Colin, to concentrate on a special word, over and over. With this word, we will help you associate it with the emotions you've experienced on our previous days."

"Any word?" Colin asked as he opened his eyes.

"Yes, but only in your mind," Nashoba suggested.

Colin had decided on the word *"wolf"*, especially since *"Ma'iingan inini"* was a mental mouthful.

"Do you have one?" Nashoba asked.

"Yes."

"Now I want you to say it over and over in your mind, keeping your eyes closed."

Wolf. Wolf. Wolf. Wolf. Colin repeated.

Colin had worn an old pair of shorts and a paint-stained t-shirt because he knew that when he shifted again, they'd be gone. His mother, of course, brought another backpack of extra clothes. Colin chuckled at a comment his mother had made that morning about how she used to have to pack extra clothes for Colin when he was a little boy *"just in case of an accident."*

"Colin?" Nashoba said. "Are you concentrating?"

"Mmm," he uttered. *Wolf. Wolf. Wolf...*

Suddenly from both sides Colin got a lick from his shifted mother and a big nudge from Richard obviously playing Quentin again.

"Keep saying it to yourself," advised Nashoba.

Wolf. Wolf.

Lick!

Wolf. Wolf. Wolf.

Nudge! Push!

Wolf. Wolf. Wolf.

Lick! Nudge!

This kept going for another twenty minutes, but no changes had occurred.

"You're doing nothing wrong, Colin," Richard indicated. "This was the hardest part for most of us."

"What is your word, Colin?" Anne asked after she transformed back to human and began to get dressed again.

"Wolf," Colin said having felt disappointed at not making it work.

"Good, good," Nashoba answered, rubbing her chin and looking towards the ground. "Hmm, well then, I guess what we could do next would be to..."

Anne suddenly screamed, "Oh, my...*AUGH!*"

Colin's mother had somehow lost her footing on the edge of the cliff while slipping on her sneakers. She toppled off the rocky lip only to grab hold of a small outcropping sixty feet above the apple trees below. Colin quickly reacted, jumping to his feet and springing to the cliff's edge. He shifted in a matter of seconds, never clearly hearing the mantra being spoken as he did so. From human to Superior the chorused words of *"wolf-wolf-wolf"* echoed in the air.

The mantra ended as he dove down to a jagged ledge, swinging effortlessly to his mother like some tailless spider monkey. He smoothly scooped her up and returned her to the top of the cliff.

Panting from the initial shock, Colin stopped to look at the funny expressions on everyone's face. In his man-wolf voice, Colin said to his mother, "*You* did that on *purpose!*"

His mother smiled, "Yes. To help things move along."

He put his hands on his knees, still out of breath from the nervous energy. He then looked back up to his mother, "Are you sure you can't shift into a *fox*?"

The others stood and laughed.

The skill of instant shifting was worked on over and over again throughout the day. Colin eventually associated *"wolf"* to the playful part of his lessons, so as not to continue to associate it with Quentin at all.

By the day's end Richard proudly announced, *"Colin is now able to walk, chew gum and shift at the same time."*

Chapter 21:
Baggy Jeans

Without using their sirens Police Chief Porter and Sergeant Harrison, along with Officers Grunwald and Henderson, drove up to 96 Edgewood Road. They had no proof that this location was going to help them find any answers to the murders, but it had been their only lead.

Mitch drove towards the simple farmhouse noticing quickly that a new wooden porch swing was empty, but still swinging. When they stopped the vehicles, they saw that Baird's Ford Truck was just inside the barn door entrance. Not much could be heard on the premises except the occasional clucking of chickens. Mitch had found the place extremely quiet especially if the presence of any canines were at all around.

"*Hello?*" Mitch said out loud as he got out of his car. "This is the Eureka Police. Is anyone home?"

He didn't get an answer right away, but suddenly heard the sounds of intensely loud hip hop music coming from behind the house. Officer Henderson pulled out his pistol.

"Henderson," the Police Chief quickly said, putting his hand up. Henderson returned the gun to his holster, but didn't let go.

A teenage boy bounded around the corner carrying a mid-sized boom box. He was dressed in a large, red t-shirt, displaying an air-bound skateboarder, and wore a pair of baggy jean-shorts; his baseball cap visor was tilted to the right of his head. The boy stopped in his tracks when he saw the police officers.

"*Whoa!*" he quickly said and turned the music off. "Sorry, like, Officers...Didn't hear you pull up." The boy then glanced up at his portable stereo. "Yeah, huh? Bit old fashion, I know, but it still works *fricken* great, so I make cassette tapes and I use it. *So*, like, can I help you?"

"Yes, we're looking for your father," Mitch answered.

"Sure. He's right in the house," the boy answered. "Probably getting dinner ready."

"And who are you?" Stephanie asked.

"Victor, ma'am. Victor Dawes."

The four officers headed to the front door with Victor leading the way. He continued to bounce up and down, as if still listening to the music. "Dad?" he announced, playing air guitar into the kitchen.

Mitch glanced around at the spotless living room as they walked into the entryway. He had asked around about this family and knew that the boy had lost his mother several years ago. For a family known to be impoverished, it looked like this Baird Dawes was doing fine as a single-dad.

"Yes, hello officers," came a clean-cut Baird, apron and all. "How can I help you?"

"Hello, Mr. Dawes, I'm Mitch Porter of the..."

"The Police Chief, sure. Doing a great job here in our town, though I'm sure it's been tough lately," Baird interrupted, shaking Mitch's hand. "Never had you guys out this way before. Good thing, I guess, huh?"

"Um, yes," Mitch continued. "These are Officers Grunwald and Henderson."

"And I'm Sergeant Harrison," Stephanie added.

"Ah, yes, the investigator," Baird took her outstretched hand, gave her a flirting wink, and shook it gently.

"You must have read about the dog attacks in the area, then?" Stephanie questioned.

"Or possibly *wolves*- yes, I did," Baird said giving a look of concern.

"Well, Officer Grunwald, here, came across pieces of a business card," Mitch explained. "It seemed to belong to one of the victims and had your address on it."

"You must mean Bobby LeClaire," Baird said. "He was visiting here the day he died."

"*Died?* What-what happened to Mr. LeClaire, Dad?" Victor joined in, displaying visible alarm.

"He was killed, son. I didn't want to upset you," Baird said to him and then turned to the others. "You see we have an American Indian background here, as did Mr. LeClaire."

"If I may ask," Mitch said, "What tribal background are you from?"

"A mix, of course, mostly Abenaki," Baird smiled. "With a bit of Pennacook on my mother's side."

"And your connection with Mr. LeClaire?" Stephanie prodded.

"Bobby LeClaire was of similar heritage and a good businessman," Baird said. "I liked supporting him by mentioning his name around town and drumming up business for him. In appreciation Bobby would come by and do us favors. He helped fix things around this old place. In fact, the extra shed out back was almost half price, thanks to him."

Mitch looked out the window to see a freshly built attachment to the barn.

"And the front porch swing?" Stephanie added.

"Oh, yes. Go sit on it if you like. Very comfortable."

"So, what you're saying was Mr. LeClaire came here from northern Maine for business reasons."

"Oh, yes. His business even reached parts of Rhode Island," Baird replied. He snuck a peek at his simmering spaghetti sauce. "He would bring the wood down himself..." He suddenly coughed having remembered the small car that he had driven.

Victor caught the mistake and quickly said, "He and those monster-looking helpers that would come in the truck. *Dude*, I didn't give *those* guys any grief."

"Yeah. They were big," responded Baird. "But total teddy bears all the same."

"Did you know their names?" Mitch questioned.

"Oh, hmm. Danny and Mike, is all I remember," Baird lied. "Bobby would bring different employees, but always his best muscle men."

"And each time Bobby LeClaire came along on the deliveries?" Stephanie asked.

"You betcha," Baird continued without hesitation. "He had come for several visits. He'd stay after sending his employees back to the lumberyard. LeClaire loved to talk about native stuff. You know, traditions, ceremonies, Pow Wows. Guess he didn't get much of that around his home or work."

"When had you seen him last that day?" Mitch asked. They had yet to have any evidence of the time of the murder.

"Oh, he would always leave by about eight pm, wanting to get back north."

"And it was the same that night?"

"Same. We said our goodbyes and he was gone," answered Baird. He looked out at the shed. "Bobby's gonna to be very missed around here. *Very* missed... So, do you have any suspects or a clear cause of death?"

"We're getting pretty close on both," Mitch lied, trying to get a reaction. Baird didn't flinch.

"Did it have anything to do with the dog attacks?" Victor asked.

"Do you own any dogs?" Stephanie instead queried.

Victor said, "*I wish!* But Dad's allergic to them."

"Ha," Baird said, reacting to Victor's act. "Indeed. Horribly allergic."

"We'd still like to look around," Mitch said, though he felt like the interview produced very little. He had hoped that some smidgen of a clue would have surfaced.

"No problem," Baird smiled, tightening his apron. "Look around all you want. *I've* got a sauce to finish, here."

"Smells good," Stephanie said. "I smell fresh garlic?"

"You bet," Baird responded. "And *lots* of meat."

As they left through the back door to survey the grounds, Victor gave a sinister grin to the nervous Henderson as he passed.

Chapter 22:
The Forgetting Formula

It had been Colin's last day of training. He was excited to get it over with and get back to some normality. *Ha. Wonder what that might look like at this point!* he thought. But there was only four more days before the new school year began and he wanted to spend it with his friends.

In the shower that morning Colin had practiced his *wolf* mantra, changing himself into the Ma'iingan inini with unemotional ease. What he found so fascinating was that his bones, skin, probably even his organs, stretched and grew without hurting a bit. And when he shrunk back to human form, it, too, was a pleasant sensation. The drawback, he had realized right away, was that his new six-foot-nine frame was too tall for the small shower.

Colin had attempted it anyway, deciding that he might as well clean his new fur coat while he was in there. *I'll be needing a good dog brush to make my coat smooth and shiny.* Colin chuckled. *Maybe I better use April's blow dryer, too! Ha- Oh, and can't forget to floss my fangs!*

He got out of the shower (still giggling to himself) dried his fur the best he could, and then stood in front of the full-length mirror. He could truly see his human side under all the fur. *Muscular, but furry...Sweet.* Colin thought, producing a big, toothy grin with his canine muzzle. "If I may be so bold: quite the handsome looking werewolf," he said aloud as he stood straight and tall. "*Girls* say goodbye to the *Big Bad Wolf*, and say hello to..."

"Colin, breakfast's ready!"

Over breakfast, Nashoba had explained that the day's lesson would be short, but important. It had to do with teaching the blending of native plants that the Sachem Tribe had used for centuries.

"What's it for?" Colin asked. "Fleas?"

"*Fleas?* Ha. That's very cute," Nashoba said. "No, it's simply an essential remedy for our kind."

"Wish we could get my friend, Jasmine, involved," Colin said. "She loves herbal medicine stuff."

"Just like all of it, Colin," Nashoba explained. "This, too, is very important to keep a secret."

A few hours later Colin found himself again in the small clearing off the Nebraska Notch Trail with three feisty wolves. He smartly stored his clothes to the side before shifting into a Superior. Though they were there in search of herbs all four were adamant about having more 'wolf time'.

Through her barks and sounds, Nashoba said, "We're looking for two plants, Colin. One sits low to the ground and has three white berries. Its light green leaves are the shape of long fingernails, and they, too, are only three. The plant is called '*oblivio lupulus*', and can be found near the smaller streams of...*ah*, here we go..."

She pounced over to a wet set of rocks near the slight trickling of water and showed off the berry bush below her. Gently using her mouth, she bit the berries off the plant and dropped them into a loose leather pouch that they all wore around their necks.

"We will need one hundred of the berries for a good, strong brew," Nashoba said.

With that the others followed the winding stream to various locations until they had all gathered enough each.

"Now we look for, '*evanesco mens mentis*'," Nashoba announced. "Our much-needed mushroom. It can only be found under or near dead birch trees. The distinguishable parts are its oval cap and its furry, bulbous stem."

The foursome meandered through the thick forest, attempting to find a patch of birch. They were constantly on the lookout for wandering hikers, but had instead come upon a small pack of startled coyotes gathered over their kill. The coyotes immediately began to growl until Colin stepped into view. Their mouths quickly closed as they backed off, tails between their legs.

"We are just passing through," Nashoba barked kindly.

"Coyotes can understand us?" Colin asked.

"Yes, and we them. But just like different cultures, our accents and words may seem unusual," she explained. "It is the tone that gets respect. Or, as you can tell, being a Ma'iingan inini helps, too."

"So, I can understand *other*...canines?"

"Yes," she answered. "But you must know, domestic dogs are not as bright, though the smaller ones and mixed breeds think they are. You just have to be patient with them."

Colin looked at the motionless pack, smiled and said hello. They cocked their heads confused.

"Hey, here's a patch over here!" Colin's mom barked. "Nine each, right?"

"Let's make it eleven," Richard answered. "That amount works the best."

They had just begun to pick the mushrooms when Colin asked, "The mushrooms make *what* better?"

"Keep picking and I will tell you," Nashoba said as she plucked another mushroom into her mouth. She counted her eleven and then sat herself down. "We, as a tribe, made two big decisions when we decided to all become Shifters; first, to be *only* wolves, and second, to never get caught. Throughout our history we have been good about keeping the second promise, despite a mistake here and there. In doing so we have held onto our love of being wolf."

"Not an easy task," Richard joined in. "Especially today with powerful binoculars and cameras, as well as helicopters and planes. But cleverness has prevailed...*Oh*, there has been stories written in them-there exaggerated tabloids."

"Being clever and mindful has always been our useful quality when needed," Nashoba continued. "But there have been times when people have seen too much. It is then that we try to use our plant concoction here. Do we have enough?"

"I believe so. You, Colin?" his mother asked.

"Yeah, I've got eleven," Colin answered, but continued to inquire. "Okay, so you use this mixture on people when they have seen too much. What does it do?"

"It's a perfectly safe mind-drug," Richard answered. "It causes a person to sleep for twelve or so hours and forget the events of the day before. All this and *no* nasty headaches."

"Do you inject them?" Colin asked as he looked down at the plants in his bag. "And how would you even get close enough? They're *probably* running away in fear."

Nashoba's snout curled into a smile as she sat herself in front of him. "We use many means to get the remedy into their bodies. As humans, we *can* slip it into a drink or, if necessary, we use a porcupine quill as a dart."

"*Dart?*" Colin repeated.

"We can throw them pretty accurately," Anne added.

"You said, *'as humans',*" Colin replied. "How would you use it as wolves?"

"The front nails of our paws are dipped into the formula," answered Richard. "We administer one quick sliver-of-a-cut which injects the drug into their bodies."

"And these people end up being fine the next day?" Colin continued. "They *never* question these strange cuts?"

"Think about your own scratches," Nashoba smiled. "I'm sure there have been mornings where you have woken to mysterious scratches on yourself and never knew where they came from. Well, these people wake up with a scratch *and* no memory of the day before. That's all."

Colin had paused, considering this. "Wait a second. I *have* had strange scratches before and forgetful days...*Mooom?*"

His mom lowered her head and placed her paw over her snout in shame. "*Maybe* once or twice."

***

The river that cut through the middle of Cochran had an excellent swimming section on its eastern side. It included deep pools and a great rope swing. The water, however, was not always healthy enough to swim in, but on this particular late August Saturday the local town officials had given a thumbs-up about it being clean and safe. Colin and his friends took total advantage of the news.

"Dude, I can't believe school's beginning already," Skyler said as he waded slowly in, his puffing along the edges.

"Yeah, summer's almost done and I feel I barely saw you guys," Jasmine added, sitting on a rock along the edge, totally enjoying the sun's warmth in her blue and white striped one piece. She then turned to Colin who was gripping the rope swing, "Especially haven't seen you, Mr. Mysterious. *'I'm taking a course in native traditions from my Great Grandmother',* he says...*'I can't text you, I'm too busy.'* Blah-blah-blah."

Colin had smiled and thought to himself. *Well, it wasn't a lie!*

He grabbed the tethered line and forgot himself as he flew through the air. His pumpkin-colored bathing suit glowed like a streak as he let go of the rope at its highest point and then gracefully back-flipped into the deep water below. When he came up both Skyler and Jasmine were staring at him.

Jasmine finally said, "So, did your *traditions* classes include Olympic diving lessons?"

"Ha-oh, it..." Colin stammered. "I've also been correcting, no, *perfecting* my balance...issue. No more *clumsy*-me, you know...like, *watch out* basketball-here I come."

Colin had come ashore to gather his towel hoping the subject could end and that they could just swim.

"Skyler," he attempted, "have you come across any good movies at the store worth seeing?"

"Oh, dude, like- yeah. I..." Skyler began.

"*No way!*" Jasmine stood, pulling Colin's towel away from him. "*I* want answers! First, there was the miraculous save you made at Perkinsville Falls and then the sudden change to meat-eater and now *you* can do acrobatics? Let alone being *perfectly* buffed."

"*Jasmine's-got-the-hots-for-Colin,*" Skyler playfully sang.

"Oh, shut up, Sky, I'm trying to *make* a point," Jasmine retorted. "So, *what* do you have to say for yourself, Trask, or are *we* not good enough anymore to be let into your circle?"

"*Whoa,* come-on," Colin reacted, and then said, "Okay, seriously, I've really missed you guys, too, but, *hey,* I've been delving into this native stuff full-on. *And*...and, because of it, have embraced the world of the *hunter*, like Skyler had said...eating meat. *All this* has produced some changes."

"Changes, like muscular *grace?*" Jasmine questioned.

"No, no, it's not just that," Colin continued, trying not to dig himself into a hole. "I've also been doing stuff at the hardware store... With Mr. LeClaire. *Oh, and* he's been helping me with his karate knowledge."

"Karate," Jasmine quietly repeated. "Karate lessons and courses in native tradition?"

"Yeah," Colin said. "Has kept me pretty busy."

A group of girls had suddenly ambled down the embankment from the park excited to jump into the river. Colin immediately caught sight of Julia among them and his stomach whirled. Colin hadn't seen Julia since that unfortunate run-in with Quentin and his gang, but was glad to recognize that her choice of friends had considerably improved. Of course, her very sexy olive-green bikini made more than just his stomach whirl.

"*Hi, Colin!*" said an enthusiastic Julia. She immediately came over as Colin grabbed the towel from Jasmine to put back around himself. Jasmine rolled her eyes, but smiled.

In a whispered voice to the two of them, Julia said, "I am *so* sorry about what happened that day with that *jerk*, O'Reilly. I truly thought I was hanging out with just my *so-called* girlfriends. Quentin just showed up and..."

"Julia," Colin answered, loving the sound of her name coming off of his tongue, "it's *okay*. I saw your dilemma. There wasn't anything you could do. Quentin just has a thing out for me."

"He's brutal *and* conceited. I still wished I could have helped," Julia responded as she placed a hand on his arm. "Are you guys still swimming? Can we join you?"

"Sure," Colin had answered quickly and then turned to Jasmine to see if she was done interrogating him.

"Yes," Jasmine responded, but just to be the usual *unusual* Jasmine she had to say more, "*If* you don't mind hanging out with us *weirdies*."

Julia smiled and said she would be honored to hang out with all of them. Julia's friends agreed.

With that Skyler sucked in his stomach (as best as he could) then challenged everyone to a cannonball contest off the rope swing. The group had a great time swinging and splashing and laughing together. Colin, all the while, found himself doing his best to be a gentleman by *not* gawking at Julia in her bikini. He failed miserably.

Just before everyone had to head home for dinner, Julia's friend, Michelle, invited the three of them to her home for an end-of-summer bonfire party. Colin and the others said yes.

Jasmine and Skyler went home for a change of clothes and came back to Colin's house to eat. Colin's father had asked them all over for some barbecued chicken. His mom promised Jasmine that there would probably be some veggie burgers of Colin's left over in the freezer. Jasmine had thought she had said this with an air of smug pride.

They sat around the backyard picnic table waiting for Colin's dad to put out the platter of chicken. He had just slid two veggie patties onto Jasmine's plate when April said, "Did Colin tell you guys about the race we did at our reunion?"

Colin and his mom quickly looked up.

"Ah, April..." was all her mom had time to say.

"Yeah, the two of us were actually blindfolded and had to follow a smell to a location where we..."

"*Blindfolded?*" Skyler asked. "What kind of a race was this?"

"Well, it was..." Colin tried to explain.

"How did you do, April?" Jasmine quickly asked, suspicion in her eyes.

"Awesomely well," April burst. "I almost did it, but had a bad fall that took me out of the race."

"You were blindfolded. That had to be difficult," Jasmine said, then quickly turned to Colin. "*So*, how did *you* do?"

"Ah..." Colin stuttered.

"He did *great!*" Colin's dad joined in. "He did *all* the blindfold section with ease and *almost* made it to the mountaintop finish line to win, but..."

"You had to climb a mountain, too?" Jasmine questioned.

"It was a small mountain," Colin quickly said. "Without the blindfold."

"The campground was part way up the mountain," his mother added, trying her best to look and sound unconcerned.

"Well, distance-wise, I believe that mountain was..." Philip was about to say.

"*Dear*, I think the gas grill is still on," Anne interrupted.

"Oh, my. Excuse me," he said and jumped up.

"And Colin would have won if he hadn't stopped to save an injured racer," April continued.

"Colin *saved* someone...again?" Jasmine said, in as much of an expressionless tone as Colin's mom had had.

"No, just helped," Colin fabricated. "She...*hurt* her leg."

"But, like I said, he *would* have won," April finished with an arm around her brother. "*I*, myself, thought he was the real winner."

"Dude," Skyler said while he looked at April. "Like, I don't think I've ever heard April say anything nice about you...*Ever*."

"*Well*," Jasmine said, a curious smirk on her face, "*I* believe this family reunion has produced some positive *changes* to your family, Mrs. Trask."

"Yes," Anne had answered in a monotone voice. She faked a smile. "I've noticed the same."

"*Hey*, look at the time," Colin suddenly announced. "We'd better get over to *that* party."

"There'll be adults there, right, Col?" his father asked.

"Yes, it's the Sullivan's house."

"Oh, nice family," Colin's dad responded. "They're all very good at flossing."

"Colin," his mother cautiously said, "are you bringing any *'medicine'*?"

"Mom, really?" Colin questioned.

"Just in case," she said, then turned to the others, "It's an allergy formula Colin's Great Grandmother made him. It helps him a lot."

"You've got allergies?" Skyler asked, before Jasmine had a chance.

"Yeah," Colin smiled. "Another change in me."

"*Probably* from the meat," Jasmine said under her breath.

Colin dashed inside to retrieve the small forgetting formula flask and tucked it into his pocket. He had given his mom a shaky smile and then joined the others.

Colin's house was just close enough to the Sullivan's to allow the three of them to walk. Unfortunately, this also allowed Jasmine the time to ask more questions.

"Colin," she said, dragging out the "o" for a full second. She was giving him the big stare.

"Jaaaaasmine," Colin returned with a grimace.

"Come on! I've been friends with you for at least four years, Sky longer, and we have seen you through many changes, *but...*"

"But she can't believe you eat meat, dude," Skyler offered.

"No-no, as if *that's* it!" Jasmine had said as she stopped to make her point. "Skyler, help me here. *You've* seen the shift in him."

Colin coughed at the word.

"Yo, like, *he's* matured," Skyler said. "He did just turn fifteen, you know."

"*You're* fifteen!" Jasmine threw back at him. "*You* haven't matured."

"Hey, that's low," he responded.

"Jazz, come on," Colin said. "I'm still me. Just been through some *new* experiences, that's all."

"What about your-your muscles?" Jasmine asked.

"Heavier work at the store," Colin answered, "and karate-exercise stuff."

"And your fine-tuned agility?"

"More karate-stuff."

"And your fingernails?"

"*Fingernails*?"

"They're long and perfect," she replied as she grabbed one of his hands. "Not *one* broken. Untypical for a boy."

"Ah..." was all Colin could say.

"Plus, what Skyler noticed," Jasmine continued. "You and April seem closer, *and* you and your mother."

"Well, like *you* said about the reunion," Colin said. He saw that Jasmine was calming down. "*Positive changes*. The realization of a native heritage brought us closer. But, ah, I think my mom still worries about others knowing of our background."

"*Really?* She does?" Jasmine reacted as she came to a stop. She contemplated Colin's mother's behavior at dinner and thought that was the cause. "*Why?* That's just...well, *that's* just stupid to me. *I* think it's so neat. I *hope* I didn't upset her. I don't care if she's shocked that I know. I'll make her *feel proud* of her heritage! You're proud of it, *right,* Colin? Huh? You should..."

Colin had pleasantly agreed with everything else Jasmine had to say happily realizing that he was clear of further query for the time being. However, this crazy night was just beginning, and all of Jasmine's questions would soon be answered in full.

Chapter 23:
Michelle Sullivan's Back-to-School Party

Michelle's party was at her family's house up in the hill section of town. This was where several of the wealthier families lived. What visually defined this part of Cochran as the wealthier section, besides the fact that they were located on the town's most picturesque piece of hillside, were their various sizes and designs of homes. It wasn't that the homes were mansions (a Colonial here, Salt Box there and many fancy Capes), it was that the houses were next to three or four car garages, had lawns that were perfectly manicured and landscaped, and of course, a pool or tennis court or private skateboard park graced the grounds (sometimes *all* three).

Michelle's family had a five-bedroom cape on six acres of rolling land that butt up against the hillside forest. Their backyard was perfectly level for the sole purpose of croquet, badminton, volleyball and an occasional lawn-bocce game. The level lawn also had one amoeba-shaped swimming pool, but for this particular evening the pool would be sharing a space with a roaring bonfire.

Both Michelle and Julia happily welcomed the threesome at the front door. Colin found himself gawking again at Julia as she sauntered up in a lacy red, spaghetti-strapped tank top and tightly fitting jean-shorts. He had blatantly blushed as she took his arm and led them through Michelle's house to the back.

Most of the students Julia and Michelle hung out with were of the popular crowd. It was the group Skyler, Jasmine or Colin might have barely gotten a "hi" from in their past experiences. So, when they found themselves among many of these students (as well as soon-to-be seniors, who were Michelle's brother's friends) the threesome felt rather out of place.

"I do have to warn you, Colin," Michelle said, holding onto his arm. "Quentin will be coming, thanks to my brother, Jake...Football-connection."

"It'll be all right," Colin responded. "Thanks for telling me."

Colin smiled at his confidence. With the strength he knew he had, yet the self-control he'd taken the time to learn, he just knew O'Reilly wouldn't be a problem this time around.

Of course, Skyler had been listening-in enough to understand Colin's confidence, too. He excitedly whispered into Colin's ear, "That's right, dude...*ka-ra-te.*"

Colin smiled.

Once in the backyard, Michelle went to help with the food table while Julia excused herself to greet some other friends. The three were left to just stand there and watch the unfolding of their first, serious high school party.

Colin could tell right away that Michelle's parents weren't too worried about the craziness and noise already happening, even though Michelle had explained to those *with* concerned parents that *her parents* were just inside the den watching television. Colin could also see that *her parents* were very focused on their television as their son, Jake, and the other seniors, snuck in six-packs of beer from around the tall wooden fence in the far back. He chuckled when he saw Tony Sagbush among them. He would probably get himself kicked off another sports team by the night's end.

The party was otherwise supplied with *legal* drinks and lots to eat. There was a massive table of sliced meats and cheeses for sandwiches, chips and dips, cut-up veggies and fruits of every kind.

"We shouldn't have eaten so much at your house, Colin," Jasmine said.

"Speak for yourself," Skyler snickered as he licked his chops.

Colin laughed as Skyler sauntered to the food table, but was glad that he, himself, had already eaten. He knew that everyone here would have remembered his avid vegetarianism and didn't want to explain why he suddenly attacked a plate of cold cuts. Instead, he and Jasmine grabbed some fruit punch and went to sit by the pool. Jasmine was just about to pick on the shirtless guys walking around (sticking out their chests) when Julia came over to them.

"Can I *please* borrow him," Julia had asked, taking Colin's hand.

"Oh, no problem," Jasmine replied, then quickly added, "Colin, you may *want* to tell her your little secret."

Colin looked wide-eyed at her.

Jasmine winked, "He's *now* a meat eater."

"Oh, *really*," Julia responded with a devious look in her eyes staring straight at Colin. "Good, 'cause tonight I'm *very much* a meat eater."

Jasmine raised her eyebrows as Colin followed suite.

Julia pulled Colin out of his seat and they maneuvered towards the fire. Jasmine watched them as they happily walked away. She had realized how things were beginning to change for all of them. She saw how easily their little trio could be split up. Would they still talk to each other, still hang out?

She looked over to Skyler while he, too, was merrily talking with a girl. *Wow!* She thought. *Many changes are happening.*

"Hello," came a non-Cochran accent. "My name is Charles," the British voice said.

Jasmine turned towards the voice.

"Charles Hartington. I'm one of the exchange students this year." He reached out a friendly hand. "And you are?"

"J-Jasmine...Jasmine Rainville." She could barely speak he was so cute.

***

Colin and Julia sat on a bench together near the fire. Colin had desperately tried to find the right words to say in this strangely wonderful situation he found himself in.

"It was a great day," was all he mustered.

"Oh, yeah," Julia smiled. "It was so fun finally spending some time with you and your friends. I posted our group-shot on Instagram, even though you were making a funny face."

"Sorry, I think a horsefly bit me right then," Colin lied, remembering how she had the phone close to his ears. "So, me and my buddies weren't as strange as others tend to see us?"

"I'm beginning to find strange and different far more comfortable to be around these days," Julia said as she looked out at the crowd. "Many of these people seem like clones, robots. *You* and your friends don't mind being yourselves."

"And what do you find so unique about me?" Colin questioned, curious to hear the answer.

"Lots," Julia said. She moved a little closer to him. "First, you don't seem to care about the need for popularity."

Colin bit his lip.

"*And* you see the world in unique ways. I see it in your artwork. *Plus,* if you don't mind me saying, you even *look* unique."

"Um, that's good?"

"Oh, yeah," she said, looking deep into his eyes. "I think you look fascinating, *handsomely* distinct. You don't look a thing..." She stopped abruptly.

"Look a thing?" Colin repeated.

"Ah," Julia began slowly, "I know people picked on you for your clumsiness *to your face*, but I had heard some call you worse names."

"Like what?"

"Like...Oriental...Spic or Ahab the Arab."

"*Seriously?*" Colin said, realizing the absurdity of students choosing *those* cultures to compare him with.

Julia gave him a thorough glance to see if he was offended and then said heatedly, "It's *stupid* racial stuff! *'Us better than them.' 'Whites better than blacks.' 'Rich better than the poor.'* It's here, too. It's *so* here. I'm so *sick* of it! *My father* is like that!"

"Your father, the doctor?" Colin said, truly shocked.

"He's *so* bad sometimes," Julia said, flecks of tears formed in her eyes. "I'm embarrassed to be his daughter."

"Would *he* see me as...like, different?" Colin asked. "You know, um, in case we-ah, if we..."

"...were dating?" Julia finished.

"Yeah," he said, feeling tingles.

"My...my dad...*yes*, he *would* have a problem with it," Julia slowly said, and then sat up straight, dropping her brows. "And I'm *going to* look him in the eye and just say, 'go to hell, Dad, *this* is my boyfriend!'"

Colin would have felt uncomfortable about the idea of Julia's prejudice father, if it weren't for the fact that he was too busy swallowing the heart that just bounced into his throat. However, the acknowledgment of dating Julia, and his fluttering heart, had fallen to the wayside at the arrival of Quentin O'Reilly.

Colin saw several seniors, including Jake, high-five Quentin near the tall fence, *plus* hand him a beer. After that the youngest star running back, and his fellow apes, waltzed onto the grounds as if they owned the place. Quentin spied Skyler at the food table and immediately scanned the party for Colin. When he didn't see him, Quentin decided Skyler would be a good way to get this crowd to focus on his awesome comedic wit.

"Hey! Hurry up, boys!" Quentin yelled, jumping up and down to get attention. "If we don't grab some food now, King Kong, here, will scarf-up every bite! *Hurry!*"

The girl Skyler was talking to slowly backed away, making him far more embarrassed than he had already been. He put down his plate and lowered his head to receive further ridicule. "Yo, buddy, no," said Quentin as he feigned a pleasant voice. "*I* didn't mean it. Eat *all* you want. Here, I'll help. Some sandwiches? *Ten* maybe? How 'bout potato salad? A *big* glob, huh?" Quentin kept piling up a plate in his hands to the laughs of everyone around.

On seeing this Jasmine sprung up out of her seat, abruptly stopping her conversation with Charles. She had begun to run over towards the food table when she saw that Colin was already there.

"*Stop it*, Quentin," Colin clearly said, at the same time focusing on his emotions.

Quentin stood straight up as he held Skyler's food-covered plate in front of him. His back was to Colin.

"*What do I hear?* After all summer long, could it be my favorite *graceful* entertainer?" Quentin then spun on his heels to crash the full plate into the side of Colin's head, however Colin anticipated as much so he simply dropped low and out of reach. The plate, instead, flew directly into the face of one of Quentin's cronies, Spencer Whimer.

"Why you little shit!" Spencer growled coming at Colin at a muscular two hundred and twenty pounds.

Colin quickly moved to his left, laying out just enough foot to catch the junior tackle by his toes. He and his weighty muscles tumbled down the slight grade to the pool's edge.

The change of events had Quentin's audience now laughing at the O'Reilly gang. This put fire in O'Reilly's eyes. He then gestured for the other guys to grab Colin so he could do some serious damage.

Colin realized that he would need to look like a person just trying to defend himself. He decided, with what little he knew of karate, to fake its movements. He remembered something about using a person's weight, like he did with Spencer, to knock them off balance. As the gorillas approached him from behind, Colin prepared himself.

Tony Sagbush had made the first move, jumping towards Colin from over his left shoulder. Colin dropped to the ground at the same time and grabbed Tony's shirt as he did so. He sent the boy flying into the large, plastic punch bowl, spilling it all over Tony and the students around him. The other two apes tried to take advantage of Colin on the ground so they came flying in for a crushing body-slam. Colin instantly rolled, putting himself out of the landing field. This allowed the smashing of two hefty bodies as they collided in midair.

Quentin stood there open jawed for only a brief moment. He was not going to let Colin make *him* look like a fool. He quickly moved to the side of the crowd and suddenly emerged with his arms wrapped tight around Julia.

"*Let me go!*" she yelled.

"Is *this* what has made you some fucking ninja-man, Trask?" Quentin remarked, putting his face close to Julia's.

Colin felt his body-tingle and knew that his eyes were transforming. He bit his lower lip to hold off the shift.

"Quentin, cut it out or I'm gonna get my father!" Michelle warned.

"Hey, like, calm down," Quentin smoothly said, sounding peaceful. "We're just having fun here. Right?" He whipped out his cell phone and took a quick selfie of himself giving Julia a kiss on the cheek. "I'll post *that* later."

"*You little...!*" she hissed. "Let me go, you scum-bag!"

Colin then walked slowly towards Quentin and Julia, breathing steadily. His face wore such confidence that it made O'Reilly falter a bit with his own.

"Come to save your girlfriend?" Quentin said, his voice shaking slightly. He squeezed his arms around her tighter and laid his face up against hers.

Colin stepped closer. He stood quietly and expressionless, then, as quick as lightning, his fist shot up and crashed between Quentin's eyes and nose, sending him spilling backwards to the ground. Colin quickly grabbed hold of Julia so she wouldn't fall with him.

"*You broke my nose!*" Quentin yelled on his hands and knees. "*And my phone!*" He cursed about the pain and blood and how his parents were going to hear about this. Quentin stood up, looking to see if any of the older football players were going to defend him. No one moved. Finally, he picked up his phone and then gestured to his buddies. The defeated gang quickly walked down and around the far, wooden fence to escape the evident laughs and giggles.

Julia wrapped her arms around Colin, thanking him for getting her out of that embarrassment, but added, "I *was* about to bite him."

Colin smiled, thrilled at the feeling of doing something he had always wanted to do, but also enjoying the incredible sensation of Julia pressed up against him. His heightened senses breathed in her sweet smells.

"Thanks, buddy," Skyler said as onlookers were still awestruck at what had just happened. "Got caught looking like a foolish pig again."

"*You* did not, Skyler!" Julia said, stepping away from Colin. "You were just enjoying yourself. Those *dirt-bags* were the only fools here, along with all these *robots* standing around laughing! You have *no* reason to feel ashamed."

"I *really* like this girl," Skyler said to Colin.

"Is everything all right?" came the British voice of Charles. "That was quite the tussle."

"Everyone, I'd like you to meet Charles Hartington of West Sussex, England," Jasmine said. "Charles, *everyone*...And, *yes*," giving Colin a long look, "that was *quite* the tussle."

Colin purposely ignored Jasmine's stare as he and the others introduced themselves to the new exchange student. After that

Charles, Jasmine and Skyler went off to sit by the fire to explore the need to resurrect *Monty Python's Flying Circus.*

Colin was about to go sit with them when Julia took his arm. She held a finger to her mouth to stay quiet. From there Julia led him to a small wooden playhouse tucked in among the trees in the far back of the yard. Michelle must have used the place when she was younger. Though it had a few spider webs and looked like it hadn't been entered in years, the children's furniture and a tea set were still inside.

Colin had to sit immediately because he was too tall for the house. He sat himself onto a pink wooden chair as Julia closed the door behind them.

She gave Colin the devious look she had given him earlier then swung one of her legs over his exposed lap and gently sat down. When she leaned close to his face, she purposely pressed her breasts up against his chest. Her soft touch, along with delicious, bodily smells, sent rapturous vibrations down Colin's spine.

"What you did for me back there was *so* wonderful," she said in a silky voice. "*And* it'll be my excuse to do this-" Julia planted her lips onto his, firm, but soft. She held them there as Colin's eyes widened with surprised pleasure. Colin acknowledged the pleasure growing in his body, but then recognized that it was the same sensation he had felt just before he... Colin barely had time to react. He lifted Julia away from him and placed her quickly in another chair. He did his best to shield her eyes just enough to get himself out through the door, which burst from its hinges.

Colin made a dash for the woods.

Hearing the commotion Jasmine and Skyler glanced over to the little house to get a glimpse of Colin running off. Jasmine jumped up to follow as Skyler went to see if Julia was all right.

Colin had dashed behind a thick white pine, having completely transformed, with pieces of ripped clothing hanging from his fur.

He couldn't believe what had just happened to him. *Of all the stupid...!* He thought, and then realized the simple fact. *They focused on the emotions of anger and laughter, they forgot about...*"

"*Colin*, are you there?" Jasmine said as she walked slowly through the thick woods.

With his mind elsewhere, and the voice of a friend nearby, Colin had forgotten what he'd become and stepped into view.

"Damn, am I glad it's..." Colin said in his gruff voice and then quickly covered his muzzle. He stared wide-eyed, seeing Jasmine looking the same. She was about to scream when he quickly said, "Jazz- no, it's *me*."

A rush of air escaped her throat as she stood with her hands over her mouth. She backed up one step, but then held her ground. What she saw was not the least bit grotesque. The handsome, muscular qualities of a powerful human, along with the dignified features of an advanced canine, had made this creature in front of her quite beautiful to look at. Its snout held the expression of a mild, calm dog, which made Jasmine feel at ease.

"Colin?" Jasmine quietly said. She recognized Colin's eyes buried slightly within flecks of fur, but they were still his eyes.

"Yes," said the rough voice. "Sorry about this, but I am glad it's you."

"*What* happened? I mean, how could..." Jasmine stuttered as she suddenly tried to piece all the ways Colin had been acting with what was now standing in front of her.

"I'll explain it later," Colin had said, deciding when and if to slip her the forgetting formula. "I've got to get out of here before others, especially Julia, sees me."

"Okay," Jasmine slowly said, "but you *will* explain it, right?"

"Yes, but you *can't* tell anyone, please," Colin begged. "Not even Skyler."

"Promise," she said.

He smiled with his muzzle, and then eventually said, "Ah, I was wondering if you could pick up the pieces of my clothes and hide them?"

"Yeah...sure," Jasmine smirked as she lifted up a pair of shredded boxer shorts.

Chapter 24:
Learning the Truth

"Could I speak to Police Chief Porter, please," Harvey said over the phone. "Sure, I'll hold."

"Porter, here."

"Yes, Officer Porter, it's Harvey Benson up here in Cochran."

"Yes, Harvey."

"I'm not sure if UVM's library was any help, but I forgot about something concerning that tattoo you saw."

"The native symbol?" Mitch questioned. "Did you find a match?"

"Yes, silly me, it was right here in my basement," Harvey continued. "I was compiling all my American Indian papers and books to bring back to the school and suddenly remembered that tattoo design."

"And," Mitch pushed.

"Well, it was sketched in an old notebook I brought home for a student."

"Who was the student, if I may ask?"

"Oh, sure. It was Colin Trask. He was a student of mine just last year that got interested in local native cultures. Nice kid."

"Was he particularly interested in the sketch of that tattooed symbol?" Mitch pursued.

"No, more interested with the tribe it represented," responded Harvey. "He'd become very fascinated by this local Mi'kmaq group, the Sachem Tribe. Their clan name was Skiri Clan, meaning Wolf Clan."

Mitch paused then asked, "Did you say *'wolf'?*"

***

Colin had breathed in the last smells of summer before autumn's musty decay would take to the air. He realized, with his new, keen senses how much he enjoyed the smells of this area around Lookout Rock.

On this particular morning, however, there was no time to focus on smells. He was here to decide whether or not to trust Jasmine with the truth about the tribe's secret and about who he had become.

"*Skyler?*" Colin suddenly blurted when he saw his friend following behind Jasmine. "You were supposed to come alone?" Colin whispered to her.

"*Alone?*" Skyler reacted, breathing heavily from the hike. "She texted me, and, like, since when am *I* out of the picture? Besides, whadya gonna talk about anyway, huh? *Julia*, maybe, and how your gonna tell *her* what had happened?"

"*You* know what happened?" Colin said, looking at Jasmine.

"No-no, he doesn't," she answered. "But he's here because I thought he had a right to know...too. In case you ever *needed* our help...ah, hiding or covering up...or something."

"Enough with the riddles," Skyler announced. He took a long drink of water. "Cover up, what? Is Colin CIA now? It would at least explain his fighting abilities."

"Yeah, cover up what?" Colin asked Jasmine.

"Well, you know, if you went...I don't know...wild," Jasmine said.

"Wild," Colin repeated.

"*Wild?*" Skyler questioned.

Before she could say anymore Colin put up his hand, "Wait, let's not confuse him anymore than we already have."

Skyler kept looking from Colin to Jasmine, waiting for some explanation. Colin, on the other hand, fiddled around with the small flask of formula in his pocket, trying to decide if this was all worth it. He considered Jasmine's point about knowing the truth so she could help. *But what if one of them leaked the secret? What if they accidentally told somebody out of fear or anger? But these are my best friends. They've kept all sorts of secrets, just maybe nothing as big as this. Plus, Jasmine saw me. She's accepted it. But what would Skyler think?*

Colin finally decided that he would explain things first, and then see what arose from there. If Skyler showed any signs of overload *both* he and Jasmine would be given the formula. He still had time to erase all memory up through last night.

"Okay, here it goes," Colin eventually said, deciding to present Skyler with the only words *Skyler* would understand, "*I'm a werewolf...A nice one, but a werewolf. Not* your typical, out-of-control type you've seen in the movies. I'm a... *different...*type...of werewolf-like-being."

Skyler paused, then laughed, "*Ha!* Weird, but funny, *so* seriously, what made you run out on sweet Julia last night?"

Colin looked at Skyler, then at Jasmine. "My emotions," he admitted.

"Well, dude, I would have felt *some* emotions, too, if *she* kissed me, but, really, dude, what...?"

"She told you about kissing me?" interrupted Colin.

"Colin, we're..." Jasmine tried to intervene.

"*Yeah*, 'cause Julia was concerned that she was too pushy," Skyler responded, with a smirk. "She thought you weren't ready for *so* much so soon. Boy, now *I* would've..."

"Sky, *shut up!*" Jasmine yelled.

"What?"

Colin hadn't been listening to any of this. He just sat there trying to figure out how he would explain things to Julia. "*Not ready?" she said! Of course, I was ready for that kiss! I really liked that kiss!*"

"*Colin!*" Jasmine blurted.

"Oh, ah, yeah..." Colin staggered. "Um, the research. Let's talk about *that* first."

"You mean the Mi'kmaq tribe stuff?" Skyler asked. "That you're half Mi'kmaq, right? We know that."

"Do you remember the shaman magic Mr. Benson mentioned about that particular tribe?" asked Colin. "Well, it was *heavily* used by my...ah, ancestors."

Colin got Skyler's full attention at the word *'magic'* and proceeded to tell of how the Skiri Tribe came to be. He reminded them of the dream he had and said how it was the first clue to his changes. He told the full story of the reunion's Sachem race and how he saved Sasha from the crumbling cliff. He mentioned the lessons he was taught by Great Grandmother Carrier, Mr. LeClaire and his mother and how they, themselves, could only turn into wolves while he could change into this other breed. He explained the importance of this being a tribal secret and how it has been kept a secret for centuries. Plus, he told them about how dogs will react strangely to him (just in case the two ever wondered) and mentioned the Tweety and Bam Bam incident.

Afterward they had sat there in silence, Jasmine looking out over the valley while Skyler stared at Colin. He was waiting for them to begin laughing, though seriously wondering if he should have been writing all this down, being only the greatest plot for a werewolf movie he'd ever heard.

Skyler eventually realized that no one was going to laugh.

"Come on, guys!" he finally said. "What's the joke? I mean, this-this is a *great* story. Whew! *What* a story."

"Skyler," Jasmine said as she turned to face him. "I *saw* him. I saw him as this, what was the name again? *Mag-an Neeny.*"

"Ma'iingan inini," Colin corrected.

"*You* saw him?" Skyler repeated. "Colin...as a werewolf." He had begun chewing on a sandwich he brought, shooting glances towards

Colin, then quickly stood up. "All right then," he exclaimed with his mouth full. "On the next full moon, I want to see..."

"Ah..." Jasmine interrupted.

"*Wait a second*," he suddenly said instead. "If *you* saw him last night, *how* could he have changed without a full moon?"

"I kinda mentioned this," Colin explained, standing up himself. "Last night's change had to do with me losing control of my *emotions*. Emotions aside, I can change at will."

"Okay, prove it," Skyler dared, as he crossed his arms, but he stepped back a bit.

Colin looked at Jasmine who shrugged her shoulders.

"I, um, first have to remove some clothing," he apologized to Jasmine, stripping down to a pair of plaid boxer shorts.

"Those look a whole lot better than last night's pair," she chuckled.

Colin gave her a sarcastic grin and then mentally began whispering his *wolf* mantra.

He slowly shifted before their eyes.

Skyler *and* Jasmine watched as their friend stretched upward and outward. They could hear the slightest sound of growing, as if someone was pulling the twisted fibers of a piece of rope. Bare skin sprouted brown and black fur with his chest, stomach and feet displaying areas of silky white. Skyler stared in awe as Colin's nose and mouth extended forward into a canine muzzle, the nostrils pressing to the front of the nose and turning a glistening, wet black.

Colin then stood there as a Ma'iingan inini, looking as non-threatening as he could. Skyler, on the other hand, stood wide-eyed and dumbfounded, while Jasmine kept a hand to her mouth with an expression of amazement.

"Now you know," Colin said gruffly.

"*You* can speak?" Skyler reacted, his mouth in shock. "*Oh-my-god!* Oh, my...This-this..."

Colin looked at Jasmine worried. He wondered if it was too much for Skyler. Then their friend began to bounce up and down in place.

"*This is so cool!*" he shouted. "Oh, *my* god! Dude-*so* cool!"

"Don't get all alarmed and scared or anything," Jasmine said, her hands on her hips.

Colin shifted back into a human and got dressed. When he was done, he noticed Skyler was still moving in a sort of excited dance.

"Skyler, you have got to promise not to tell anyone," Jasmine pressed. "No secret videos put on YouTube...*nothing*."

"Yeah. Yeah," Skyler promised as he shook his head up and down. Then he turned to Colin, "Like, *dude*, you are...Wow-*It's* really true. Like, this totally explains Perkinsville Falls, and you whooping Quentin's ass, *and* his buddies. Oh, man...So, like, *your* mom, too? A wolf? Crazy cool. Think she'd show us how she does *that*?" Skyler asked.

"*No*," Colin quickly said. "You *can't* let her or Mr. LeClaire know that you know. Understand?"

"*Okay*. Okay. *Big* secret. Get that. Right," he said as he finished his sandwich excitedly. "So-so cool."

Chapter 25:
The Invitation

On the first day of school, it took Colin three whole classes to get acclimated again, especially with students looking at him with praise instead of giggles. Nothing had been more satisfying, though, than the silent mouths of Quentin and his gang. They kindly made it a habit of keeping their distance from Colin *and* his friends.

As for Julia, Colin hadn't seen her yet, but was prepared to face her with a practiced lie. Jasmine had thought of it after their day up on Lookout Rock.

"Just be yourself and be confident," she had coached him. "Then throw out that vulnerable side. She'll love it."

"Which is what again?" Colin had asked.

"*I'm sorry, Julia,*" Jasmine performed, "*but I-I just wasn't ready to get so close without- without a proper first date. You know, just you and I...* I think she'd love that."

"She will?" he questioned.

"I hope," Jasmine had responded. "It would work for me."

"*I don't know,* Jazzy," Skyler had joined in. "I believe *this* would work for you..." Skyler suddenly sprouted a British accent, "*My dear Lassie, I would cherish a warm kiss, but not before my afternoon tea. Would you like to join me? Do you take one lump, or two?*"

Jasmine had given him a punch in the arm, but not before blushing.

So, that was the plan for this particular day as Colin stood nervously staring through the cafeteria windows at Julia and Michelle, both laughing over their lunches.

"Here goes..." Colin whispered to himself.

As he stepped into the large room, Julia jumped to her feet, ran over to him and gave him a warm, but cautious hug.

"Oh, Colin," she said emotionally. "I tried to text you and you didn't answer, so I thought..."

"I, ah, gave April my phone," Colin quickly said, though confused by Julia's tone.

"*I am so sorry.*"

"W-why?" he reacted, feeling like he missed something.

"Jasmine told me all about your *golden rule* of dating first and getting to know the person better. I think that's very honorable."

"Well, ah, yeah," was all he could say.

"It was just that I was so moved by your heroics, I just couldn't stop myself," she smiled. "Can I... can I say that we're, like, together?"

Her words had caught him so off guard that he almost didn't catch the familiar tingling of a pre-shift. He quickly bit his lip to stop the change and blurted out an enthusiastic *"Totally"*.

"Are you sure?" Julia pushed, not certain why he had delayed.

"Oh, *I'm* sure," Colin announced, feeling the tingling subside.

Right then the bell rang so Julia took both his hands and quickly said, "I've got World History next, but wanted to boldly ask you two questions. Would you like to be my guest for my dad's dinner party this weekend?"

"Sure, I'd love to," Colin said. "What's the second question?"

"Would *that* count as a *first date* under your golden rule?" she playfully grinned.

***

Dr. Philip Trask had entered the kitchen and then flipped through the day's mail on the table. "Hi, Sweetie," he said between the sounds of an electric hand drill Anne was using to hang a new shelf.

"Hi, Sweets," she returned as she got off the ladder to give him a kiss. "How was work?"

"Fine," he remarked. "Had Richard in today. You've got to keep on that guy about flossing. He's got great teeth, but, wow, do I find weird stuff between them. I swear he eats meat with the *hair* still attached."

"*Ha*, really?" Anne half coughed, but recovered with, "Weird... Anyway, I think we received a rather elaborate invite in our mail today. Did you find it?"

"Yeah, here it is. Oh, it's from Dr. and Dr. Baker. Isn't Colin in their daughter's grade?"

"Yes, he is," remarked Anne. She drilled in another screw for the shelf.

"Well, isn't this nice," he said, reading the invitation. "Ken Baker and his wife are inviting us to a fancy dinner party at their house," Philip read off the elaborate card. "It says, *open bar, exotic dishes, music and a silent auction in honor of reelecting Senator Heston.*"

"*What?* You've *got* to be kidding!" Anne suddenly blurted. "*That* slime-sucking environment *killer*! I wouldn't *step* a hundred feet near *that* party if they're honoring *him*!"

Philip stood there quietly trying to count how many times he had seen his wife's eyes change when she got emotional. "Okay...I hear you," he slowly said, "How 'bout you don't even go one *thousand* feet of the party and leave it at that. But I do feel I should make an appearance as a fellow doctor. I'll go talk some business, eat, then come right home. *No* donations, I promise."

"Just an appearance," Anne calmly acknowledged.

"Yes."

"*Fine.*"

***

Stephanie had stood fuming outside the house of a domestic crime scene in the pouring rain. *Damn these depressed, emasculated men.*

Too weak to handle the words, 'It's over between us!' *like real men. No! They've got to break in and show that woman how much they truly loved them by beating or shooting them...shit!*

It had been the third type of domestic murder in two months and they all involved the killing of women. Stephanie knew she was exhausted when her next thought was how to use the *Pack Dogs* to rid Vermont of these dejected, violent males.

She reached for the buzzing cell phone in her rain jacket. "Hey, Mitch."

"Hey, Steph."

"Any new leads?" she asked. "Jack Richmond of Fish and Game is waiting to hear from us about more wolf connections."

"He'll have to wait," he answered. "But *I* have something new. Harvey Benson called, the Indian enthusiast we talked to. He found an actual match to LeClaire's tattoo."

"Really? Did you find out which tribe it represented?"

"Yes, but we have a Colin Trask from the same town who was recently at Benson's house, extremely interested in the same tribe."

"What's the connection?" she asked.

"I'm not sure yet," Mitch continued, "but he just happens to work for Bobby LeClaire's father up there in Cochran."

"Really?" said Stephanie as she got into her car. "Are you going up to talk to both of them?"

"I was considering going up there next Monday."

"Then I'll join you," she said, buckling up. "Think there'll be a link to the Dawes family?"

"You really got a bad feeling from them, didn't you?" questioned Mitch.

"Oh, yeah," she responded. "Something wasn't right. Are you still keeping an eye on them?"

"Yes, I've got Henderson on it," Mitch said, but paused on the line. "Hey, Steph, can you hold? I'm going to take this call."

There was a long wait before the Police Chief was finally back on the phone. "Are you available tomorrow?" he quickly asked.

"*Tomorrow?* What's up?"

"This might not have anything to do with the local murders, here," Mitch began, "but I just got word that our recent acquaintance, Pinket Worthington, was murdered in her library a few days ago."

"Oh, my-" Stephanie reacted.

"She was shot," said Mitch.

"Why would someone shoot that sweet librarian?"

"It's supposed to be an easy case," replied Mitch. "The police chief in Burlington defined it as a murder-suicide. Do you remember the custodian that passed through the archives while we were there?"

"Yes."

"Chief Ford said that they found the bodies of the custodian, a Francis Galton, and Mrs. Worthington among a complete mess of books, documents and files, looking like there was a struggle. He speculated that Galton had lost his head with Worthington, shot her, and then shot himself. A note was left behind talking about struggling with the bad wages he received and losing his wife because of it."

"*Unbelievable*," Stephanie reacted, and then quickly added, "I'm sorry, but I still don't get why he called *you*."

"This *Police Chief* said that there were records *we* had just been up there in the basement archives, and simply called to find out why."

"Do they think we're implicated in some way?"

"I don't know," Mitch floundered. "I had mentioned our search for Native American families in the area and the lead about finding addresses contained in the Eugenics Project survey."

"And that sent up red flags?" Stephanie pressed.

"He responded with a suspicious, *'really'*, then slowly asked if Mrs. Worthington had helped us. I said, yes, of course, that she found us some useful documents."

"That was true," Stephanie responded. "So, what was the big deal?"

"Just that he spoke so quickly asking about what documents we had. When I asked what this had to do with the murders he instead inquired if the addresses we found were recently recorded, then suddenly asked who had suggested we go to the library in the first place."

"Did you tell him?" she asked.

"No, *I* started to get suspicious from all the questioning, as if we *were* somehow involved."

"Or maybe it has to do with those *more recent* Eugenics surveys that Harvey Benson first told us about," Stephanie responded. "In fact, I bet *that* was what this Police Chief was talking about. So, no mention of Benson's name?"

"Not at all. I thought it best to keep him out of it," he said, and then paused. Mitch knew that all this was happening because they were following a lead for the dog murders, and it just happened to bring them to the library. "We don't have time to be suspects in someone's document-mystery and don't want to be around for any interrogation."

"Right," Stephanie understood. "I'm going now to pack. We're going up there *tonight*."

Chapter 26:
Victor's Army

A blustery, rainy Friday night saw several cars and trucks parked in the back lot of *Howard's Used SUVs*. The anxious group had to gather first in the service garage of the closed establishment before they were to leave in the two rented passenger vans.

"Thanks for arriving on such quick notice," Victor said to the eager, almost salivating crowd. "We arranged all of this at the last minute so as not to attract attention and expose our plan. We can thank Police Officer Henderson for a marvelous job at keeping any more snooping souls out of our...fur. I must regretfully say, however, that you won't get the opportunity to thank him personally. Maul and Talon, here, conveniently made sure our European informant wasn't going to accidentally mention our little excursion."

The two subdominants snickered.

"If I may say so," a nervous Johnny Dumont challenged, "Isn't the killing of a police officer only going to bring us...more attention?"

Victor's face was expressionless as he walked up to Johnny. He suddenly burst into a grin, saying, "It could, except that we had done some *snooping* ourselves and found that our Officer Henderson sadly had a dreadful divorce in his past, leading to an intense bout of depression. Well, it just so happened that this deep depression resurfaced. They'll be finding his unscathed, hanging body with a very heartfelt, goodbye note nearby. Something tells me that won't drum up too much attention for us."

Johnny cringed inside at the thought that all of this was brewing into a total nightmare and whatever their idea for the weekend was he had to find a way to let Richard, and the others, know. At this point, even if he knew what was happening, he couldn't easily sneak away to make the necessary call.

"Okay, troops," Victor smiled as his arm presented the awaiting vans, "grab your few belongings and let's go. When we reach our safe quarters for the night, my father and I will let you in on our wonderful plan. Until then, enjoy the ride."

As they all piled into the awaiting vehicles Johnny tried to envision a way to call for backup, but saw no window of opportunity yet. He would just have to wait and hope that whatever the plan, Colin and the others would somehow be ready to respond. Then Johnny nervously thought about Colin, *A fifteen-year-old suddenly having to go into battle. Fuck!*

His fears increased when he saw Carl drive in late with a young passenger. It was Benny Carrier. Carl must have had the responsibility of picking Benny up at his home. The boy and Carl were pulled into the first van, where Victor was, and they drove off.

As Johnny's van began to move, he mentally said a quick supplication. *Please don't mention Colin!*

***

Dr. Kenneth Baker had been earnestly pacing back and forth in his home study. Each passing day made him a bit more nervous. The loss of the *Operation Eugenics* documents was not only serious, it could easily mean his life. The variety of wealthy, powerful men and women involved out-surpassed his status as the next generation guardian of the documents. He had earned this position after the death of his father and after thoroughly proving his devotion to the cause. In fact, he was more than guardian; it was he who had been the pivotal part of reinstating a new sterilization program ready to be implemented before the coming winter. If it hadn't been for the disappearance of the documents, his reputation within the hierarchal society of the *Well Born* would have easily escalated. But now...

"Is Senator Heston going to make it to our dinner party, dear?" Kenneth's wife asked from the living room.

"Probably not. He's a very busy man," the doctor answered. "Dear, I've *really* got some things to wrap up here. I promise I'll help you set the table for dinner."

"That's okay, honey," she said. "I can get Juanita to do it."

Dr. Baker slowly pulled the sliding doors to his study shut and returned to his desk. He reached for his cell phone and dialed the number for the Burlington Police Department.

"Hello, Henry?" the doctor asked, his voice was almost a whisper.

"I thought I said no phone calls here, Ken" the aggravated police chief responded.

"Relax, it'll be brief," assured Kenneth. "First, I personally wanted to acknowledge your expertise in dealing with the library debacle concerning Worthington," he paused. "*Thanks*. It *was* very believable. However, my concerns still are for those papers. I have several of the program's original architects showing up at my party this weekend. I would like *missing documents* to not be the focus. Any word on that?"

"No, except for this strange connection with the Eureka Police Chief and that state BCI Detective," answered Chief Ford.

"Do you know any more about the two?" the doctor asked.

"Just that they were recently looking for the same documents," the police chief explained.

"I still don't understand how the fuck they would have heard about them?"

"Yet, it was how Mrs. Worthington found them missing in the first place...she claimed. Do you really believe she betrayed us and gave the officers the documents?"

Kenneth sat there thinking about what he had deduced. *It all happened days after she asked for more money to keep protecting those papers. Maybe she was getting me back for turning down her request, but...maybe not. He didn't make the call to terminate her!* "Well, she's too dead to ask now, huh?" Ken replied.

The Police Chief sighed and then responded. "*So,* just to let you know, I'm sending some men down to Eureka to see why the officers were up here. If they do have our documents, these guys will get them back."

"Good. The sooner, the better," said Kenneth. "Do you know why they wanted them in the first place? Do you know whether they're pro-eugenics?"

"I don't know about being pro, but this Mitch Porter said something about using its addresses to look up Indian families," explained the police chief. "He said it concerned the dog-related murders down there."

"Right, I've heard about them." Then came the quiet, sinister voice of the doctor, "You know, Henry, it seems that somebody down there came up with a creative way to be rid of people. Maybe *we* wouldn't have to repeat the old program here if we simply hired those trainers and their pets to do our job for us."

On the other end of the line Police Chief Ford winced.

***

The vans had just entered Burlington when an excited Victor Dawes thought to praise his youngest warrior.

"So, pup," said Victor from the front seat. "Come up and sit near me."

Benny slowly moved his way to the front.

"Carl told me you lied to your mother again," Victor said with a smirk.

"I said I was going to a friend's house for the weekend," Benny answered quietly.

Victor ordered one of his subdominants to move so to let Benny sit next to him. He placed a muscular arm around Benny's shoulders. "I commend you on your determination to be with us. You have my full trust now. As for this weekend, things are about to get pretty exciting. Tomorrow night we will personally face the actual perpetrators who have secretly attacked our people. Are you ready to go to war?"

"Yes," a nervous Benny Carrier had answered, his head left low.

"Ah, *dude*, a stronger *'yes'* could convince me," Victor said. "Look at me."

Benny looked up, worry in his eyes.

"That's right," pondered Victor. "You *desperately* had something to tell me a few weeks ago, didn't you?"

"Yes," Benny said.

"Then I give you permission to speak."

"Really?" Benny nervously began. "Well, th- there's another boy here...in the north. I-I met him at the Sachem Reunion. He-he's...a *Superior*, too."

"*What?*" Victor screamed as the driver of the van swerved a bit from the noise. "*Why the fuck didn't you tell me you...you...!*"

"You told me I..." Benny began to say as he tried to move away from him.

"*Just shut up!*" Victor yelled, then turned to the driver. "Stop the fucking van!"

The driver quickly slipped into the parking lot of small shopping center as the other van followed. Watching from his side of the vehicle, Johnny got a bad feeling when Victor hopped out looking furious, with Benny in tow.

"*Dad!*" Victor yelled towards the other van.

Baird popped out. "What is it?"

"It would seem fucking-*Pup*, here, *did* have something important to tell us!" Victor growled as he held Benny in the air by his shirt collar. "He fucking claims that there's *another* Ma'iingan inini living nearby from the Sachem family."

"Another? How...?" Baird first said dumbfounded, and then he turned to Benny. "What's his or her name?"

Victor dropped him to the pavement. When he got up, he said, "Colin Trask."

Johnny stared out of the van window at the discussion that was taking place. He knew he had to get out there.

"Wheredya think *you're* going?" one of the women asked.

"None of your damn business, Paylon," Johnny growled.

Johnny got out of the van to see Victor angrily pacing back and forth.

"Get back in the van, Sinclair," Baird immediately said when he saw Johnny approach.

"I might be able to help," Johnny said with strong conviction.

"In what way?" Baird asked skeptically.

"I overheard everything and, yes, it's fucking strange as hell," Johnny said. He really hoped his idea would work. "But I have a friend in the area that might know the local Shifters. If you needed to find this-this *other*, I bet she could help."

Victor gave him an intense look, then looked at Benny. "Hmm, yeah," Victor considered. "I'm sure as hell not going to stand for my weekend being interrupted by some fucking European-compassionate Superior. We find him and then perform one of our late-night attacks. *I'll take this fucker out quicker than LeClaire!*"

"I can call her from that gas station over there to see if she knows any Trasks," Johnny said as he slowly moved towards the lit up Handy-Mart.

"No, wait, it's 10:30pm," Baird quickly said. "We're sitting here in an empty lot with two suspicious vans. I say we get to the motel and call from there."

Victor agreed, dragging Benny and himself back into his vehicle. Reluctantly, Johnny went back to his, still attempting to play out the next scenario that might help warn the others of their local presence.

The vans pulled out of the lot and proceeded to the Uncommon Grounds Motel. As the group piled out, Baird signed them in. He had them registered as the *Howard's Used SUV, Employee Appreciation Weekend*. Baird had explained how they were there to enjoy the local Shelburne Museum and the scenic boat trips on Lake Champlain.

"Here's the key for room 10, Sinclair," Baird said when he came back from the office. "Use the phone in that room for your call while we unpack."

Trying hard not to look hurried, Johnny moved steadily to the upper level. He hoped to warn the Trask family in time.

Half the crew was already moving in his direction when he reached the top of the stairs. He was about to dash to the room when an enthusiastic Carl yelled to the group to come look at his room's decor. He was laughing about how it had one of those old-style paintings portraying five dogs sitting around playing poker.

"We all ought to try that some night, huh?" cackled Carl.

Johnny jumped into the room and closed the door. He quickly dialed Anne Trask's number and prayed they'd be home.

"Hello, this is April."

"April, quickly, is your mom home?" Johnny heavily breathed into the phone.

"*Who* is this?" April suspiciously asked.

"It's John. This is urgent."

"Oh, hi, Johnny, I'll go get her," she said.

Hurry... Johnny thought. He heard the others laughing as they were leaving the room below.

"Johnny?" Anne whispered, an obvious touch of fear in her voice.

"You've *got* to get out of there," He had almost yelled, covering the phone. "*We're* here, *in* Burlington. *They* know about Colin. They're coming to kill him as soon as they find your house."

"*Oh, my!*" Anne responded. "We'll leave right away. What do I tell Richard and the others?"

"I'll let you know," Johnny quickly said.

"Let her know *what,* Sinclaire?" a smiling Baird asked as he came through the door.

"Oh, she wanted to know why I was here and if I were free," Johnny produced. "She's an old girlfriend and fellow Shifter, but such a damn *European compassionate.* No way I'd include her. She's just really fucking hot, you know."

"Guess it's hard to find a good *bitch* these days," Baird said, eyes slightly probing for any signs of betrayal. "Did she know where this Colin lives?"

Here was Johnny's big gamble, to tell them the exact address. He knew Anne would get them out of there in time.

"Yes, she knows the family well," he began, thinking that he could be making the biggest mistake of his life. "It's Eleven-eleven Bridge Street, in Cochran. I think it's about two town south of here."

Victor, who had positioned himself outside the door, suddenly appeared in the room carrying the motel's telephone book.

"Trask, is it?" he asked with a questionable air.

"Anne and Dr. Philip Trask," Johnny said. "He's the human. She's the Shifter. That's what my source told me."

"A Chief Born from a *one-half* couple? What's this world coming to?" Victor announced. Then sounding shocked, "Well, well. Here it is, Eleven-eleven Bridge Street. Dad, why don't you give them a call and see if they're home."

Johnny had bit his lip hoping that, at least, a phone machine would pick up to explain that it was truly their home.

Baird punched in the numbers, giving Johnny a big smile. "Yes, hello," he said with a salesman-like accent. "Would I be speaking to a Mrs. Anne Trask? Yes? Well, we're doing a quick survey tonight concerning our area's teenagers. Are there any in your house...? Two. Boys? Girls...? A boy *and* a girl. How nice. Their ages...? Thirteen and fifteen. Great. And who is the fifteen-year-old...? Ah, the boy. Oh, Colin, you said. What a nice name," Baird said with raised eyebrows. "Well, Mrs. Trask, I'm calling on behalf of McKenzie Meats. We were wondering here at McKenzie if your son, Colin, enjoys our delicious and local meats? He does! Wonderful. And your daughter...? In sandwiches, for dinner? That's great. It's what we like to hear. Thank you so much for your time, Mrs. Trask and have a wonderful evening, and make sure you and your family 'like' us on Facebook."

Baird got off the phone, looked towards Johnny again, and then flipped through the drawers of the room's dressers. He pulled out complimentary pamphlets and found a map of the area. He placed the map in Victor's hands and pointed to Cochran.

Victor glanced at Johnny, giving him a baleful grin. "Thanks, Sinclair. See you soon!"

He leapt out of the room, calling to his subdominants, "Maul, Trapper, get the others-let's go!"

Johnny had begun to clear out his small bag of clothes while some fellow roommates came in to do the same. He was glad to not be suspiciously focused on anymore, but was confused by Anne's interaction with Baird, and the amount of information she gave him. She must have known the survey was a fake, but why would she give Colin's name? She must have had a lot of faith in herself and her

Ma'iingan inini son. He wanted to have faith, too, and hoped they were already on their way to safety.

***

Anne had pushed Philip, April and Colin out the door and into the family car. She couldn't take any chances on how fast these antagonistic Shifters would be. Her excuse to leave was pretty lame, but would have to do.

"Are you serious? Tonight? At eleven-ish in the evening?" Philip had kept questioning. "Who the heck has a survey contest at this time of night and gives out prizes? Let alone two nights stay for four."

"Faith Peterson won a pair of tickets from a radio station to see *Raine Dylan and the Sisterhood* at seven in the morning once," April offered, obviously excited about the spontaneous circumstances.

"Hey, give me some credit. At least we won," Anne kept pushing the lie. "And didn't I just say how sad it is that we never do anything spontaneous anymore."

At least it was the weekend, giving her lie some validity.

Anne had thrown a set of clothes into a nearby backpack for each of the kids, so they wouldn't have to think about it. "I remember now hearing about these unusual contests," she continued. "To get us more aware of our local businesses. It was a promotional thing or something."

"Well," Philip smiled accepting the sudden turn of events. "I guess I won't argue promoting our local Sheraton. I'm just not used to winning anything."

Colin, all the while, had remained quiet and observant. He didn't know what was going on, but picked up the scent that his mom was scared about something. Once in the car Anne had relaxed a little bit, so Colin figured an explanation would be coming his way soon and he knew that his father and sister would not be a part of it.

When they got to the hotel Anne convinced her husband that she'd go take care of the prize logistics with the front desk. While Colin gathered what little things they had, he observed his mother quickly presenting her credit card to the clerk.

Once the family had settled into their rooms Anne took Colin's arm and explained to the others that they were going to look into the complimentary all-you-can-eat buffet brunch they serve in the morning.

"Okay, dear," Philip said. "April and I will park ourselves in front of the tele. She's been wanting me to watch some teen drama series."

"Really, Dad, you'll watch?" responded April.

"Sure. What's the name? *Teen...Wolf?*"

"Oh, my god-yes!" April reacted. "The guy in it is so *hot*...I mean...cute."

Once out the door, Anne dragged Colin into the stairwell. She turned to him and grabbed his shoulders, "Here's what you need to know before I call Richard," she said, a mother's worry was in her eyes. "We're up against something big. Richard and I hadn't mentioned it because we didn't think it would happen so soon and we wanted you to get used to your new self. There's another Superior...An angry, vengeful one who has gathered a *pack* to literally go on a killing spree against...*we don't know who.* Johnny Dumont hasn't..."

"Johnny?" Colin interjected. "Is he part of them?"

"Yes and No. He's our spy," Anne continued as she looked at her watch. "He just called. This pack is here...in the area, and they've found out about you and are-well...they were coming to kill you."

"*Wha-* Kill? Why?" Colin said, absorbing the intensity of her words.

"Tradition, *maybe.* There's never two Superiors in one area without a fight," his mother quickly explained.

"And *he* wants to fight me for leadership?" Colin asked.

"No, not this one. He's the werewolf of folklore, the killer of humans. He's *exactly* what you didn't like in those movies. This Superior is strictly here to kill."

"The second phone call. The survey. Who were you talking to then?" Colin questioned.

"One of them," Anne admitted. "Johnny had no choice but to tell them where you lived or be killed himself. When the phone rang again, I knew there was a connection. I just hope it saved Johnny's life. *We're going to need him.*"

"Need him for...*what*?" Colin had been afraid to ask.

"To know when to go to battle. These vicious wolves are to attack some group of people, but we don't know where or when," Anne explained as she turned to head down the stairs. "I've got to call Richard."

Colin watched as his mother ran around the corner. Replaying the information, he had just received Colin suddenly sucked in some air. *Nashoba said that when the tribe was in trouble and was without a Chief, a Superior had been born to be the next leader...Mom said battle. I'M SUPPOSED TO LEAD A BATTLE?*

Chapter 27:
Visits to the Trask House

Across the road from Eleven-eleven Bridge Street stood a tall hedgerow outlining the Gifford family's yard. The weather-beaten holes throughout the brush allowed a perfect vantage point for Richard LeClaire and Carolyn Royal to watch the Trask house.

Due to the late call from Anne the two Shifters had barely settled into their location when a van pulled into the Town Hall parking lot just next door.

"You think?" Carolyn whispered.

"Let's see," answered Richard.

Shadows exited the van and moved swiftly to the backside of the building. They made their way along some fencing to the far end of the Trask's back yard and to the house. The porch lights were left on so Richard and Carolyn could make out the silhouettes of one human and a group of canines running towards the house. The human figure quickly extinguished the light as the slightest snapping of glass could be heard. In a matter of minutes, the two could make out the cussing words of frustration. The perpetrators were out of there fast.

Richard was happy to count that all six had returned to the van and had driven off.

"They're gone," a nervous Carolyn said.

"I hope for good," Richard responded.

"Now why didn't the Superior shift before going into the house?" Carolyn asked.

"I get the feeling this Victor Dawes had wanted to impress Colin before he shifted and killed him," Richard answered. "He obviously thinks highly of himself. That could work in our favor. Now, let's go over and see why they left so easily."

They emerged from their hiding place and walked across to the road. Upon entering through the damaged back door Richard saw that some furniture had been abused. They cleaned up what little mess there was.

On the kitchen table there sat a big note written to Richard explaining that Lizzy had suddenly fallen ill and immediately needed their help at the Carrier Farm. The rest of the note mentioned feeding April's goldfish and watering some plants. It had looked honest and clear, and, evidently believable.

"Good job, Anne," Richard said to himself.

***

On Saturday morning Police Chief Porter and Sergeant Harrison turned onto the Trask's driveway and parked. Though they had come in Mitch's police cruiser they were both unarmed and dressed in plain clothes. Mitch didn't see the urgency for firearms for what they were investigating here, but they were in the back trunk, just in case.

The two had wanted to meet with Colin to understand his interest in this Mi'kmaq tribe and if he knew of any living Skiri Clan people in the area. They were also curious about his relationship with Richard LeClaire, who Mitch and Stephanie had not met when he retrieved his son's body. Mitch had planned all this with the hope that there would be a connection to the son's murder. However, there was still not enough to go on except for the design of the tattoo matching this specific tribe and the tie-in to a *wolf clan*.

The police chief walked up onto the back porch and knocked on the door. When he heard no answers, he cupped his hands over his eyes to look through the door's window. It was then that he noticed a brand-new pane placed in one of the door's window frames, the smell of fresh pine trim held in the spotless glass. Mitch stepped away from the door and noticed small shards of glass on the porch floor.

"What do you see?" Stephanie asked as she came up the steps.

"Don't know," Mitch said, bending to pick up some of the glass. "Seems like a window here was just recently broken."

"A teenage boy," Stephanie offered. "Shouldn't be too unusual."

"They weren't too good at cleaning up either," Mitch responded, as he was about to stand. Just then something caught his eye near the floor. On a small section of one of the porch's wicker chairs a tuft of fur clung to a partially frayed back leg. Mitch pulled off the fur and brought it into the light. Just seeing its recognizable hues and the familiar feeling between his fingers told him exactly what he was dealing with...again.

"That's not what I think..." Stephanie began.

"Unless this family has a brown and white Husky, it is," Mitch said.

"No dog house or back yard cable," she replied with concern in her voice. "We've got to break in."

Mitch quickly returned to his car and grabbed their two handguns, broke out the new window and entered the house. Slowly the two of them moved through the rooms listening for any unusual noises. They looked in every dark corner. Stephanie could see right away that the house was in perfect order, neat, clean and untouched.

After sweeping the whole place Mitch had returned to the note on the kitchen table he had seen earlier. On studying it, he had truly hoped all the members of the family *had* gone to this Carrier Farm.

"I found more fur on the stairway," Mitch told Stephanie when she entered the kitchen. "Do you think these attackers broke in, saw the note, then left?"

"Fixing their broken window behind them?" Stephanie pondered aloud. "That doesn't sound typical."

Stephanie went back upstairs, walked around, then came back to the kitchen. She picked up and glanced again at the note. "Something *did* happen here tonight," she began as her fingers rubbed the top of the table. "I just don't have an explanation for the repaired window in the door."

"What are you thinking?" Mitch asked.

"Besides the recognizable fur, two things. First, the note, it was done on a paper towel, the nearest writing material. What did they use to write with? A permanent marker. This easily went through the towel and marked up the table underneath." Stephanie pointed to several black streaks on the fancy walnut surface. "Anyone who so obviously cares about their neat home and furniture wouldn't have used a paper towel and permanent marker."

"And the second thing?"

"Upstairs, clothes were scattered throughout the boy's and sister's rooms- yes, typical- but the parent's bedroom, if you really looked, was left very tidy and organized. However, five empty coat hangers were on the closet floor among clothing that had fallen, *and* their luggage was just behind the mess."

Mitch squinted his eyes in mild confusion.

"Well, wouldn't these obviously *orderly* parents have picked-up their closet and properly fold their clothes into luggage to go away for the weekend?"

"Ah, well, *I* didn't for this weekend," Mitch had awkwardly smiled.

"Because you don't have a woman in your life," Stephanie remarked with a smile. "So, what I'm trying to say is that this family may have been tipped-off about our furry visitors. They left before the attackers came. Which, of course, leaves us with the most important unanswered question..."

"What is our Southern Vermont killer dogs doing way up here in the north, *and* here at the very house *we* were coming to visit?" Mitch responded.

"*Plus,* if it were truly them, why, out of all the places they've been to, did they *fail?*" questioned Stephanie.

Mitch put his hands on his hips having noticed that the street outside of the Trask home was beginning to increase with morning traffic. He turned to Stephanie and said, "Well, with no Trask boy around, I say we pay a visit to Bobby LeClaire's father instead."

Stephanie went back into the car while Mitch left an apology note on the door about the broken window, explaining that he was a Boy Scout, selling gourmet popcorn, and accidentally put his elbow through it.

As he got back into the car, Stephanie said, "Mitch...look at this." She pointed to the pages of the Eugenics survey photocopies that were still in his vehicle. "Just like the Dawes family name and address, *Carrier* is mentioned here under *Indians.* It even gives the name of Lizzy as one of the Carrier children."

"Lizzy Carrier? The one the Trask family is supposedly visiting?" Mitch asked. "Is *Trask* part of that list of names?"

"No," responded the Sergeant, "but Carrier might be the mother's maiden name, and this is all old data."

Mitch stared at the page for a few seconds. He started up the police car and began to pull out saying, "I believe Police Chief Ford's intense need to question us has just reversed. I think it's time to ask him some questions about these newer documents *we* now need."

***

Colin hadn't slept well having had *leadership worries* throughout the night. This was why at breakfast he haphazardly mentioned the fact that he was invited to the Baker's dinner party that night.

"*What?*" Colin's mom reacted. "And you're just telling me now?"

They had just been finishing a filling brunch when Colin announced the news. Before that April, Philip and Colin had watched in amazement while Anne ate several rounds of eggs, bacon and sausage.

"So, I'm *late* telling you something," Colin said between the sips of his fifth cup of coffee, "I hadn't considered this sudden hotel stay or any of the other unexpected events to interfere with *my date*."

"A *date*?" April exclaimed, lifting her head from her food. "Wait, you mean *you're* dating Julia Baker?"

Colin looked at her partly embarrassed, having realized he had finally admitted this fact in public. "Well, I..."

"You're not upset with Colin being interested in the Baker girl, are you dear?" Colin's dad interrupted. "I doubt she has anything to do with the senator *or* her father."

"Why would mom not approve of Julia?" Colin suddenly asked.

"No. It's not that. It's..." Anne began to say, frustrated by the sidetracked questions and frustrated that she couldn't speak to Colin alone right then and there.

"Well, I think it's perfectly fine that he was invited to this big shindig tonight," his dad proudly said. "Since I'll be going to the event, too, we can go together as father and son."

"Right, I'll be there with dad," Colin said, watching how upset his mother was becoming. "I'll be someplace safe." *But, hey, it beats sitting around here preparing to go to war against a bunch of vicious wolves and their vengeful Superior.* He thought.

"You're *really* dating Julia Baker?" April said again, not truly convinced.

Anne sat there, staring out the restaurant's window. She wasn't upset with Colin. It was wonderful he was interested in somebody. The fact that Julia happened to be related to such a conservative father like Dr. Baker felt a bit awkward to her, but *that* wasn't the pressing issue at the moment. She wanted, no, she *needed* Colin to be ready to fight, just in case. *Of course, that's why he's so upset.* She thought. *In the confusion, in the hoping that all this wouldn't come to be, we didn't prepare him. We could soon go into battle and we didn't prepare our own leader. And since Johnny hasn't called yet, we have no idea if and when there'll be a fight.*

Anne had notified the front desk of a possible emergency call to her. Richard knew of their location and had already started rallying the troops, just in case. *But what was Colin going to do to be ready?* Anne continued to consider. *Sit around a hotel? The party would be just up the hill in Cochran. He would at least be accessible.*

"Okay," she finally said.

"Okay, what?" Colin and his dad chimed together.

"I think it would be great if he went to the party," she responded, shooting Colin a look that said, *but we still need to talk.*

"Good." Colin responded with a sigh of relief and then he suddenly looked up and said, "I don't have any nice clothes with me."

"No problem. I've got to pick-up my dress clothes at the house, anyw-..." his father began.

"*No,*" Anne interrupted, not wanting them to go near the house.

"No?" Philip repeated.

"Ah, *oh...no*, I mean," Anne said. "*I* totally forgot bathing suits for myself and April. We could be enjoying the pool and hot tub while you two are at the event."

"Darn, I'd love to use the hot tub," said April. "Can we go shopping for new suits?"

"Ah, yeah, maybe, dear," was all Anne said, giving Colin a solid glance.

Colin understood his mother's concern about returning to the house and said, "We'll just come and go quickly."

"Oh, fine. It'll be fine," his mother calmly said as she considered one possibility. "Besides, I have Richard there to water the plants."

"So, it's okay to go back to *our* house because *Richard's* there?" Colin's father questioned. He had begun to get suspicious with all that had been happening. "Are you upset that Colin and I aren't going to fully enjoy our stay here at this four-star hotel or are you planning something? *Wait...My* birthday! That's it, isn't it? I see it in your eyes. Early surprise party, huh?"

"Oh, Philip. You ruin all my best plans," Anne replied. She quickly produced her fake smile. "*And* your birthday is two months away. How *did* you figure it out?"

"Sorry, dear. You can't pass too much by me," he said smugly.

"Richard will be frustrated that you know."

"I'll pretend I'm surprised," he grinned, so proud of himself. "Okay, April, are you ready for that walk by the lake? Your mom is wanting to push us out the door again, for *what*, was it? Have some things to talk to Colin about? *'Wink-wink! Say no more.'*"

"But *when* can we go shopping for bathing suits?" April desperately asked.

"Maybe, later," Anne lied as she fiddled with the forgetting formula in her pant pocket.

***

Richard sat in his office at the hardware store about to call Desmond Sachem and his daughter, Sasha. They had been the last on his list of potential tribe members who could come and help. As he started to punch in the numbers, he noticed a handsome couple at the service counter who didn't seem to be customers.

"May I help you?" Richard asked as he put down the receiver and stepped towards the counter.

"Yes, we're looking for a Richard LeClaire," Stephanie said.

"That's me."

The detective and police chief introduced themselves, said where they were from and gave their condolences about the death of Richard's son. Richard thanked them, trying hard not to look too rushed. He was, however, caught off guard when they explained the reason for their visit and the mention of Colin. The two officers had thought it rather coincidental that Colin was so interested in the same particular tribe represented by his son's tattoo and just happened to be Richard's employee as well.

But Richard had more important things to think about then how these two had connected his tribe with the murders in the south, as well as finding their way up to Cochran to question Colin, too.

"I'm afraid it's all my fault," Richard said. "Yes, it would seem a coincidence that my employee, Colin, would be interested in a tribe you yourselves are inquisitive about, but I was only trying to spark a young man's curiosity for our native cultures in the area. I sent him to look for the information on the Sachem tribe after he had researched Abenaki and Penobscot history."

"So, *you* sent him?" Mitch asked.

"Well, sure," Richard said, lifting his sleeve to display the same tattoo. "The tattoo, you're referring to, happens to come from my lineage. I thought Colin would find it interesting to learn about *my* tribal ancestry."

"Interesting as in the *Skiri Clan* part?" Stephanie pressed.

"Especially that," Richard continued, impressed by their homework. "The tribe was devoted to the wolf. It was our power animal, hence our clan's name. Long ago we had trained them to hunt for us."

"*Really?*" both Mitch and Stephanie chorused.

"In fact, a native friend of mine, Ms. Carolyn Royal, is still very much a trainer of big dogs," Richard had decided to fabricate, knowing Carolyn would be perfect in delaying these two. Her two huskies and the one malamute were able to totally obey her every command because she could literally speak to them. "If it's true that these southern murders were done by a trainer of canines, she may have some insight on how it was being done. Otherwise, I don't fully see the connection with my tribe."

"Wait," the police chief suddenly said, "does this Ms. Royal know the Trask family as well?"

Richard wasn't sure where the question was going but he dared to answer, yes.

"Then that could explain the fur," Stephanie chimed in.

"Fur?" questioned Richard.

"We found fur on a porch chair and...*and* we were concerned it was, you know, *our* dog-problem, *so*, we kind of broke into the house to investigate more. Please apologize for us."

"Oh," Richard reacted, but breathed a sigh of relief, he was impressed at how observant these two humans were. "No, Carolyn comes by with the dogs a lot. Colin loves to wrestle with them."

"Well, your information will surely help. Thank you, Mr. LeClaire," Stephanie said. "And Ms. Royal's address?"

Richard gave them Carolyn's address and had planned to quickly call her once they left to prep her for the visit.

"One more question," Mitch began. "Out of all the victims of these past murders, your son Bobby had seemed to be the only one to put up a decent fight against his attackers. Any clues as to how?"

"It saddens me to think of how my Bobby may have died, but I am grateful you told me that he had put up a fight," Richard said to Mitch as he came around the front of the counter. "As for possibly how, I'll be glad to show you. Give me your hand."

Mitch slowly gave the older man his hand. Richard took it and immediately flipped the husky, ex-football player unto his back as if he were coiling a garden hose.

Richard smiled down at the shocked police officer and said, "We did years of karate together."

Chapter 28:
Unwanted Guests

"I also need to pick up my gun invention," Colin's dad said as he pulled the Subaru Outback into their empty driveway at about 3:30pm. "I promised the Granda's that I'd shoot some filler into their chimney. Ms. Granda is writing a story about it if it works."

Colin had immediately perked his ears for any unusual sounds as they opened the doors of the car (his mother's suggestion before he left). What he quickly heard was the rustle and bustle of several people up on the porch and inside their house. When Colin's dad was in full view, they all looked at him in shock, streamers and some balloons tucked behind their backs.

Philip stopped and looked at them, a grin spreading across his face. "Sorry, Richard," he innocently said.

"Philip?" exclaimed Richard, feigning disappointment. "Anne didn't even warn us."

Philip smiled when he began to acknowledge the others. "Well, hello and welcome back Lizzy, Bill and Trisha, too...Dr. Sachem...Desmond and Sasha. *What* a surprise. Wow! It's like the family reunion all over again. Wish my younger brother could have come."

"Oh, man, we tried," Richard lied.

"Oh, well. He and his family are probably off on some cruise or something," Philip mused.

Suddenly Carolyn Royal bounded around the corner to the back of the Trask house where they all stood. She came to an abrupt halt in front of Philip and Colin.

"Oh, shit."

"Philip caught us red handed, Carolyn," Richard quickly said.

"Caught...*us*," she returned, knowing full well that the two of them, especially Colin, should not have been there.

"Sorry about the surprise party," Colin's father apologized again. "So, Anne really got you guys all down here just for me? I bet the *two-nights-for-four* over at our Sheraton was just to get us out of the house, huh?"

"Can't pull the wool over your eyes, Birthday Boy," Richard continued. "We all chipped in on that one."

"Darn! That's not good," said Philip, perturbed. "And here Colin and I just left it all behind for this dinner party."

"No, no," Great Grandmother Carrier interjected. "You still have time to enjoy it. Besides, we were putting this together for when you returned on Sunday afternoon. Anne must have gotten distracted and forgot to warn us. Oh, well, it'll still be fun."

"It sure will. Thanks," Philip expressed, as giddy as a ten-year-old.

How or why his father fell for all of this Colin would never know. But, he, himself, understood the coincidence of so many relatives suddenly converging at his house. The fact that these killer Shifters were truly planning something had become evident and clear. He was impressed at how many of his relatives heeded the *battle cry*.

Looking towards the porch Colin had been pleased to see Sasha again, especially up on both of her legs. When he heard his dad excuse himself to get dressed, Richard whispered to him intensely, "In the house, *quick*."

They all filed through the back door and towards the living room. Trisha and Sasha went upstairs to help Colin prepare some clothes for his party. In the living room Richard and Nashoba suddenly looked at him with signs of worry on their faces.

"We are *so* very sorry for the secrecy," Nashoba said, taking his hand. "We were waiting for word from Mr. Dumont to let us know where and when things were happening."

"Last night's call was the first we heard from him in weeks," Richard explained. "But we still don't know anything. We do know that they're here, having paid your house a visit, looking for you."

"They came here?" Colin said, looking around.

"Yes. Luckily, they didn't stay long thanks to your clever mother," Richard replied.

"But, that's why we're all here," Nashoba smiled, nervousness in her eyes. "Things could move quickly. If Johnny can tell us the details in time, we may be better prepared to stop this madness."

"With *me* as your Superior, to help *lead you* into battle," Colin sarcastically said. Nashoba and Richard looked at each other with concern. It was then that Uncle Bill stepped into sight.

"*Yes*, you *are* a Superior. You are *our* Superior," he had begun in his deep, baritone voice. "There isn't *anything* you can do about that. And as our leader... Well, my boy, here's the truth... We need only *see* you in our presence and we'll, *I promise you*, have the strength and will to fight. Understand me?"

Colin stood there speechless. His brain raced with the simple fact that he was *only* fifteen. He had found out just a month ago that he was this-this *Ma'iingan inini.* He then looked over and saw Dr. Grandpa standing there and recalled his words during the Sachem race, *"Think about what you have already done and find it in you to know that you will do more."*

"I understand," said Colin in a quiet voice. "So, what do we do next?"

Uncle Bill smiled wide as Richard clapped Colin on the side of his left shoulder producing a hearty, "That's my boy!"

"*Richard!*" Nashoba protested.

"Oops, my bad," Richard said, bowing respectfully, but with a devilish grin.

Aunt Trisha appeared from upstairs holding Colin's navy-blue suit jacket and navy slacks, plus a white shirt with a thin black necktie. "Is this okay?" she asked. "Sasha helped pick it out."

"But we've got a possible battle to fight," Colin challenged. "I can't be at the party, now. It could happen tonight."

"We want you in a safe location and nearby," explained Nashoba. "This dinner party will be the perfect out-of-the-way place for you. Steve, *Dr. Grandpa*, will follow you and your father to the event."

"We've got *sound-friendly* walkie-talkies to use to keep in touch," Uncle Bill added, "in case of an immediate change of plans."

"We're hoping Johnny will call soon with the precise time, day, location of the raid...*If he's*..." Richard began, but stopped. "Go get dressed. Your dad still has to get his invention ready to do that chimney-shooting-thing."

Colin grabbed his clothes from Aunt Trisha and dashed upstairs. He passed his father going down the steps wearing a dark gray suit and a maroon tie. The tie clip was sporting a flat, silver tooth in the middle of it.

"See you at the car," Philip said. "I've got to mix some sealant in the garage. Oh, and I think I heard Sasha drop and break something in your room. Hope it wasn't anything important."

"Doubt it's a big deal," Colin said as he watched his dad go around the corner at the bottom of the stairs. "Don't get anything on your suit."

Thinking about it, he didn't understand why Sasha would still be in his room, especially with the door shut.

"Sasha," Colin said as he opened the door, "whatever you broke, don't..."

Colin stopped dead. Across from him, wrapped in the husky arms of a wiry, longhaired boy, was his wide-eyed cousin. The boy's grimy hands covered her mouth.

Colin noted immediately that this intruder had entered through one of his windows, though it was a ten-foot leap. He focused back on the boy. His positioning was the same as that of Quentin's when he had held Julia, except for a bed between them.

Colin had begun to move towards the renegade Shifter, but as he did so his bedroom door slowly closed behind him with a creak. Colin whipped around to see an emo-looking girl dressed in a tight camouflage tank top and cut-off jeans. She held a finger to her mouth, requesting silence.

"Am I in the presence of Mr. Colin Trask?" Beta said quietly as she bowed with an exaggerated flare.

"Who wants to know?" he asked.

"Oh, just a really cool dude we're acquainted with, that's who," snickered Maul.

"Oooh, yes, someone *very* interested in meeting you," Beta answered.

"So, according to your little girlfriend here," Maul responded, faking to kiss Sasha, "Daddy's *muggle* relatives and friends will have to eat birthday cake without you."

"And if you come real-peaceful-like," Beta explained, "Maul, here, won't have to *rip* your *girlfriend's* head off. Just say the word and we'll let her go."

Colin looked over to Sasha. When she caught his eyes, she found her strength. Anger quickly took over her fears and her pupils began to shrink.

"No, don't," said Colin calmly to Sasha, but her captor thought he was talking to him.

"Oh, Beta, look. Our *compassionate* Superior, here, is concerned about his European sweetheart," Maul crooned as he grabbed her head with both his hands, as if ready to break her neck.

It was all Colin needed to see. This time he wasn't going to control his anger. Colin shifted so quickly that his clothes burst across the room in shreds.

Completely shocked by the speed of the shift, Maul rapidly deduced that he couldn't kill the girl and transform at the same time. Instead, he flung Sasha over the bed where she hit the opposite wall and fell to the floor.

Maul barely transformed before Colin was on him. His attempt to fight as a wolf was futile as Colin simply gripped his head, twisting it with ease until it faced backwards.

"Is everything alright?" came Aunt Trisha's voice.

With the slight sound of footsteps coming up the stairs, an already stunned Beta made a quick shifting dash out the window. Her clothes were still intact as she jumped through the sill's opening.

Sasha had pulled herself off the floor just as the bedroom door opened with Aunt Trisha stopping in her tracks. "*Oh, my,*" was all she said as Colin continued to stand there holding the remains of Maul.

She quickly closed the window and the curtains and called down to the others. Sasha was apologizing for being totally caught off guard when everyone arrived.

Nashoba took in the scene and turned to Sasha, "It was not your fault, dear. We should have watched every inch of this house. We're the ones who should be sorry."

"I did tell them I was Colin's girlfriend," Sasha added, "and that we were all the relatives of Colin's dad."

"Good thinking," Uncle Bill said. "I hope that sticks."

Richard grabbed Colin's bedding and held it up so he could change back into a human and get into his dress clothes.

"Did my father see or hear anything?" Colin asked as he carefully laid Maul's head and body down to the floor.

"No, I don't think so. I sent Carolyn out there to distract him," Richard said.

Colin looked again at the dead wolf at his feet and realized precisely what he had done. "*Richard...*I've killed someone," he responded.

"Yes, as he would have you and Sasha," he calmly said.

"He didn't change back to human."

"No," Nashoba offered. "We stay as the body we are at death."

"Come on...We don't have much time," Richard insisted. "You need to get going before this Victor comes back in full force."

"What about all of you?" Colin said as he slipped into his shirt.

"A few of us will stay here pretending to decorate more, because *you* would have hidden this dead body from us as if nothing happened," Richard explained while handing Colin his suit jacket. "Some of us will go back to the hardware store where we're hoping Johnny will call us. Put your tie on in the car...Now *go*."

Colin said goodbye to everyone first, but gave Sasha a big hug saying, "You were very brave." Then he dashed down the stairs and continued out onto the porch. Carolyn was standing there talking about her chimney and *its* cracks to his dad.

"Well, maybe next week I can take a look at it," Colin's dad had said looking up at Colin. "You ready? I'm all loaded up."

"Great."

Richard hurried them towards the car saying, "Have a wonderful time at the party, you guys, and good luck with that chimney, Philip. Don't shoot the family dog."

"Hope not," Colin's dad answered with a smile. "It'd be a pain getting this sealant out of its fur."

***

Beta had dashed towards the far end of the Trask's backyard finally stopping a few feet beyond a thick patch of pine trees hiding her pack mates. Talon, Fang and Trapper jumped down from a large maple and walked towards her.

"Beta, *what* the fuck?" Talon said.

"And where's Maul?" asked Trapper.

"*He's fucking dead!*" barked Beta.

"Dead?" Fang reacted. "By who? The Superior?"

"Yes-yes," Beta said, panting heavily.

"He shifted? He fucking wouldn't dare unless everyone else were Shifters in the house."

"No-they're from the dad's side," she argued, transforming back to human "decorating for some stupid party for him. I mean that's what his European girlfriend said."

"And *you* believed her?" Talon challenged.

"She was so fucking *weak*, she had to be a European. And *this* Superior, he just shifted *so* fast. Maul didn't have a chance."

"*Regular* humans would have fricken heard something," Fang commented. "They had to have seen him."

"*I got scared*. The Superior probably shifted back to human. He was so fast."

"Really? Just shifted?" Talon questioned. "He would have been *as* naked as you and with a *fucking* dead wolf next to him!"

"Doesn't make sense," Trapper pondered aloud. "Did *he* fuck'n jump out the window?"

"Well, *I* didn't see...*Fuck!*" yelled Fang, pointing. "*Obviously not!* The Superior and the father are driving away!"

"*Goddamnit!*" Talon said. "Trapper, go find a phone and call Victor. Fang, keep an eye on the fucking house, then get up to that party as soon as you can. I'll follow the Superior."

"What about me?" Beta argued. "I don't have any clothes."

"*You* can hang out with *me*," Trapper winked, licking his lips.

Beta growled at him as Fang slapped him on the arm, but Talon had no time for this. "Just steal some fricken clothes and do it quickly!"

Talon went into a run. He realized immediately that another car was following the Superior's car.

Chapter 29:
Information Relayed

Johnny Dumont had spent most of day with several of the other Shifters hanging out on Burlington's Church Street Marketplace. The outdoor pedestrian mall was four blocks of stores, restaurants, cafes and street vendors. On this sunny Saturday the marketplace was bustling with both tourists and locals. Victor's pack just sat on the benches and the well-placed rocks laughing at the variety of Europeans coming and going. Johnny had thought that his fellow derelicts would have stuck out in a place like this, but the marketplace was riddled with strange looking people.

Their job was to stay there until Baird came by to bring them back to the motel to get ready. Baird and Victor had only recently explained where the attack was to happen, how they would implement it and who exactly the families were that they would be *"afflicting appropriate revenge on"*. Baird described this event as being the largest gathering of these evil perpetrators in one place.

Johnny could now understand the rage against this overly racist group and what they had done to his people, but this type of revenge was wrong. A lot of the guests attending this party would be innocent victims who were never involved with the original act. It was because of this that these fellow Shifters had to be stopped. He needed to contact Richard and the others, but even in an area full of people with cell phones he could find no easy way for himself to let his friends know.

Johnny sat on a rock as the rest of the pack abused an outdoor table promoting the reelection of a Senator Heston. When he saw two tough looking boys standing near an outdoor cafe, he suddenly had an idea. Johnny threw a small stone at them to get their attention. They reluctantly came over, expecting to be part of something illegal.

"I need your help," Johnny began as he tried to sound authentic. "This wild group I got involved with over there has two brothers who've been hassling me about dating their younger sister." He pointed at one of the Shifter women. The two boys cringed at the sight of her.

"You're kidding, right?" one said.

"Oh, man, wish I was," Johnny continued. "They won't give me any peace and I want out. So, here's my plan. I need to look like I have to leave quickly. This is my wallet. There's fifty bucks in here for you if you do this thing for me. I already took out the important papers."

He showed them the empty wallet containing only the one bill. "I want you to steal it from me."

"No, way, dude. We could still easily get in big trouble," the other boy said.

"Please, I really need a way out. I'll chase you to that far corner there near the jewelry store. The alley way will be your escape," he pressed. "Besides, the nearest police officer is way over there on the other block."

The two looked towards the cop, then back to the fifty. "Okay," they both said, then one offered, "*I'd* sure as hell pay something to get away from *her*, too."

"Damn straight. So, wait until I'm tossing it up out of boredom," Johnny told them.

They stepped back towards the cafe just in time for Carl to plop himself down near Johnny.

"What did *they* want?" he said suspiciously.

"Thought I might have some drugs," Johnny lied.

"Ha," Carl reacted. "Here we are about to kill off a handful of these Europeans while their own children are trying to do it to themselves."

"*Crazy*, huh?" Johnny replied as he lowered his head to look like he was fed up with being harassed by the unattractive woman's brother. The two boys looked on with pity.

Carl joined the others again now hounding a group of punked-out teenagers. Johnny had begun to toss his wallet in the air, attempting to look bored and heavy in thought. The boys glanced towards the police officer at the far end of the street one more time, pulled up their hoods around their faces and made their move.

"*Hey!*" Johnny yelled after one of the boys caught the wallet in mid-air and both began to run. "That's *my* wallet!"

Johnny jumped off the rock, purposely slipping on the ground. He never looked up at the others hoping his fellow Shifters had picked up on what was happening.

Johnny yelled again as he ran towards the boys who were already at the corner alley, he was glad he had picked good runners.

The other Shifters sat back in laughter as they watched their fellow compatriot look like a fool.

"Didn't know Sinclair was such an old wolf," Carl laughed.

The Shifter next to him (who really wasn't his brother) looked on in disgust, "He'd suck in a hunt, wouldn't he?"

Through the alley Johnny waved goodbye to his saviors and sprinted to the nearest restaurant. Inside he asked to use their landline phone to call Richard.

***

It was five in the afternoon when Mitch and Stephanie finally walked through the doors of the Burlington Police Department. They had spent several hours with the dog trainer, Ms. Carolyn Royal, who showed them how talented she was, as well as her dogs. She had proven that her three dogs were able to do many tricks from the impressive fetching of specific shoes out of her closet, to the passing of a rubber ball from dog mouth to dog mouth, as well as the subtraction problems they solved by the number of barks they expressed. But after all their accomplishments, Ms. Royal had little to say about teaching them how to kill. She just couldn't understand why one would ever train their dogs to murder, especially a fellow Indian like herself.

"The trainer would have to severely abuse them," Carolyn had said. "Starve them, maybe. Ah, it sounds so horrible... However, if it were true, I would bet you this type of training would cause them to be attacked themselves. This could lead you to some possible clues in your area."

"How do you mean," Mitch asked.

"Injuries such as continuous dog bites," Stephanie surmised.

"Exactly," answered Carolyn. "Ask the area hospital and health clinics to keep you informed of similar looking injuries by one or more people."

Writing the idea down, Mitch had been excited by its possible potential. "Thank you, Ms. Royal. That's going to be very helpful."

After the visit they then headed to Burlington to question Police Chief Ford. Inside the station Stephanie introduced them both to a middle-aged woman on the other side of the lobby's check-in window. They saw right away that the woman was into cats with her desk and side walls covered in everything feline.

"What can I do for you officers?" the receptionist asked.

"We know it's getting late in the day, but we're looking for Police Chief Ford," Stephanie said. "Is he in?"

"Well, you just *barely* missed him. He got himself all spruced up and is heading to a dinner party," the woman explained. "Quite a fancy to-do, I heard, but that's all I can say. Is it very important business?"

"Oh, we just needed to check with him about some information he has that could help us with a case down south we're involved with,"

Mitch lied, then decided to give the lie a little extra. "Sadly, it's concerning something you might not want to hear about...looking at your decor here."

The women glanced at her cats and kittens. "Gosh, *what* is it?"

"It's some horrible killing of neighborhood cats in our town. *Brutal.* By some miracle, Officer Ford may have an unexpected lead to solve this case."

"Oh, my," the woman expressed, concern on her face. "Well, this sounds *extremely* important. I don't think the Chief is going to be that upset about being interrupted for helping fellow officers. Here, I'll write down the address of where the party is being held. It's Dr. Kenneth Baker's house. What you want to do is get back on the highway, south, to the Cochran exit, about twenty-two miles. At the first light in town, you take a left up into the hill section. It's called The Wolf Creek Estates."

"Of course, it is," Mitch remarked. "*We* thank you, and the cats of our town thank you."

"My *pleasure*," she returned with a wide, proud smile.

***

Skyler had patiently leaned back on his chair awaiting his pepperoni and pineapple, double cheese pizza. He and Jasmine sat in their usual seats at The Grill feeling incomplete without the company of Colin.

"Ma'iingan inini or not, I miss Colin," Jasmine announced.

"Hey, these types of *shifts* in a person's life can be a big deal," Skyler said, making a silly face. "Besides, that's not the reason he's not with us tonight, is it."

"I know. It's Julia," she responded. "I *am* happy for him."

"Well, one of us had to find a soul mate eventually," Skyler replied. "I just figured it would have been me first."

"Oh, you're looking for your soul mate...at fifteen?"

"True love knows no age."

"Right. In any case, I'm hoping that even with boyfriends and girlfriends we'll still all hang out."

"Speaking of...whereabouts is that old chap, Charles Hartington, dear girl?" Skyler asked, with an improved accent. "Are you still *hanging* together and snogging?"

"Snogging? No. We talk at school, sit together in the cafeteria, and, yes," she admitted. "I even invited him out with us tonight, but he was busy with his host family."

"Guess you're stuck with me."

"Hey, here's an idea," Jasmine suggested. "Let's ride up to the Baker party and see if we can get a glimpse of Colin *hanging* with the hoity-toity."

"Spy on Colin?"

"No, just check in."

"Sounds a bit creepy, if you ask me," Skyler said, excited by the pizza that was headed his way. "Besides, their house has a complete wall around it with an alarm system."

"An alarm system...in Cochran?" Jasmine reacted, as the waitress handed her a Caesar salad.

"Julia's mom *and* dad make enough money to be paranoid," Skyler replied. "However, I happen to know of some holes in the system."

"*How* do you know about *holes* in their alarm system?"

"Hey, it wasn't my idea to spy on Julia," he had said after swallowing his first bite. "My parents were over at Ms. Granda's house doing a photo shoot of our Siamese cats, Huey, Duey and Irving. I got the wonderful pleasure of having to hang out with their eleven-year-old son, Ricky. *He's* a strange dude."

"And?" Jasmine pursued.

"Well, Ricky seems to have a big crush on Julia and he showed me the backyard of her house where she supposedly sunbathes a lot."

"*Aaaand*?"

"And Ricky found a section of wall where the security alarm had burned out and hadn't been fixed."

"So, you're saying we could go there tonight?" Jasmine finally asked. "I'm not sure if we should trust an eleven-year-old peeping tom."

"Aaaand *you* want to do *what* tonight, *girlie*?" Skyler responded.

Jasmine blushed, "We're protecting Colin?"

Chapter 30:
Dr. Baker's Dinner Party

"Does that gun of your father's really work?" a partially curious Ricky Granda questioned. It was just past six as Colin and Ricky stood away from the Granda's house waiting patiently. Ricky had just been inquiring how strange it was that their highly rambunctious Pomeranian, *Attila*, was simply sitting quietly at Colin's feet as if she had always known him. Colin didn't comment.

Dr. Trask (who was all decked out from head-to-toe in rain gear) had been fiddling on the side of the house preparing his invention. Ricky's parents stood in the driveway watching.

The only reason Colin's dad was asked to try out his invention in the first place was because of Jeannine Granda. Jeannine was a freelance photographer and writer who worked part-time from home for the Burlington Times Newspaper. Once a week she wrote a column about the interesting people and places around her. When Dr. Trask mentioned his hobby of inventing gadgets (over the cleaning of Jeannine's teeth), she immediately saw a story. So, there she stood, next to her skeptical husband, taking notes and photographing the event to go in the newspaper's Monday issue.

"My father's shotgun?" Colin finally said. "I *don't* know if it works."

Colin had been still dazed by what had happened in his own home. But thinking about the evening more, he realized he was getting just as nervous about meeting Julia's dad. *Hi, Dr. Baker.* He thought to himself. *What? You have a problem with me being Indian? Well, what's your view about werewolves?*

The thought almost lightened his mood.

With the blast of the first load of sealant onto the chimney, Colin was transported back to reality. His father's converted weapon had actually put the specially mixed sealer (in an inventive mini-baggy) right onto the broken section of the chimney, spreading it in and around the crack. His father had pretty good aim, too, Colin realized.

"Hey, mom, can I take some pictures?" Ricky asked while his mother continued snapping away.

Colin took notice to her camera. It was a high-end digital 35millimeter, with a large telephoto lens, that must have been able to get incredible close-ups of the mortar hitting the chimney. "I use it to also shoot wildlife on my days off," Jeannine had told Colin and his father earlier.

"Can't I take a few, Mom? Huh?" Ricky continued to ask.

"No, dear," she said. "You *know* you're not supposed to touch my equipment."

He came back over to where Colin stood. "My phone shoots almost just as well," he remarked, opening up the camera app and shooting Colin's dad at work. "Just can't shoot close-ups."

Colin cringed at the screechy pitch.

"Why are *you* dressed up?" Ricky eventually asked. "Got a date?"

"Yeah, I do," said Colin with a chuckle. "My father and I are invited to the Baker party next door."

"*Really?* Julia's house?" Ricky asked, suddenly excited. "I'd *love* to go to that! Who's your date, your father?"

Colin gave him a deadpan look and simply said, "No, Julia."

Ricky's smile disappeared as he stared more intensely at Colin. "*Julia?*" he repeated.

"Yeah," Colin said, attempting to read Ricky's changed expression.

Rick stared a little longer as if to argue, but instead lowered his head.

"*You* have a crush on her, don't you?" Colin smiled.

"Ummm, *yeah*," Ricky finally said in a defeated voice.

"I've had a crush on Julia, too," Colin admitted, "for years."

"Really? She's *so* cute," he responded. "Have you kissed her?"

"Ah, well..." Colin stammered, then changed the subject. "Look, you know, I promise to be very good to her, okay?" He put out his hand to shake.

Ricky almost considered not shaking it, just so he could stay jealous. Then he realized he really liked this Colin guy and decided he'd just have to trust him with his girl.

"Well, you *better* be good to her," he replied.

Colin promised again that he would.

"All done here," his dad yelled as he placed the rifle back into the car. "Let's get over to that party. We're already fashionably late."

They said their goodbyes to the Grandas and began to drive the short distance to the Baker house.

"Did they like the results?" Colin asked, making conversation to hide his nervousness.

"We'll see tomorrow after it dries," his father answered. "I'm surprised it took only four rounds, though. I've still got a round of mixture in the gun."

They drove onto a small, open grass lot across from the Baker's house, specifically to be used for parking that night. The two got out of their car and approached the central gate entrance of the surrounding nine-foot wall.

"They must like their privacy," Colin's dad whispered as he made a face.

Four hired security guards were stationed at the gate. Philip showed them their invitations and the gate immediately opened.

"Oh, hey, are you Colin?" one of the guards had asked. "Dr. Baker's daughter had asked me to tell you that she would meet you in the kitchen."

"Oh, thanks," answered Colin.

"Well, I guess that puts me on my own," Colin's dad responded.

"No, dad, come in with me," Colin decided as he realized it wouldn't feel *as* awkward if his own dad was with him during introductions. "I'd like you to officially meet Julia."

"Okay," he smiled. "First, I want to call the hotel room and let your mom know we're here."

"Oh, the Bakers ask that you deposit all cell phones in the entryway," said the same guard that spoke to them earlier. "They want no distractions at their party."

"Sure, fine," Philip said. "Just this one call."

As Colin and his dad walked towards the entrance, Colin remembered what Julia had told him about her house. Looking around at what he could see he acknowledged that Julia's home was not at all like Michelle Sullivan's. The doctors' display of extravagance had surpassed the Sullivan's with two tennis courts, an outdoor, as well as a small, indoor pool, plus an elaborate collection of antique rifles, clothing, paintings and many other items honoring the Revolutionary War (one of Kenneth Baker's expensive hobbies). Colin's dad had jokingly saluted the life-size, brass statue of a 1776 soldier in the entryway right after he deposited his phone in the slotted box provided. They were then escorted to the kitchen.

The Baker's kitchen, Colin quickly surmised, was the size of *their* house's first floor. The kitchen, at that moment, was filled with platters of food, servers and frantic cooks running back and forth.

As Colin came to the entrance of the kitchen door, he could see Julia helping a young African American woman fill a plate of smoked salmon appetizers. Suddenly her father appeared at the other end making Colin nervous enough to push himself and his dad off to the side of the doorway and out of sight.

"*What?*" Philip whispered.

"Not yet," replied Colin.

As they watched, Dr. Baker was staring at Julia with a shocked expression. He quickly pulled her hand away from the platter as he harshly said, "*We* are the ones hosting this party!" Then he gave a degrading gesture towards the workers in the room, "*They* are the help. You're embarrassing me."

"No, Dad," Julia said defiantly, pulling her arm away. "*You're* embarrassing *me!* I will not be treated this way, and sure as hell won't stand for you treating these people so poorly...*anymore*."

"*You don't talk to...*" he began, as he turned red in the face while pointing a finger towards Julia. As he looked angrily around the room the hired help pretended to keep working. He looked back at Julia and slowly hissed, "*We* will talk *later*." He then turned on his heels just in time to produce a big, welcoming smile, "Dr. and Mrs. Carmichael, *how good* of you to come. Wait till you taste the salmon appetizer...delicious." And he left the room.

Colin had then stepped into the kitchen just as the hired staff began to lightly clap for Julia. She stood there holding back tears. On seeing Colin, she ran into his arms.

"D-did you hear that?"

"Yes," Colin said. "You were great. That must have been hard."

"I just don't know what to do sometimes," she said.

Feeling uncomfortable with his dad right behind him, Colin cleared his throat and simply said, "Julia, this is my dad, Philip."

"Oh, my, gosh, I didn't...Welcome, Dr. Trask," Julia smiled, taking his hand. "I'm so glad you could come."

Colin's dad shook her hand with concern in his eyes. "It's good to be here," he said. "Especially with Colin."

"I'm glad he's here, too," she smiled at Colin.

"And, Miss Baker," his father expressed, still holding her hands. "If it's any consolation, my father was the same way. It can be hard."

Chapter 31:
The Converging of Many

"*What?*" Victor yelled into the telephone, having earlier been in a fit of rage over the death of Maul.

"It's Talon."

"No fucking kidding. Where the *hell* are you?"

"I'm in an empty house just down the street from *our* party," Talon said as he looked around the affluent surroundings for something to steal.

"Why are you at the party without us?"

"Okay, ready for this- the *other* Superior is at *the* fucking party," Talon proudly said. "All dressed up and here at *theee* party."

Victor paused at the news. *Well, happy fucking birthday to me!* He thought. *I'll be able to kill my one rival* and *the slimy Europeans in one easy location.*

"We are about to go pick everyone up as we speak," Victor said on the phone. "Stay put. We'll be in from Burlington as soon as possible."

Not wanting to be weighed-down with stolen goods, Talon stepped through the broken door of the house grabbing only some sliced meat from the fridge to nibble on. He snuck back to the grassy parking lot where he had left the body of the old man. Blood covered the ground from the severe neck wound, which he figured he should at least clean-up for now. He could clearly see the road from this vantage point, so he would stay there and wait for the others.

As Talon was about to lift the body back into the car, he suddenly wondered why the old man followed the Superior to *this* party if he was at the other house decorating for *that* party? Out of curiosity Talon bent over and rolled up the left short sleeve of the man's shirt. Nothing. He pulled back the other side. There it was, the Skiri Clan emblem.

Baird had told them that the older tribesmen proudly tattooed the symbol on their bodies when they were young.

I knew it! The people at the house are Shifters! Talon thought.

Then Talon heard the small electrical crackle of a voice, "*Steve? Any signs of anything strange?*"

Talon dropped the body back to the ground and pulled out the small, silver walkie-talkie from the old man's pant pocket. He quickly put it all together. *The goddamn Superior and his pack know about us! How?... A... spy? Fuck! They planted a fucking spy!* Talon looked across the backyard to the house he was just in. *Got to get back to the phone!*

"Hey, what's going on there?" a young security guard questioned. He stared wide-eyed at Talon, then saw the lifeless body on the ground. The guard went for his gun. *"Don't move!"*

"I don't have time for this," Talon hissed about to raise his arms to shift.

The amateur officer, however, saw the silvery glimmer of the walkie-talkie in the dark and thought it was a gun. At that very moment a car full of loud teenagers passed the lot screaming and beeping. When they threw out a handful of firecrackers the blast spooked the guard just enough to make him pull the trigger. He sent two bullets into Talon's chest.

Talon faltered back against the car and dropped the walkie-talkie. He put his hand to his chest and looked down at the slightly bloody holes around his favorite *Iron Maiden* shirt. "I really *like* this shirt," he slowly breathed. He gathered his strength and changed instantaneously into a wolf, not even bothering with his clothes as he pounced. The stunned officer didn't even have time to emit a sound.

Talon dragged the dead guard and old man under the front of the car relieved that none of the other officers had heard the gunshots. However, he was just about to leap across to the house with the phone

when he saw a police car drive up onto the grass. Talon crouched low in the dark to watch and wait.

***

Mitch and Stephanie had stepped out into the dark parking area among several cars, most of them large SUVs. In this one lot alone, Mitch could count four Hummers.

"No one is panicking about high gas prices, here," he commented.

"Wealthy people," Stephanie said. "Good place for a Police Chief to mingle, I guess."

"I prefer to mingle with farmers," Mitch offered. "Bit more down to earth, I believe."

They had begun to walk towards the front gate when Mitch spied what looked like glowing eyes near one of the only economical cars around. He blew it off as a reflection and proceeded on.

"Good evening, officers" Mitch said as they showed them their badges. As the hired guards looked them over Mitch continued, "We have some important business to discuss with Police Chief Ford. I believe he is here at the party?"

"Yes, he is, sir," said one of the guards. "In fact, he actually congratulated me about my polished attire."

The other guards rolled their eyes.

"Is there a way to page him so as not to bother the other guests?" Stephanie asked.

"Ah, well, that's Cromwell's job, being the only one who works here full time," answered another guard. "But he's out walking the grounds, though he shoulda been back by now."

"He probably chased off those rowdy teens who just drove through," proposed the third.

"Soon as he comes back," the polished guard said, "we'll see what the procedure is in contacting the Police Chief."

"Thank you," Mitch responded. "We'll be waiting in my car there. Just signal us when you're ready. And you do look mighty polished." "You know what?" the polished guard quickly said, "I believe I'll take it on myself and find the Police Chief for you."

***

Atop her mountain bike, Jasmine had just crested the last hill to the Granda's house. "Come on, slow poke!" she yelled behind her.

"Oh, s-sure, Miss Health-Nut," Skyler huffed. "I haven't been on this thing all summer. Besides it *is* kinda hard having these heavy binoculars around my neck."

"Besides the heavy pizza in your belly," she answered. "So, there's your goal for this fall. *Ride more.* Now where should we hide our bikes?"

"O-over here." Skyler pointed to a grove of white spruce down from the Granda's driveway.

They pushed their bikes into a dark area of brush. Skyler grabbed his water bottle and a bag of potato chips he had hid under his shirt.

"Really?" replied Jasmine looking at the chips. "You look like you're ready to see some kind of a show."

"Well, you never know how long it'll take to spy on a party."

"We're not *spying*," Jasmine reacted. "Besides...I'm just feeling a little protective of Colin now, knowing his...*uniqueness*."

"Yeah, I can picture how helpful we're going to be to a werewolf," Skyler smiled.

"He's our friend. Of course, we will help him if we can," Jasmine argued. "And he's not a werewolf. He's a Ma'iingan inini."

"Huh," Skyler suddenly expressed when they reached the wall. "This was all easier during the day."

"You mean you can't find the broken alarm section?" Jasmine asked, looking up and down the bricked barrier.

"Calm down, calm down. We'll find it," he assured.

***

Police Chief Ford twisted his way through the jovial partygoers gripping his whiskey glass as if it were precious gold. Sporting a slick navy-blue suit for the event, Henry had hoped that this affluent crowd would still recognize one of the area's most visible officers without his uniform on. From the start he had been mindful of his standing amongst the wealthier of the area, but through a variety of successful police scenarios he had reached quite a celebrity status, which he *thoroughly* relished. His most publicized heroics, however, had been an unexpected accident. Henry smiled, remembering the ironic event. As reported in the local news, an irate man had taken a black family hostage out of sheer anger over a failed poker game. It so happened that this was the same person Henry owed *a bunch* of money to from a similar game the night before. The police chief saw the opportunity to not pay this low-life back and he took it. *Sure, the little colored-girl wrapped in his arms could have been hit,* Henry recalled, *but I pulled the trigger anyway.* As a result, it saved the girl and her family, making Henry look like a hero.

If I could be so lucky in my card games! The police chief considered.

"Henry!" Dr. Kenneth Baker had exclaimed for the second time, pulling Henry out of his daydream.

"Oh-hey, Kenny, there you are," Henry said as he walked over to the tuxedo-clad doctor. He was among a group of distinguished people standing by the pool.

"Come. I'd like you to meet some associates of mine you might not know," Kenneth said. "Now, I'm sure you recognize Representative Patrick Robertson and Attorney Dick Donalds?"

"Ah, Mr. Donalds," the Chief said, shaking his hand. "*If I recall*, an excellent job getting the Governor's son off on those *alleged* drug charges," he added with a wink. "I'm sure the Carmichaels are quite appreciative...being an election year and all. And Representative Robertson. Nice to finally meet you. I admired your legislation against raising minimum wage. Can you imagine *those types* making over ten dollars an hour?"

"Yes-yes, well, Henry," Dr. Baker said, pulling him away, "I'd like you to meet these three gentlemen here, and this lovely young lady. They are the next generation of Vermont's top businessmen, *and women*, of course. This is Jeb McDaniels, owner of the *Mega-Burger Palace* franchise throughout the state. Vincent Caprinelli, president of *Only Caprinelli*, the construction and renovations business I've mentioned to you. This is Trent Wintworth who runs *Modauffe Financial Advisors*, and, last, but never least, Eva Coulter, our area's most aggressive developer. I *do* like that dress, Eva. It's such a *yummy* lime green."

"*Kenny-Kenny*...May we *focus* on the main issue?" Eva remarked with a devilish grin.

Dr. Baker smiled and gestured to the others to follow him to the far corner of the backyard past the tennis courts. The party was now in full swing between the house and the pool's edge, so Kenneth didn't need any stray ears around.

"Police Chief Ford, here, has been a big help with regenerating part two of our resurrected sterilization project."

"And how do you plan to distribute the new batch of serum state-wide this time?" asked Mr. Donalds.

Just then two younger boys ran past the group, attempting to follow the perimeter of the Baker Estate wall.

"Hello, Jonah, Zev. Be careful of Mrs. Baker's roses at the far end, please," Kenneth said to the boys, and then turned to the others. "Dr.

Cohen's kids, Ha, Ha...he's one of our best surgeons and a big contributor to the arts. Um, *that's* why he's here- Okay, to answer your question, Mr. Donalds... It'll be in the *flu vaccine* this time," the doctor said smugly, quite proud of his clever scheme. "And, yes, though it may be wasted on many reputable senior citizens, our statistics show that almost all welfare and lower income families will be receiving the vaccine this fall and winter. In fact, we have developed a big ad campaign in specific neighborhoods and towns promoting the importance of protecting the family from the winter flu. As for the *well-born* in Vermont, we have the regular vaccine available to them. In conclusion, our special mixture is ready within my father's warehouse on the waterfront just waiting for my say-so. Distribution will be immediate."

"Very good," Representative Robertson said, sipping his glass of scotch. "Your father would be very proud; God rest his soul."

"But, Kenneth, lower income doesn't always include...you know, *certain* families," Dick Donalds commented.

The Police Chief jumped in saying, "You mean the Orientals and Indians and what-not, well, *I've* got that covered. I have obtained updated town records in nearly every county about where those certain *types* live in our state. We'll know just where to place the vaccine."

"Well, that sounds very good," Mr. Donalds had said, putting his drink down on the grass and then folding his hands in front of him. "I guess there's just that one apparent issue needing to be addressed then."

"Ah, issue?" Kenneth repeated.

"About our *documents* disappearing," he said.

Dr. Baker looked at the Police Chief.

"Kenny, of course we know about the missing papers," Representative Robertson made clear. "Whom do you think ordered the termination," he said to the Police Chief.

"We had a short meeting concerning the problem just last week," Trent Wintworth arrogantly added.

"We were all *truly* hoping that the Baker family name would not be tarnished by this incident," spoke the gruff, but always clear, Vinny.

"No. *Hell*, no. We *are* on it," the police chief immediately said as he nervously fiddled with his empty whiskey glass.

"We believe it was *simply* misplaced," Dr. Baker explained. "I'm paying some trustworthy university students to thoroughly search the archives at the library, even as we speak."

"I do hope you can find them, Dr. Baker," Dick said over his spectacles. "Especially since we *can't* ask poor Mrs. Worthington to help us, hmmm."

"I promise this should all be cleared up by Monday, sir. Right, Henry?" Kenneth responded, praying for some certainty.

"Yes, indeed. *I* also have several of my boys on it. I will *bet you* they'll have answers even by tomorrow morning, if not tonight," he said, absentmindedly saluting.

"Good," Representative Robertson said. "Senator Heston will be pleased to hear that and, of course, the evident progress of our new program."

"Of course- of course. And *speaking* of him," Dr. Baker smiled awkwardly, "I need to check on the progress of his silent auction. Excuse me, gentlemen...Miss Coulter."

The doctor had walked up to the house leaving the police chief standing there uncertain as to what to do next. He was about to politely excuse himself when he was suddenly rescued by one of the servers.

"Pardon me, sir?" a petite Vietnamese woman said. "You have some visitors at the front gate who need your attention."

"Please excuse me," he said to the others.

As he made his way through the doctor's home, he prayed to his God that *what needed attention* had to do with recovered documents.

***

In a dark brush-covered section of the Baker's backyard, a young eleven-year-old boy leaned strategically against the eight-foot wall, suspended by the branches of a well-placed tree. Ricky Granda had propped himself in place only minutes after Skyler and Jasmine had found their vantage point deeper along the wall. He had been continually scanning the grounds to see if he could find Colin and Julia. *Nice or not*, he wanted to keep a watchful eye on this Trask dude.

The Granda boy put his small spy binoculars in his pocket, still looking over his shoulders now and again. Ricky had thought earlier that someone else was in the woods with him, but the noises stopped so he figured it had only been the local wildlife. He then reached behind himself to a broken branch and took hold of his mother's camera. Having learned to sneak off with this heavy toy was only half the fun. Its telephoto lens could reach a good distance allowing detailed visuals of Julia, and her friends, around the pool or tennis court. Ricky considered his collection of photos to date that he had acquired on his own personal memory card, all of them downloaded and hidden within folders on his own computer. He'd shoot frame after frame, delete any bad shots, then save or print out his favorites (his Julia Baker photo album was secret, too).

Tonight, he steadied the camera on a small tripod to work with the low light. He positioned his pudgy face up to the viewfinder and began to scan the crowd near the pool lights and tiki torches.

***

More Shifters had showed up at the LeClaire Hardware Store either standing around in the back lot waiting, or wandering along the isles inside. Nashoba had relaxed in a chair near the office while Anne paced back and forth in the paint supply section. Richard, on the other hand, had been putting away heavy pieces of lumber that somebody left on the floor of the warehouse.

"Why don't you rest, Richard?" Bill suggested as he watched him lift fifteen 2X4s at a time and sliding them into their slots.

"No, this is good for me. Keeps my head clear. Besides, I can get so much more cleaned up when there aren't any human eyes watching," responded Richard. The two began walking back to the main building. "What's Trisha up to?"

"She's over there in the car working on a winter sweater for me," answered Bill. "She says it's how *she* relaxes."

"My Sally used to sew and quilt the nicest blankets," Richard reminisced as they stepped back into the main building. "She used to meet with her friends over at..."

The phone from the office had begun to ring as Richard looked at Bill intensely. Richard leapt across the store.

"*Johnny?*" he asked, gripping the receiver.

Nashoba got out of her chair and appeared at Richard's side along with Anne.

"Yeah, it's me. Okay, quickly..." Johnny Dumont had said. He sounded winded. "The plan is to attack a big dinner party tonight. The guest list includes people involved with some unauthorized sterilization program that targeted specific ethnic groups, Indians included, of course. *Their* Superior has a significant army here ready to kill *everyone* at this party, even the innocent family members *and* their children."

"When and where?" Richard responded.

"Tonight. Out your way," Johnny continued. "The Wolf Creek Estates, they said. A Doctor Baker's house."

"*What?* It's where Colin and his father are," Richard blurted.

Anne gripped Bill's arm.

"*Our* Superior is there?" Johnny questioned and then said, "Crap, the vans are here...You guys get going."

Richard stared for a second at the phone, then looked at the others.

"They're attacking the *same* party?" Bill repeated in disbelief.

Richard simply said, "We've *got* to get there first."

The group was about to leave the office, but quickly turned towards a commotion at the back of the hardware store. They saw Trisha and Desmond outside struggling with a young girl.

"*Let me go, you fucking sons-of-bitches!*" the rough looking teenager screamed.

"We found her prowling around the building," Trisha said.

"*Get your fuck'n hands off me! There's no way you bastards are human!*" Fang screamed.

Richard caught her reducing pupils and immediately looked around the back lot of the building. "She's one of the rebels," he responded, and then to Fang, "*Is there anyone else?*"

"I ain't telling you, you fucking traitor!"

"Desmond, take a quick look. Trisha, you're going to have to stay with this fowl-mouthed pup. There's cable in the store to tie her up. Anne and Nashoba, prepare the others outside. We need to get up to the Baker's now."

Chapter 32:
The Attack

After Julia had finished helping another server with some stuffed mushrooms, she escorted Colin and his father out to the back patio where a local jazz band was playing. There they bumped into Julia's mother, Carol, trying to talk to a young couple holding a toddler.

"*I* am *so* glad you came, Paige!" Julia's mom said forcefully to the little girl. Her voice was a high, childish pitch. She looked at the parents, completely gushing. "She is *sooo* cute!"

"Thank you, Dr. Baker," said Paige's mother.

"Oh, *please*, call me Carol."

Colin understood why she was a bit over exaggerated when he noticed the empty martini glass in her hand.

"You *know*," Carol continued as she leaned towards the couple, "Kenneth was not *at all* interested in having the guests bring their children, but *I* insisted. I just love the wee *kiddles*. Now...we do have three professional childcare people in the living room area to watch your cutie. Especially if you'd like some free time, *okay?* Enjoy...*Bye-bye* Paigey."

"Um, Mom," Julia had slowly said, already embarrassed.

"Well, *hi*, Sweetie!" her mother smiled. "You enjoying yourself?"

"Yeah, *and* I'd like you to meet Colin...and his father, Dr. Trask."

"Oh...well, Dr. Trask, *yes,* the dentist," Julia's mother said. She took his hand gently in a flirtatious fashion. She paused, staring at him, then suddenly said, "I've got this one *pain* right about here..." She pointed inside her mouth, then burst into laughter, "*Ha!* Isn't that *sooo* typical, right? I get that *all* the time as a doctor."

"Ha, yeah..." Philip responded. "I guess we all do. How is your practice, Dr. Baker?"

"Please, call me Carol," she said in a sultry tone. "And *it's* doing fine. Cardiology is never boring...you just have to keep up with the *beat*- Ha!"

"Mooom..." Julia pushed.

"Oh-oh, *my*, yes. It's Colin, right?" she sputtered.

"Yes, ma'am."

She looked at him up and down. "*You've* grown."

"Ah, yes...ma'am."

"I *heard* that you and my Julia are, well, ah...*an item*," Julia's mother spoke cautiously. "I mean, *I* think it's fine!"

"Mom, you promised," Julia said, now completely embarrassed.

"*Welll*, dear, *you* know how picky your dad is *about*..."

"About what, Dr. Baker?" This time Colin's father spoke up.

"My, ah, my Kenneth is *a bit* old fashioned, like his father was, mind you."

"And he seems to have had a thing against my wife and kids, is that right?" Philip continued. "Then you have my permission to let him know my wife's background, and, of course, Colin's. It's American Indian. *There*...he finally has a racial label to give them."

Colin's eyes rose.

"Oh, please, *don't* take me wrong," said Carol as she backed up, realizing a few other guests had overheard. "*I'm* perfectly fine with diversity, even here, in Vermont. *Really,* I am. My Kenneth *does not* represent my..."

"Ah, Dr. Baker," interrupted the young server who Julia had helped earlier, "there seems to have been a splatter of paint in the *day care*-living room. Um, it has to do with your husband's George Washington painting, I'm afraid."

"*Oh, my,*" Carol said in shock, but looked totally relieved to have a reason to escape. She politely excused herself.

Julia had watched her go then returned her attention to Colin and his father. "Here's the second time I have to say *sorry*. This is by far the most humiliating day I've had in my life."

"Please, don't apologize, Julia," Colin's dad kindly said. "I understand the stress of being a doctor. It can follow us home."

"It's more than that," she said, her head lowered.

"Go see if you can help your mother inside," suggested Philip. "She'd appreciate it a lot. Meet us over at the food table. If that's all right with you, Colin?"

"Yeah, sounds good. I wanted to mingle with the guests, anyway," Colin joked.

"Talk about anything to do with investments, tropical vacations and *what do you do to stay in such wonderful shape?* You'll fit right in," Julia smirked, and then left.

Colin watched her go into her house and then followed his dad over to the outdoor feast. The tables were twice the size of Michelle's party and the amount of food was doubled. Of course, the number of people attending this party was doubled, too, not including the children. Colin guessed that there had to be over one hundred and fifty guests, as well as the thirty or so employed cooks, servers, the band and gate-side guards. He looked out towards the various, well-dressed adults and wondered if a lot of them held the same beliefs as Julia's father.

"Don't be hard on her," Colin's dad said, breaking his train of thought. "I can tell she's a sweet girl, considerate and strong."

"Yeah, she is," Colin said, and then simply asked, "How long have you known Mom's native background?"

"From the start."

"So why the secret from me and April?"

"I think your mother was tired of people like Dr. Ken Baker and their narrow-minded belief system," Colin's dad responded. "She thought that if you saw yourselves as no different than the other children, you wouldn't grow up feeling different."

"Well, I've learned...especially recently, that different is okay," Colin said.

"But you learned that on your own. It wasn't forced on you. So, it has made you stronger," he smiled.

Oh, much stronger. Colin thought.

"Shall we go chow-down?" offered his dad.

"Sure."

They had started through the line until Colin realized he wasn't the least bit hungry. He instantly blamed his lack of appetite on his nervousness about meeting Julia's dad. When his father proceeded on (stopping to talk with some fellow acquaintances), Colin stood to the far side to quietly observe his surroundings. He considered his nervousness again and finally understood that the uncomfortable churning in his stomach had nothing now to do with Julia's dad. He was anxious about the impending battle with a bunch of crazy, blood thirsty Shifters out there, somewhere.

One I already killed! Colin thought anxiously as he made his way over to the meat table and filled a small plate. *Have the others heard anything yet? Is Johnny Dumont even alive? Is the attack tonight or tomorrow? Am I even ready?*

"*Whoa*, slow down there, flesh eater," Julia said as she watched Colin fill his mouth with several roast beef slices. "Are my parents making you *that* nervous?"

***

Talon had stayed low to the ground to listen for any more movement by the two officers who were only four cars away from him. He was about to dash to the nearby empty house again to warn Victor of the other Shifters when he heard and felt the ground move. It's subtle, but evident rumble meant the presence of more than one heavy vehicle.

The two vans. He thought. If it were Victor and the pack, they would be parking far enough away to allow the element of surprise.

Talon put his ear to the ground. The vehicles had stopped somewhere to his left. He waited, and then slowly heard the vague pounding of many feet stepping out onto the pavement and grass.

It's them.

He would wait for the others to get closer and make a clean dash in their location to warn them.

***

Mitch and Stephanie had been waiting in the car for a sign from the guards that Police Chief Ford was available.

Stephanie eventually crossed her arms and asked, "So, *when* we see him, then what?"

"Ask him questions," Mitch answered as he sipped some old, cold coffee. "Ask maybe, *'Why were you so curious about our visit to the library?' 'What does any of this have to do with the death of Mrs. Worthington?'* and also, *'Those Eugenic documents you were asking us about, well, we would now like to see them ourselves.'"*

"What about the Trask boy?" she said.

"We can see if he's home tomorrow, but from what Mr. LeClaire said, he sounds like just an academically curious kid. Then again, if he is part of the same native background as LeClaire and this Carrier women, we may have to examine all of these people a little closer...Hey, look."

Mitch pointed to where the polished guard was waving his arms. They got out of the car and walked over to the front entrance. A broad, balding man stepped through the gates at a brisk pace. His stern face had shown determination until he noticed the badges being held out by Mitch and Stephanie.

"What's this all about?" Police Chief Ford exclaimed.

"We are the two *suspects* you were curious about just the other day. Something to do with important documents, I believe," Mitch boldly said.

"Officer Porter?" Henry said.

"Police Chief Porter, yes."

"Y-you're *here*?" he curiously questioned, obviously caught off guard. "But, I..." He quickly looked towards the house.

"But you what?" Mitch asked, trying to grasp his look of fear.

Whether it had been the intense conversation with Dr. Baker's associates or the two whiskeys in his empty stomach, Police Chief Henry Ford suddenly blurted out an unexpected confession, "I sent my men to Eureka to retrieve those documents. The *missing* documents," he exclaimed, then with a pleading look he said, "You *do* have them, right? They *want* them back. *They'll* pay. *I bet* they'll pay a..."

"Who wants *what* back?" Stephanie questioned. "Are you talking about the Eugenics papers we have? They were copies of..."

"Copies? But-" Henry muttered.

Mitch was about to barrage this fellow officer with more questions when he glimpsed the slightest movement gliding along the left wall. He had barely registered the presence of a large canine before it leapt out of the darkness, trailing saliva over its bared teeth. With unconscious reflexes Mitch pulled Stephanie and himself backwards to the ground and out of range of the beast. It, instead, hammered into the side of Police Chief Ford, spilling him onto the driveway's pavement. Henry's struggles were futile as the vicious killer ripped his throat open in a matter of seconds.

Stephanie and Mitch were now only several feet away from the wolf when it turned to concentrate on them. Yelling and shots from inside the gates, however, suddenly distracted it. Mitch and Stephanie stared in the same direction only to see more wolves take down the three security guards. Their mouths dropped open when two of the wolves transformed into humans, closed the iron-gates and immediately wove a thick chain around it. Once the gate had been securely locked the two aggressors changed back to wolves and proceeded towards the house.

Mitch and Stephanie had no time to analyze what they just saw as the original attacker turned its snarling attention back to them. The two slowly began to shuffle backwards towards the parking lot. The salivating wolf lowered its head and drew back its mouth, as if smiling. Slowly, almost teasing, it approached the unarmed officers. Then, out of nowhere, just as the wolf was about to pounce, there was a bounding swoosh over Mitch and Stephanie's head. In front of them had leapt yet another large canine. This one, however, growled viciously at the first wolf, putting itself between it and the police officers. In an instant the two were fiercely fighting each other, evidence of blood and fur spattered across the pavement. Stephanie and Mitch continued to inch away as they watched the brutal battle in front of them. Mitch had thought that a dash to the car could now be achieved and was about to suggest the idea to Stephanie. Instead, he found himself staring into the eyes of an older, gray-faced wolf. The wolf simply raised a clawed paw across Mitch's neck drawing very little blood. When Stephanie attempted to roll away at its left side, the wolf took his other paw and stuck a nail quickly into her leg.

In no time the formula had entered their bloodstream and they were both fast to sleep.

***

Beta had been one of the inside wolves whose job was to let Victor know when the guards were dead and the gates secured. She also wanted to prove herself worthy again after the Trask-house tragedy. Beta's front yard partner, an older subdominant, was left at the house entrance to kill anyone who might try to escape.

The rest of Victor's army lined the left section of the wall awaiting the signal to make their dramatic appearance. Victor Dawes stood there as a two-legged, dressed in his now signature black muscle shirt and charcoal jeans, looking up and down at the rows of his salivating pack.

"What Beta mentioned makes sense," barked Baird next to his son.

"What? About everyone having phones?" Victor scoffed. "I have wolves ready to stifle anyone who tries to make a call."

"Everyone?" his dad pressed.

"Then we kill them all quicker than planned. Now where's Talon and Fang?" he inquired, getting annoyed. "They should be here to enjoy this great event."

"They're probably still cleaning up the outside stragglers," Baird barked.

"Well, I *won't* wait for them."

"They'll be here," assured Baird, then said with strong conviction. "Tonight, son, *we* are going to make our rebel elders *very* proud."

"*Yes*," Victor considered. "This shall be recorded as one of our tribe's greatest battles."

"Are you ready to face the other Ma'iingan inini, if necessary?" Baird asked.

Victor looked down at the mostly black-furred wolf that was his father and scowled. "*That's* a stupid question. Now, shut up, I think I hear Beta returning."

***

Skyler and Jasmine had pulled themselves up along a vine-covered section of the wall. A patch of taller maples just behind them had leaned their branches over for perfect camouflage. Skyler checked along the top of the wall for the alarm wiring and found several disconnected sections.

"I bet the whole alarm system is busted," he realized. "I guess any area of the wall will be accessible."

"At least we're hidden," Jasmine said. "Now where are the binoculars?"

"I feel kind of naughty doing this," Skyler replied as he handed them to her.

"As if you hadn't already thought of using these for this sort of thing," she teased, peering through them. "Hey, I can already see Colin and Julia. They're near one of the food tables."

"Food tables? Sweet. Tell me what they're serving."

***

Julia put together a small plate of food for herself while Colin nibbled on the rest of his meat slices. From there the two stepped down to the pool area where several clusters of guests mingled among themselves.

"Where's your dad?" Julia asked as she took a bite of some carrot sticks.

"I think he's talking to some fellow colleagues," Colin answered.

Julia paused for a second and then said, "Sorry again about my parents."

"You don't have to apologize anymore, though, *whew*, it must be tough. But how I see it," Colin smiled, grabbing her hand, "I think *your* kindness dwarfs any of their actions."

"You really think so? *That's* so sweet," Julia said, leaning in and kissing his cheek.

Colin made the move to kiss her on the lips, but suddenly pulled back. He immediately smelled something that would have never been invited to the party, a canine smell. Multiple canines.

"Colin, what is it?" Julia said, seeing the concern in his face.

Colin's brain searched for an explanation. He considered that his fellow Shifters had just appeared outside the wall to retrieve him for battle, but then that thought quickly changed. The canine air he smelled was that of *hate*.

At that moment Colin could hear the sound of galloping paws as several wolves leapt the barrier wall and landed along the length of the lawn. They immediately encircled terrified guests who all stood in frozen horror. Those who found their voices screamed, those who found their legs turned towards the house to escape, only to be blocked by several large, growling canines guarding the exits. The band stopped dead in mid-song.

Colin quickly translated what was happening into one possibility, the other Superior discovered where he was and had sent his pack to come and get him. Now he, alone, had to somehow protect Julia and the others without the help of his tribe.

Colin scanned the grounds and had counted fourteen Shifters in and around the lawn. It would be a difficult fight, he realized.

He was about to step away from the others to present himself when suddenly the crowd turned towards the top of the wall. Colin followed their gaze to a tall teenage boy with dark, flowing hair. He stood as proud as a drill sergeant; hands wrapped behind his back. The guests, and wolves, fell silent.

"Well, hello," the boy on the wall bellowed with a strong, projecting voice. "Before my friends and I indulge in the merriment of your party tonight, I'd like to ask you all two simple questions, and remember, raise your hands. First, how many people here *truly* believed they were going to succeed at ridding Vermont of, what you called, *undesirables*? Huh? How many? Anyone? Okay, let's try this one...How many of you involved in the *forced* sterilization of *my* people could have known it would someday come back to haunt you?"

Colin looked confusingly at the people around him. He didn't understand the questions being asked. This was obviously the angry Superior, yet he spoke to the crowd as if the guests here had done something to him *and*, what would be, *his own people.*

Forced sterilization? Colin thought. *That's insane!* And then he thought: *Does this include Dr. Baker? Could even he go that far? These renegade Shifters seem to think so.*

Colin suddenly gasped. *This is the event! They're attacking here...with children...with Julia!*

"What, Colin?" Julia nervously whispered. "Do you know what's happening?"

Colin looked at Julia, but didn't speak. All he knew was that he had to do something fast. He began to step forward to protest the allegations when two older men emerged from the guests.

Dick Donalds and Patrick Robertson strode just below the area of the wall where Victor stood. They had attempted to express no fear, but even Colin could smell them.

"Excuse the interruption, but as someone who feels I may speak for the others," the State Representative smoothly said, "I have to say *we* have *no idea* what you're talking about concerning the sterilization of *your people*. But believe me, with the resources at my reach, I can easily get down to the bottom of these complaints."

"Sterilizing *people*...without their consent?" Attorney Donalds repeated as he looked from the representative to Victor with exaggerated shock. "*That's* the most disturbing thing I've heard in years. As a lawyer I would *certainly* be willing to help in the pursuit of this heinous act. And, if I may, would gladly help you with your legal matters concerning your evident raising and training of wild wolves...*pro bono*, seriously."

Victor looked down at these pathetic, yet entertaining, Europeans with a lengthy, sardonic grin. "Um," he slowly said, "and you two are...who?"

"Dick Donalds," said the stalky, bald man, standing a strong 6'2" in his black tailored suit. His vague white mustache had begun to twitch nervously.

"State Representative Patrick Robertson," said the chunky, round one. He attempted to mimic the confident posture of the young teen, but failed miserably.

Victor took his eyes away from the two men and proceeded to pull out several folded sheets of paper from the back pockets of his jeans. He scanned the pages quickly, and then looked back down at them.

"It seems *you're* on the list," Victor exclaimed.

"List...?" the representative slowly said only to recognize the documents in Victor's hands. His mouth dropped.

"*Carl, Dad*, you may have the honor."

Two of the closer wolves sprung with lightning force at the unsuspecting men. With no time to utter a single scream, the two were mauled in a matter of seconds.

Colin, having been consumed by the older men's attempt at negotiations, was suddenly brought back to reality. The crowd of guests had begun to scream and cry again, all desperately seeking a way out. They scrambled and fell over each other in panic. Any who had been brave enough to make a running escape or an attempt at the opposite wall were taken down by the surrounding wolves and killed.

Colin grabbed Julia's hands and quickly said, "You've got to trust me- Stand very *still* with the others. I'll keep you safe." He immediately let go and took a bounding leap over the terrified crowd. He landed beside the two ravaging beasts still ripping apart the dead men near the wall. Without the need to shift, Colin tore the attackers from the bodies and flung them across to the back lawn. Baird and Carl angrily regained their feet, but held their ground.

Colin then turned to face his opponent. "*Stop this now!*" he yelled to Victor.

The older teen looked down from the wall and smiled. "Oh, *there* you are," he said. "Colin Trask, I presume."

"Stop this. You want me," Colin implored. "Take *me* and leave the others."

Victor bent down to place the folded papers onto the top of the wall and then he jumped to the grass below, landing between Colin and the petrified guests.

"Dad, *you* were right," Victor said aloud. "Mr. Trask, here, would give his *life* for these *destructive* Europeans...Why? *Why...?*"

"*Because*, Victor Dawes," came a powerful voice from the top of the wall. It was Great Grandmother Carrier, in human form. "We all live here...in this state...in this country. And we have done so *peacefully* for centuries, following *human law*."

Victor looked up and then followed the north part of the wall. What he saw positioned there were eleven wolves ready to spring to the lawn below.

"Hooray! The *Just-and-True* Calvary is here," Victor mocked. "But I'm afraid, old wolf, that you're *totally* outnumbered."

Using that as his cue, Johnny Dumont, at the far end of Victor's pack, quickly turned and leapt upon the wolf beside him, catching it firmly by the neck and biting down hard. From there the Sachem wolves sprung off the wall to fight. Nashoba transformed, discarded her clothes and joined the others.

Chapter 33:
Protecting the Innocent

"*Dammit,* don't move, Carol," ordered Kenneth Baker inside the kitchen. He and his wife had just entered the heavily staffed room on their way to see what all the commotion was about. As they did so, they stepped in front of their workers all pasted up against the cabinets and walls. In front of them stood two growling, pacing wolves.

Kenneth backed the two of them slowly towards a counter where a Hispanic girl shook uncontrollably, a large, silver tray of appetizers still in her hands. In a swift, twirling move, the doctor grabbed the girl and one of the carving knives on the counter. The appetizers sprayed everywhere. Kenneth then began to move towards the exit using his frightened employee and her tray as a shield.

"Follow me," he said to his wife as he forced the server forward. "We're getting the hell out of here."

The girl, however, had begun to scream when the wolves wove back and forth in front of them. Kenneth believed that the knife in his hands was what kept them away so he waved it side-to-side. In an abrupt burst of fear, however, the serving girl swung her tray above her head to make a run for it. The tray fell behind her and across the bridge of Kenneth's nose sending the doctor sprawling backwards. As he fell, his flailing arms pushed his wife to the side, knocking the knife out of his hands. Two timely employees pulled Carol away.

The wolves kept their ground as the serving girl ran out a side door. The doctor shuffled backwards on his hands and feet. He kept slipping on the appetizers and the blood from his nose. He looked on in horror as the larger wolf gestured to the smaller one.

Benny Carrier gave a wolfish grin as he acknowledged Beta's unexpected charity. With a powerful leap, he proudly and swiftly killed his first European.

***

Pressed flat to the cold stone of the wall, Jasmine and Skyler peered in shock at the phenomenon in front of them. They had instinctively known to not make any sounds or these animals would easily hear them. What clearly could be seen on Jasmine and Skyler's expressions was the fact that they *were not* going to be able to help Colin out of this mess.

***

Colin had stepped away from a very angry Victor Dawes who stood in awe as his own army wasted precious time fighting fellow Shifters. Within seconds, though, a burst of energy blew across Colin's face as particles of clothing floated to the ground around him. Colin now looked up into the blazing eyes of a seven-foot tall Ma'iingan inini. It towered over him, flexing muscles covered in a black fur that faintly glimmered from the surrounding torchlights. Colin would have taken the time to acknowledge its stunning appearance if the werewolf hadn't turned its vicious attention on him.

"*You stupid idiots! These goddamn fuckers are the enemy!*" Victor growled as he pointed to the guests. "*You should be attacking them!*"

Colin knew that there would be no reasoning with this Superior. Victor was here to kill, and to kill him, too. Still, with this werewolf focusing mostly on him, Colin was unable to concentrate on making himself shift.

Victor erupted with anger. He had had enough of this untimely interruption and this *pitiful* Superior in front of him. Ready to pounce, Victor was suddenly hit from behind by the golden-gray wolf of Johnny Dumont. Nashoba, at the same time, had body-slammed him on his left side. The highly muscular creature did not waver, but grabbed the two with quick arms. He threw Johnny far into the back corner of the tennis courts and then effortlessly lifted the old wolf to his open muzzle, biting into the graying fur of her neck. He shook his head vigorously.

Victor, brazenly grinning, discarded Nashoba's dead body as if it were a boring chew toy.

"*No.*" Colin barely whispered as his emotions went wild. He then sprang with such speed and fierceness that his hands were already around Victor's neck before he had even transformed. But Victor had no time to acknowledge human hands, as they became Superior claws in mere seconds, digging deep into his flesh.

Victor twisted backwards and out of Colin's grip, regaining his balance. He realized that this Ma'iingan inini was as fast and agile as he was, nothing like the aged Superior, Bobby LeClaire. However, Victor also knew he had an advantage over this compassionate wolf. *All I have to do is this!* Victor thought as he reached into the crowd for two unsuspecting victims.

Colin stepped back in shock when he saw his father hanging by his collar along with a blonde-haired woman in a short lime green dress. Victor gave a sinister werewolf grin as he threw the woman hard into the crowd of guests. Then, just as easily, he tossed Colin's dad over the opposite stonewall.

"Oops, slippery claws!" Victor teased.

Colin had only seconds to consider whether his father was alive or dead, or whether Julia was still okay. When he saw Julia dashing through the crowd to help the injured, he returned his attention to the imminent battle. Thoughts of his father would have to wait.

Colin dove for Victor's exposed midsection when Victor made another attempt to seize more guests. It sent them both careening down to the pool, landing them in the deep end. They slashed and bit underwater, attempting to keep each other down or cut each other's throat.

Victor instead dropped quickly to the bottom, then, with the effects of a missile, sprung out of the pool and back onto the lawn. He quickly leapt towards the house.

The children! Colin realized as he jumped out himself.

***

Ricky Granda's expression was wide-eyed and slack-jawed. One of his hands lay over his mouth to keep it silent. Though several feet away from the party, he was able to view this whole inconceivable event unfurl. What he had been witnessing tonight was something he'd only seen in the horror movies secretly watched in his bedroom. *This time,* he knew, there were no special effects. Ricky could barely breathe as he fought an incredible urge to make a run for it. Then it occurred to him what he could be doing in this precarious position. He had his mother's digital camera, and *it* barely made any sounds. He slowly raised the heavy instrument to his eye, adjusted the lens and began to shoot one frame after another.

***

Anne Trask had just taken down the older wolf guarding the front door. She made her way towards the sounds of weeping and whimpering and found herself at the side entrance of the kitchen. There she saw a young boy-wolf finishing a kill as his counterpart inched her way towards a withering, crying Carol Baker. Anne made her move just as Beta leapt for the doctor's throat. She caught Beta in her haunches and they tumbled into the refrigerator.

Leaping back to her feet Beta growled, "Who the *hell* are you to stop me?"

"A Sachem," Anne barked.

"It's the other Superior's mother!" snapped Benny. He recognized Anne even as a wolf.

Anne made the mistake of turning towards her young relative, "You have disgraced your Great Grandmother, Benny."

Beta took advantage of the distraction and dove for Anne's exposed neck. Anne had barely reacted as she skirted to her right, but was still caught on her left thigh. Beta bit down hard, shaking and twisting her head. Anne was able to pull herself away then jumped back onto her good leg. She could feel the sharp sting of pain and the trickle of blood down her backside. She had known full well that a fellow Shifter's bite heals that much slower so she was quite vulnerable. Beta knew this, too, as she and Benny savored the easy kill. They drew back to attack when suddenly a bone-splitting sound stopped Beta in her tracks, her bluish-green eyes widening.

Standing behind Beta (trembling in fear and anger) had been a drunkenly brave Carol Baker. She had taken the carving knife that her husband had earlier and pierced it through Beta's back, unknowingly stabbing her stomach.

"*Die you fucking, goddamn satanic beast!*" she screamed, and then fainted onto the floor.

As Benny watched Beta drop to the floor, Anne went for his neck, shaking until he eventually went limp. She sadly staggered away from his body.

"You chose poorly," she whispered.

***

Colin sprinted towards the Baker house after Victor. While he ran across the grass past the paralyzed guests, he found himself in arms-length of a battle between Desmond and a rebel Shifter. He quickly reached his arm out, not losing his stride, and flung the aggressor backwards to the tennis courts below. Carolyn was there to finish him off.

Still only inches away Colin couldn't prevent Victor from crashing through the living room window where the children had been playing. The angry Superior went straight for the frightened huddle of caregivers and kids, ready to snare several in his claws. Colin used Victor's arched leap as his only chance to derail this hideous beast's intentions. He dove straight forward, with incredible force, sinking his nails deep into Victor's sides and sending them both smashing through the far wall. The paneling and timber had ripped apart at the weight and strength of these two Ma'iingan ininis, producing a gaping cavity into the next room.

They tumbled into Kenneth's private study where Victor catapulted Colin onto the doctor's work desk. As its top caved in, sending papers scattering around the room, Colin tried to regain his balance. His opponent was too quick. Victor grabbed Colin and threw him against the opposite wall that displayed Dr. Baker's framed achievements. A supporting beam had broken Colin's impact, sending him back to the floor in a dizzying heap. He shook his head to focus only to see the werewolf diving in for the kill. Colin rolled to his right sending Victor into the same beam.

They both jumped to their feet as Colin crouched low in preparation. Expecting a continuation of biting and clawing Colin was taken by surprise by Victor's sudden karate kick to the chest. He was sent crashing through to the main entryway and slammed headlong into the brass sculpture of Dr. Baker's Revolutionary War soldier; cell phones spilled across the tile floor. This time Colin lost consciousness and did not move.

A tired and bleeding Victor walked arrogantly into the space, grinning widely. He would now get to show his pack and the others that *he* was their true Ma'iingan inini. He would tear off the head of *this* Superior and hold it high to his warriors. This, he was sure, would inspire the pack to finish what they had come here to do in the first place.

"*Fool*. Your compassion for these fuckers only killed you in the end," he stated as he slowly drew back his clawed hand.

Suddenly the front door burst open, as he was about to strike. There in front of Victor stood a battered and leaf covered Philip Trask swinging a shotgun to his shoulder. He had closed one eye to aim.

Victor stared down at him dumbfounded. He had recognized the man quickly as the one he tossed over the wall. Now here he stood aiming a gun at Victor's chest. *Oh, well,* thought the Superior, smiling. *This guy won't survive a second shot.*

Dr. Trask had the creature in focus, but decided instead to send the chimney mortar higher. He lifted the barrel quickly and ignited wet sealant over Victor's eyes and nose. The Ma'iingan inini screamed in shock, falling back onto the stairway behind him.

Colin stirred from the commotion and then leapt to his feet. What he found waiting was a disheveled (but very much alive) father, and a blinded Superior. Thinking quickly, Colin grabbed the brass statue beside him and thoroughly sent the erect soldier and his upright musket through the stomach and back of Victor Dawes.

Victor stood there in total shock. The one visible eye only stared straight ahead. His snout slowly, but clearly said, *"no-"* as he dropped hard to the ground.

Colin turned to his dad. "How did you...?"

"I luckily landed in a pile of leaves," his father smiled.

Colin stared back at the dead Superior. "You saved my life."

"Hey, I'm glad to have been some sort of help," his father responded.

"*You* were great," Colin answered as he brushed dry wall pieces off his fur. Only then Colin realized who he was in front of his father. "Shit, *Dad*, I-..."

"Hey, it's alright," his dad smiled wide, shaking his head as he took in his son's amazing new look. "I've known bits and pieces of this mystery. You see, your mom's formula didn't work so well on me after a while."

"You're kidding?" Colin said. "But that means you know she's..."

"A wolf changer-shifter-thingy, yeah," his dad finished. "But I've only seen her change once. It's pretty cool... Then, *you*- I mean, *damn*..."

"Sorry. I should have told you," Colin said.

"No, you shouldn't have, but I know now and the secret is mine to keep- Let's go help the others."

"Wait, I have an idea that may help," Colin said.

***

Outside on the back lawn, the Sachem pack had continued their fight to protect the Baker's guests. The remaining few had to constantly prevent Victor's subdominants from diving into the huddled masses and taking out the helpless humans. The guests either crouched low, hugging each other, or stood pasted to the side brick wall, praying for an end to the madness. Julia was one of them standing and watching each scenario unfold, wanting to be prepared to fight if she had to. Though in shock at seeing what had become of Colin, Julia didn't let it get in her way of wishing that he were still safe and alive.

***

Out in the middle of the tennis courts Richard LeClaire laid injured. He had tried to use his body to knock Baird away, in a heroic move to save the life of Johnny Dumont. Instead, Baird had rolled with the hit, and then kicked Richard into a metal net post, breaking his back hip and leg. From there Baird ended the life of the spy, then proceeded towards Richard to do the same.

"I know who you are, LeClaire," Baird growled as he approached the older wolf patiently. "It is going to be an honor to be the one to end your life after *my* son did so to your own flesh and blood. And in your next life...please *stay* out of the way when *true justice* is being carried out."

"True justice doesn't kill blindly, Dawes," came a low, steady growl.

Baird turned to see the husky wolf of Uncle Bill behind him.

"Old man, I will be through with LeClaire, and onto you before you can even blink!"

Baird would have attacked Richard right then, but a loud, projected voice pierced the night air, stopping both Bill and Baird where they stood.

"*Your Superior is dead!*" came the voice of Colin Trask, holding the limp Ma'iingan inini body of Victor over his head. "*I am the Superior here and I order all this to end now!*"

The whole of the grounds had come to a sudden standstill. Wolf and man stood silent staring towards the back patio of the Baker House.

Eventually a loud, anguished howl was heard from a shocked and disbelieving Baird. In a sudden fit of rage, he turned blindly back to the incapacitated Richard to pounce. Uncle Bill, however, intercepted the attacker bringing Baird down in a swift tear of the neck.

Chapter 34:
Making Many Forget

Three of Victor's remaining subdominants had stood in awe, frozen by the unexpected turn of events. One was the female Johnny had pretended was the unintended girlfriend, and the other two were Carl and Trapper. Within seconds the three realized their plight and instantly retreated over the wall.

Colin lowered the body of Victor to the ground and returned his attention to the scene in front of him. He happily saw Julia weaving through the crowd as she helped those who were hurt. Many of the guests just swayed, trance-like, where they stood. They gradually, however, understood that the danger was finally over, though several wolves still lingered among them. At this point they had learned there were good among the bad.

Preoccupied by the violent battle, reality eventually set in for Colin. He had to accept that one particular wolf would not be changing back to her human self. He stepped over to the remains of Nashoba, and knelt next to her. Richard, with great trouble, limped to his side, and then plopped himself to the ground, exhausted.

"To pass on after such an honorable fight has been the wish of many Native people for centuries," Richard said, still in wolf form. "She had a good, long life. Now her story ends as incredibly as it began."

"Still, I will miss her...a lot," Colin said sadly, then, "*Wait*, Richard, have you seen my mother?"

"Here," came a bark from the back entrance of the house.

Colin looked up to see his wounded mom, her hip bleeding less, but her fur discolored by the dried blood. He quickly leapt to her.

"It looks bad," he said.

"I'm all right, dear," his mother assured. "It's already..."

"*Honey*, you're hurt."

Anne Trask showed the human expression of shock when she saw her husband. She turned to Colin.

"Yes, he knows. Has known," Colin told her.

"*How*?" she asked with a tilted head.

Understanding the tilt, Colin's dad smiled, "Your *'forgetting potion'*, whatever you call it, has a small glitch. If you use it on the same person too many times, we get immune to it."

He smiled at his wife, gave her a kiss on her furry forehead and started dabbing a few paper napkins on the wound. "Oh, and I'm okay with why my surprise birthday might not happen any time soon," Philip smirked.

Anne, with her long, wolf snout, smiled back.

Colin stepped away again to the lawn and daringly approached Julia as his Ma'iingan inini-self. He understood that he and the others had to start administering the formula, but wanted one chance to speak to this brave girl after the immense trauma she had been through. Having seen Julia's weeping mother kneeling over the torn body of her father, Colin knew Julia would need to stay brave.

As he approached her, the crowd reacted to him differently. Half were still too awestruck to respond to his presence, the others stood back uncertain. Julia stood her ground, as Colin got closer. Instead of fear, her eyes beamed with the gratitude of seeing him alive, a single tear had rolled down her cheek. "You saved us," she said to him, her voice cracking from the strain of the night. "You and... your friends."

"I'm glad I was here to help, but...your father, he..."

Julia lowered her head.

"I'm sorry."

"My mother?" Julia asked.

"She's fine," Colin answered.

"Where is she?"

"In the kitchen," Colin began.

Julia looked at the non-threatening man-wolf in front of her and simply said, "I don't understand any of this...but, thank you, Colin," and went into the house.

***

Desmond and Sasha had jumped the sidewall to get to his car. The two had parked near the Granda's house and had left leather pouches containing flasks of formula just inside the shadowy bushes beside it. They grabbed one pouch each in their mouths and ran back to the others.

The Sachem protocol for administering the mixture had always been within thirty minutes to an hour of an unfortunate event or accidental sighting. This helped set up the necessary time for sleep. Forgetfulness of the day before, though, lasted a whole twenty-four hours. *This* incident, for the remaining guests, would soon be a night that will seem to have never happened.

Each wolf dipped their nails quickly into the potion and sprinted from guest to guest, lightly scratching their legs or arms before they could react. The fearful, who had begun to see their fellow patrons fall to the ground, tried to make a run for it only to be easily caught by Colin and the others. The fast-acting formula dropped them gently where they stood into what would be a well-needed deep sleep.

Desmond had come to Philip Trask who was still helping Anne.

"No, Des, he won't need any," Anne said.

Desmond gave her a confused look, but moved on.

Colin and Sasha went to Julia and her mother. Sasha scratched the neck of the mother who was still crying over the body of her dead husband. Colin explained that he would take care of his friend. Sasha continued into the other rooms to help with the children.

Julia watched as her mother drifted off to sleep like the rest of the kitchen help had done.

"It's a harmless sleeping formula," Colin explained. "It will make you forget everything that happened."

Julia gave him a sad look and eventually asked, "Will I remember who you are?"

"Not as I am now, no," he said.

"So, I won't know how my dad died," she slowly said.

"No," Colin answered. "I'm sure that will make it very hard for you in the morning, but...it has to be this way, I'm afraid."

"I'll be all right," she responded, and then said, "Will I see you in the morning?"

"Yes, I'll be here," he smiled.

Julia put her arm out for him to scratch her. "Thank you again...Colin."

He gave her the slightest incision, barely drawing blood. Her eyes closed as she slowly swayed into his furry arms. He gave her a light kiss on her forehead.

Colin had been about to pick the sleeping Julia up off the floor when Uncle Bill alerted them to the sound of distant police sirens. He knew she would be safe there next to her mother in the kitchen.

Colin, instead, went out and quickly tucked Richard and his mother under his arms to run them down the hill to their clothes. His dad followed beside him. As they ran through the parking lot, Richard had suddenly remembered Dr. Sachem.

"Quickly," he barked, "We need to remove Dr. Grandpa's body from the area. I'll use his car to get down to the hardware store."

"Naked?" Colin asked.

"I know, but I'll duck low behind the wheel. Now tell your father to get his car out of here, too, and then get back inside. They're going to need *your* help."

"Right," Colin answered.

He was about to explain the idea to his father, but his father quickly responded, "Got it."

***

Uncle Bill had shifted to human, dressed in clothes left in his hidden Ford Pick-Up and then rapidly maneuvered the truck outside of the right wall. From there Colin joined Desmond and Carolyn in tossing wolf remains into the back of the truck. They had to be rid of everyone who hadn't been invited to the party.

Colin stood on the wall above and questioned the inclusion of the rebel Superior and his dead pack members among their deceased tribesmen and women.

"Disappearing corpses are more important, right now," his uncle hastily explained.

Colin turned to jump back down to the few wolf bodies left. As he was about to leap Colin noticed the folded documents that the angry Superior had previously displayed in his hands. They were the very papers that their opponents claimed was the reason they came to kill. He would hold onto them tightly until he and the documents were safely home.

After all the bodies were gone and the surviving Shifters had left, Trisha did one last sweep with the formula for any guests who might still have been awake. Four police cruisers showed up just as the last stragglers quietly snuck away; Uncle Bill and his truck had already escaped along a dirt road on the backside of the Wolf Creek Estates. The officers would be unprepared for the odd and morbid scene they were about to witness.

***

Whatever had transpired in front of Jasmine and Skyler had finally come to an end. The *good side,* they understood, had thankfully won. Just the same, the two knew they were *not* supposed to have witnessed any of it, especially after watching all non-Shifters being given the forgetting formula.

They quietly and accurately slipped away, slowly moving back towards the Granda house. Skyler kept his heavy breathing down as best he could all the way to their bikes.

"Just-just can't believe..." Skyler eventually tried to say. "It was-was...*insanity.* People were killed."

"I know, I know," Jasmine responded, just as traumatized. "You've *got* to remember, though, right? Got to remember, *we-didn't-see-a-thing.*"

"*Damn!* Wait...*Shhhhhh,*" Skyler whispered, whipping one finger to his mouth. "*Wolf?*"

They ducked into the brush that hid their bikes and held their breaths. The evident cracking of dried leaves could be heard behind them from within the woods. As it got closer Jasmine dared herself to peek.

"*Ricky?* Ricky Granda?"

"*Augh!*" he yelled as he jumped out of his skin.

"Shhh! Shhh!" Skyler motioned.

"Wait, *what* were you doing?" Jasmine questioned as she walked towards him. Then she saw the camera. "*No,* you didn't...at the Baker's...with...*that?*"

"Um, well, I mean," stuttered Ricky still in shock by the same event they had seen. "Why? *Did* you guys see?"

"Yeah," Skyler answered.

"Ricky..." Jasmine spoke slowly, "if you...if there are *pictures* on that camera...you've *got to* get rid of them."

"What?" Ricky responded, snapping out of his daze. "No *fricken* way am I losing these pictures. This is *news*-stuff. Like- *this* is money. No way."

"But there are people to protect," Jasmine pleaded. "That's why *they* put the guests to sleep. They needed those guests to forget everything."

"Forget? So that's what they did," Ricky said. "Then- *no.* No, because of *that.* Now I have proof of what happened so-so Julia, *especially*, will know the truth."

This time Skyler spoke, "*What* truth, dude, that a werewolf and his wolf army attacked Julia's houseguests? That Julia's mother and father may be dead now because of the attack? What images do you want to *shock* poor Julia with, Ricky? She'll have enough pain from the fact that people died right there at her own home."

"The *good* wolves, like Colin," Jasmine tried to explain, "came to save these people. Otherwise, they'd probably all be dead now. *Julia* would be dead now. It's Colin, and the ones who protected the others...they need your help in keeping this secret."

Ricky stared down at the camera. "Well, like, how did Colin and the bad guy train all those wolves to-to do what they did?"

"Werewolves can do that," Skyler lied, knowing exactly who some of the wolves must have been.

"Fine," Ricky said.

He pretended to fuss with the dials of the camera before Jasmine and Skyler could get close to him all the while secretly slipping the memory card out and into his closed fist hand. He dramatically hit the delete button just as the two were looking on.

"You did it?" Jasmine asked.

"Yeah. See-" Ricky showed them the *"no images"* screen.

"Please do not speak a word, Ricky," Skyler insisted. "The immense investigation from- *oh, man,* probably every government agency would be huge. It would *not* be good...understand?"

"Yeah, I do-I do. Promise," Ricky said, tired and annoyed.

Jasmine, however, didn't believe him. She had thought that if Colin knew about this tonight, he could take care of the problem with his potion.

"Okay, *we* better get going, Skyler," Jasmine quickly said. "It's been a *long* night."

***

As the constant sounds of police cars, ambulances and buses continued outside on the street, Colin entered the room of an emotionally exhausted Ricky Granda. Having been too tired to undress and shift again, Colin had run to the house in human form. He climbed into Ricky's window and swiftly gave him the formula using one of his human fingernails.

Afterwards he sniffed-out the digital camera used that night and took it home to destroy (just in case).

"Sorry, Mrs. Granda," Colin had apologized as he smashed the camera and hid the pieces deep in the garbage. He then finally went off to bed, having no need for the sleeping potion himself.

Back at the Granda house (unbeknownst to Colin) Ricky had earlier emptied his pocket containing the camera's memory chip. He had placed the chip inside the pages of one of his science fiction novels on his bookshelf. Colin's formula, however, made Ricky forget the card had ever existed.

Chapter 35:
The Saturday that Didn't Happen

"Good morning," Colin's mom softly said after knocking on his bedroom door.

"*Huh?*" Colin stirred, and then bolted upright in bed. "What time is it? I need to get to Julia before she wakes."

"Calm down, it's only nine o'clock. You still have an hour," she smiled.

"Really? Good," Colin responded and then asked, "How's your hip?"

"Fine. It's still a little sore in the muscle, but the bite marks are barely visible."

She limped slightly to the end of the bed. "How are *your* cuts?" she asked.

Colin assessed his wounds. "Huh...*gone*."

She smiled, but paused for a second, staring at her hands on her lap. Eventually she said calmly, "So, *ah*, do you want to talk about anything?"

He looked at her briefly, rubbed his eyes, then replayed the previous night in his head. Eventually he said, "I'm going to miss her."

"Nashoba, yes. Me, too," his mother responded. "She was a great woman and I know for a fact that if she were here right now, she would be saying how proud she was of you. *I'm* proud of you. You fought well, and...and I know it must have been very hard. Hard to suddenly be put in such a serious situation."

He took in a deep breath, recalling the battle. "It really happened, didn't it?"

Anne said nothing.

"Strange..." Colin began. "The wolf side of me knew what to do and how to respond to all the craziness, but it's the human side of me that has to deal with all the mental aftershock."

"Like what?" Colin's mother cautiously asked, knowing it was important for her son to sort it out.

"Like having to kill others," he said. "I ended two people's lives yesterday, maybe three."

"It's difficult," Anne said in agreement. "But you know there was no negotiating with this Victor Dawes...There was no *'talking-it-out'*."

Colin nodded.

"And you understand now that it was basically up to you to stop him," his mother continued. "You *do* know that, right? This Victor was powerfully strong, and a killer. He and his vicious pack would have kept on killing. If they had succeeded the local authorities, or even the government, would have found out and have to get involved."

"Do you think last night's events could be traced back to *us*?"

"Hopefully not. Our kind have been in, well, similar situations throughout history. We clean up well."

"What do you think would happen *if* the authorities found out about us?" questioned Colin.

"Oh, my. I don't even want to imagine," she reacted. "Some in our government, in the *military*...well, they might be very excited about getting to know us...scientifically."

"*Scientifically?*"

"This is all speculation. A subject for another time," Anne said. "Let's just get through these next few days first. Have some breakfast then go see how Julia's doing."

"Right."

***

Mitch Porter had stirred slowly awake to find himself in two very precarious situations. First, that he was laying on a mat in the middle of a school gymnasium full of people, and second, that somehow Sergeant Harrison was snuggled up beside him.

With his right arm under Stephanie's head, Mitch gingerly moved his other arm up to see what the time was. At the sight of 9:45am, Mitch reacted to the fact that they were losing precious hours. From his startled shudder he awoke the Sergeant.

"Wha-Huh? *Mitch?* What the *hell* are you doing in my room!" she yelled.

"Stephanie, *shhhh-*" he said in a lowered voice as he quickly retrieved his right arm. He pointed to the darkened gym around them.

Stephanie leaned up on her arms to see that it wasn't her motel room at all. She now found herself among several sleeping, well-dressed strangers.

"How...?"

"I don't know. I was just about to find out."

Stephanie rubbed her eyes hard, and then lifted herself off the matt with the help of Mitch. "Wondered why the motel bed was so hard," she said.

The small gymnasium was in an elementary school showing signs that the room was also used as the auditorium and cafeteria. The two could hear voices coming from what looked like the door to the kitchen. As they made their way towards the lit entrance (stepping over men, woman and children) Mitch read an inscription on the cinderblock wall.

"*Cochran Elementary?*"

Stephanie looked up in amazement, too. "How are we already in Cochran?"

"Hey, you two-," came a surprised voice coming from inside the kitchen entrance. The door flew open revealing a nervous police officer about to reach for his gun. His partner was at the ready behind him.

"I'm Police Chief Porter of the Eureka Police Department. And this is Sergeant Stephanie Harrison, BCI for the state," Mitch quickly said as he went to produce his badge.

"Keep your hands where I can see them," said the hefty and gruff officer.

"They fit the description, Seamus," said the thinner, younger officer.

"It's *Officer McDougal*, Ploof. How many times...!" argued the older man, and then turned back to Mitch and Stephanie. "Okay, then...Police Chief. Sergeant. Sorry. Had to be sure. Besides, we have your identification information here inside."

Mitch checked and felt empty pockets.

"Since you two are the first to awake, we'd like you to come answer some questions."

"Fine," Mitch said, not liking the tone this officer had.

"Coffee?" the other officer asked as they stepped into the kitchen.

"Sure. Thank you," Mitch answered.

Mitch noticed at once that these must have been the only two officers here. They had set up two chairs around the kitchen's cutting-board table with one big percolator between them, and a box of donuts. On a metal counter to the back were dozens of wallets and cell phones.

"Sergeant?" the burly officer said as he handed Mitch his coffee.

"No, no thanks, but I could sure use a donut," Stephanie responded.

The two officers laughed making Mitch feel more at ease.

"As you must have gathered, I'm Officer McDougal and this is Officer Ploof."

"Raymond," Officer Ploof added with a wave.

Officer McDougal rolled his eyes as he produced two more chairs to place around the table, and then pulled out a large pad of paper and a pen.

"Before we start, *I'd* like to ask a question," Mitch said. "Where were we last, since we must have all been brought here from another location?"

"Well, that was gonna be *my* first question," Officer McDougal smirked, giving that sense of suspicion again.

The more he observed these two officers, the more Mitch realized that they were either very new at simple inquiry or that they were jumping the gun before the real professionals arrived with questions.

"You see, me and Officer McDougal found you two ourselves," Officer Ploof offered, "*just* outside of where all of it happened."

"All of what?" Stephanie asked.

"The attack," Raymond continued. "*Thirteen* people were killed."

"*Killed?*" Stephanie reacted.

"Where?" Mitch questioned, spilling his coffee.

"Where?" Officer McDougal repeated. "At the dinner party you two *weren't* invited to. Which would be my next question, *why* were you even there?"

"*What* party?" Stephanie pressed. Then she turned to the gym door and said, "That's why all those people in there are dressed up."

"You were at Dr. Kenneth and Carol Baker's house. You don't remember?" said a frustrated Officer McDougal.

"*No*, we had simply arrived in the area Friday evening and immediately went to our motel rooms," Stephanie argued. Mitch shook his head in agreement.

At this point Seamus had begun to question the credibility of these officers. Here were two people who had come all the way up from southern Vermont, got obviously drunk at a party they weren't invited to, and somehow passed out in the parking lot just feet away from where these horrendous attacks took place.

"Ma'am," Seamus slowly said, "*it's* Sunday."

"*What?*" Stephanie blurted.

Mitch sat wide-eyed as he racked his brain for answers. He eventually perked up and said, "Police Chief Ford. What about him? Is he one of the investigating officers here?"

The two officers put down their coffee mugs at the same time. Officer McDougal cautiously said, "Why?"

"He was one of our reasons for coming up here in the first place."

"*He* was one of the victims *ripped* apart last night," Raymond responded.

"Ripped?" Mitch repeated. "How..." He stopped abruptly, and then asked, "Was there fur everywhere?"

"Whoa, fur?" Officer Ploof reacted, animated by the amount of coffee he'd been ingesting all morning. "Fur was *everywhere*, all over the lawn, all over the house, in the pool, too. *Totally* creepy. I mean... Hey, wait now. If *you* can't even remember where you two were last night, *how'd* you know about the fur?"

"*I* get it," Officer McDougal stood as he eyed Mitch a little closer. "Aren't you...*and you?*" he pointed to Stephanie. "You're the two who've been investigating this same kinda stuff down your way. What again...? 'The Killer Dog Murders'?"

The police chief and sergeant didn't respond.

"Then I'll ask again," Seamus continued, now writing crazily on his pad of paper. "*Why* were you two there and *how* could you be *that* close to one of your own cases only to be passed out *just* outside the crime scene?"

"Passed out?" Stephanie responded, understanding the implication. "You mean drunk?"

"Yes," Officer McDougal stood again tucking his pen and pad into his back pocket. "*Maybe* it was the two of you all along who trained those canines, huh?" he paced, now trying to look and sound like an investigator.

"Yeah," Officer Ploof joined in. "And *maybe* it was your way of cleaning up your jurisdiction, huh? You sick rabid dogs on the unsuspecting dirt-bags in your area. Sounds like a good way to rid yourselves of any *riff-raff.*"

"*And*, for some strange reason," Seamus continued, "you two came up here to pull the *same* attack on our rich and powerful of the area. *Political* reasons, maybe. Some big wigs who stepped on your toes, maybe. Or *maybe*, trying to get Police Chief Ford's position in Burlington... However, *this time* you must have gotten cocky and partied with your *victims*, passing out while your dogs did all the dirty work."

The two, proud officers stood there with their arms crossed, curious to see how their suspects would react to this obviously thorough inquiry.

Mitch stared at them in amazement. He shook his head, and then finally said, "First, *where* are our so-called dogs?"

"Run off, probably," Seamus answered. "Because you were passed out."

"Second," Mitch continued, "did you smell alcohol on us?"

"Ah...well, no," Officer Ploof said as he looked at Seamus. "'Cause you just totally looked passed out."

"*And* would you say that *all* those people out in the gym had passed out drinking, too?"

"Well, yes, kinda, I'd say some truly had," Raymond responded. "Some of them *really* reeked."

"The children included?" Mitch asked.

"Oh, well, now...They're probably all just exhausted from such a scary night," Officer McDougal quickly offered.

"If we were found asleep," Mitch said, "how were all these other people found? Awake? Hiding? Contained in one of the rooms?"

"Ah, no," Seamus said, his hand on his chin as he considered what he was told by the other officers. "I heard they were all out cold, like yourselves, throughout the house and backyard."

"Throughout?" responded Stephanie turning to Mitch. "A sleeping gas, maybe?"

"Outside in the fresh air?" Mitch considered. "But, maybe something like that. To have us forget, too. How and why?"

"And, Mitch," Stephanie had said slowly, "*those* people out there, with us included, *all survived the attack.*"

Mitch stared towards the gym door amazed he had missed such a relevant fact.

"Okay-okay, back to the canine involvement," Officer McDougal continued to pursue. "If it *wasn't* you two, how did you happen into the exact area of one of your own dog attacks...a hundred something miles from your own jurisdiction?"

"LeClaire and Trask," Mitch eventually said, pressing fingers against his temples. "We were here to see a boy named Colin Trask and a Richard LeClaire."

"Well, Mr. LeClaire is the owner of the hardware store," Seamus commented. "I thought you had said you came to see Police Chief Ford? Why'd you come up to talk to Richard?"

"He had a son killed," Mitch said, "by the... 'pack dogs'."

"Well, *I* didn't know that," responded Raymond. "Did you know that, Seamus?"

"And this Trask boy?" asked Officer McDougal, ignoring Raymond.

"He's an employee at the store who knew the owner's son," Mitch then decided to lie, not wanting to delve into the American Indian connection. "And Police Chief Ford knew all of them and had some possible information concerning that son's murder."

"He did?" Officer McDougal had reacted. "Ford knew Mr. LeClaire and his son, *and* this Trask boy? I wonder why he..."

"Yes, *I'm* now wondering, too...*That* is why we came to question these people," Mitch interrupted, changing his tone of voice to one of authority. "None of this is making sense so I *need* to get back to that crime scene right away. Who's your commanding officer here in town?"

Officer McDougal took offense to the question, but eventually said, "Chief of Police Rockwell. He's probably still up there."

"Up where?"

"The Wolf Creek Estates," Officer Ploof answered. "I'll draw you a map."

"Thanks," Mitch said, standing up. "Um, Steph?"

She jolted, half asleep still, nibbling on a blueberry-glazed donut. "Yes- right," she quickly said.

"My car?" Mitch suddenly asked.

"Ah," Seamus muttered. "Still up at the house. You were all brought here in buses...I'll, ah, drive you up there." Then in a last effort to keep some authoritative dignity, he commanded Raymond to keep an eye on the others.

***

Not caring about the distance, Colin had run all the way up to Julia's house after breakfast and a much-needed cup of coffee. He wanted to be there when she awoke from her drugged sleep, though he wasn't quite sure what he'd say when he faced her. His mother, however, was very able to prepare him, *"You and your father were invited to the party, so either say you didn't make it or you had forgotten the whole night, too. Then let her know that you heard, say, on the radio, or internet, that something bad had happened and that you came over as quickly as you could to see if she was okay. That's it."*

When he arrived on her street, police cars were still actively present, as well as a barrage of media people and trucks from local and regional news agencies. He ran up to the front gate, now blocked by police tape.

A female officer put up her hand and said, "Are you with the Press?"

"Ah, no, but-..."

"Family?"

"Well, no."

"Then, sorry, you can't be here."

Colin looked over her shoulder to see several officers and men in suits surveying the grounds. Some were taking photographs and bottling evidence. Behind him reporters and cameramen were huddled near the grassy parking space questioning a high-ranking police officer, obviously, Colin guessed, speculating as to the cause of the whole mess.

Colin turned back to the woman officer and said, "My girlfriend lives here. I need to see...well, if she's all right."

"Anybody found alive was moved to the elementary school," she said, then felt bad about her wording. "Hey, ah, I didn't see anyone who was left inside that was, you know, your age, so she's probably at the school."

"Okay, thanks," Colin responded. He turned abruptly and was about to run in the direction of the school when he barreled into Ricky Granda. Ricky tumbled backwards to the ground.

"Whoa, like, sorry, are you alright?" Colin said as he helped the boy to his feet. "Hey, Rick."

"Oh, hey, that's alright. Colin, right? I know who you are from high school basketball."

"Oh."

"And my mom just mentioned you and your dad's name this morning. Something to do with having fixed our chimney," Ricky said while scratching his head. "I just don't remember you being there. Weirdness. *So*...Colin...do ya know what's happened. Is the girl, here, *Julia*, okay?"

"Did you say, Colin?" came a voice from behind the two of them. "Colin Trask?"

"Yes?" Colin turned towards the unrecognizable voice.

Police Chief Porter and Sergeant Harrison had just arrived from the elementary school and overheard the exchange of the two boys as they approached the front gate. Mitch was excited to finally question this tall teen who had been one of their reasons for traveling to the area. Since they were in regular clothes, he had decided to approach Colin as if they were reporters.

"Hi, I'm Carl McMichaels of the Eureka Gazette and this is my assistant, Betty," Mitch said. "We've been wanting to hear something, *anything*, about the massacre that took place, but can't seem to get anyone to talk."

"*Massacre?*" Ricky said. "You're kidding!"

"*Massacre?*" Colin repeated as he tried to sound like Ricky. "I didn't know it was *that* bad. I just got here."

"If you aren't sure what happened, why are you...*two*, here?" asked Stephanie, joining in on the ruse as she pulled a pad of paper and pen out of her coat pocket.

"I came to see if my girlfriend was okay," answered Colin. "I was just told..."

"Girlfriend?" Ricky said and then hesitated. "Wait, do you mean *Julia?* Julia's your girlfriend?"

Colin wanted to apologize (again) but one of the reporters continued his questioning.

"Girlfriend, huh?" said Mitch. "Hmm. And she just *happened* to be here at...do you know if she's okay?"

Colin studied Mitch, briefly sensing extra meaning behind his questions, then cleverly responded with emotion, "*I* don't know. I'm *really* concerned. They won't let me in to see if she's all right."

Mitch had looked at Stephanie. The only clues they had about this boy was that he was connected to Bobby LeClaire's father and that he happened to be interested in the native symbol found on Bobby's arm. These connections were rather thin. But a full Saturday had mysteriously gone by where more clues had to have surfaced. Now there were murdered partygoers where fur was involved. All this bothered Mitch greatly. So, having the boy right here at the very scene of the crime had seemed quite significant.

He decided to dig deep. "We think there may be a connection between these killings here to those of the 'Pack Dog Murders' in *our* area."

Colin finally understood what these two were looking for and was certain they were not reporters. He also knew that he had to be far more cautious in what he said.

"Do you mean those attacks in southern Vermont?" Colin asked, feigning deep concern. "You think people here were attacked by dogs? Who'd do such a sick thing?"

"Wolves or dogs, yes," Mitch pushed. He was ready to spring everything he had on the boy to spark a reaction. "We've been following the story from the get-go and think there's a possible link between the killer dogs and a Mi'kmaq Indian tribe. I believe they called themselves the Skiri Tribe."

Colin had to muster all of his talent to suppress the slightest signs of emotion. *How could these two have learned that much!* He looked back at this Carl McMichaels, and said, "Skreeky-what...? Wait, I remember this...*they* were that interesting tribe from northern Vermont."

"Yes."

"I had done a paper for a class on Indian tribes in our area. That Mi'kmaq tribe was barely mentioned. But, come on, you were just talking about dogs attacking people, here, in my girlfriend's house. You think Indians are involved?"

"You did a paper for school?" Mitch continued to ask. "Whose class?"

"Dude, like I haven't even seen whether my girlfriend is safe or not," Colin suddenly said.

"I do hope she's okay," Stephanie said, sounding positive and concerned.

"Yeah, I do, too," added Mitch. "So, was it Harvey Benson's class?"

"Yes, yes," Colin answered, acting like he was looking all around the grounds for Julia. In reality, though, he had finally understood where this man and woman were getting some of their facts, but was still surprised that they had connected it to Victor's attacks. He decided to tell the two reporters more of what they probably already knew. "Mr. Benson has a basement full of Indian stuff. That's where I learned about the Abenakis, Penobscots and this Mi'kmaq tribe. If you want more info on this, my boss at the hardware store knows a lot, too. Richard LeClaire. But, seriously, I've got to keep..."

"*Colin?*" came a surprised, familiar voice from behind them all.

"Julia!" Colin said, eyes widening (feigning surprise). He had turned to see Julia and her mother standing in the middle of the road wearing the same wrinkled remains of their party clothes from the night before. A police cruiser was by their side. Dr. Carol Baker stood there dazed, simply staring at her home.

"She's okay," Colin excitedly said to the two *reporters* and then dashed off. Mitch and Stephanie smiled in agreement and looked on.

"At least *she's* alright," Ricky said mostly to himself. He then crossed his arms, "Can't believe he's dating *my* girl," and stormed off back to his house.

"*Well*, our Mr. Trask seemed to have told the truth," Stephanie commented. "Does explain why he showed up in the first place."

Mitch still pondered aloud, "But *so* many coincidences. His Mi'kmaq interest, the fact that he works for Bobby LeClaire's father, and, *now*, dating the girl who *happened* to be at the very place attacked last night."

"Oh, just look at him, Mitch," Stephanie smiled. "He's a strong, athletic fifteen-year-old who works in the local hardware store, who *happens* to be dating one of the local girls. I don't think we have much on him."

"*Hmmph*," Mitch grunted, still not fully satisfied.

"Let's just get onto the grounds and see if we can find anything that resembles a new clue, shall we?" she suggested.

"Fine."

"*So*," Stephanie eventually said as they walked towards the gate, "You *actually* had your arm around me this morning?"

"Well, you were quite snuggled and comfortable on my shoulder, there, Betty," Mitch retorted.

"And *where* do you come off calling me *'Betty'*?"

***

Colin had to remind himself that he knew nothing about last night as he approached Julia and her mom. "Are you okay?" he simply asked as they hugged.

"I'm not sure," Julia answered. She then exclaimed emotionally, "*I don't know anything*! Why *can't* I remember?"

"Yeah, I know."

"Were you here?"

"I *think* so," Colin explained. "I, um, woke up at my house dressed in my suitcoat."

"*You* ended up at your home?"

"Ah, yeah. Weird, huh?" Colin saw his mistake, but continued the lie. "Just can't remember going anywhere. I did wake up with smoked salmon in my coat pocket...but, no memory, sorry. My father couldn't remember either. He heard about it on the morning news."

"So, you heard, then, that...my dad...Is it true?"

Julia's words had awoken her mother from her stupor. The doctor's eyes immediately welled with tears as she broke into a run towards the house screaming her husband's name. Julia stood and watched. Tears slowly trickled down her cheeks.

Colin pulled her close to him and quietly said, "I heard."

"There *was* a party," Julia exclaimed, pressing her face into Colin's chest. "The police told us there was... here, at *my* house. With all those people here, how could not one of us remember what had happened? *Now* my father and others are dead and no one knows why!"

Colin couldn't find words of comfort, so he just held her tight.

"Ma'am?" said a female officer to Julia. "Chief of Police Rockwell would like a few words with you."

"Ah, yeah, sure," she answered. She looked up at Colin and sweetly asked, "Will you be around?"

"Yeah," he smiled. "All day, if you need me."

"Good," she replied and began to walk away with the officer.

"Wait," Colin suddenly said.

"What?" Julia asked.

Colin leaned in and gave her a long, passionate kiss.

She eventually pulled away, gave a thankful, but sad smile, and then walked to the house.

Chapter 36:
Honoring the Dead

That Sunday evening Colin sat around the dinner table with his father, mother, Uncle Bill, Aunt Trisha and, of course, Richard. The rest of the tribe returned home as quietly and quickly as they had come. As for April, she had been sent to a friend's house for another sleepover, after being reassured that all was safe. Everyone remaining in the Trask house spoke of the battle, its thankful outcome and the proper procedure to put it all behind.

"How will you explain Nashoba and Johnny's deaths to friends and neighbors?" Colin questioned. "They died as wolves."

"Right," joined Philip, "*And* what about Lizzy's farm."

"We'll take care of the farm," Trisha smiled.

"As for explanations about their deaths," Uncle Bill added, "I've got a fiery car crash for Lizzy that ends up in Seymore Lake just south of her farm. The body is never found."

"Oh, you're going to crash that cute Volkswagen Beetle of hers?" Anne said.

"Oh, Lizzy would have liked the idea, sweetie," Trisha mused. "But what about Johnny Dumont?"

"Let's make it that he drowned in the deepest part of Lake Champlain," explained Richard. "He has a small boat and liked to fish the lake. Shouldn't be a total surprise to anyone. He couldn't swim well."

"And Dr. Grandpa?" Trisha continued.

Uncle Bill paused. "Hmm, tough one since he died a human."

"I know," Anne suggested. "Let's put him in the Volkswagen. He came to visit Grandmother Carrier and died in the crash, too."

"Yeah," agreed Bill. "We'll burn his body in the car, but we'll tear Lizzy's car door off, making it look like her body was lost in the lake."

317

Colin had had enough. All of this seemed far too inappropriate. "You're all making this sound like a game. These *were* people- our friends. It's, like, disrespectful."

Uncle Bill smiled. He stood and walked over to Colin's chair placing a rugged hand on his shoulder. "No disrespect to you, our Superior, but you must understand our view. These lies we must tell of our tribe members are meant to help us, the living. We have our secrets to keep in this life, but to use the word 'disrespectful'...oh, no. We cannot disrespect those who were valiant warriors, or be disrespecting the shells that they left behind. *Because*, as we all know, these shells of theirs, of ours, are temporary. When we discard them in death, we become *spirit*, and *we* as spirits can be still the warriors, teachers, and friends we were in this life. All you need to do is to quiet yourself and the voices of our fallen ancestors can be heard, their presence sometimes felt."

"Colin, all your life this is what I have said, especially around our dinner table," Anne added, "'*Give thanks to what nature has given us'*. It was my way of talking to our ancestors, our elders, those who are now of the sky and of the earth. Nashoba, Johnny and Dr. Sachem are now part of that world, and they will always be there for us."

"Then what about the spirits of the rebel wolves and *their* Superior?" Colin queried. "What becomes of them? Do they become the negative parts of earth? War? Hatred? Does *their* anger live on as bad spirits?"

"We can only hope that's not the case," Uncle Bill said quietly, not sounding sure. He returned to his chair and his meal.

"Our ritual for burial includes a prayer for the spirits to find peace on the other side," Aunt Trisha continued. "We believe those who just died and the ancestors of our past will help guide these negative spirits. But enough about this, I'm hearing Great Grandmother Carrier saying that *our* Superior needs his nourishment. *Eat*, dear boy."

She was right. Colin had realized his irritability had to do with lack of food, so he finally dug into the steak and potatoes in front of him. As he did so, the thought of Victor, up on the wall, entered his mind.

"Wait- the *papers*," he blurted as he put down his fork and dashed up to his bedroom. He returned with the folded documents from the night before.

Richard stood and said, "The papers Baird and Victor Dawes had all along? You found them?"

"On the top of the wall."

Richard glanced over the first page, and then passed it to Anne, who continued it around the table. All were silent as they absorbed its contents.

"So, this is what started it all," Richard said first.

"It's horrible what these people of power did...but," Anne commented.

"But *not* enough to go on a warpath? I could think of many cultures who would have rebelled over these circumstances," Uncle Bill questioned aloud.

"So why *did* we stop them?" Aunt Trisha suggested, an intense, inquisitive look on her face directed, Colin thought oddly, towards him. "*Why* did we stop our fellow tribesmen from seeking revenge on *those* who attacked us in another way?"

Colin knew quickly that the question wasn't directed at him (the fifteen-year-old) but him (the Superior). "Hatred only causes more hatred. Though these eugenics people held a similar level of anger to that of this Victor Dawes it wasn't right for the rebel Shifters to continue the negativity with violence and death. It would have continued the cycle and have attracted far more problems."

"Indeed," Richard agreed.

"Yes," Aunt Trisha concurred.

"*You know,*" Colin suddenly said as he stood, "it doesn't mean we let the Eugenics folks off the hook. Nashoba said it on the stonewall last night, '*We do live here...And we have done so peacefully for centuries, following human law.*' *We* have proof of this crime these people committed. We'll let the law decide the fate of those who had been involved and expose the truth to the public so it can't happen again."

"And if I'm not mistaken," Philip surmised as he held the papers in front of him, "I think our local journalist, Mrs. Jeannine Granda, might *just* be the person to unleash this story to the unsuspecting public, *especially* if she finds copies in her mail tomorrow afternoon."

"This is good," remarked Uncle Bill. "If justice is fulfilled, these actions alone could calm the spirits of our rebels."

"Here-here," agreed Trisha.

"*Here-here!*" the others joined in.

***

School had been canceled throughout most of the county, due to what was pegged as the *Baker Party Murders*. Students stayed close to home as their parents vehemently called around in search for answers. The investigators, too, were in search of answers as they continued to question the survivors, but it was the truckloads of persistent media agencies that struggled the hardest to get the slightest speck of recollection from anyone.

It wouldn't be until later in the week that another story would attract the attention of the hungry media. Jeannine Granda would share her unexpected find with the area's news crews and Chief of Police Rockwell. In the end, the *Well Born* did not fare well. The truth *did* hurt the reputation of many important families involved.

On this day, however, three friends were finally getting together after a *crazy-freaky* experience. Colin, Jasmine and Skyler were also attempting to reclaim some day-to-day normalcy. They met at The Grill, seeing each other for the first time since the tragic night. Colin had heard only bits and pieces of why his two friends witnessed the *event* in the first place. Their only response was, *"we were hanging around to help, just-in-case".*

Colin, looking his buddies over, could tell emotions were running high. It especially showed with Skyler, who had only ordered a glass of orange juice. Colin finally broke the silence when his two burgers appeared, "So, anyone want to talk about it?"

"What, in *here*?" Skyler quickly asked as he looked to his left and right. "Those *two* guys over there are..."

"*We'll* be subtle and quiet," Colin suggested, interrupting him.

"Subtle," Skyler returned. "*I've* been questioned three times on my way over here. I'm just hoping my fabricated story stays consistent."

"Twice for me. Even CNN asked if I knew anything," Jasmine joined in, then finally said, "Okay, the other night you had mentioned your mom and Mr. LeClaire were hurt. How are they doing?"

"Fine, both of them. We, like, *heal* quickly," replied Colin. "Ha, but Dad keeps babying Mom as if she's incapacitated. *She's* loving the attention."

"He knew, huh?" added Skyler in a whisper. "For how long, I wonder?"

"He won't tell us, but it hasn't changed him a bit," Colin smiled as he thought about his dad. "Have to say, he's a pretty awesome guy."

"He *saved* your life," remarked Jasmine.

"Yeah, he did."

Jasmine leaned-in and whispered, "What about the *wolf* bodies?"

"Uncle Bill took care of it," Colin said. "Buried them in a deep pit off of some old logging road."

"Does that include the, ah...*bad* Ma'iingan inini?" Jasmine asked.

"Yeah, all of them."

"*He* was *really* bad," responded Skyler.

"Yeah," Colin answered.

"Like, dude, I don't think I'll be able to see another horror flick with...*you know* in them, again," he admitted. "I'm still a bit curious, though. What are all those news people going to do with this story, since none of the guests know what happened?"

"Well, I do know now that those two police officers, calling themselves reporters, had already linked last night to the southern Vermont murders. They even had somehow made the connection to our Mi'kmaq tribe. That kind of investigated knowledge, unfortunately, is getting too close to the truth," Colin said.

"But with '*you-know-who*' gone, those pack dog killings, obviously, won't happen anymore," Skyler deduced. "Then, hopefully in time, *this* will all go unsolved and slowly go away."

"I hope so," replied Colin. "Our *kind* doesn't need any more press, no matter how vague the stories all seem. Our secret *must* be kept *quiet*." Colin had bit hard into his hamburger at the same time intensely eyeing the two of them.

Skyler got the gist and replied, "*Dude*, like, *I* totally get it. *Mums* the word. Not even the smallest Tweet. Like *right*, Jasmine?"

"*Obviously*," she answered, rolling her eyes with a smirk.

Colin smiled.

Skyler finally called over a waitress for a pizza. When she left with his order, he pushed his seat onto two legs and then turned to Jasmine saying, "You know, Jazz, that Colin Trask is *sure* persuasive nowadays. Whatever happened to the quiet, clumsy boy we used to love *and* dared to pick on? Man, he thinks he's soooo *superior*."

"What do you expect from a carnivore," Jasmine replied, mussing-up Colin's hair.

Epilogue:
Lookout Rock

The cool evening breeze tugged at Colin's fur as it pulled him back to reality. He could tell the hours had passed now by how quiet the town was below him. He took in a deep breath once again, savoring the gorgeous autumn night.

The two coyotes were long gone having had their fill of the tender doe. "Not even a thank you," Colin whispered in his gruff voice.

Colin looked at the positioning of the moon and knew it was time he should head home. It was a school night and his mother still had a curfew for him. "Even a Superior needs his sleep," she had said.

He reached over and grabbed the deer thigh for his mother, got to his feet and then leapt off the forty-foot drop to the apple trees below. He vaulted towards one particular tree where he had hidden his clothes and shifted back to human form. Fully dressed he slowly made his way back to eleven-eleven Bridge Street. As he walked along the quiet road to town, he looked up towards the glowing full moon above him. He suddenly had an urge to howl.

Hmm, no, he thought to himself smiling. *Too cliché.*

The end

About the Author

Marc Hughes is an author and cartoon illustrator who has written and designed children's books and activity books. He helped explain the political stories of a World Citizen in picture form, and worked on this *World Citizen's* full-length documentary film. He just finished drawing a book about a monk who hands out positive statement stickers and is currently illustrating a graphic novel about the importance of plankton.

Marc's love of wolves and American Indian culture goes back to the movies and documentaries that finally began to depict both in a positive light.

CPSIA information can be obtained
at www.ICGtesting.com
Printed in the USA
BVHW060724100222
628127BV00006B/19